THE CRESCENTS OF THE MOON

Also in Arrow by John Matthews

BASIKASINGO

The Crescents of the Moon

John Matthews

Arrow Books

To all wartime children, and to all displaced persons, past and present.

Acknowledgements
My thanks go to the many people who have assisted me in research: the various staff members of the Croix-Rouge, Geneva; the offices of the United Nations; the Lebanese Embassy, London; the Bank of England, and Reuters.

Arrow Books Limited
17–21 Conway Street, London W1P 6JD

An imprint of the Hutchinson Publishing Group

London Melbourne Sydney Auckland
Johannesburg and agencies throughout
the world

First published in Great Britain by Arrow 1984

Set in A.M. Times by
Photobooks (Bristol) Ltd

Printed and bound in Great Britain by
Anchor Brendon Limited, Tiptree, Essex

ISBN 0 09 932940 9

Contents

The sinews of war are infinite money.
–Cicero, *Orationes Philippicae,* v, *c.* 60 BC

Ah! wealth takes wings, and leaves our
hands all bare,
And death's rough hands delight our
hearts to tear . . .

–Omar Khayyám

PROLOGUE

Beirut, March 1975

A low drone, subdued yet persistent, echoed in the darkness of the large auditorium. Slowly it built up, alternating with a high-pitched whine, then becoming constant again as the stage lights gradually rose.

At the centre of the stage was a steel-framed globe over twenty feet high, reflecting on its bars in hues of red and gold the growing intensity of light. Then another object, obviously the source of the sound, became apparent – a man on a motorbike manoeuvring deftly and swiftly around its inner curves. The lights, sound and movement matched tempo, totally captivating the audience as the tableau became clear.

The show had attracted a crowd of almost three thousand to the Casino du Liban auditorium that evening. Imported from the Paris Lido, the show had also appeared in Las Vegas – these being the only two cities apart from Beirut in that March of 1975 that either held or attracted the wealth to support its extravagance and grandeur.

Only a few rows at the front were lit by the glow from the stage, and two men sitting in that light seemed slightly distracted from the spectacle. They both wore traditional Arab *thobes*, common among the more expensive front tables and seats, although most other Arabs and tourists in the audience were in Western dress.

The larger of the two, Amir Khourem, wore a brighter head-dress band, and appeared more aloof and resplendent than his colleague. Khourem played nervously with a set of beads on the table between them.

'An interesting dilemma, Fuad, but do you seriously

expect me just to accept the implications?' Khourem turned to face his colleague more fully. 'And if I am to concern myself with this now – what am I to do about it?'

Fuad Al-Hakim was a banker and now he exhibited a banker's true caution. 'You could dissociate yourself from the party – or at least try and sway the party more away from the left. So many factions are dividing further now, becoming more and more extreme – it can only lead to disaster.'

'But why *me*? Why am I alone in danger?'

'It isn't just you; there are others – but you would be a more obvious choice for removal.'

On the stage the lights and sound had risen as the motorcyclist negotiated the roof of the steel globe; as they reached a crescendo, the lights dimmed abruptly, the drone dying a fraction afterwards, and a wave of applause swept rapidly through the audience. Khourem maintained a faintly inquisitive expression, and as the applause died Al-Hakim turned to him again.

'Before you were Khalil's right-hand man in the PSP. But Khalil was much too extreme – there was little hope of the party being elected. He posed no threat. To remove you or him at that time would have served no purpose.' Al-Hakim paused significantly. 'But now with the Karim Sha'b it is different. Whatever the policies at heart, the guise is more moderate, the face more acceptable – they *do* pose a threat. And you, Amir, as their leader . . . with the elections now so close.'

'But you, too, are in a similar position,' Khourem rejoined.

'I fully realize that – both in my capacity as your friend and adviser. It was, in fact, recognition of my own personal danger that made me aware of *your* situation, Amir.'

'I'm sorry, my friend, I did not intend to be harsh and indelicate.'

They had talked about the matter before, but never had they touched the real core of Al-Hakim's feelings; both their schedules disallowed meetings of any length, and this particular night had been arranged for some weeks now.

'Perhaps I should have known of this earlier,' Khourem commented. He looked around. The main lights were now on, and a gentle hubbub of conversation and clatter of cutlery arose from the surrounding tables. 'Who would such a situation serve best?' Khourem asked at length.

'Any faction of the Lebanese Front – the Bloc National, the al-Kata'eb – your guess is as good as mine."

Khourem considered. 'But a conflict on any scale would be like turning the clock back. We have only in the last five or six years got fully on our feet after the troubles of '58. And a country that has been financially broken – what good would that be for either party to control?'

'There are those that even *that* situation would benefit.'

Khourem raised an eyebrow.

'Outsiders,' Al-Hakim said flatly. 'And again those inside who would not consider the full implications of their actions – some can only see good rising out of destruction. They cannot gain what they wish with the balance as it is, so they change the balance, change the power structure, change whatever they have to – a means to an end. The loss of blood they see as a cleansing, a martyrdom to the cause . . .'

Al-Hakim gripped Khourem's hand tightly across the table. 'But does it matter *who*, Amir? The fact is that if harm should come to but a handful of men in our country, we will be plunged headlong into total conflict.'

Khourem looked up slowly with his deeply hooded eyes. 'Is that why you've transferred so many interests to Bahrain of late, Fuad?'

It was a delicate question, one that would never have been asked outside of the heated situation, and Al-Hakim flinched slightly. 'I have been transferring interests there for many years now. That is purely good business sense. But there are those still here who would not be able to transfer, perhaps won't have the same foresight . . .' Al-Hakim calmed himself momentarily. 'And don't think that the effects would stop just here. Consider the effect on the whole of the Middle East, including the Bahrain market. Investors and traders would ask themselves: if it can happen here, then why not there, and there, and there also.'

Khourem sat back and looked straight ahead. On the stage a new tableau had formed: a pasha seated on a large raised throne, drawing on two hookah pipes. The giant glass bulbs of the hookahs were capped in gold and filled to within a few inches of the brim with water; inside each swam scantily clad girls, their hair flowing in serpentine strands with their fluid motions. To each side of the throne, servants in ballooned trousers fanned the pasha with large white ostrich feathers. It was a scene that in every way befitted the regality and splendour of the large auditorium.

Khourem waved his arm in an expansive gesture. 'Are you trying to suggest that everything – all the strength and goodwill our country has built up in the last ten years – could be lost, sacrificed?'

Al-Hakim looked down again. 'In the past we have enjoyed both wealth and splendour – and we have sacrificed them time and time again for our ideals, however misguided they might have been. What makes now so different?'

'And I suppose that while this is happening, the rest of the Arab world would just sit back. That would never happen!'

'No, Amir, you're right – that *wouldn't*. Each nation, each faction would take its side, as they've done in the past. It would no longer be the west bank of the Jordan, Damascus, the Sinai – our own country would become the battleground.'

From their position on the hillside the three men could see the glow from the lights of the Casino du Liban from around the promontory of the Bay of Jounie. A faint glistening was the only relief on the sombre darkness of the water. Above the bay, the lights of summer villas twinkled magically; but on their side there were few dwellings, and they huddled among the pine trees and rocks in thick darkness.

Their leader was taut, his attention fixed on the road below; his two companions were more noticeably uneasy and at intervals chattered nervously. Most of the traffic had passed by in the early evening, and then there had been another heavy flow when the Casino floorshow had ended. There was no other road back to Beirut and the three men rested secure in the knowledge that their patience would be rewarded.

They had planned this well. Each of them wore rough green army canvasses and *khoufia* head-dresses, so that the loose trail of the towelling could be drawn across to conceal their features. Their leader carried a Simi rifle with infra-red telescopic sights and high-velocity bullets; the other two had Kalashnikovs. The leader tested the sights on some of the passing cars, as a matter of identification as much as anything else.

He could just imagine the scenes in the nearby Casino, celebrated as one of the world's largest, the 'Jewel of the Middle East'. He felt both sickness and excitement as he zoomed in closely with his sights on the people inside their limousines – the men, either in *thobes* or evening suits and bow-ties, the women with their dark veils or Dior evening gowns, the glistening jewels; this was the heart of Middle-Eastern wealth. It was that element that he resented the most – not the wealth itself, but the hands it was in – and he was sure that was why he had been particularly attracted to the contract. He wondered whether this was a legacy of his upbringing and just how far his hatred of semites would take him beyond plain professional judgement. He would watch that in future; it could create a traceable pattern.

After a while the lights on the road seemed monotonous, and his mind drifted to other assignments, other contracts, *Mannheim*. Though vital, there should be no problem with *this* one: it was quite straightforward. He remembered the rain-swept carriageway of a German autobahn – a barrier looming suddenly before him, the bloodied bodies left behind, the wailing of the Polizei sirens – but his attention was back quickly.

After a quick confirmation through the infra-red sights, he was sure – he could pick out the elongated headlamps of the Cadillac Seville quite clearly now; it was just rounding the last stretch of the Bay of Jounie. He made a small signal to his two companions and they tensed in anticipation.

In the back of the Cadillac, Khourem sat with his thoughts. The chauffeur negotiated the last of the curves high above the bay. To one side they were almost level with some small palms, but now they were rising steadily as they reached the promontory, and the pine-clad hills encroached more sharply the other side.

After the floorshow their conversation had become less tense, and Khourem had gradually worked his way around to accepting that something would have to be done. It would be too drastic for him to step down as party leader, or for it to be swayed further from the left, but for the benefit of the media there *were* certain steps that could be taken. They could recruit known moderates without giving them any real political power or say, could even change small elements of their manifesto. These would be placebos; in reality they would keep the same tough line, keep their integrity. The same thoughts had preoccupied him almost totally towards the end of the floorshow and during the gambling afterwards; he had lost almost twenty thousand Lebanese pounds between the chemin-de-fer and the roulette.

Al-Hakim steered clear of such excesses and had merely laid a few small stakes to hold his interest. Now he silently studied his companion's grave expression, wondering what decision would finally be made. At that instant he saw something else in Khourem's expression – a flicker of sudden surprise – and his attention was ripped away.

The high-velocity bullet hit the windscreen in that same instant. All the windows were tinted and bullet-proof, and Khourem gasped at the impact of the bullet entering, spreading a score of spider strands. The shock froze him for a second, then he directed the chauffeur.

'*Kawam.* Move faster!'

Khourem knew that the tinting would obscure them, but the first bullet had weakened the windshield . . . any other hits around the same position would likely break through.

He scanned the nearby hillside, but the darkness was impenetrable and he couldn't see any movement.

The car had picked up speed considerably when the next two bullets hit – both within inches of the first. The windscreen stayed in place, but the fourth bullet hit the centre of the rough triangle and a foot-round hole was pumped through.

The remainder of the windscreen frosted instantly and the chauffeur was hit by some of the shards of flying glass. He swerved and braked at the same time, still trying to pick out the now obscured road. He saw something dark loom up to one side, then nothing.

From the side window Khourem saw the large rock flash by, and then they were dangerously close to the low barrier.

'Push the windscreen through,' he directed tersely.

The chauffeur lifted his arm up, but at that moment a fifth bullet pumped the windscreen through for him, and the glass and the rush of air hit them as one.

They could see clearly now. Another, smaller group of rocks was directly ahead but they were still steering sharply into the barrier. Khourem wasn't watching the barrier now, though. His eyes were set towards the bend beyond the rocky outcrop; if they could make it to there, they would be clear.

The chauffeur swerved away from the barrier, but the motion was too abrupt – the back swung sharply around and broke through with a sickening rending of metal, the far-side wheel catching over the sheer edge. They started careening wildly towards the small rock outcrop, and the chauffeur fought hard to stop the car sliding over the cliff. He braked and swung the wheel in at the same time, and they had slowed amidst a shower of sparks when they collided with the rocks and finally came to rest. The damage to the wing was heavy, but they weren't badly injured, merely shaken. It took a moment for them to come to their senses and realize their position.

At Khourem's side the view was dizzying. One back wheel was still hanging precariously over the cliff edge, and far below he could see the white horses of waves breaking over the jagged rocks.

'*Gahan'nam ennar!* God in hell . . . get us moved!'

The front of the car was jammed hard against the rock outcrop, and the chauffeur opened the door to see if there was anything he could do manually to pull the wheel in. The interior light picked him out immediately. The shot cleanly removed the lower side of his jaw.

Khourem sat frozen with fear. The light could pick out the back seat also, and for a moment Khourem wondered when the next bullet would come. Which of them would be next? Al-Hakim tried to reach over to shut the door, but it was too far, and they both resigned themselves to keeping as low as possible in the back seat.

Al-Hakim saw some movement in the hillside – some scurrying among the pine trees – and then a man showed ghostly in the slanted front beam; another two came quickly to his side, but remained among the shadows. They moved hurriedly towards the car with their rifles held waist-high and stopped within only yards.

'*Harak!* Move! Out of the car!' one of the men ordered.

Al-Hakim and Khourem climbed out tentatively on the side facing the three men. They stood in uneasy silence for a moment, and then Al-Hakim spoke.

'You intend to kill us?' he asked flatly.

The man the question was directed at, who had come to the forefront, did not answer.

'Yes,' one of his companions answered in an equally flat tone. Al-Hakim looked more directly at the first man – in that instant he had seen a glimmer of hesitation in his eyes, as if he had wanted to answer but couldn't. The eyes were light blue, whereas his companions' were dark, and a heavy scar ran from the corner of his right eye, giving it an unsightly droop. At first the scar had been shielded by the heavy shadow of the *khoufia*, and Al-Hakim hadn't noticed it until the man had turned fully to face them. Al-Hakim thought again about the rumours he had heard; now, faced with their reality, they seemed altogether too accurate to be merely happenstance, too convenient . . . And he began to wonder if they could have been engineered to bring him and Khourem together at the same time.

Above his fear, Khourem felt somehow cheated that this should happen now; especially since his course of party moderation had now been determined, and he had begun to even relish a part of it, the duping of the right-wing. Al-Hakim's warning turned over and over in his mind: *'Our own country will become the battleground.'* Khourem's sense of defeat was overwhelming.

'Why?' he protested weakly. 'To what purpose?'

The three men remained silent and their leader made a simple movement with one hand.

One of the other men stepped purposefully forward. There was a fraction of an instant in which the full horror hit Al-Hakim and Khourem.

'Shyatin! . . . Bnadik' ibne zine! . . .' Khourem raised one hand in protest and continued a chain of curses as the volley of rapid fire hit them.

The bullets ripped through his hand and on to pound his body, then arched up to consume Al-Hakim. They were both thrown harshly against the Cadillac, Al-Hakim almost somersaulting over the boot and coming to rest close to the rocky edge.

The leader made another small movement and the last man moved in and turned Khourem's body face-up, ripping the *thobe* brusquely from his chest. He took a large curved knife from a side sheath and made a small incision just below Khourem's neck. Then he forced the blade deep in and drew it viciously downward, snapping the hard ribs and slicing through the soft flesh of the stomach; then again horizontally so that his butchery formed a rough crucifix, the blood that welled up quickly marring its shape.

Sweat was raised on the man's brow from the effort, and he wiped at it impatiently as he sheathed his knife again. He stood back and the leader leant across and felt for the pulse behind Khourem's ear. After a moment he appeared satisfied, then looked briefly towards Al-Hakim in a manner that suggested he was now of minor importance.

With a final small signal the three men moved away, disappearing once again into the darkness of the nearby hillside.

Al-Hakim lay with his face against the road, watching the three men cautiously. He could hear the soft pump of his own heart against the cool tarmac. He knew that at least two of the bullets had hit him in the chest and another had entered his back as he had been spun around. Only moments before he had resigned himself to die, but now he was filled with an overwhelming compulsion to live, to discover the purpose and identities of their three attackers. He only hoped that someone would reach him in time.

Part One

Croix Rouge, Beirut: Geneva Desk

1

18 August 1976

With the siege of Tel-Zataar, the hostilities here have reached a new level. An estimated 1600 people have been killed in the shelling of the last few days, and the injured run close to 4000. Evacuations have been increasing, but the total number has probably still not reached 1000. 16 medic trucks and 2 ambulances have been employed in the operation, with evacuation capabilities limited accordingly. So far 2 site infirmaries have been established and casualties are being dealt with in turn, according to their seriousness.

Leorah Ajlan, Croix Rouge, Beirut

Daniel Grade huddled against the late November chill as he walked along Fleet Street. It was almost seven at night, but many lights were still on in the five- and six-storey dull stone buildings on either side. Some newspapers had adopted more modern façades, but even with the marble and smoked glass there remained an air of solidity, of timelessness.

Grade walked past the *Sunday Express* building and turned into Wine Office Court heading for Ye Olde Cheshire Cheese, a small pub dating from the late seventeenth century which had been a favourite watering-hole of both Samuel Johnson and Dickens, among other notables, and, being so close to Fleet Street, was doomed forever to be connected with scribes. Grade pushed his way past a small crowd of drinkers around the main serving counter which had survived the pub's many renovations, then down the narrow stairs to its cellar bar. There the ceiling was low and supported by heavy oak beams, and the rough stone walls, pillars and archways were painted white. The bar itself and the bottles behind were back-lit, giving, with a few table lamps, a subdued, mellow atmosphere.

The bar was crowded but Grade must have made an imposing sight as he peered into the room; he was large and quite stocky, wore a heavy leather coat, and in the corner of his mouth was perched a fat cigar. His hair was tousled stone-grey, his features rugged, except his blue eyes which were babyish and rounded, giving him a softly inquisitive look. He could just pick out Billy Stoner on the far side and made his way across.

'Hello Billy, how's tricks?'

There was no formal greeting between the two of them, just a brief knowing look that encompassed the many years of their acquaintanceship.

Stoner indicated the bar. 'What will you have, Danny?'

Grade ordered a pint of best bitter and settled on a bar stool as the barmaid pulled the hand pump, then set the drink down on the counter.

Both men were of a similar age and mould, but their lives had taken different directions. Theirs was a friendship that went back over thirty years, to the small boxing gym where they had both been apprentices, both keen amateurs. Stoner nearly always wore Slazenger pullovers – Grade often thought in memory of that age – although now he was well past his athletic prime.

Stoner looked up thoughtfully. 'Have you done much reporting on the courts lately, Danny?'

'Oh, I don't know – I think the last time was when you were standing in the dock, Billy.' It was a delicate tease, one that he knew would be taken in good humour now that sufficient time had passed, the wounds had healed. Stoner had never really had the speed for his weight in boxing, and had turned to petty crime to supplement his income. Grade had made it to professional, but it was a short-lived career; eight of his ten first fights had been stopped due to injury above the eyes, and he had drifted rather than planned his move into boxing journalism. That had been the start. A personal hunch on a 'fixed' fight had given him his first break into investigative journalism, and since then – through more general and investigative reporting – he had built up a certain reputation. It was then that he had found himself suddenly on the opposite side of the fence to the Billy Stoners of this world. Now he could see that his comment had fallen flat. Stoner remained thoughtful.

'It's trouble, isn't it, Billy?' Grade said. 'I thought you'd left all that alone.'

'Leave it out. Successful wholesale greengrocer goes back to blagging – what for?'

'I know that, and I know your looks too, Billy. It's trouble.'

Stoner leaned closer. 'Yer, well, it's more of a little scrape than anything else – a brush with the law.'

'How hard did you brush them?'

'Quite hard. I hit one of their boys in blue on the nose.'

Grade looked up incredulously. 'You hit a policeman?'

Stoner held his hands up defensively. 'Yer, but not without undue provocation. That's why I wanted to get the "sp" on the courts.'

'I don't know how much I can help you, Billy,' Grade commented. 'You really want a lawyer.'

'I've got one already, Danny, but you know what it's like – too often they're looking out for their own interests as much as yours.'

Grade took a sip of his beer. 'Well, most of my cases either start or finish in court – that's about the strength of it. But now you've got me intrigued. How did it happen?'

Stoner collected his thoughts for a moment.

'It all started with me running this mate's Roller home after a pub birthday celebration. He was pissed, you see – out cold – so I had him laid out across the back seat and I had his bird in the front. Anyway, I must have had a bit more than I realized myself, and of course the inevitable happened. We hit a slippery patch on this bend and skidded into this cul-de-sac just on the turn – then we hit this lamppost, bang! It wasn't too bad, we weren't hurt, but the wing was badly smashed up and the steering had snapped – I just couldn't shift it. Then it hit me. Joey only had named driver insurance, and I wasn't one of them – I wasn't covered. And I was pissed. *And*, by the way that we'd spun off on the corner, I was pretty bloody sure he had a couple of Kojaks on the front. So we decided to leg it. I bunged Joey over me shoulder, told the bird to keep her knickers on straight and we started doing a Houdini.'

Stoner took a quick slug of his drink. 'That's when the doctor showed up – trust me to pick the stockbroker belt – going on about trying to leave the scene of an accident and all that. His wife was already on the blower to the police.'

'How did you know he was a doctor?' asked Grade.

'That came out later – "a responsible, upstanding member of the public",' Stoner mimicked a magistrate. '"Assaulted during the course of a citizen's arrest".'

'You hit the doctor, too?'

'Yer, well that's debatable as well, but for other reasons.' Stoner fought to stay credible, even in the face of Grade's apparent doubt. 'You see, this doctor was trying to keep us there – grappling away like a madman, he was. I don't know where he got the strength from. In the end I managed to shake him off with one arm, and the silly sod goes and falls over.' Stoner paused heavily. 'That's when this copper arrived.'

Grade couldn't resist a faint smile. 'Not your lucky day, was it?'

'You're not joking. Smarmy bastard he was – got his notebook out straight away. Started going round the car, checking the tyres, talking to the doctor, breathalyzing me – everything. Then he starts reading out the charges. Bald tyres, no insurance, Joey had let the tax disc run out, drunken driving – you name it, it was wrong. Then he goes right over the top – starts going on about me assaulting the doctor and all that crap. "Fuck off", I muttered under my breath.

"Right", he says in his smarmy manner. "That's assaulting a police officer in the performance of his duty", and he writes something down in his little book. "No it isn't", I said – and I thought to myself, if I'm going to get done for it anyway, I might as well have the pleasure . . .'

'And that's when you hit him?'

'I couldn't think of a better time, could you?' Stoner said flatly; then he leant forward with an ingenuous smile. 'That isn't the best part though. This copper gets up, brushes himself off, lifts up his notebook, wipes the bit of blood from under his nose, and as cool as a cucumber, in the same smarmy bloody voice he says, "Correction, that's assault *and* battery".'

There was a long silence while Stoner took another sip of beer, and then he looked up with an air of concern. 'What do you think I'll get, Danny?'

Grade had been drinking his pint throughout Stoner's story, and now he contemplated the last few inches in the bottom. 'Well, for a start you want the case heard in the Crown court in front of a jury – ask your brief to apply for it. You won't stand a chance of getting off in a magistrate's court – they're no better than police courts. Not that you've got a chance of getting off anyway, but just that in the magistrate's court you'd get the standard sentence: six months in prison, a one-year driving ban and a heavy fine.'

'And the Crown Court?'

'There you've got a chance of missing the six months, and if you're very lucky you'll only get a couple of endorsements on the driving offences. But you've got to claim mitigating circumstances. Say that you were distraught and shaken after the accident, that you were worried that your friend in the back had been hurt during the accident. All you could think of was getting him to hospital.'

'What about the doctor?'

'He didn't tell you he was a doctor, and he didn't come to the aid of your passengers, so how were you to know? But for God's sake don't mention the smarmy attitude of the copper – the jury will just think that you've got an inbuilt dislike for coppers, and that that was the real reason behind you thumping him. They might think you make a habit of going round thumping coppers on the nose.' Grade smiled at the fleeting mental image. 'Compliment his efficiency, but politely point out that he seemed a bit more concerned with his duty than your friend's welfare – and it was this that finally pushed you over the brink and made you momentarily forget yourself. Let the jury draw their own conclusions. And I know it'll be difficult, Billy, but above everything else, appear apologetic.'

Stoner looked up hopefully. 'Do you think it'll work?'

'It's your best chance. More to the point, it's your *only* chance.'

'That's a great consolation,' Stoner said with doleful sarcasm.

'Listen, if you play it right, there's no way they'll send you down for six months,' Grade reassured him. 'How long is it since your last offence?'

Stoner thought for a moment. 'Over twelve years now.'

'Well what are you worried about – straight for twelve years, now with a respectable business. And on the other hand one brief, regrettable incident under unfortunate circumstances – and all because you were doing a drunken friend a favour.'

The general clatter of conversation around the bar had built up slightly, and Stoner looked around sheepishly for a moment, still deep in thought.

'Yer, well, I suppose you're right,' he said at length. He eased a smile, and Grade could see it was merely reassurance he had wanted all along.

Stoner seemed momentarily preoccupied with the movements of one of the barmaids, then turned back to Grade. 'Here, we've been talking about all my problems – how's life been treating you?'

'Can't complain. I've just finished a case a few days back, just writing it up now.'

'Anything interesting?'

'So, so. It's a Swiss pharmaceutical fraud – money hidden

in different bank accounts. You know the type of thing, Billy. The same goes on here, but with the tax-man. The most difficult part –'

At that moment Grade was disturbed; he could see one of the newspaper's messengers looking above the crowd, then picking him out and coming across. Grade broke off.

The messenger was careful to keep to Grade's side and, as he spoke, at intervals he looked over cautiously, almost guardedly, towards Stoner.

From his position, Stoner couldn't tell what was said, but he could see the faintly puzzled expression on Grade's face.

Stoner offered him another drink, but Grade held his hand up. He talked a moment longer with the messenger, then looked back at Stoner.

'Something's cropped up, I'm afraid. I'll have to go.'

'Still burning the midnight oil, eh?'

'Something like that,' Grade quickly knocked back the last of his pint. 'And let me know how the case goes, Billy. Good luck.'

'If it goes well Danny, I'll owe you one,' Stoner called after him.

'Yes, Billy, you'll owe me one,' Grade muttered under his breath, but his expression stayed thoughtful as he made his way out of the small bar.

'Is that him?' Grade asked, looking through the glass window into the managing editor's office.

Bob Golding didn't seem too perturbed at having to vacate his own office, and now he stared, too, at the rather dapper man seated on the far side of his desk.

'Said that he would only see you alone,' Golding commented blandly.

The man was middle-aged and dressed in a grey suit, his dark brown hair cropped primly; a pair of steel-rimmed glasses completed the image of stern efficiency.

'What does he want?' Grade asked.

Golding turned away and started making his way through

the busy newsroom, leafing through some small notes in his hand.

'You'd better ask Mitchell – he saw him first. But I don't think he said much.' Golding looked up. 'Mitchell had the feeling that the same man called a few days back, asking for you. When he inquired who it was, he said he preferred not to give a name, and when asked what it was about, he rang off.'

Grade looked mystified, and Golding pointed back to his office. 'Your best bet's in there. Ask him yourself.'

'But he's Swiss – you're sure of that?'

'Yes. Said he got your name from that pharmaceutical investigation you've been on, and that was it – stumm!'

Grade looked down. 'That's what I'm worried about – one of the drug company lawyers slapping an injunction on me.'

'Look, if I see him getting anything official looking out of his jacket, I'll come to your rescue. If it's anything else, forget it!'

Grade returned his smile; at times Golding played up his custodian image, and that brief acknowledgement was all that was necessary between them. Grade turned and made his way into the small glass-fronted office, shutting the door firmly behind him.

Golding's intrigue over the purpose of the man in his office was growing. He stayed looking through the glass as Grade settled into his conversation, watching each small change in his expression, each nuance. After a few moments some papers were passed across, but there was no hesitation from Grade, who accepted them with interest. Grade hunched over the table, and Golding could see the man picking out different portions of the papers, then flicking the pages, seeming to stop and explain at intervals. Gradually, Grade sat back and the conversation appeared to continue normally again. Golding tore himself away, started doing his rounds of the newsroom.

Golding thought he had seen something in Grade's expression – a faint shadow of shock or surprise as the papers had been put away – but it had been too fleeting to read anything into. He pushed the thought away. He stopped off at the sports editor's desk and left a few notes, then went over to his sub-editor to discuss the final details of the 'Focus Abroad' page. It was a more complicated layout than he had first envisaged, and he had been in conversation almost twenty minutes when his attention was drawn back to the glass window. The door was opening; the two men were shaking hands.

He could see Grade smiling, but there was something withdrawn, uncertain beneath, and Golding's curiosity peaked. He cut his conversation short.

'We'll pick this up later, Jem – or I'll get Wyman to go over it with you.'

Golding came across as Grade had said his goodbyes and led his visitor out through the main office door.

'Well?'

Grade turned away, appearing hesitant. 'We must arrange a meeting – as quickly as possible.'

'Okay, so we'll arrange a meeting. Now you can tell me why.'

Grade half ignored the comment. 'We'll need Nabens in on it, and someone from financial – you can recommend someone on that score.'

'Danny?'

Grade could sense Golding's building impatience, and he looked directly at him for the first time. 'I'm sorry Bob, but if I told you straight out, standing right here, it just wouldn't come out right. You just wouldn't believe me.'

'Try me.'

Grade had hoped to wait until a meeting, which by its convening alone would make the gravity of the situation fully apparent. Now he realized that Golding wouldn't be so easily put off. He indicated the office and they went back inside. Grade closed the door and leaned with his back to it, inhaling almost in a sigh.

'That man who was just here works for Switzerland's largest banking consortium,' he said, then paused. 'He claims that they were instrumental in starting the war in the Lebanon.'

The statement seemed somehow too simple, too banal to carry the full weight of its meaning, and for a moment there was an awkward silence.

Golding felt numb, and then a first chill of realization touched him inside. He looked up slowly. 'You're right, I wouldn't believe you.'

Anton Reiner checked out of London's Tower Hotel and hailed a cab for Heathrow airport.

He was still in the same dark suit that he had worn in Fleet Street earlier, and there was a nervousness about him that went beyond plain business anxiety; he looked at his watch repeatedly as the taxi sped west. The call to Milan would be relayed to Swenkel by early morning, and he felt relaxed about that at least; it was becoming increasingly difficult to call from Zürich.

There the game would start again. It would be more vital now than ever to keep up appearances.

The same paranoia was returning, as it had done so often in the past weeks; he was sure he had been watched, but could they have possibly followed him here? Could they be watching him now?

Unconsciously, he found himself studying the passing cars, fighting to pick out their occupants from behind the lights reflected on their darkened windows.

It was late and traffic was light on the motorway west. Those cars that did pass didn't seem to stay close for any length of time, and there were no cars that had followed consistently, as far as Reiner could make out. After a while he settled back.

As Swenkel had said, if anyone was following, *they* would be watching too, keeping his interests at heart. He thought again of the contact they had supplied – Leorah Ajlan. He had only spoken to the woman once on the telephone – a faint distant voice – and she had seemed particularly intrigued as to where he had got her name. That would have been the ultimate irony, if she ever found out, and he hoped now that his explanation of having read her old newspaper articles had been accepted; and that Swenkel was right – that she would prove the best source. He gazed blankly out of the taxi window.

It would be good to plan a weekend away. Perhaps take Piai and the children to one of the mountain resorts near Murren or Lucerne. That would take his mind off things. It seemed suddenly hard now to attach any certainty to their lives.

He broke out of his contemplation only as they turned off the motorway heading for the main Heathrow tunnel. He looked at his watch again: 9.40 p.m. They would be having their meeting in London that same evening, or first thing in the morning at the very latest.

The Heathrow tunnel lights distracted him and slowly phased out his thoughts. His part was done. Everything would take its course now.

Catherine Grade sat alone in the large house, a hearty fire burning in the stone fireplace before her. She looked at the fire as a sort of companion, but she felt nothing of the comfort and warmth it should have afforded. This had happened too many times before, she thought. She glanced up at the clock on the mantelpiece: 10.12 p.m. There had been the one call over three hours before, something about 'only an hour or so, darling', then nothing.

Obviously something else had cropped up – another crisis, another deadline, another 'hot' story – and she was meant to understand. It was the picture that she resented the most; the lonely and doting housewife, bored and frustrated . . . Then all the worn clichés about 'change of life' came to mind. *Christ*, that she could never stand, and so in the end she said little, kept her frustration and annoyance bottled inside.

Sometimes she felt like a prisoner in the house. At first, the large Georgian house in Wentworth with its acres of woodland and golf courses had been like a dream, but at times the house somehow felt much larger than it was, more isolated. She was free to roam its many spacious rooms, each of them equally empty, and it was then that she would sense the depth of her loneliness, the subtle captivity.

She would imagine she heard feet running, the sounds of laughter and screaming in the rooms, where the toys and then the pop posters and college mementoes had been.

Almost in a daze she walked to the side of the fireplace, to the cabinet on top of which were found photographs of the two girls. Pauline, the eldest, had emigrated to Australia with her husband – almost eight years ago now, she reflected. Julie, the youngest, was still on a college exchange in Paris, but she had never felt quite so close to Julie; she was always the tearaway, the difficult one, who somehow could only be calmed and directed by Daniel. Those two had an almost unspoken understanding, which she appreciated but at the same time partly envied.

But now as she looked at the photograph, she knew that Julie was the last remaining tie with what had been eroded over the past few years, and suddenly she felt an unaccustomed affinity with the girl, even though there was now more time and distance between them. Perhaps she was lonely, too, she thought.

She put the photograph down gently and, as she settled back and stared again into the flickering fire, made up her mind to write to the Sorbonne.

The four men were grouped in a small office at the back of the newspaper building; from there they could just hear the faint mechanical sounds of the presses two floors below.

Grade and Golding flanked one side of the boardroom table; Rolf Nabens, the international editor, and David Wetherall, the city editor, the other. Golding was the oldest of the four, with Nabens and Grade next in seniority.

Nabens had worked as the paper's Middle East correspondent based in Cairo in the late fifties and early sixties. He was the product of a Maltese mother and Iraqi-Jewish father, but the variation and scope of his articles over the years, in particular some pro-Palestinian, had earned him the reputation of having an unbiased, objective viewpoint.

David Wetherall's acquaintance with city finance was absolute, but his knowledge of international banking – apart from a spell reporting on the EEC in Brussels – was usually used to translate its effect on the city market.

Golding's patriarchal influence was evident as he considered the information from his colleagues. A pair of heavy tortoise-shell rimmed glasses were perched towards the end of his nose, contrasting with his thinning grey hair, and at intervals he adjusted the glasses and played with a pencil in his hand, as if visually underlining some points in his notes.

The papers left with Grade had been passed around the table several times, and the conversation quickly focused on the implications of Grade's news. David Wetherall held onto the papers increasingly as the conversation turned more to finance, and now he elaborated on his answer to one of Golding's questions.

'Suisse Banque Exchequer Collectif – SBECSA. As the name implies, they combine a number of Swiss banks – five or six if I'm not mistaken. The power of the one or two major banks left out is dwindling day by day, and mainly due to SBECSA's virtual monopoly. As for the coterie of small non-member banks – in SBECSA's eyes, they will always remain small, and so just aren't important. So, yes, their position is very strong. But their responsibility? That's another matter. In many ways they can afford to be a law unto themselves.'

Nabens was making some notes. 'You paint a bit of a tyrannical picture. The "SA" is their company registration?'

'Yes, their form of *Limited.*'

'It is a public shares company as such?' asked Golding.

Wetherall considered the question. 'A sort of Bank of England with its primary tie to the banks it serves rather than government, might be a more apt description.'

Everyone took in the comparison, and then Golding spoke again.

'And what do we know about Anton Reiner?'

'Very little,' Grade said quickly.

'Do you think that, in essence, what he says can be trusted?'

'I've only met the man for a few moments – I'd more likely misjudge him . . .' Grade broke off. He remembered Reiner's extreme nervousness, the way it could have so easily obscured his true character – but there was something else beneath, a strong conviction or a deep hurt, he had never quite made his mind up. 'Well – I liked him, but he was edgy. Perhaps if I had to commit myself to trust, that show of vulnerability helped; but that might be what he intended all along. On that side of things, if what he says *can't* be trusted, then we have an even more curious question of ulterior motive: why a man in his position would put in the time and trouble to set us on a wild goose chase? If he was part of another bank, then you could see the sense in him damaging SBECSA shares. At present until I research more, that's the only firm thing in his favour.'

'What exactly is his position?' asked Golding.

Wetherall flicked through the papers in his hand. '*Sous-directeur.* A sort of executive manager. But he's also one of the principal directors of one of their member banks – Banque du Martigny.' Wetherall looked around the table. 'It's quite standard – they like to keep things as much as possible within the circle.'

'That brings up an interesting point,' commented Golding. 'Why does Reiner attach guilt to SBECSA in particular? Why not one of the member banks?'

'From what he says, he only sees the point of this kind of operation coming from a collective purpose,' offered Grade. 'For one bank there just wouldn't be sufficient gain in trying to affect banking patterns on this scale.'

'And Reiner got your name from your recent pharmaceutical investigation?'

'Yes.'

Golding pushed his glasses back slightly. 'Even though your investigation wasn't connected with any of the SBECSA banks?'

'A large proportion of my investigation was conducted through the Swiss Banking Institute,' said Grade. 'A sort of "watchdog committee" to all the Swiss banks. I have a good contact there: Simon Mendel. Reiner claims he was referred through him.'

'Okay, check with Mendel on that. As for the question of scale, we'll be coming to that later,' Golding said, looking briefly towards Nabens. 'First of all, what facts have we got? There's no point in going into the situation in any depth unless the foundations can be proved solid.'

Grade studied his earlier notes. 'The main piece of solid information is a supply of arms to a Lebanese Phalangist group through one of SBECSA's subsidiaries – Securitee Maslegeisen.'

'Is this subsidiary's normal function supply of arms?' asked Nabens.

'Import-export mainly – it could cover a variety of sins. Doesn't really give us much.'

'SBECSA are widely diversified,' supported Wetherall. 'Insurance and property companies, even a supermarket chain.'

Golding was pensive. 'I don't know – do we have anything there or not? The French sold Mirages to Israel, yet at the same time showed open support for opposing Arab nations, and even at times the PLO. The Israelis helped South Africa develop the atom bomb, yet stand strong on human rights. The fact that arms were supplied doesn't really prove a lot. If I remember correctly, the Swiss supplied the Germans with an abundance of arms during World War Two.'

Nabens nodded his head in grim agreement.

'I think the main point will be proving a strong purpose in their involvement,' Grade said. 'There's no doubt from the papers I've seen that this company is tied to SBECSA, and that arms *were* supplied. There was one other piece of information that won't be so easy to substantiate . . .' For a second Grade considered; it was this allegation that Reiner had been particularly vague and hesitant about, yet still it was potentially the strongest. 'It concerns the assassination of two prominent Muslim politicians.'

Golding met the steadiness of Grade's gaze. 'Again, what facts?'

'Only a claim – Reiner believes that the assassin was an independent hired by somebody from within SBECSA. From there it's a research job. All he's given me is the name of a contact in Beirut, an ex-correspondent with one of the large Muslim dailies – Leorah Ajlan.'

Golding held his hands up to heaven. 'Please, please, spare me. In effect we come back again to trusting this man Reiner's claims – or establishing a probable cause or motive for SBECSA. Okay David, just for the moment saying *if*, what would they have to gain?'

Wetherall seemed to mull over his answer. 'As far as I can find out, deposits in Lebanese banks at the time were somewhere between twelve and fifteen billion dollars. Within weeks of the war starting, over forty per cent of the deposits were removed, but to where, nobody can trace exactly . . . Another twenty or twenty-five per cent disappeared over the following six months, and since then there have been even further withdrawals.'

'So a very large proportion of their banking deposits,' Golding considered. 'But can we assume a proportion of *that* to be deposited now in Switzerland?'

'All I can say is that Switzerland would be a likely prime choice. Bahrain has been expanding, but a lot of investors feel wary of the Middle East in general since the war started. To a large extent Beirut's banking was modelled on the Swiss system – advantages of freedom of movement, tax, secrecy, etcetera . . . So it's easy to see *why* Switzerland might be an alternative choice.'

There was silence around the table, and Wetherall expanded on the point. 'A lot of Arab investors were already investing in Switzerland, and so in that sense a large transfer might seem quite normal, but I think what should also be mentioned is the potential at that time of Middle East banking. If Beirut had proved itself over the years as a good alternative to Switzerland, there would have no doubt been the question of changing allegiances – of perhaps considerable future deposits. In that sense the loss to Switzerland is almost incalculable. Since so much of the world's money is now in Arab hands, the Swiss could have started to lose the balance of free-banking power worldwide.'

Grade thought how the British Government had been sweating over the last few years to pay back a loan of three billion pounds to the IMF. It made twelve to fifteen billion dollars seem monstrous.

Golding looked up from scribbling a brief note. 'You're saying that there is sufficient motivation for Swiss involvement?'

'Yes and no,' Wetherall hedged. 'The motives are strong, and I portrayed them as such so that you could see each side clearly. On the other side we have a matter of principle – we happen to be talking about one of the world's most principled establishments. Given *that*, it seems unlikely.'

'But what would they put at risk in real terms?' asked Golding. 'Apart from principles, of course.'

'Well for a start, a discrediting of this sort would lose some investors right across the board. On top of that there would almost certainly be an embargo on Swiss banks, similar to that now imposed on Jewish banks.'

'And we all know how effective that has been,' Nabens commented wryly.

Wetherall himself smiled; where terms had appeared favourable at Jewish banks, Arab investors had simply deposited through bearer bonds, which were almost impossible to trace.

'The point is that the Swiss banks are concerned about their world image to the point of almost total distraction,' Wetherall continued. 'Take their company title for instance. Being based in Zürich, the language is German, and in fact they are known in Switzerland itself by their German title. But *internationally* it is almost unpronounceable, and I think they feel that in some quarters there is still a lingering aversion to German. And the initials don't fit as conveniently as SBECSA, so for the international market, as they are down here,' – Wetherall indicated the papers in his hand – 'they are known by their French title. It's the same with Schweizerische Kreditanstalt, also based in Zürich – to the world they're more commonly known as Credit Suisse. So that gives you some idea how Swiss banks feel about *image*.'

Golding wrote something down. When he had finished, he touched one end of the pen thoughtfully to his chin. 'On one hand we have an extremely strong motive – on the other an equally strong matter of principle. The question is: at what point does one overcome the other?'

Golding let the mood of his question settle for an instant, then turned towards Nabens.

'Again, with the emphasis on *if* this claim was proved, what would be the effects on the Middle East?'

'It's hard to judge. At present all the Arab nations are extremely sensitive to *any* outside involvement. The most important, and perhaps most pertinent factor is the position of Switzerland in Western society.' Nabens was gathering his thoughts as he went along. 'While most Arab nations decry their neighbouring Arabs' ever changing allegiances and attitudes, they almost accept it as par for the course. But they seem to expect something more from Western society. Talking of *principles*, as we were, they feel we have certain standards – both political and moral – which should be upheld above all else. In their eyes, if those should crumble, then God knows . . .' Nabens folded his hands on the table before him. 'Bit of a simplistic view – but as the one country that has waved the flag for peace more than any other, Switzerland would epitomize those standards. Talk of them being implicated in starting a war could be damaging beyond belief.'

Everyone was lost in their own thoughts and notes for a moment; Wetherall was the first to look up. 'Why would SBECSA's actions necessarily reflect on the nation as a whole?'

'Believe me, the Arabs find things like that particularly hard to separate,' Nabens said flatly.

Golding was still writing. 'And the effects?'

'That's the part that's hard to judge – the reaction could take a variety of forms. At the least it would certainly make Western mediation in any Middle-Eastern affairs more awkward.'

Nabens sat back as everyone completed their notes and looked towards Grade. 'There's something else about SBECSA that rings a bell – but I just can't put my finger on it.'

'They were heavily involved in a London property deal a few months back – that's probably it,' Wetherall commented.

Nabens considered this uncertainly. 'Yes, could be.'

'If you're ready, gentlemen,' Golding looked up. 'I think we should recap at this point. Danny, your man Mendel at the Swiss Institute – could he prove useful again on this one?'

'I think so. Mendel's a bit of a piggy in the middle as far as Swiss banking is concerned. He has a very solid reputation, some think he's virtually unapproachable. But we managed to work out quite a good arrangement during the course of my last investigation.'

'No backhanders on expenses I hope, Danny.' Golding feigned annoyance.

Grade smiled faintly. 'Please – let's not forget good Swiss principles.'

'Of course not,' Golding agreed blandly, enjoying the first hint of lightheartedness since they had entered the small room almost an hour beforehand.

Golding looked towards the clock on the far wall: 10.14 p.m. Everyone appeared to have offered their views. Wetherall had likely exaggerated – the two conflicting views of Swiss principles and warmongering seemed somehow too far apart. Nabens' theory of a harsh Arab reaction was more readily acceptable and sobering, one fact he wished could have been more easily discounted. As for Grade, only a few slim leads backed Reiner's claim; for the most part it would be a matter of seeing where, if anywhere, they led: a SBECSA subsidiary, Maslegeisen, involved in a supposed arms deal? The assassins of two prominent Muslim politicians apparently paid out of Switzerland? Golding studied his notes again, looking for something that might guide his decision further. He decided finally to tackle it another way.

'This man Reiner – if we didn't take the story, would he go elsewhere?'

Grade was pensive. 'He was particularly nervous about the whole thing, almost frenetic, and he expects to hear back from me immediately. I think the answer is yes.'

'I feared as much,' Golding commented. 'And if he goes to one of the tabloids . . . as we all well know, sometimes to our own expense, the motto of "print and be damned" still echoes in some quarters. They'd just leave the mess to be cleared up in the crossfire of counterclaims and innuendoes – and as they sat on the sidelines and watched, they'd milk *that* for all the publicity it was worth.'

'Does that mean we go with it?' Grade asked.

Golding gathered his composure. 'Yes Danny, it does, but mainly by default. I'm by no means convinced of your man Reiner's intentions, or the validity of his claims. And I'm even less happy about the possible consequences, but then that's not meant to be the concern of a good newsman.' Golding took off his glasses and placed them down summarily. 'I'm only going with it because it's simply too big to lose to somebody else. But I want it proved Danny, right down to its last sordid detail. Because that's the only way it's going to get printed.'

Golding played nervously with the pen in his hand. 'And if you should feel for one moment that we are on a wild goose chase, then I want you to pull out. We could expend an awful lot of money and manpower on a story like this – and perhaps to no avail.'

The outburst seemed to tire Golding; he was conscious of everyone staring at him. He placed his pen down. 'I think the best way to work it will be for Danny to follow the main story, and for you Dave and Rolf to act as the anchors, and supply any other input and sidebars as you might think appropriate.' Golding put his glasses back on. 'But it's late now – we'll make the final arrangements in the morning. We all might have some clearer thoughts to add then.' He started collecting his papers.

The realization of the commitment suddenly hit Grade; only two hours before all they had – all they *still* had – was some slimly connected evidence and allegations from a rather dapper Swiss banker, something 'that would have to be discussed at some length'. Now he was embarking on probably the largest news story of his life. He had worked with Nabens on several occasions before – most recently on a story about the repatriation of a Jordanian doctor from England after the murder of his own children – but he had only once relied on Wetherall, for some information related to a computer fraud.

It was clear that Golding didn't wish to entertain too much further discussion, and there was silence as Nabens and Wetherall started collecting their things. Grade remained seated as the three men cleared their papers from the table and moved towards the far end of the room.

'Aren't you leaving now, Danny?' Golding asked from the door.

'No, it's okay, I just want to make some final notes.'

The small office was particularly quiet after the door had been closed; the smell of stale coffee and cigarettes, which always reminded Grade of late nights in the newsroom, hung thickly in the air. In the distance a clock chimed above the dull churning of the presses.

Fleet Street had seen its golden days, Daniel mused: Profumo, Burgess and Maclean and, on the international scene, JFK's assassination, Suez, Watergate. There was little doubt that the story could rank among them, *if* he could prove it. The prospect felt somehow distant, and not only because what they had traded at the meeting had been mostly tentative; size, in itself, seemed to make it all the more elusive.

Grade tried to concentrate – to plan out some sort of schedule for his forthcoming meetings with Mendel and

Leorah Ajlan – but one thought stayed prominent, the same thought that had entered his mind just after his meeting with Anton Reiner. He looked towards the calendar on the far wall, identical to the *Daily Post* calendar in Bob Golding's office: 29 November 1976. It had been over eighteen months since the start of the Lebanese war. Why should the information come through now?

2

It was almost midday, but the sun appeared quite low over the jagged, snow-capped peaks above Mürren. A faint mist encircled Schilthorn, the highest peak; a mist that moved imperceptibly with the breeze, at times completely shrouding, at others only slightly veiling the mountain tops.

The sun seemed somehow to shine up towards the peak, and when the mist cleared, the people in the cable-car could make out the circular edifice of the Piz Gloria restaurant and the main cable station, glistening down at them like faint beacons.

The cable-car trundled slowly up towards the summit.

Anton Reiner wished now that he had brought his binoculars. The panorama was breathtaking. Far below and behind them, the small village of Mürren clung to its narrow ledge high above the rich green of the Stechelberg meadows. Ahead, beyond Schilthorn, the Monch and Eiger could be seen quite clearly, and further to the south-east the peak of Jungfrau edged starkly above the sheer limestone cliffs at its base. The snow level was quite high, covering mainly the peaks and some of the higher, north-facing ledges.

'I'm glad that we came here now,' Anton remarked. 'It's beautiful, isn't it, Piai?'

'Yes, but I think it's better in the spring.' Piai looked out to one side. She was tall and blonde and ten years younger than him, a slight darkening in her eyebrows and the deep-set roundness of her eyes betraying her Italian background.

'Did we come here in the spring?' he asked.

'No, we went on the lift at Chamonix – remember? We were on our own, we left the children with Clara.' She turned slightly, taking in a wider panorama through the large glass window. 'There was much less snow, and the fields were greener, more vivid.'

There were about a dozen other people in the cable-car. The two children were at the far end, looking back towards Mürren. They tore their attention away and moved across as the vista of Schilthorn loomed nearer, and the valley floor became more distant, insignificant.

Marc, the eldest, was almost ten, and his enthusiasm was quite obvious. He pointed towards the peak.

'Is that the restaurant?'

'Yes, yes, it is.' His father put a calming hand on the boy's shoulder. 'Look, Marc, don't move about so much. You might disturb people – perhaps even rock the cable-car.'

The boy seemed almost excited by the prospect. His little sister didn't really understand, and merely looked on expectantly. She was small and blonde, almost a miniature of her mother. Anton reached across and touched her head lightly.

'We'll be there soon – only a matter of minutes.'

The cable-car tilted slightly, then righted as it took up the slack in the wire and started the steepest part of the ascent. Anton could feel the car swaying, accentuated even more by the stronger breeze at that altitude.

Anton felt a new sense of exhilaration. There was something about the sheer grandeur of the scenery – combined with the element of excitement – that possessed the mind strongly. *Problems* were easy to forget.

The car was now close enough for them to gain a full view of the restaurant and cable station; the light patches of mist had cleared even further, and they could now see above the preceding snow-covered ledges. Anton could make out the movement of people in the restaurant, and those queuing by the station for the next car down, but they were still distant enough to be no more than vague shapes.

For a second something caught his attention – a small irregularity in the pattern of the scene ahead – and he fixed his gaze more intently. He held it there for a while, trying to pick out more clearly the figures around the cable station. Unconsciously, he found he had been gripping his son's shoulder tighter.

'Father?' the boy looked up at him questioningly.

'I'm sorry,' he murmured after a second. He could feel that some beads of sweat had come to his forehead, and he dabbed at them with a handkerchief.

He looked back at the cable station. There were a number of people milling about behind it, and a few people on the platform itself: someone at the ticket kiosk, a guard, and two men in overalls, probably engineers or operators. He concentrated on the concrete housing above the platform. The movement was clearer now – someone was edging among the shadows of the giant steel wheels and cables. At first he thought it could be an engineer, but the overalls didn't match the light blue of the two men below – the colour was much darker, probably dark blue or black, and there was something dark obscuring his face.

Anton dabbed his forehead furiously. '*Himmel!* For God's sake.'

His wife had noticed his increasing anxiety. 'What's wrong?'

'I don't know yet,' he snapped. He swung around and surveyed the other passengers inside the cable-car. His eyes rested on a man in a flannel suit at the far end, and he moved across.

'Your binoculars – could I borrow them please?'

There was something in Reiner's tone that prevented the man from asking why. He passed them across with a faintly quizzical expression.

'Yes . . . okay.'

Anton took the binoculars with a polite nod and turned them towards the cable station, pressing them as close to the glass as possible to kill any reflection.

The cable station was out of focus at first. Anton adjusted

the binoculars quickly, panning in on the interior of the concrete housing. A small flicker of movement showed to one side of the frame, and he held his focus on that position. Gradually the figure became apparent among the shadows. There was another movement, the figure coming into a stark beam of sunlight breaking through a gap in the large steel wheels, and there was no longer any doubt.

Anton watched intently. There was something directly in front of the man, attached to the large supporting cable, demanding his full attention: a white, moulded plastic object with some loose wires protruding. Anton watched the man strip one of the wires, take something from a side pocket, and attach it to one end; then press it hard back into the plastic. The man started working on the other loose wires.

Anton held the binoculars limply to one side. Fear gripped his stomach like an icy claw. *Where the hell was Swenkel?* His man had been watching on Friday; he had seen the car in its usual position – they *must* have known that he had gone away, and *should* have followed.

He gazed at the vista below, but suddenly it held none of the beauty of only moments before. Now it looked rugged and barren – hostile. He could picture the scenario in his mind's eye: the explosion, the cable reeling rapidly out from its housing, the car plunging into the depths of the valley below. He studied the valley closer. There was a ledge a hundred feet or so below, shrouded in faint mist, but the car would likely be only slightly faltered by that, perhaps splitting open, then would continue its journey down, rolling and bounding over the sharp rocks until it reached the bottom. There would be no chance of survival; the valley floor was so distant it was barely visible

Suddenly Anton was aware of all the small movements of the car – movements that he hadn't really been aware of before: the gentle rocking as it rose on the curve of the wire, the swaying with the breeze that whipped sharply around the upper levels of Schilthorn. Anton felt the cold fear rise as nausea to his chest and throat. Some vomit trickled into his mouth, and he wiped at it brusquely with his handkerchief –

and at the now thicker perspiration on his forehead.

Piai gripped at his arm tightly. 'Darling . . . what is it?'

'Please . . . please,' he gasped. He looked desperately past her to the two children. The boy was old enough to sense that something was wrong, but the girl looked on so innocently. So unaware.

Anton wrenched his attention away and looked back through the binoculars.

There was a flicker of movement in the bottom of the frame, but Anton kept his attention on the figure inside the upper housing. The man was connecting the last of the wires – then he looked down suddenly. Anton panned down, following his vision. Something had dropped, or some movement had alerted the engineers below; one of them was looking up, signalling his colleague as he moved towards the steel ladder at the back. The engineer glanced up again momentarily, then started making his way along.

Anton panned back to the figure above; the actions were more hurried now. Anton could see now that it was a ski-mask covering the man's head, with only his eyes showing, making him appear even more ominously executioner-like. The man was turning again, looking down, struggling with the last of the wires.

The first engineer was halfway up the ladder, and the second had now come to its base appearing to call up. Anton began a silent prayer. He willed them on, fighting to relay his thoughts across the distance between them. *For God's sake, quicker!* Look there, *there!*

Anton clung to the faint hope. The first engineer was at the top of the stairs, looking around, but at that same instant the figure started moving away towards the back. Anton began to wonder if he had finished setting the device, or if he had been disturbed. The thought obsessed him in the passing minutes, as the engineers walked deeper into the housing in a slow, deliberate search.

The figure was obscured by one of the steel wheels for a second, and then Anton picked him out again, clambering down from the back of the platform, out of sight of the two guards. The ski-mask was gone, and he was heading into the crowds milling at the base of the platform. Anton panned back; one of the engineers had discovered the device.

Anton's pulse raced harder. If the charge had already been set, what were the chances that they would know how to defuse it? He saw the second engineer, directed by the other, head back down the ladder. It was unlikely that he was in pursuit of the escaping figure – they didn't seem to have been aware of his movements at the back, and by now it would be too late; he would have already merged into the crowds below. *No*, it had to be some form of emergency prevention, or an effort to defuse the device. God in hell, *hurry!* There couldn't be much time; it would surely have been set for a couple of minutes at the most. Anton wiped at his forehead again.

He watched the other cable-car load up and start its way down towards them. At that same instant it struck him that the escaping man would likely not want to stay around the restaurant or the cable station, and he began to inspect the car closer. It was too distant as yet to make out the huddled figures clearly, and he turned the binoculars back to the housing.

The first engineer was lifting up some of the wires tentatively, at intervals looking around for the return of his colleague. There was nobody on the ladder, and no apparent activity from the main office below. Anton felt a sudden sense of despair that they wouldn't defuse it in time, and clung again to the hope that the man had been disturbed before the charge had been fully set.

The other cable-car was closer now. He panned in, but the angle obscured the passengers in the centre and on the far side. Anton waited until it levelled out and drew nearer, by which time he no longer needed the binoculars. It was quite crowded, with a thick grouping of people looking away from them towards Jungfrau, but nothing significant. Then, as the car was almost alongside, a man looked around from the group towards him quite directly, meaningfully. As the man's eyes bored hard into his, Anton's slim hopes faded.

*

Daniel Grade got up early on the morning of Bob Golding's final meeting and busied himself in the kitchen making toast and hot coffee for breakfast. He had just buttered two slices of toast and poured out his first cup of coffee when Catherine walked in.

'Yes, please,' she muttered in a half-yawn, indicating the pot he was about to put back on the stove.

He poured out a second cup and passed it across, and they sat at opposite sides of the kitchen table, both in silence.

'You were late last night,' she commented at length.

'Yes, I'm sorry,' he answered. He suddenly didn't feel like expanding on such an obvious comment. He took a first bite of his toast and glanced at the morning paper lying on the table to one side.

Catherine studied him more intently – his sober, taut expression – and she felt both sorrow and contempt for him; sorrow that the extra work had obviously tired him as much as it had aggravated her, so that when he had come to bed the night before she had turned her back on him, feigning sleep; contempt that now he should pay her back with similar treatment. After all, it was *his* job to explain. She contemplated him a moment longer above the rim of her cup, then pressed a bit further.

'Something urgent, no doubt.'

He looked up briefly. 'Yes, I'm afraid so. I might have to return to Switzerland for a while.'

'But you've only just got back. I thought that the story was finished.'

'It is,' he said, folding the paper to one side. 'But this is something else. Same town, same banking community, same contact – but a different case.' He smiled wryly. 'It was referred through the last case, but there the connection ends.'

She knew that he was teasing, but decided to play along. 'I always did like playing twenty questions in the morning.'

'It was through Mendel. Simon Mendel – you remember.'

It was a ridiculous question; Simon Mendel was difficult

to forget. In the space of only six weeks Daniel had brought back numerous gifts from him for her and Julie. First, chocolate bars for Julie, then, when he realized she was older than he'd thought, a few top-quality one-pound boxes. And an ornament for herself – a porcelain mountain goat complete with brass bells. It was now on a side table in the hallway. Though they had never met, Mendel had become almost an extension of the family. She could also tell by Daniel's expression that the mention of his name should somehow make this new errand more acceptable. She wasn't softened by it.

'Well, at least you seem happy with it.'

Grade sipped thoughtfully at his coffee. 'I shouldn't be,' he said. 'Just as I'm ready to leave last night, a strange man walks into the office with the wildest claim imaginable. The only thing that sweetened the bait was the mention of Mendel's name. Two hours later Bob Golding dumps the whole thing in my lap. Investigate!'

'Then why didn't you say no?'

'It's simply too large – and it's as intriguing as hell. Besides which, it was me who started talking Bob into it in the first place, but he's usually so sceptical I didn't think he'd go for it.'

Catherine held one hand up to her head. 'Sometimes I think you're crazy, Danny. And I suppose it's the challenge?'

Daniel could sense the sudden edge in her voice, and he looked across the table more seriously. 'Look, I'm sorry about last night. Things got bogged down a bit and went on longer than I expected. I should have phoned again.'

'It's not that. It's just that I can picture it dragging on much the same as the last investigation. Christmas is just a month away now, you know.'

'Don't worry. It should all be wrapped up by then.'

'Yes, just like the case the same time last year was meant to be,' Catherine mocked.

'For God's sake!' Daniel folded the paper to one side. 'Is there anything else on your mind – or are we going for a full review of the year's most annoying events?'

Catherine turned away and bit her lip. 'What would be the point?'

Daniel went back to reading the paper. He could feel the tension in the silence that followed, almost sense Catherine's thoughts coming across in waves. He'd felt the same tension before, as if there was an invisible barrier growing between them, but this was one of the first times that Catherine had really aired her thoughts. She'd made small comments at times, but nothing that had amounted to much. It always seemed that she kept most of it in reserve.

Catherine looked back slowly. 'I wrote a letter to Julie last night.'

'That's good,' he said on impulse, though he quickly realized the significance; they usually took turns to write to the two girls, and if Catherine ever wrote out of sequence it was usually to Pauline in Australia.

'Anything special?'

'Need it necessarily be?'

'No. I just wondered.'

Catherine put down her cup. 'I just thought that with Christmas coming up, it would be good to make some arrangements for her visit.'

Daniel looked up. 'We're not back to that again, are we?'

'Perhaps we are,' Catherine said sharply. 'You seem to forget that she has spent most of the summer over there – we've seen her only a matter of weeks in the past year. So I think the least you can do is make sure you are *here*, and available, and unpreoccupied for Christmas. After all, she's *your* special daughter.'

Daniel got to his feet. 'Then why the hell did *you* write to her.'

Catherine could sense that the conversation had escalated far beyond what she had intended, but suddenly she felt the stopgap break, her emotions flood over.

'Because I was lonely. The same way I've been lonely so many nights in the last few years.'

'*Now* you tell me,' Daniel glared at her. He felt a pang of softness towards her, mixed with his anger, but he was too confused to say anything. He threw the paper down and stormed out of the room.

He was still in a daze as he went upstairs and shaved and dressed. Was this the reason for all those increasingly awkward silences and half-spoken thoughts of the passing months? He had always thought it to be some private inner problem that she would tell him about in time, in her *own* time. He had never pressed, perhaps he had even been too busy to do that – Christ, how could he have been so blind, so unfeeling?

Then again, Catherine was intelligent, sophisticated. All too often she would appear very private, very aloof; she could hide her thoughts with a half-smile or even a sharp rebuke. You wanted to delve, to ask what was wrong, but all the time you could feel her silent defences warning you off. In that way, it was as much her fault as anyone's.

He finished dressing and left the house without saying goodbye.

The sun on the A25 into London slowly relaxed his mood, his thoughts beginning to gel. He would book his flight to Zürich straight after seeing Golding again. If things went smoothly he would be in Beirut within another two days.

It was the worst possible time for the problem with Catherine to surface. There would be so much to think of in the coming weeks. They were slowly splitting apart, but what could he do about it?

Leorah Ajlan woke with a start as the roar of the fighter plane receded. She went quickly to the window. Her apartment was on the third floor, and she could see the flames from the bombs and incendiaries in the distance above the spread of Beirut's grey and white rooftops. Two, perhaps three, miles away; she measured distance against St George's Bay to the east.

She glanced up at the sky. The jet was beyond the hills encircling Jdaide, she guessed from its faint roar. Only its vapour trail now remained.

Leorah went over to the dresser and started changing. It was a practised routine, and she had cut the time down to under two minutes. A shirt was already inside her khaki jacket, and they went on together; then came a pair of khaki trousers with a canvas belt through the loops, from which hung a large sheathed knife; lastly, a pair of combat boots. She picked up a first-aid box as she got to her feet, and reached for the holstered gun from her wardrobe: a Llama .45. From the same shelf she took a small peaked cap; her long black hair was already in a bun, and she perched the cap on and pulled it down sharply.

The uniform concealed her softness and femininity but, as with the sign of the Lebanese Croix Rouge on her jeep, she had found that little deterrent against getting fired at, so it was best to keep to practicalities. Already she felt both fear and apprehension at the numbers of dead and wounded that would await her. Her adrenalin raced harder as she made her way down. Almost in a panic she took her jeep out from its garage and onto the Rue Maamari. She turned east and then cut off onto the Rue Rebeiz, heading for the bay.

She passed behind the cluster of luxury hotels that had been the scene of intense fighting over eight months ago; the scars weren't so apparent from the back, but it was still clear from carbon staining around the window frames that many of the rooms on the middle and upper floors were burnt out and empty. The few residential and office buildings in between had been badly battered by the crossfire and short-fall of mortars; what remained was little more than wasteground.

Shortly after the fighting, Leorah had been both amazed and disgusted by the spectacle, but now so many districts of the city had gone the same way that it had become a common backdrop. Now her attention was drawn by the *other* districts – the traders and bankers of the Rue Hamra and Emir Bechir – their outwardly untouched opulence in itself seeming to defy the grip of war on the city.

Often she would reflect on the way that fortunes had changed. Certainly, the path of her own life had changed radically; it had been less than four months since the bombing of the *Yaumi Rassul* offices. There had been bombings of other Muslim newspaper offices during the previous months – usually followed by swift retaliations against Phalangist counterparts – and full production had been delayed until a fresh review of the war situation. Most correspondents had either become stringers for those remaining newspapers or had contributed to the wire service for foreign newspapers.

Leorah felt that neither alternative would make proper use of her past experience, so she might as well aid in *other* areas; a position at the Croix Rouge had become vacant at the time. 'Information officer' had been the initial title, but the rigours of war had quickly demanded other skills: general first-aid, family resettlement, comforter and counsel to both soldiers and victims.

The post had made little use of her journalism, but the children had made up for it; they were always the ones to suffer most in wartime, the ones she felt really needed her. After all, Jamil, her brother, had been little more than a child during the troubles of '58. She had kept his photo in her diary, had marked off his birthday each year – he would have been twenty-seven now – two years younger than her. At times, she wondered what he might look like now had he lived.

The roar of the jet returned. Leorah looked out across the bay as she sped along. The jet had circled around to the far side of the harbour and was now heading out to sea.

A slight cloud cover was moving in, casting its grey on the water, and the fighter's vapour trail was now only visible towards the hills. It was the sort of weather they usually chose. Probably Israeli, she judged, watching its path swing south – the border was less than seventy miles away.

Leorah turned her attention towards the smoke on the horizon as she came onto the Avenue Charles Helou, then crossed the Beirut bridge, heading towards Jdaide. As she got closer to the village, winding through the narrow backroads, she could tell that the smoke was coming from the hills slightly further north, probably the encampment at Zalqua. She put her foot down harder; it was less than another three miles now.

The rising smoke had trapped itself in small pockets among the hills, some of it spreading out across the road ahead; she could just make out a Red Cross truck heading through it towards her as it climbed over a small ridge. It was windowless, and she gave it no more than a passing glance; the injured inside would be with the doctors at the East unit soon, while those in the village below who perhaps couldn't be moved would need her attention more.

She gained her first sight of the refugee encampment as she crossed the same ridge, looking down into a small gulley. Most of the buildings were constructed of clay, water and breeze-blocks; the roofs were slate, and corrugated iron, sandbags and advertising hoardings had been used to patch the damage caused in previous raids.

The fire was coming from three or four houses towards the back of the village. It had burned them out almost completely, though there seemed little danger now of the fire spreading, the blast had levelled most of the surrounding houses. There were about a thousand people in the encampment, most of them Palestinians and leftists; a large number of them were now out on the streets, adding more confusion.

Leorah could see that one Red Cross jeep had remained behind. She meandered her way down quickly, parking as close to it as possible.

As she surveyed the scene, she could see Dr Halaafa from the ICRC unit in East Beirut, coming from one of the houses close to the edge of the fire. She went across.

'How many injured are there?' she asked him.

He looked up briefly from some notes he was making on a clipboard. It took a moment for the question to register.

'About twelve or thirteen. But I'm not counting the minor injuries – there are a score of those or more.'

'And deaths?'

'We were lucky. Only three.'

She looked out across the battered buildings. 'What defence was there?'

'There's a guerrilla unit a couple of miles away – apparently they've got a rocket launcher. A few of them came down on reconnaissance, but by then it was all over. They've probably pulled back into the hills by now.'

'And that was all? They didn't offer any assistance?'

'They rarely do. They just fight the wars – they leave the injured for us.'

Leorah studied the fire and the hills behind more thoughtfully. The doctor started to move away.

'Anyway, you're a bit premature aren't you? We won't be issuing a full report until tomorrow.'

'I'm not here just for that,' she said sharply, then shrugged. 'You know me doctor – always seeing in which other ways I can be of use.'

He looked back more directly; for the first time he was aware of the soft lines beneath her heavy khaki canvasses, the inquiring compassion in her eyes.

'I don't know you that well Miss Ajlan, but I know of your activities. And yes, you are right – we need every bit of help we can get. In that respect, you are welcome.'

'You don't mind if I look around?'

He waved his clipboard to one side. 'Of course not. Go ahead.'

Leorah acknowledged him curtly and made her way back towards the fire. The ground was littered with displaced rubble, boarding and sandbags, and she picked her way through carefully. The crackling heat and smoke of the residual fire threatened to smother her.

The smell hit her as she got closer, as it had done at Damour and Tal-al-Zaater – the smell of paint and plaster burning, of decay, of burnt flesh. It had been much worse then and at most other sights she had visited. *God*, she quickly reprimanded herself, is that how she saw things now? Did the size of the attack make it any less atrocious? The loose rubble and concrete was hot beneath her feet as she got closer to the heart of the fire, and she trod lightly.

At that moment she heard something which stopped her in her tracks. Her skin prickled. It wasn't the crackling or hissing of the fire, nor the wailing and crying from the confusion in the village behind. She listened more intently. It was coming from only a few yards ahead: a faint groaning, muffled among some loose rubble and a sheet of boarding. She scrambled forwards quickly.

She was more certain now; she could pick out the position it was coming from. She threw aside a few of the loose rocks and moved a part of the boarding. An arm appeared.

Her breath stopped, then came back in a faint gasp. She clawed desperately at the remaining rocks, drawing blood from her fingertips, but not caring, not feeling the pain. She rapidly cleared enough to view most of the head and chest.

It was a young boy, probably no more than eight or nine. His body was blackened by the heat and carbon, the surrounding fine white dust adhering in parts. His hair was thickly matted, and he looked up with both relief and suspicion as the light hit him. Leorah felt a lump rise in her throat. She wiped gently at his face and tried to force a smile from behind her sadness and revulsion.

'*Ikame hudu.* Don't worry – you're safe now.' She swung around and looked back towards the village. Dr Halaafa was by his jeep. 'Doctor, please, come quickly!'

She clawed at a few more of the rocks as the doctor made his way across. Together, they moved the remaining rocks and hauled the boy out. They carried him across and laid him close to the doctor's jeep.

'So much for the recovery team,' Leorah snapped.

'We haven't got time to go into that now.' Halaafa took his bag down and took out some cloth and surgical spirit.

He started cleaning off the loose grime and dust, and a gaping wound quickly became apparent on the boy's leg. The boy hissed in pain. The carbon had coagulated the blood in a thick cake which had sealed the wound. Now the blood ran freely again.

'If you'll do a tourniquet, I'll clean the wound further,' Halaafa instructed.

Leorah took out a bandage and tied it high up on the boy's leg. Halaafa continued wiping with the cloth, but he could see now that the wound was much deeper than he had first thought.

'I'll have to give him a local.' He took a needle and syringe, and rolled a cloth and put it to the boy's mouth. 'If you'll bite on this it will help.'

Halaafa waited for the anaesthetic to take effect, then started cleaning deeper; after a moment he could see that the bone was showing through. He took out some instruments from his bag and probed tentatively.

'How bad is it?' asked Leorah.

'Some shrapnel has broken through the muscle tissue and at least one tendon has been severed. The cartilage might also be damaged. It's very dirty and difficult to clean – there could be a danger of gangrene if he's not operated on quickly. He could lose the leg. You'll have to take him to the East unit straight away.'

Leorah showed her surprise. 'Why can't you do it here?'

'It's just not possible. There's a woman here with a haemorrhage, she can't be moved. I have to operate on her here, and *quickly*.'

'But, as you said, the boy might lose his leg!'

'Yes, but with the woman it's her *life*. I have to make that choice!'

Leorah stared back defiantly a moment longer. She suddenly sensed the futility of arguing further; that in itself was killing time. If she drove hard, it would take her less than twenty minutes.

'Where's his mother do you think?' she asked.

The boy muttered, '*Juwa eldai'a*,' and pointed

The doctor looked towards the confused mass of people.

'There's no way of him knowing since the attack. Besides which it could take too long – we just haven't the time. I'll ask around for who's missing a child while you're gone.' Halaafa bandaged the arm and cleaned some marks on the boy's stomach. He looked up again. 'There's a couple of shrapnel marks on his stomach which aren't so serious, but have him checked for internal injuries – you can never be too sure.'

Leorah nodded. They lifted the boy and put him in the passenger seat of her jeep. She confirmed a few final details regarding the East Beirut unit, then put her foot down hard, heading out on the dust road.

As she cleared the hills surrounding the village, she reached over and gently cleared the boy's matted hair away from his eyes. Suddenly it felt like she was trying to save Jamil all over again.

3

There were nearly fifty CRS, the special French riot guard, facing the crowd that morning in the Place St Michel. They were in total black, the gleam of their visors and body-length shields making them appear faceless, impenetrable. Behind them, the crumbling stone façades and steps of the Latin Quarter looked out of place against their display of uncompromising efficiency.

Ahead, the crowd – mostly students from the Sorbonne and a few outside activists – were in disarray, and becoming increasingly agitated as the guards advanced slowly. Some shied to the back with their hastily daubed banners.

Xavier Peton stood his ground. The girl with him, Julie, he had met eight months before. She was the daughter of a London journalist, on student exchange from Radford College, Oxford.

'*Bien assez*, they will do nothing, you will see,' he muttered indignantly.

In the months he had known her, he had discovered that at heart she was not a radical. That her father had indoctrinated her in what he would often term 'the class-conscious values of the *nouveau riche*'. Not quite *haute bourgeoisie*, but supporting similar traditions because they had done well by them. Now Xavier felt he should even the balance by enlightening her as to his own view of the social revolution: that some degree of militancy was vital, if nothing else to provide politicians with a necessary degree of insecurity.

The guards moved slowly forward, but with purpose.

'Are you sure they won't do anything?'

'Sure, sure?' he mimicked. 'You always want a guarantee. How could I know? I am as far from reading their minds as they are from mine.' He shrugged and conceded as an afterthought. 'Perhaps they are a bit more predictable.'

The crowd split apart even further, their numbers thinning, the unease settling deeper. Panic sparked and spread like a wave as the first break showed in their ranks. The guards picked up pace, but maintained the same heavy marching stomp.

Xavier tugged at Julie's arm.

'*Vite, vite.* It is no good. It's too late now.' He looked to one side, towards a small street heading in the direction of the Pantheon. 'Over there!'

He began to run with Julie at his heel, but as he looked across, the CRS were narrowing the angle to the small street. He wasn't sure they could make it. He scanned the square once again – there were two other exits on that same side, but they were blocked by the surge of the crowd. He yanked back at Julie's arm.

'It's our only chance.'

Julie's heel caught in one of the rough flagstones, and she half-stumbled, only keeping balance by her tight grip on Xavier's arm. The last group of CRS were within yards of the street entrance, and she was suddenly seized by fear.

The guards came across in an arc, forming almost a shiny black wall of plastic and steel. Xavier brushed past a few, but Julie could see that the last was directly in her path. His shield was held firmly before him, and his baton was raised. She saw it lift higher as he bore down upon her. Her legs seemed paralysed.

She braced herself and ducked down to protect herself from the blow. But at the last second he pulled back the baton and pushed out his shield, brushing her aside. Julie felt the glancing impact to her ribs and one shoulder, knocking the wind from her, careening her off into the side street just behind Xavier.

When she looked around, fully ten yards into the street, she was clear. She stood still for a moment in the relative quiet and safety, catching at her breath. Part amazement and relief swept through her. It left a space that was quickly filled with shock and sickness.

The last line of guards passed in a rush, now almost at full pace, their heavy boots clattering on the rough flagstones. As the guards clashed with the crowd, the two became hopelessly tangled, people beginning to spill out from each side.

Julie turned away.

'Are you all right?' Xavier asked.

'Yes, but no thanks to you.' She leaned back and brushed some of her hair out of her face. The colour slowly came back into it. 'I hope you don't have any more bright ideas for a Sunday outing.'

'I'm sorry, okay?' He seemed suddenly vexed and looked further up the road. On the corner was a bar with a small *Martell* sign. 'Look, this is no place to talk, come on.'

He turned away, but she stayed for a moment before following. Never again, she thought to herself. Only a few weeks previously, water cannons had been turned on a crowd in the Place des Invalides. She must have been mad to agree to the idea in the first place. It wasn't so much the consequence that annoyed her, more Xavier's damn cocksureness. She caught up with him as he entered the bar.

'So they wouldn't attack, eh?'

He led the way to a table through the smoky atmosphere and they sat down. He looked across directly.

'But they wouldn't have, I tell you. I know this from before.'

'In your own words – if I remember them correctly – they are brutal, cold-blooded enforcers of the capitalist status quo, and will grasp at any excuse to crack a few heads . . . Now you can't have it both ways.'

Xavier held Julie's hand across the table. 'It's true what I said. They *are* ruthless and brutal, but they are also cowards. They were outnumbered by the crowd today ten to one – if the crowd looked organized and even a bit angry, they would not go in. They are not so stupid. It's part of their job to intimidate, to weaken the crowd – create fear, anxiety. And when a weak point appears, *then* they go in.'

An old man in the corner appeared to be listening to them; probably with more curiosity than normal because they were speaking in English. Julie looked unconvinced. Xavier leaned further forward.

'Don't you see, it's the same every time. The crowd becomes weak, begins to split up, and they attack. It is simple.'

'Then what made you think they wouldn't attack this time?'

Xavier lifted his hands up. '*Pah!* I would have thought the students would have learned their lesson by now. They have been told what I have just told you time and time again about these marches. So I give up – I don't know the answer any more.'

The *patron*'s wife came up for their order. Xavier sat back again.

'*Oui, pastis* . . . And you, Julie, you should have a brandy.'

Julie nodded dumbly. The *patron*'s wife understood the order in English and went back to the bar.

They settled into silence as she went away, and were still in silence when their drinks arrived, apart from some small comments from Xavier spurred by the noise in the square having died down.

At times, Julie thought, she didn't know how to take him. Often he would seem wise and intuitive, then just as quickly the opposite. Even his appearance was confusing; with his horn-rimmed glasses and his dark hair waved back, at times he looked erudite and sophisticated, one of those few young men who actually looked good wearing glasses. At other times, it would make him look childish and weak, inarticulate. She liked to think of him in the better light, but on occasions she found it difficult. Perhaps his expression gave him away; perhaps it changed along with a part of his personality.

She knew the fundamental mistake she made. She would compare him with her father. For as long as she could remember, her father had seemed so reliable, so strong in spirit, it was probably unfair to compare. She often thought that he had always been like that, even when he was a teenager; that he hadn't suffered the same fickleness as the young men she knew. Even his boxing photos – testament to his 'wildest' period – had a certain rough elegance about them.

It brought her mind back to the letter she had just received from her mother. Although nothing was mentioned directly, she felt something unsettling in its underlying tone. She felt suddenly she should be there, if only for the assurance that she was wrong. But it was impractical; she pushed the thought away after a moment. She had enough problems coping with Xavier's moods of late.

Xavier was sipping repeatedly at his pastis. 'Anyway, we are finished with demonstrations like that. Never again!'

'Well at least we gained something from today,' Julie commented dryly.

'No, no, I don't mean in that way. Just that we are finished with anything so disorganized. There are more powerful, influential pressure groups than the student body here.'

'And more dangerous to be involved with.'

Xavier leaned back across the table. 'That is where you are wrong. They are not so dangerous simply because they *are* organized. People like Le Marteau Rouge.' Xavier's eyes were suddenly fevered and distant. 'In fact, I have already made contact with them, and things look favourable.'

Julie felt growing apprehension. She was reminded of her cold panic earlier, in the square. 'Xavier, please. Today we were lucky – next time . . .'

'You are worrying for nothing. They are still only a mild pressure group – they are not terrorists, for God's sake.' Xavier knocked back the last of his pastis. 'Believe me, it's safe.'

*

Daniel Grade took a taxi from the Bellerive au Lac hotel on Zürich's Utoquai, heading towards the city's banking centre. He had initially wanted to stay at the St Gotthard so that he was within walking distance, but there was little available at such short notice.

The changes in the city in the last couple of months were small but noticeable: there were fewer coaches and tourists evident, and the water on the river Limmat as they crossed the Quai bridge now looked almost grey with a faint mist. The clouds were low, shrouding the nearby mountains.

As they turned into Banhof Strasse, it was easier now to judge the city's austere banking mood; the façades of the grey stone buildings seemed stern and unapproachable under the heavy sky. The only contrast was the elaborate hotels and shops of the street, against which some of the banks had made an effort to compete with more modern foyers in glass and chrome.

'Schweizerische Institut?' The driver confirmed over his shoulder.

'Ja.'

The building was most of the way up Banhof Strasse, and the driver stopped just past the back of Werd-Muhle Place. It took a moment for Grade to get his bearings; on earlier visits he had approached from the Banhof Bridge end. He thanked the driver and paid him.

Grade looked up at the building. He had wired from London, then had phoned earlier that morning to confirm the appointment: Mendel would be expecting him.

Golding's directives from their final meeting played over in his mind as he made his way inside, then up in the lift. 'Try to prove Wetherall's theory of monetary gain; balance it against this question of principle. Find out the feasibility of a rogue element within SBECSA'.

Golding had thought it expedient to have a meeting with Mendel before making contact again with Reiner; it was vital to test independently Reiner's claims before taking the investigation further.

The seventh-floor bell rang. Grade stepped out into a small open reception area and approached the girl at the desk.

'Mr Mendel, please. My name's Daniel Grade. I have an appointment.'

The receptionist remembered him vaguely from his last visit. 'Ah, yes. One moment please.' She paged through the intercom, then indicated the leather chairs to one side. 'He won't be long.'

Grade glanced out of the window while he waited. After a second, his attention was drawn back to the desk; a light was flickering for an outgoing line. Golding's doubts resurfaced: 'If a rogue element existed, could one or even a small group of men exercise such power?' Grade tried to focus his thoughts, but they were broken by Mendel's office door opening.

'Daniel, you gave me such a surprise when I received your wire. Please, come in.'

Grade walked ahead into the office and took one of two armchairs opposite Mendel's desk. The room was in neutral shades of beige and brown, with abstract prints at almost precise set intervals. Somehow, as before, it reminded Grade of a psychiatrist's office.

'It's so soon after our last meeting, you see,' Mendel added. 'I would have thought that any further loose ends could have been dealt with by phone.'

'It's actually something quite different. I hoped you wouldn't mind.'

'Ah, now I'm at a loss. Two visits in almost as many months. To what do I owe this pleasure?'

Grade felt awkward in the face of Mendel's levity, but purely because of the subject he had come to tackle. Mendel's attitude *had* leaned more and more in that direction during his last visit, and they had developed a very amiable working relationship, almost a friendship. It was quite a contrast to when they had first met; then Mendel had been reticent and guarded, living up to his reputation as Zürich's 'ferret', gained from his ability to seek out financial information.

Applied to his appearance, the term was unfair: Mendel's features were small and angular, but he was still a good-looking man at fifty-five, his light brown hair greying and swept back slightly, but with no thinning.

Mendel's grey eyes suddenly lost their friendliness, became more piercing, searching.

'Was there something wrong with the information I gave you?'

'No, no, it's not that,' Grade put him at ease.

Grade mentioned Reiner, then began to explain his visit to the newsroom of the day before. He watched Mendel's expression gradually change from polite interest to concern. Mendel stopped him at one point and ordered coffee through the intercom. He settled back again.

'This is quite a claim this man Reiner of yours is making. Can he substantiate it?'

Grade homed in on the 'this man Reiner'. 'Doesn't the name ring a bell? According to him, he was referred to me through you – from the CYBAL investigation.'

Mendel frowned, searching his memory.

'No,' he said finally. 'I remember a woman contacting me a while ago – asking about the CYBAL investigation. A Miss Grenouille at the Banque du Martigny. I passed her your name.'

'Yes, that would be it. Reiner's a *sous-directeur* at Martigny.'

Mendel nodded. 'As far as names are concerned, has he given you any leads here in the banking community?'

'Apart from the fact that he suspects someone within SBECSA, no . . .' Grade pandered to Mendel's raised eyebrow. 'Though vague, our *desk* view seems to go along with that. No other bank is large enough to have a worthwhile interest.'

Mendel stared at him pointedly for a moment, then swivelled his chair to an angle, glancing out of the window, stroking his chin thoughtfully. '. . . Accepted.'

Grade filled in the details, giving the fuller extent of his newspaper's views on Reiner's claims. Mendel remained silent, pondering. The only interruption was the arrival of their coffees. Mendel showed surprise at Maslegeisen's possible arms shipment, but promised to find out just how much that went outside of their normal activities. As a last point, Grade covered the suspected connection with the assassinations of Amir Khourem and Al-Hakim.

Mendel opened his hands out. 'And these assassinations alone were meant to be the root cause of the war starting?'

'No, just the spark to an already highly volatile situation.' Grade raised his eyes as he sipped back the last of his coffee. 'Khourem was an ideally placed leftist with an almost fanatical following. It was a measured act – little else would have been necessary.'

Grade could see by the expression on Mendel's face that only then did the total impact dawn. Mendel's gaze was distant. Slowly, he swivelled his chair straight.

'I just hope you're wrong,' he sighed. 'For all of our sakes, I hope you're wrong.'

Mendel got up from his chair and stood by the window, looking out.

Grade sat anxiously in the passing seconds. Despite their friendship, he was in awe of Mendel and the banking system he represented. It was indisputably the world's largest, handling money that could buy many nations tenfold – and the vital key to its unrivalled success had always been secrecy. The very same secrecy that Grade was now attacking. And Simon Mendel was a kingpin, an arbiter of that system, those traditions. Yet without him, Grade knew that he would never be able to penetrate its inner sanctums.

It was a thin line to walk. If Mendel decided the system was threatened from within, he could decide that these people, these renegades should be set apart from it, made an example of – so that the system itself would remain mostly unscathed. But if he should decide that the system would suffer through *either* path that was taken, the barriers would come down; at the worst, article 273 of the Swiss penal code would be evoked – the clause which strongly dissuaded prying into Swiss banking affairs. Breaking it was comparable to a charge of treason in most other Western nations.

Mendel's judgement was absolute, but Grade trusted it above any other; he was both respected and respectable, an arbiter of fine principles and fair play, incisive criticism and judgement. Above all, as their final judge, he had to be a man that the system looked up to, who exemplified all their best traditions and practices. Grade had seen that all too well on his past investigation. On that side of it, Mendel would be as eager as he to flush out an enemy in the camp. Grade held his breath as he looked at Mendel's taut face. Silence had settled like a cloak.

'Do you realize what all this suggests?' Mendel commented finally.

'Yes, fully.'

'And where it could lead? Do you really know *that*?' Mendel turned and looked hard at Grade. 'It will reflect badly on *all* Swiss banks, even if SBECSA is cleared. There could easily be a run. Then there is the thorny question of Swiss neutrality.'

'I'm quite aware of the significance – moral and otherwise,' Grade said, his voice matching Mendel's gravity. 'But I was hoping to get away from that factor and more to the facts. If SBECSA is cleared, the story won't be printed; it's as simple as that.'

Mendel was silent. He had shown shock at first, as if not accepting it, not *wanting* to believe it. Now his face gave a different picture: of someone studying a puzzle for the first time, analysing it calmly, then finally slotting its pieces together.

'Yes, yes, of course,' he said quickly. 'I'm sorry. If what I am thinking is correct, the whole thing is unlikely anyway, and I am already beginning to think of the implications. So silly of me, really. Please, let us get back to facts. What first made Reiner suspicious?'

'Many small things, a lot of it circumspection. Apart from the assassinations, the main hard fact is of course the Maslegeisen link.'

Mendel sat down. 'And is this true? Have you actually checked that arms were shipped?'

'If Maslegeisen have something to hide, I don't think they will so readily let me look at their records. I won't know about that until I check with the receiving warehouse in Beirut. I decided to come to Zürich first.' As the words came out, Grade began to think that perhaps he should have reversed things.

Mendel's eyes flickered rapidly. 'And talking of names again. Do you have something there, in the Middle East perhaps?'

'Only contacts,' Grade said. 'But it wouldn't help much, even if I could discuss them. It's really the Swiss end I'm interested in.'

'Yes, yes, I see.' Mendel took a cigar box from one side and offered it to Grade. 'I know they're smaller than the ones you like, but you'll find them good Havana.'

Mendel tilted his chair while Grade lit up. He put the ends of his fingertips together, as if he had followed a particular line of thought and had now come to its end. As quick as his shock had appeared, it had dissipated.

'You see, Daniel, with something like this . . .' He seemed to be searching for words. 'You don't really want to believe it's possible; in fact, by all rights, it simply is *not* possible. And that is apart from my fear of the consequences. Those still stand – though that is probably as much my natural protective instincts at work as anything else. As I say, I think you have to get back to square one and ask some very necessary questions. In that respect, we have hardly begun to scratch the surface. If you had said to me that so and so at whatever branch of SBECSA was suspect, then we would at least have a starting point. As it is . . .'

'I know how it looks, Simon, but at this stage it really is *only* feasibility I'm interested in.' Grade suppressed an ironic laugh. 'In fact my editor echoed almost exactly your sentiments. That's why I'm here, instead of with Reiner. We're not committed as yet.'

'And that will depend on what I have to tell you now?' Mendel held his hands inward.

'To some extent. And of course other factors . . .'

'Yes, of course.' Mendel looked down with a thoughtful air, then started leafing through a drawer to one side. 'It would seem so ridiculous just telling you straight out that you're wasting your time, Daniel. I mean you are *here* now, having come all this way. So I think it best to show you something.' Mendel passed across two sheets of paper.

They were both graphs, with dates at the bottom and figures along the side. Grade studied them for a moment.

'Both show the inflow of investment capital in Switzerland,' Mendel informed him. 'The first shows it in relation to the value of the Swiss Franc against the American dollar. The second against the interest paid to investors in Swiss Francs over the same period. Both run up until April of this year.' Mendel left a significant pause.

'You will notice that although the interest rate paid goes down considerably, the investment keeps increasing. Also, if you compare the interest charge with the Swiss Franc value against the dollar, there is an almost direct relationship. One is coming down, the other at the same time is going up.'

Grade put the papers down. 'How does this affect Reiner's claims?'

'Very simply. Swiss banks just don't want foreign investments at this moment.'

Grade drew deep and long on his cigar. 'Isn't that a bit of a contradiction in terms for a banker?'

'No, not with the type of investments we are talking about,' Mendel pressed his point. 'As the value of the Swiss Franc rises, money flows in, but they are using the franc as an investment medium. It could be any other currency – the dollar, the pound, or a commodity, or gold – it doesn't really matter to this type of investor. He will ride the wave, then try and sell at the peak. Meanwhile, the Swiss Franc is artificially high and we can't sell our products abroad because they are no longer competitively priced. Don't forget that a large proportion of Swiss industry is international; we have too small a country for much internal trade. And we still have the crash to face, when our investor decides to bail out.' Mendel pointed back to the papers. 'As you can see, no matter how much we reduce the interest rate payable – even to the extent of a negative rate – we cannot deter investors. The banks just don't need the money, Daniel. And certainly not to go to the lengths this man Reiner has described.'

It took a moment for the gravity of Mendel's words to settle, then Grade's first thought was why Reiner would concoct such a story? *And why didn't Wetherall pick up on the same point?* 'Is this widely known?'

'In Switzerland, yes, because we have had to face the problem the most. In the West you term it "hot" money – but then on the other hand you are still fighting to attract investors, so perhaps you are not so paranoid about it. Your time will come.'

So that could explain Wetherall, but still there was Reiner! 'I'm sorry, but I'm still trying to assess all this.' Grade took out his pen and leafed through his notebook. He looked blankly at the notes he had made on that first day with Reiner, then on the first clean page wrote: *Ulterior motive?* And to himself thought, perhaps Reiner had some sort of internal grudge with SBECSA; if that was so, no doubt he had expected him to take the case just on face value all along.

'Let's just not leave it at that, Daniel,' Mendel continued. 'As I say, you're here now, so we might as well cover it thoroughly. Tell me, what figures do you have for total deposits that *could* have been transferred from Lebanese banks?'

Grade started leafing through, but the notes were too jumbled to pick out quickly. He thought back to Wetherall covering the point. 'About eight or ten billion dollars. I can't remember exactly.'

'Okay, whatever – in that region.'

Mendel went over to the far side of the room and picked out a file, came back and laid it on his desk. Almost ceremoniously, he opened the cover and ran his finger down one of the first pages. He stopped halfway.

'Last year, portfolio funds – in other words those handled for investors mainly outside of Switzerland – topped one hundred billion dollars. In addition, assets made up another sixty-five billion dollars. So against that we have, even being generous, ten billion. And obviously it would be ridiculous to say that *all* of that would automatically come to Switzerland; perhaps at the most fifty per cent would be more realistic. So then we have only five billion. Something like three per cent, in all.' Mendel closed the file. 'Not exactly worth starting a war over.'

Grade found it hard to hide his disbelief. He felt suddenly uncomfortable with the information; he had been previously aware, in vague terms, of the vastness of Swiss funds, but had never really applied it to the Beirut situation. The many objections and counter-statements passed through his mind, but there was little point. They just weren't founded on the same solid ground as Mendel's information. As he well knew: facts were facts. He forced a nervous smile. 'You know, I came here with so many questions, and we've hardly got past square one.'

'Questions in what sort of vein?' asked Mendel.

'Well, it doesn't really matter now. If we can't satisfy motive, then it's not worth going into the finer points of a Swiss banker's good principles.' Grade tapped his cigar into the ashtray. 'I'll have to rethink my strategy.'

'As is my job, I could uphold those same good principles, which *are* the general rule.' Mendel laughed faintly. 'But as I found out to my cost during your last visit, I could find myself at the wrong end of the argument. There will always be the one bad apple. But then there is usually a reason . . .' Mendel opened his hands out, then interlocked them smartly on the desk top. 'I'm sorry, Daniel, I wish I could be of more assistance.'

Grade's cigar tasted suddenly stale and acrid. He stubbed

it out. 'Some you win, others, well . . . It's a newspaperman's occupational hazard.'

'Also a banker's,' Mendel complied. 'Which hotel are you staying at?'

'The Bellerive au Lac.'

They indulged in small talk for a few minutes – how Grade was finding his hotel, the change in the city's character each season, the final outcome of the last investigation. Then Mendel stood up.

'Look, if I have any more thoughts on this, Daniel, I'll give you a call. I feel almost guilty sending you away so quickly.'

'That's alright. Your efforts on my first trip more than make up for it.' Grade forced a smile, but inside the shock waves were still washing through him. He felt numbed.

They shook hands and Grade made his way back down the seven floors to the Banhof Strasse. He hailed a taxi within minutes.

The sun was trying to break through some of the distant clouds to the south-east, but Grade was lost in thought as he looked out across the still waters of Lake Zürich. Only two days into the story, his first real interview, *and it was all over!* He dwelled on that one point until the taxi had almost reached the Bellevue intersection. Nobody could have guessed that outcome at the London meeting, not even Golding at his most sceptical. Thoughts of Beirut, Reiner, Leorah Ajlan milled through his mind . . . But if Mendel was right, if *motive* couldn't be proved, the whole thing became futile, worthless. The aftertaste of his cigar was even sourer now. The defeat should have been total, but something still nagged at the back of his mind; whether just reluctance to accept so quick a turn around, he wasn't sure.

When Grade got back to his hotel, there was a message waiting regarding Reiner. He would have troubled himself with why it was not from Reiner directly, but the meeting with Mendel was still strongest on his mind. He read the message, going back over it for fully a minute . . . then crumpled it slowly and deliberately in one hand.

*

The school at Ma'alot Torchiha was similar to many of Israel's outlying village schools. Built of whitewashed breeze-block, the sun had first bleached and brightened the white, then faded it, so that the grey showed through with a mottled effect. Only two storeys high, it merged well into the surrounding white-grey rock desert landscape.

Abel Menachet, the school bus driver, had been waiting outside for fully ten minutes now. He stood by the doors with his back rested against them and tilted his cap to shade his face some more. He had seen taxi drivers in Tel Aviv wearing similar caps when he had first arrived from Rumania twelve years ago, and he had bought one as soon as he took the job; now he wore it everyday. In the winter, if the sun wasn't too fierce, he would turn the peak to one side, 'like Popeye' he would sometimes joke with the children.

The bell rang high up on the school roof; then there was fully two minutes of silence before the shouts and screams of the children filled the dried clay quadrangle, echoing from the building behind.

Abel stood nonchalantly to one side as the children filled the bus. Then he began to hurry the last few who were playing or lagging behind.

'*Ajal!* Come on, we will be late for those in Parod.'

Parod was the last call on the round trip that wound for twenty miles on the desert roads through the nine surrounding villages from which the children came. Abel stood up on the steps and counted the numbers as he scanned the seats. Should be thirty-eight, thirty-eight came in that morning, he recalled.

'*Kullmin hene?*' he asked.

'*Aiwa*, I think so,' one of the first boys answered.

He looked around a second more, then swung the heavy door shut, climbed across to his single seat and started her up. Turning out onto the dust road, he accelerated hard, the diesel engine responding sluggishly and noisily.

Often, some of the children would sing on the journey back – hardly ever on the way there – and Abel liked that. They rarely talked to him, so he kept a small radio strapped around his rear-view mirror, and he would turn it on if things got too quiet, too monotonous; but somehow the children would then talk and shout louder, until it became almost deafening, and he would finally turn it off for some peace again.

In age, the boys and girls ranged from seven to twelve; the classes were small at Ma'alot Torchiha, no more than fifteen in each.

Abel was distracted by a 'clicking' noise. He glanced back. Two of the boys were playing a game with large ball bearings and cubes, trying to guess how many the other had in his hand. One of the boys was called Benedict, 'Beni' for short; Abel knew the names of some of the more popular children, and 'Beni' was a bit of a leader among the older boys.

The winter sun was quite low, and it blinded Abel for part of the road that headed almost due west towards Kabi. He squinted against it as he powered his way along.

The first stop was at Yehi'an – an old white stone village with some pre-fabs on its outskirts – where he let out three children. Next was Ga'atonne for another four. Abel drove away quickly, eager to reach Kabi, which marked the intersection for the long run down to the villages of Beit Ha'amek and Joudeida. There was a five-kilometre stretch of winding, rougher road ahead that he was always glad to have past, and somehow he felt once he'd turned again, he was on the homeward run.

He could now see the start of the rougher road ahead. A faint dust rose a few feet from its surface, even in the slightest of breezes. The hills each side encroached sharply in parts, but were mostly meandering, of virtually white rock, with the first signs of greenery displayed by some small cypresses on the taller hills.

The children were becoming noisier, and seemed oblivious to the extra bumpiness of the road. Nobody was singing, just high-pitched talking. Abel turned on the radio, catching the middle of a news broadcast. He spun the dial. Eventually he found some music: an Israeli version of 'Mammy Blue' with orchestral backing. He started to hum along faintly with it.

Then he broke off. He could see something on the road, appearing white and ghostly in the dust. He slowed down, as he got closer, then his eyes adjusted and the dust settled slightly. It was a goat. A dead goat!

'*Jahan' nam.*' Abel cursed under his breath. It was blocking the narrow road and he couldn't get past. He applied the brakes heavily and the bus came to a halt with a hissing, almost sighing, sound.

Someone had run over a stray and not stopped to move it. Abel had a nervous afterthought and glanced hesitantly at the gun in the open glove compartment, then quickly discarded the idea. If it was an ambush, they would be in the hillside already, almost upon him. Better to leave it where it was. If anything happened, he would have to make it back to the bus in any case; his place was in there, the doors locked, the gun in his hand, not outside, exposed. Abel scanned the hillside again, and shrugged off his expanding thoughts. There was obviously nobody there; the rocks were too shallow for concealment, and there were virtually no trees. *No*, someone had hit a stray; he had seen a few in his time.

Abel opened his door and got out. Curse it, the goat would be heavy and he would have to move it alone, unless some of the children helped him. He glanced back briefly, then quickly forgot the idea; if any of the goat's blood got on their clothing, and if they also happened to be from Ribyan, newly settled families, he might never be forgiven.

Abel walked towards the goat. Then, seemingly from nowhere, a herdsman appeared on the nearby hillside. Abel squinted up and tilted his cap some more. He could see two other goats on the same hillside now. The sun was against him. Perhaps that was why he hadn't seen them before.

The herdsman was waving furiously at him. As he got closer, Abel could hear his shouts.

'*Haramayi!* Thieves! Please, you help me.' He continued mumbling and shouting as he came down and confronted Abel.

He was dressed in a very old *thobe* and his *khoufia* was soiled and ragged at the edges. As with many Arab herdsmen of the district, he spoke only broken Hebrew. He was out of breath for a moment as he pointed down the road ahead.

'They have stolen five of my goats in a *Katamya*, a big truck. They kill this one and leave here so my brother cannot follow quickly. Please, you help me move.'

Abel leant down and felt the goat's body; it was still warm. 'This must have been only minutes ago.' He straightened up and looked at the herdsman.

'Yes, yes, they have just gone,' the herdsman agreed hurriedly. He reached into his *thobe* and held the scabbard of his knife. 'They cut its throat. Sometimes it takes many minutes to die. My brother brings his jeep around any minute now. Please, we move . . .'

The herdsman bent down without another word and gripped the goat's front legs. Abel glanced back to the bus. He had been momentarily suspicious of the herdsman, but that had passed with his explanation; what he had said Abel had heard of happening quite often in the region. He scanned the hillside again. Nothing. He made a small signal to indicate he would just be a minute, then took hold of the goat's back legs. They began to drag it back.

The goat was heavy, and after a second Abel straightened up to ease his back. He caught a movement on the hillside in the corner of his eye. He turned.

Abel saw the man stop in his tracks less than fifty yards from the bus. He was dressed in a green combat uniform and had a striped, ragged *khoufia* like the herdsman. In his hands he gripped an automatic rifle. Another similarly dressed man emerged on the other side. They must have come from higher up, or must have virtually dug burrows!

Abel looked back to the herdsman as if for an explanation. Little could be seen of his face under his sun-bleached and grizzled beard and moustache, except his eyes. Abel saw the intent that was there, and fear spread like an ugly mushroom inside him.

The question thundered through his mind as he back-stepped. Why? Where? . . . How? He had looked at the hillside – there was *no* place to hide. Then he noticed the sand-coloured robes cast aside, almost indiscernible among the rocks . . . *Meshuganah!*

His first thought was that the bus door could be locked from the inside – Benedict was near, he remembered. He turned and started to run and shout.

'Beni! Beni! Lock the door!'

A secondary thought was the gun, but it was both too dangerous and ambitious for a twelve-year-old to handle. Abel saw two other men appear. One of them raised his rifle, then lowered it again, slowly. Suddenly Abel sensed the herdsman close behind him from the flapping of his *thobe.*

He shouted 'Beni!' once more before he felt the knife spear his guts from behind like a cold needle. Then he felt it turn, and his guts dissolve to liquid.

He saw the shaking image of the bus and someone moving close to the front, and heard the rattle of gunfire striking the bus; then it faded and the dust road rushed up towards him. He felt his own breathing for a moment more in his own private darkness.

The herdsman lifted off his *thobe* with a dramatic gesture. Underneath he wore green combat trousers and his chest was bare.

'*Ajal!* We have not much time. We have made a bad start.'

His four companions knew him as 'El-Hasik' – The Fire; a revolutionary name he had chosen to replace his own awkward five-worded name. Two of the men took large kit bags from beneath the same camouflage robes on the hillside. Another followed El-Hasik inside the bus to inspect the damage from firing his automatic into its roof. One stood on guard outside. El-Hasik stood at the front of the bus and cast his eyes around slowly. He turned off the radio that was still playing.

There was fear in the children's eyes, but something else too: coldness. They were young, Hasik thought, but they could certainly show their hostility. Somehow their youth and innocence made it all the more marked. But in time he knew that he would make them a slave to that fear, to his command; in time, they would beg and crave for the merest hint of friendliness or companionship from him or his men. He knew the psychological game well.

'Some of you will speak and understand Arabic. You will convey to the others that this bus is now at the command of the Palestinian Liberation Organization.' El-Hasik faltered slightly as he spoke the words. He knew that their organization was too small – and in the past too fanatical – to be recognized by the PLO. That recognition was dependent on the personal endorsement of Abu Ammar* or Abu Jihad, PLO co-founder. Hasik surveyed the bus as the agitated murmurs of some of the children grew.

They were within fifteen miles of the border. Hasik knew that once they had driven the bus to the tunnel, the situation would be secured. There would be doubt at first as to the whereabouts and fate of the children. Then the Israelis would track them from news of the first vehicles stopped by the tunnel, and would begin to take up position outside. He would demand an audience only with one of the leading generals. Then he would make the declaration! There was no doubt in Hasik's mind as to Fatah's acceptance then. It would be viewed as one of the finest coups of the conflict, if not *the* finest. He began to feel mounting excitement inside, further fuelling his already nervous anticipation.

He raised his arm in the clenched-fist Fatah salute.

'*Hurriyi!* We must prepare. There is much to do.'

The last two men came into the bus with their kit bags. They nodded eagerly towards Hasik. But one of the other men, Jahleb, in the middle of the bus, stood motionless and stared back worriedly; then he beckoned with one arm.

Hasik made his way down, past the broken glass from the shattered windows along one side. Jahleb pointed first to the roof.

'When I noticed one of the children moving near the front, I fired a short burst. But as you see, I was careful – all the bullets are here and here.'

Hasik studied the marks; two or three had pierced the metal, and some were still embedded in it. Yes, he thought,

* Palestinian name for Yasser Arafat.

as he'd directed, if there was any initial resistance. But what was the point of this display? He nodded impatiently.

'But there were some ricochets . . .' Jahleb faltered as Hasik's expression darkened. 'I'm afraid this boy here . . .'

It was not necessary for Jahleb to point. Hasik had already picked the boy out. He was about eight or nine, with dark, wavy hair, in tighter curls at the side. The children around him were subdued and quiet, probably too shocked and fearful to speak.

He pushed Jahleb aside and tilted the boy's head back. The eyes weren't glazed or cloudy as yet, and he felt for the pulse. Nothing. Tilting the boy's head further, he examined him more closely.

He could see where the bullet had entered – a jagged, slanted hole on the cheekbone – but there was no exit wound. Hasik knew that if it had been direct, it would have removed the far side of the face. The bullet was still lodged inside. He opened the boy's mouth and felt inside to see where the bullet had been deflected. After a moment he could feel it close to the back of the throat. The boy had probably been unconscious from impact, then had choked on his own blood.

Hasik felt his anger rise; the ricochet couldn't have been avoided, but Jahleb should have been quicker to notice the boy's condition. He reached out and pinched Jahleb's cheek with his bloodied fingers, smearing it slightly.

'A minute earlier and this boy could have been saved, Jahleb. You should be more careful. Next time it could be one of your colleagues.' He smiled disdainfully, then turned his back.

His mind began to race: the driver was one thing, but the boy was a totally different matter. If the Israelis discovered the boy's death, they would amost certainly be more loath to meet his demands. They might even completely refuse to negotiate. It could also seriously jeopardize his acceptance by El-Fatah. Overall, how he dealt with it would probably be more vital than the planning already laid.

He studied the boy again over one shoulder, almost

ironically, thinking what a tease fate was that one small boy might stand in the way of freedom for Palestine.

At 10.34 that same evening, London time, a message came through on the *Daily Post* wire:

> School bus reported missing in northern Israel. First sources suspect hijacking. No confirmatory information as yet. Will try full report for morning – Tel Aviv desk. Harvey Boylen.

Rolf Nabens was informed, and minutes later he laid the message on Bob Golding's desk.

'Should we pass it on to Danny?'

'No, not yet. Let's see what develops. Run it normally for now.'

Nabens shrugged. 'Could be a good sidebar.'

'Yes,' Golding agreed. 'It could also be a whole lot larger than that, or a complete waste of time. It's just too early to judge.'

He contemplated it a moment more, but couldn't think of any connections worthy of a sidebar. He passed it back. 'He'll have enough on his plate for now, I don't want to distract him unnecessarily. But let me know the instant anything else comes up on it.'

4

Daniel Grade was ushered by one of the staff nurses along the corridors of Zürich's Waid hospital. It was a large, rambling structure looking out onto the Kaferberg forests and meadows.

The corridors were scrubbed and spartan, with intermittent wood panels and paintings to soften the tone; but

Grade found it as cold and clinical as any hospital he had visited. He felt its atmosphere unsettling him more and more deeply as he followed the nurse to the far end of one of the wings.

'Room 309.' The nurse opened the door and held her arm out. She spoke in stilted English. 'Visiting hours finish in just over forty minutes. Call me if you need any more assistance. Thank you.'

Grade nodded and walked in. He fixed his eyes on the bed as he shut the door. He found his surprise difficult to hide.

'Are you sure you're alright? You certainly look fine.'

Anton Reiner was sitting up in the bed with no outwardly visible injuries. He frowned slightly.

'Why, yes. Shouldn't I be?'

'But your message – and the fact that you are in hospital. I thought you'd almost been killed!'

Reiner raised one hand. 'That is true. But it wasn't a case of serious injury or anything like that. If it *had* happened, myself and my family would have been killed outright – or I would be here. One or the other. And I *am* here.' Reiner allowed a faint twinge of humour to break his seriousness. 'I suppose you were expecting a mass of broken bones and plaster. Like a skiing accident, perhaps . . .' Reiner noted Grade's still quizzical expression. 'Oh . . . the hospital bed was doctor's orders, I'm afraid. Like many others, I suffer from heart problems – angina in my particular case. All the shock and tension sent my blood pressure up to one-eighty over one-twelve.' Reiner reached over and took some tablets, grimacing as he swallowed. 'Without some rest, our friend's task – whoever he was – would have been accomplished anyway.'

Reiner made another waving motion and Grade took a seat by the bed.

Grade smiled. 'I should have learnt long ago in this profession not to take anything on face value. I'm sorry if I appeared unsympathetic.'

'No, no, you were right. A hospital, the mention of an attempted killing –I too would have thought the same. But I must admit in one way I *did* want it to alarm you. To let it strike you as it did me that very day at Mürren. As I thought of Piai – and the children. The children . . .' Reiner's face suddenly contorted.

'How close was the attempt?' asked Grade.

Reiner leaned over and lightly gripped Grade's hand. 'Even now it upsets me to think about it . . . let alone relate it . . . I will have to take it slowly.' Reiner settled back again and let his eyes roam the ceiling as he began with the ascent to Schilthorn, his first noticing some movement; then his taking the binoculars and panning in, following each action of the 'hooded man' in the motor housing. At intervals he paused, allowing his breath to come steadily. '. . . Then the man was disturbed by two of the engineers from below, and made his way down a ladder at the back and away into the crowd. I suspect that he disappeared quickly, probably in the next cable-car down. We only found out later that he hadn't had a chance to set the device. But everything else was in place. A moment later and . . .' Reiner took a hurried gulp of water from a glass to one side.

Grade noticed Reiner's steel-rimmed glasses on the side table, and was reminded suddenly of his frailty. If this story was true, he now understood better Reiner's nervousness, his near-paranoia, at their first meeting. He had a picture of Reiner as a faithful and conscientious servant of an all-powerful, awesome 'system' for the past twenty years. Now he posed a threat and was in real danger, something that must be completely alien to him. But whatever compassion and concern he now felt for Reiner, the confusion of his thoughts since his meeting with Mendel still plagued him. He took out his notebook.

'Did you inform the authorities?'

'Yes, the police at Mürren were involved – an Inspector Bante.'

'And were there any witnesses?'

Reiner's eyebrows furrowed slightly. 'Why yes, of course, the engineers for a start. Why do you ask this?'

Grade could sense that perhaps his own doubts were

apparent, and covered quickly. 'Just that if we can't track our SBECSA man through the Zürich banking community or through Beirut, your "assassin" might turn out to be our only lead. That is, assuming the two are connected.'

'Of that, there is absolutely no question,' Reiner said.

Grade decided to ease off. Any further questioning was just making Reiner more uneasy and irritated, and now that he had Inspector Bante's name, it seemed unlikely that Reiner would have fabricated the story; he would be able to get more information from Bante direct.

'Talking of "tracking" – how are things going at your end?' asked Reiner.

Grade tucked his notebook away. 'It's coming along. It's always difficult, often protracted on an investigation like this.'

'But you've met with your contact here in Zürich – Mr Mendel?'

'Well, yes.'

'And what was his initial reaction?'

'One of shock, of course,' Grade hedged. 'But it will obviously take a while for something concrete to emerge.'

'But there must have been some sort of indication?'

Grade looked hard at Reiner; he could sense it sounded unlikely that Mendel hadn't voiced any sort of reaction. He cursed inwardly. It would have to be said at some time: if not now then when he got back from Beirut.

'I should stress first of all that this is only one man's view. Firstly, he sees a problem in that we have no particular suspects. Apart from the export company, which is yet to be verified, you've given me no names. But more importantly there's a serious question mark over general motive.'

Reiner looked nervously around. 'Names, names! You know I can't help you in that respect. That's what I thought *you'd* find out.'

'I need a starting point,' Grade urged.

'And motive! That is even more ridiculous. I thought we'd satisfied that quite adequately while I was in London.'

'Yes, but you neglected to mention that right now Swiss

banks are up to their ears with foreign investments – to the extent that the interest rate is a negative one – and *still* they keep coming.'

'But of course!' Reiner stared back as if Grade had missed the obvious, then leaned forwards. 'Don't you see? If they weren't in a strong position, they wouldn't be able to reduce the interest rate and still attract investors. If the Middle East was an easy and readily available alternative, they would transfer there. Also, you are talking about a rate designed only to deter short-term speculative investors. There is nothing to say that transfers from the Middle East would necessarily be of this type. Just as many would be long term investments, bearer bonds, etcetera.' Reiner lay back. 'Then, of course, there is nothing to stop them depositing in other currencies: dollars, pounds, Deutschmarks . . . whatever. For which they will receive a much higher rate. And still, of course, with the same benefits of secrecy, which is what attracts them mainly. It is only designed to deter speculation on the Swiss Franc, not turn away investors totally.' Reiner looked over from half-closed eyes. 'My God, they are the lifeblood of Swiss banks – the banks would never survive if those investments ceased.'

Grade stared at Reiner blankly. The explanation was convincing, one that he would have normally believed. But Mendel's facts had *also* seemed solid; besides, he had relied on Mendel's judgement once before, and he had been proven right.

'But deposits in Swiss banks are already very large – and most certainly in comparison to the gain from Beirut. What would be the point?'

Reiner eased his breathing for a moment before answering. 'Did your friend also tell you how much of that money was already Arab – how much would have eventually gone to Beirut, if their banking centre had been allowed to gain strength?'

Grade's doubts grew. 'Are you saying that he's totally wrong?'

'No, the two aspects are very close. It's very easy to

overestimate the investment implications of Swiss currency protection. Most cautious bankers do exactly the same.'

There was a long silence as Reiner watched the gradual acceptance of what he was saying dawn on Grade; then his eyes narrowed.

'Of course, I should have realized . . . When you were asking about the incident at Mürren, it wasn't that you wanted to *track* anyone, was it?' Reiner paused markedly. 'It was just that you doubted me. Perhaps you thought I made up the story! Perhaps you think the whole thing is a hoax even from our first meeting . . . That's why all the questions. That's why! I should have known . . . *Should* have known . . .' Reiner's exasperation was mounting and his face began to redden.

There was a short but tense silence.

'Please, leave me now. Please. I am too upset.'

Grade was still staring at Reiner; the turnaround, the dismissal had been so sudden. One part of him believed Reiner, but another part had long since trained itself into a healthy scepticism, resisting the acceptance of any information until it could be checked out, *thoroughly*. He cursed himself now for letting it show.

Grade stood up and made his way to the door; he stopped just before opening it and ran a hand lightly through his tousled grey hair. 'I'm sorry – I don't know quite what to say. You should know it's my job to doubt, to question . . . all too often things aren't quite what they seem.'

Grade made his way out and back down the corridor. He regretted having to leave Reiner on such a note, but suspected that Reiner shared his feelings; either way, it was obvious that no amends could be made at that moment, nothing further of any substance discussed.

Later, his suspicions were confirmed. Reiner telephoned him at his hotel at almost 9 p.m., apologizing for his earlier outburst, and said he fully realized there were bound to be some obstacles on such an enquiry. 'I am also forgetting that you too are now putting yourself in similar danger.'

Visiting Reiner had been the first time that Grade had really considered it, but he had pushed the thought away. Up to now the greatest danger he'd faced since his boxing days had been a missed deadline, a dead-end source, maybe only a page six placing.

Reiner got to the point of his call; the apologies were over. He had a name to pass on. He hadn't passed it on previously because he would have preferred the case to be proved more strongly first. He was afraid he might falsely implicate an innocent individual, a man in a position of considerable trust and responsibility. He paused significantly.

'His name's Schaarer . . . Dr Emil Schaarer. Up until two months ago he was very high up on the board of SBECSA – *Directeur Conduite* – and it was said that he resigned due to his increasing political duties. But this was never publicly disclosed, and rumour has it otherwise, quite otherwise . . .'

Immediately the name struck a chord in Grade's mind, but it eluded him exactly from where. As it finally dawned on him, he realized what had thrown him – he was not used to associating the name with banking.

'If you are well up on Switzerland's position in the Middle East peace initiative, you will know him well,' Reiner said. 'Dr Schaarer will be co-chairing this year's Geneva conference.'

Shortly after his meeting with Grade, Simon Mendel sat in silent contemplation. He always liked to think of himself as a moderate in the Swiss banking community. Not a moderate like the others on Banhof Strasse; they just kept on with their strict and cautious practices, and had long since forgotten the meaning of the word.

He had been a part of them once. A *sous-directeur* at the Leuflen Kreditanstalt, one of the big six along with SBECSA, though not quite on the same scale. He had been fresh out of university with his PhD in economics after six years – four at the University of Basle, two at Harvard – and had stepped in at Leuflen as manager of foreign credit. He had stayed with them fourteen years, rising to *sous-directeur* after only six, and then the lack of opportunity he saw ahead had coincided with the formation of the Swiss Institute. It took him less than another five years to rise to be its Chairman. He had made the right decision.

In that time, he had seen and experienced, and *predicted*, nearly all the great scares: the Penn Central Railroad and its shares crash, the IOS swindle, the UCB. Then there were the monetary crises of 1971 and 1975, and all the small ones in between. He often thought that it was his two years in America, his exposure to all that *bullshit*, as they so succinctly put it, that helped him see through it.

The other bankers were cautious, so cautious and strait-jacketed, you knew exactly what they would do to safeguard themselves, what precautionary measures they would take. By observing one, you could almost predict how they would *all* act and think; they became as predictable and reliable and precise as their precious watches. You only had to make something *appear* safe – usually by appealing to their greed – to attract them; in the rush they ignored all other factors, they would suddenly throw that treasured caution to the wind. He had warned and cajoled and nursed them through many a crisis.

Now he considered himself very much apart from them, an arbiter of fair play between their cautious and greedy banking practices and the equally greedy, unscrupulous world outside. He would laugh at their naïveté, but at the same time hold no misconceptions about their efficiency, the strength and capacity of their calculating minds, and their capabilities if they should decide – God forbid – to be unscrupulous. He had even less illusions about those outside who had dealings with the community, supposedly for *mutual* gain.

It was for those reasons that he now held a worried frown. On first meeting Grade, he had shown that same suspicion of outsiders – but, then, that was a natural Swiss trait. Then, as he'd sensed Grade's openness, directness, he had warmed to him.

Now, on this latest visit, he began to worry that he may have appeared to short-change Grade. True, it was his job to uphold the 'system' whenever it should be upheld – but then he had momentarily forgotten his lack of illusions. *Anything* was possible, he should have remembered that. It was just that Grade's claims had come across as so tenuous, so full of rumour and innuendo. He bit his lip. He shouldn't have made such a hasty judgement of the situation. It could be viewed as a lack of *moderacy*, even by his own standards. And that would never do.

The telephone rang in a small back room of a hotel on Paris's Rue Saint Lazare. It was answered within seconds.

'Yes?'

'Jaalgen. Herr Vruger calling.' The voice sounded distant and tentative. 'The name I gave you the other day, Julie Grade – have you been able to formulate any plan as yet?'

'On the girl, nothing. But on her boyfriend, Xavier Peton, something interesting. Some talk with activists at the university, some with old contacts – it turns out that our friend Peton has been in touch with a pressure group here. A bit of money in the right hands, it won't be difficult for me to step in as his contact.'

'Good. Let me know your progress.'

The tunnel was an awe-inspiring and daunting sight to the children as the bus approached. Above its entrance, sheer rock rose almost three hundred feet, then sloped, bare and jagged, to its summit at fifteen hundred feet. It was on the main road between Mount Hermon and the Golan in the north-eastern corner of Israel, less than twenty miles from the Lebanese border, and almost as close again to Syria.

The bus stopped within twenty yards of the entrance. Two of Hasik's men got out and ran towards it – quickly swallowed up in its darkness.

The children sat in awkward silence. They had been acutely aware of the dead boy's presence, but never more than in these passing moments. He was at the back of the bus, tucked behind a set of seats so that he was obscured, and covered in a tarpaulin that Hasik's men had found in the luggage compartment, usually used to cover the roof rack in bad weather.

Hasik had at first been angered by the boy's death, in particular because it might affect his negotiations with the Israelis. Now he had accepted it, and began to consider its compensations; nothing else could have served as a better warning to keep the other children in order. Hasik looked around the bus.

'They are good children, no?'

Jahleb grunted his agreement and smiled back.

They waited in silence for a while, and then a small explosion sounded at the far end of the tunnel. Hasik looked at his watch: less than ten minutes since they had gone in. Not bad for scrambling the far rock face and setting the charge. If all had gone according to plan, a small number of boulders would have fallen, effectively blocking the road on that far side.

Jahleb started up the bus again, but waited until his two comrades appeared before edging forwards.

'It went well?' Hasik shouted from the open door as they came alongside.

'Yes, five or six large ones, and a pile of loose rubble,' Aman answered. 'No one will get through.'

Hasik indicated for Jahleb to put the lights on, then stared straight ahead as the sheer rock-face cast its shadow slowly over them, blocking off the sunlight from outside. The twin beams began to wash the inside tunnel walls.

A murmur stirred among the children. Beni stared blankly out of the side window. Before they had been in light, and even that had offered its own form of hope. He had been able to look around at the passing landscape, at the few people evident in the small villages they passed, hoping that the villagers might be able to read something into his lost, confused expression. And if that alone was too optimistic a thought, it was at least a form of contact, something to relate to in the world outside. Now they were going into darkness, and he began to realize with sinking despondency that this could be their prison, their tomb.

He felt the coldness and damp of the tunnel reach out its claws to his very soul. He looked around at the dark rock, then, having judged its confines, its monotony, turned his attention inward – to the men and their guns, and to the other children. A small girl towards the back of the bus began to cry.

Hasik had let the sounds of the children's agitation ride, but now the soft weeping drew his attention. He took a torch from one of the kit bags and flickered it around.

He couldn't pick out the girl, but he shouted '*Irtah!*' in quick warning. After a second the crying became more muted.

The silence settled more deeply in the passing minutes. The bus had edged almost fifty yards into the tunnel and now stood at a standstill with its engine idling. Aman and his accomplice had stayed by the entrance, and at length another explosion sounded, this time much louder, and with a heavy, ominous echo. The ground shook, then there was a growing rumble as rocks began to fall behind them.

The large boulders came first, but were quickly obscured by a deluge of finer rocks and dust. The second was ear-shattering. As the dust cleared, they could see that the road had been blocked by a fall up to four feet high in parts.

Some of the children had turned to watch. Now their imprisonment was complete. Hasik was already facing in that direction, looking the length of the bus aisle, past the last member of the gang stationed stolidly halfway down. He smiled thinly and scratched at his grizzled beard. He began to think ahead to the forthcoming negotiations. He would need a spokesman for the children. He remembered the name that the driver had shouted just before he died. He looked around.

'Which one of you is Beni?'

Nobody stirred, and he surveyed more intently. 'Come on, which one of you? Which one . . . I can easily find out by looking at the names on your satchels or schoolbooks.'

A boy a few rows back raised a hand slightly. He had curly dark brown hair and his eyes were bright and attentive. At twelve, he was one of the eldest boys.

Hasik smiled at him. 'So you are the brave one.' He nodded knowingly. 'So it follows also that you will do our bidding – as much for yourself as for the other children. When the Israelis come, you will assure them that you are *all* alright.'

Beni returned the smile wanly. With one child dead, he was sensible enough to know that two might not make that much difference. He had been determined not to raise his hand, until the mention of satchels – for he knew that he could never allow Hasik or any of his men to learn, or even suspect, what was inside *his* satchel.

He had grasped the gun amidst all the early confusion, as the rifle-fire had sent him sprawling to the floor – he could no longer reach the door – but the gun was there, right there, less than two feet from his grasp. The terrorists were still a good twenty yards away. So he had leant across and grabbed it, and scurried back on his belly and his elbows, and thrust it quickly inside his satchel. Not knowing what to do with it, or what he *might* do with it, but feeling frightened all the same.

With that fear still in him, he sensed that he might never use it. It was bad enough now having the thing just inside his satchel, let alone pointing it, aiming . . . pulling its trigger. But if the right moment ever did come along, he would see how he felt then. The postponement took his mind off it a bit, allowed him to breathe easier. He was a patient boy; he had learnt that much from his father.

Aman and Fayek had scrambled back over the rock-fall to the bus. Taking two further kitbags, they busied themselves attaching the plastic explosives inside the emergency exit, and at set intervals down the length of the bus: seven packs in all. Each had its own detonator cap, which they connected to a continuous wire leading to a central multi-firing box outside, so that they could be fired individually or all together.

The childrens' fear had now reached a pinnacle. They were young, but they understood in their own simple, panicky ways the danger of the devices now set.

Jahleb and the last man then took care of the final detail: running the cord of a field-telephone the length of the tunnel and standing guard at each end. Hasik had the third line to the telephone, and there was one spare. He looked at his watch; less than forty minutes since they had first entered the tunnel.

Now came the long wait.

It was 9.38 a.m., London time, when Grade got hold of David Wetherall. He started on the tedious explanation of the conflicting stories of Reiner and Mendel. At points he paused, collating and reassembling the information in his mind, so that he was sure he related it as close to its original sequence as possible. Wetherall whistled softly as he came to a finish and mentioned Schaarer.

'If it's solid, you've got a hot one there, Daniel. Rolf could have a field day with that snippet alone.'

Grade agreed, but turned him back to the financial meat of the conversation.

'In their own way, they're both right,' Wetherall said at length. 'Switzerland has been in a very strong position and has been almost 'stonewalling' investors . . . but then Reiner is also right to point out that this is really only aimed at short term speculative investors – in particular on the Swiss Franc.'

Grade voiced the thought that had nagged at him repeatedly during the passing hours. 'Do you think that Mendel has misled me in any way?'

'No, I really don't think so.' Wetherall mulled it over, but spoke with conviction. 'In a way it's his job to portray the Swiss side as best he can. Also, there are a lot of people – it's not only him, and not only staunch supporters of the Swiss banking system – who find it hard to view Arabs as anything else but short-term investors. Because they have such large sums of money and are prone to speculate, everyone's attention is drawn by the market fluctuations that arise. *That's* the talk of the city; everyone ignores the fact that almost as much again will probably be on long-term deposit. In fact, not only does this not draw attention, but it's pretty hard to trace, even if you are looking for it. It's very easy to be secretive with long-term investments in any banking system, but *particularly* in Switzerland.' Wetherall paused. 'No, I'm afraid your friend Mendel merely fell into a common trap. I could have made the same mistake myself – probably would have in his position.'

'And Reiner?'

Wetherall considered a second. 'Well of course, he's got an axe to grind, so although I go along with his basic premise – he might well exaggerate. But then there's no way of finding out *exactly* what the figures are.'

'So how do I make my decision?'

Wetherall seemed faintly baffled by the question. 'In what way?'

'Who do I put my money on?'

'I'm sorry, Danny, but that's what I'm trying to tell you. You won't prove much through the financial route. Timeless energy has been spent shrouding the Swiss banking system in secrecy – so people depend on *theories*, because the hard facts are hidden from them. And you're not going to get anywhere examining general theories. Start with something small – like Emil Schaarer.'

'You call that small?' Grade gibed.

'Just an unfortunate turn of phrase,' Wetherall said lightly. 'Have a search done on him: which companies he's a director of, what shares he has, etcetera. There's a lot that can be told from hard figures and the dates that relate to them.'

Grade quickly saw its value. He had already thought of investigating Schaarer, but more in the conventional sense of having him tailed, seeing if he went anywhere or met with anyone outside of his normal pattern of work and home life.

'While you're at it,' Wetherall continued. 'If you're really concerned about the allegiances of Mendel and Reiner, or want to read a bit more into why their views conflict – have *them* investigated too.'

Grade was put off balance. He had asked about Mendel, but had never really suspected his involvement. Mendel had been as good a contact as one could hope for on his last investigation, had almost played the part of a host *and* confidant – which brought to mind the gifts he had showered on Catherine and Julie. But apart from that, he *trusted* Mendel. Although his staunch Swiss banker's view on Arab investments largely explained Mendel's views differing from Reiner's, Wetherall was obviously suggesting the journalist's normal insurance policy. What was the motto? '*Everyone is suspect until checked out.*' Grade accepted its good sense, though resignedly; in the end his newsman's instinct prevailed over the uncomfortable feeling that it would be almost like cheating on Mendel.

'I suppose you're right,' he said finally.

'Searches like that usually take a few days to come through.'

'Yes, well, I'll use the time to go to Beirut.' And he began to push his thoughts on. To him, Zürich had become a maze – and it wasn't only what Wetherall had said. He had sensed it before – even from the first day with Reiner – and then the *theories* and contradictory information had just piled one on top of the other. If there was a key, it was in Beirut, with the assassination of Khourem and Al-Hakim, and with Leorah Ajlan.

'Talking about that neck of the woods,' Wetherall said, 'something came though on the wire last night – and again this morning. Rolf and Bob Golding were discussing it just a while ago . . .' Wetherall related details of the bus hijacking.

Grade considered the information for a moment. 'I'm afraid it's no use to me, at least not until I see some light on the rest of this. Let Rolf follow it up.'

*

Xavier Peton had arranged to meet his contact in the cafeteria of the George Pompidou cultural centre, the new architectural controversy of Paris. The open-plan café was crowded; his 'contact' had wanted it that way, knowing from past experience that you were more unlikely to attract attention from an unwanted observer amongst a crowd than in a seemingly deserted place.

Xavier knew him from the rolled-up copy of *Paris Match* he was holding; that had been prearranged. He was a man in his early forties, wearing jeans and a windcheater, but somehow still appearing smart. The man stepped forward.

'I am François Duffal.'

'Xavier Peton.' Xavier nodded curtly. He immediately recognized Duffal's voice from their one previous telephone conversation. They took a seat by the front windows. Outside, in the foyer, a mixed crowd of young students and tourists milled about.

'So, let's see if we might be of use to each other . . .' Duffal paused a moment. 'One thing that I must ask, first of all, is why you should want to join our organization?'

'Well, I've admired Le Marteau Rouge's actions through the years.' Xavier grinned slightly. 'I thought the fruit and vegetable pelting of D'Estaing at his conference with the farm leaders was particularly appropriate.'

'So you are familiar with our organization, and what we represent?'

'Yes, precisely measured political demonstration. To me, you represent everything that the other student demonstration bodies would like to represent, but don't . . . or can't.'

Duffal sat back. Xavier knew that this was the final testing ground, the personal meeting; everything would hang on what he said now. Duffal lit a cigarette; Xavier noted its mild and sickly smell – it was not French.

'And you know from which backgrounds we draw our members?'

'Yes, students and ex-students of the three major Paris

universities – and some outside activists with left-wing sympathies.'

Duffal asked a few more questions in the same vein – interrupted only by a noisy group of tourists by the entrance – then he leaned forward, gripping Xavier's hand suddenly.

'What is our motto?'

'*La machine n'a pas de coeur, ni de cerveau* . . . The machine has no heart or mind – you can only steer it, try and alter its direction.'

'Good!' Duffal sat back.

Xavier had noted Duffal's blue eyes earlier, but he hadn't noticed how cold and piercing they were. And there was something else. Almost unreal. The skin around them was smooth and taut, out of keeping with the crags and lines of the rest of his face. This hardness was only broken by Duffal's easy and confident smile.

'You realize that we have already been into your background in some detail,' Duffal said at length. 'This is only to confirm *your* knowledge of *us* . . .' Duffal looked away, for a moment taking in the scene of the artists and mimes in the large courtyard below. 'At this stage I think we are satisfied: you would be a worthwhile member.'

Xavier felt his enthusiasm growing. He had never thought that acceptance would come so quickly. But he controlled any sign of his feelings, realizing that would appear unprofessional. He was about to utter his thanks when Duffal held his hand up.

'But, please, not so fast . . . First we have a small test, or *duty* should I say, which will mark your introduction to Le Mateau Rouge.'

Duffal opened his copy of *Paris Match* and passed across a small padded envelope. 'You have no doubt heard that on occasions we send out 'flash' letters to – how should I say – *individuals* who we think have deserved them.'

'Yes, I know – small magnesium strips which ignite on opening,' Xavier quickly showed his knowledge; he couldn't help thinking that it was all part of the 'test'. He was still under observation.

'That's right. The intention is only to startle, not to cause injury . . . but the warning is equally effective.'

Xavier took the envelope and read the address. He looked up with faint surprise. 'But this is in Switzerland.'

'Yes, a French industrialist of German parentage,' Duffal said easily. 'One of the many who live in Switzerland to turn the tax laws to their advantage. He is quite an important target for us. You should consider it an honour.'

'I'm sorry, I didn't mean to question it,' Xavier was flustered. 'Just that I thought your targets were only in France.'

'Time was when that was true . . . But now, with the tax laws, as I say . . .' Duffal glanced around, then looked at his watch. 'Anyway, my friend. We will meet here at the same time next week, by which time we will know from the newspapers the results of your action.' Duffal stood up. 'Good luck. From there we will discuss your final acceptance and other duties.' Duffal clapped his hand on Xavier's shoulder and smiled faintly, then turned away and headed for the glassed-in, caterpillar-like walkway which led down to the street.

Xavier watched him disappear, and then began to allow his enthusiasm full vent, feeling a wave of fulfilment sweep over him. My God, what he had wanted for the past two years, virtually ever since he had arrived at the Sorbonne. And for it to all happen so quickly, so easily – without ceremony. But then ceremony was something that belonged to *them* – the establishment, the *haute bourgeoisie*.

To *them*, he urged himself, looking again at the name one the letter – the Anton Reiners of this world.

Grade had been busy that afternoon. He had both sides of the story now, Mendel's and Reiner's. And of course Wetherall's view, which in effect said that both were right in their own way. He still had mixed feelings about the financial searches, but at least it would shed some light: it just couldn't be as simple as that, two such opposite views to the question of Arab investment in Swiss banks.

Most of the morning had been spent in the offices of Semleche and Bunt. Company searches were their speciality, but they would trace in reverse and use an associate private detective agency, if necessary; it would take much longer – a company search could be provided within hours – but they *could* do it. Grade had paid them a flat fee in advance. On expenses.

On the way back, he'd called into the main Swissair offices on Hauptbahnof, and booked a flight to Beirut for 10.12 the next day.

Then, back in the quietness of his hotel room, he had started contemplating what had been on his mind throughout the day, growing stronger as the hours rolled by.

He didn't realize till then how hard the paranoia had gripped him.

Usually on an investigation he spent the early parts – whether hours or days – asking questions. Often the same monotonous, persistent questions. Grade termed it the 'plodding' part, because that's how it felt. But a part of that plodding he enjoyed. Because people would talk, and *talk*, and often – especially if you stayed quiet at just the right moments – they would fill the gaps. They would over-talk.

At first it might be a small snippet, even a part of a statement, a sentence – but then you could play that against someone else, and sit back and let *them* talk. Talk themselves right into the silent noose you were slowly weaving.

It was then that the word *investigation* really came into its own. Tying all those loose ends together; seeing which ones didn't quite fit. But it hadn't happened on this one so far, and the paranoia had begun to set in.

He recalled his earlier hunch that the main clue was in Beirut, that everything would start falling into place there. Reiner had provided only a few slim leads, mostly based on rumour and innuendo, and as he went back over and examined the threads, he had little more than that now. Reiner saying one thing! Mendel another! And then

Wetherall compounding it by being as cautious and noncommittal as good newsmen often are.

Even from that first day in Golding's office, it seemed they were stabbing in the dark. The size of the story had blinded them. The story that *must* be taken because they had it first – rumour or whatever – so someone had to be sent out to try and prove it, because they couldn't, just *couldn't* let anyone else get it first. *Get what*?

It seemed odd, now he was mentally ridiculing Golding, whose view he so respected. He stopped himself suddenly, searching back into his own soul. He himself had been just as bad. *Hypocrite!* He had wanted the story, and badly, and now in his confusion he couldn't remember why.

Was it just its size? The added prestige to his career that it could doubtless bring?

Perhaps that was the trouble! The one thing that had attracted him – and them – was what also made it so ludicrous, so preposterous. They never had a hope. The world's largest and most respectable banking community involved in a clandestine plot! A plot which would embroil a whole nation in war! And, at that, a community in a country which stood for the very essence of peace. And now Schaarer had been implicated: a man who stood as a spokesman, a figurehead of that country's peaceful intent. His mission now directed towards the Middle East – the very region to which he was supposed to have sent his assassins, his soldiers of fortune. It was all too much!

Grade went over and lay on the bed, staring up at the ceiling, unseeing. The room seemed suddenly claustrophobic, and he decided to go for a walk.

Making his way out of the hotel, he crossed the Bellerive Strasse and found himself in the park-like grounds along Seefeld Quai. Autumn was crisp in the air. A time of dying. The leaves had turned gold and brown, and those already fallen had curled inward, fluttering back and forth in the breeze.

Dying! He remembered that first investigation. It had all seemed so natural to Tony Dwyer. Just another game. In

Dwyer's eyes: okay, they were gangsters, but they were also friends, mates. Christ, they had been brought up just a couple of streets away. And then Grade had told Dwyer about Gennini, the club manager, how those *mates* had clubbed him and nailed his kneecaps to the floor before they blew his head off with a shotgun. It was desperation time. *'I'm getting past it, Danny. I've only got a few fights left. If I fix this one, they'll see me alright. I owe them one.'*

Where was that sporting principle? That young man with bright eyes and high hopes and ideals?

The book he'd written on the subject, *Demise – the rise and fall of a champion*, had long ago settled the score, for both of them. Dwyer's share of the royalties had meant that he wouldn't need any more fixed fights. For Daniel it had been a second transition, from sports journalism to investigative; the first transition, equally as demanding, had been from boxing to journalism. Those on the paper with a more formal education had had their doubts; but he'd been as factual and informative as any of them, and more stylish than most. A poetic throwback from his Welsh-Irish blood, Julie often joked. *Tony Dwyer!*

It seemed strange thinking now that at one time Tony Dwyer and he had shared the same thoughts. So much time had passed.

Dead leaves rustled beneath his feet as he walked. He made his way slowly along and sat down on a bench. Of course, that explained how two people could have such differing views. Mendel and Reiner! How even one person's view could change with time. Wetherall's view he had known all along, and Golding's and Nabens'. They would try to balance both sides. On one hand, and on the other . . . Perhaps not wishing, perhaps even fearing, to make a bold move in the wrong direction.

Grade sat there for a long time, listening to the leaves rustling, the hooters and motors of boats on the water, the traffic . . . and it struck him that perhaps that was what was frustrating him; his newsman's instinct was to find an inconsistency, something that might indicate guilt, and perhaps that just wasn't there as yet. Mendel's and Reiner's differing viewpoints, the arguments on ethics and motives for or against Swiss involvement, the Middle East reaction, all of it *could* be balanced. Perhaps he simply needed more – some names on the import sheet from Maślegeisen, a snippet of information from Leorah Ajlan, or something in the financial searches. One good clue and the inconsistencies might begin to show.

The realization swept over him suddenly, as if what had been troubling him all along had finally surfaced. He was in the right position; all he needed was the key. He remembered with surprise that it had only been three days since the messenger had walked in on him and Billy Stoner in that bar. With the size of the story he should allow for the early stages taking longer.

He left the park feeling more positive about the forthcoming trip to Beirut, and even about what had already passed. The wheels were in motion, with Semleche and Bunts' report, and the interplay of the statements of Mendel and Reiner. And Schaarer!

How quickly thoughts can change! Not only Tony Dwyer's, he reflected with a hint of sad irony.

He made his way back to the hotel and lay on the bed in much the same position as before; the counterpane still carried his imprint. He felt more settled now.

Grade wasn't sure exactly how long he had lain there when the room bell rang. He went across. He felt a flutter of apprehension as he opened the door. A room-valet, complete with pill-box hat, stood there.

'Yes?'

'A message, sir. It came in just a few minutes ago.'

Grade took it. 'Thank you. Oh, and could you tell service to send me up a drink? A Scotch, please.'

The valet nodded and he shut the door. Grade recognized it as a wire message from their Zürich news agency, Dalckener. He fumbled at the envelope, opened it, and began to read. As the words sank in, he wondered whether to love or hate Golding's casual bluntness.

Got your message from Wetherall. Have considered it at length, have had a meeting with Rolf as well. If he is involved, we have to prove it soon. The conference convenes in just over three weeks. We can't break the news while it's in session because it would be catastrophic. Need I say more! Even if we were as hard-hearted as some make out, I can't think of anything more likely to attract a censure. Also, it can't be too soon beforehand, because that doesn't give time for a replacement, and the two would be linked anyway. It would have the same effect. Know what I mean!

You've got ten days! Good luck.

The *he*, he knew, referred to Schaarer. The *conference* was perhaps more obvious. And the trouble was, he knew exactly what Golding meant.

The Arab sat alone in the resplendent room. Outside, from the small villa annexe which served as his own private mosque, strained the sounds of the muezzin reciting from the Fatiha, calling the faithful to prayer. Through a window to one side, he could see the moon formed in a slim crescent – quite fitting, he thought. He slowly looked around as two men were ushered in at the far end of the room. He adjusted the folds of his silk *thobe* about his feet, as the men settled themselves. He studied them carefully.

'What news?'

'He was stubborn, I'm afraid,' answered one of them. 'We had to burn both his arms in acid almost to the elbow before he spoke.'

The Arab's eyes flickered only slightly; these were words that not along ago would have made his flesh crawl. Now it only served to make his resolve firmer.

'But he *did* talk?'

'Yes, yes. He confirmed the involvement of the German, and whoever hired him in Switzerland, as we had already suspected. The name Vruger or Vrugen was mentioned.'

'And Al-Ben Salmad?'

'He was in Cannes for almost six months, throughout the summer. A large villa, but discreet all the same, well guarded. He was using another name and identity – something Ashonni, an Iraqi diplomat. Now he is in London.'

'Do you know exactly where in London?'

'Not as yet, but we are close to finding out.'

'Let me know your progress.' The man in the *thobe* lowered his eyes slightly. 'I think you know what must be done when you find him.'

The two men nodded solemnly, and he allowed another moment's silent.

'We have also another problem – that of the English journalist I mentioned recently.'

'Is he to suffer the same fate as Salmad?'

The man in the *thobe* seemed annoyed at this presumption. 'No. You are to watch his progress, nothing more. I already have someone close to him. I don't yet know if he will be acting in our interests or not. As it is now, I think it more likely that he will be our ally.' As he finished, he looked down again. He didn't want them to see just how desperately he clung to that hope.

Kent Ehnbridt had mixed feelings about working for Herr Vruger. The work itself was okay; it was very close to what he was used to: tracing, finding large debtors to the banks, investigating frauds, picking apart the skeletons of previously solvent companies that had mysteriously gone bust. That had its ups and downs, like anything else.

But Vruger and their method of meeting he could never quite get used to. All five meetings had been in Vruger's large Mercedes, where he could only pick out a dull outline of the man through a tinted glass screen. All further contact had been by telephone. And then, after all those precautions, on one occasion recently when Vruger had dropped him off at the Glarnischof hotel, he had opened the side window. They had hardly talked on that occasion, and it was as if he had done it just to say, 'Yes, we know each other well enough now; it's about time you saw me. In future we will talk business as usual.' With his short brown hair and steel-rimmed glasses, he looked very much as Ehnbridt had imagined him: quiet, restrained and cautious, with the merest hint of civility – nobody would ever go so far as to call it friendliness. The normal Swiss attitude meted out to strangers. The 'feeling out' stage. Ehnbridt had practised it as much himself; it served his kind of business well.

Vruger had even allowed the barriers to go down at just the right juncture, in very much the 'normal' fashion of someone cementing a working relationship. But despite the gradual turnaround, he still sensed something more guarded about Vruger's attitude than was warranted by their dealings.

It had been almost two years since Ehnbridt's first case for Vruger, and Vruger's air had intrigued him almost immediately. If only he could piece together the purpose behind the various assignments, it would likely make quite a story. Probably it would go a long way towards explaining Vruger's preoccupation with remaining anonymous.

Perhaps one day he would tell it all to the newspapers, he thought whimsically. But not yet. Not while Vruger was still in grace. The newspapers only paid the once, Vruger had employed him now seven times in the last two years. He had to look to the better paymaster.

The tannoy broke rudely into his thoughts. He listened partly to the French; the German had finished. He looked up. The board confirmed it: SWISSAIR FLIGHT MESR 216 TO BEIRUT. BOARDING GATE 12.

He got up and mingled with the small crowd that was forming. He could just pick out the broad back of the tweed jacket he had identified earlier, and the curly, stone-grey hair. About thirty, thirty-five yards ahead. Perfect, he thought. Not too close, not too far.

Part Two

UN Press Center, New York: Reuters London

5

NEW YORK: 11.42 29 NOVEMBER

When Kurt Waldheim and co-chairman Dr Emil Schaarer go to the peace conference in Geneva next month, a key issue on the agenda will be the Middle East. First call will probably be for a Christmas ceasefire in the Lebanon before they embark on talks over longer-term peace plans. Among these will be a resolution over the combined problems of almost daily Muslim – Phalangist clashes and the presence of Palestinian refugee camps; in response, from the Arab nations, will no doubt come a call for resolving the now long-standing and thorny questions of a Palestinian homeland and Israeli occupation of the West Bank. However, in light of the recent hijacking of a bus of Israeli schoolchildren by Palestinian terrorists, Israeli responses are not predicted to be warm.

UN Press Center

The East Beirut unit of the International Red Cross was busy that morning. It had been used mainly as a drugs distribution centre for the surrounding medical units, but this morning, as with many mornings recently, it had taken the overflow from the main hospital in Beirut. The normal wards were filled, and the overflow had come down into the basement, among the pipes and pillars that fed and supported the giant above. Virtually every space was filled, leaving only two clear aisles, and even the pipes had served a purpose by supporting traction ropes.

The basement had been cleaned and scrubbed, but the

rough-cast walls and floors quickly built up dirt from the belching fumes of the pumps and boilers.

There were fifteen new casualties in that morning, to add to the forty already there. Daniel Grade tried to shut off his ears from the sounds as he walked along one of the makeshift aisles past rows of beds. The babble of voices was broken only by the biting commands and instructions of doctors and the occasional wheeze and moan of those in pain.

He had been directed down to the basement from above, and now he asked one of the doctors, 'Where will I find Leorah Ajlan?'

The doctor pointed towards the far corner, where the pillars were closer together. Grade could just make her out among the shadows. Two bare bulbs were strung over the pipes, making the shadows more pronounced. He made his way across.

It was much hotter there from the large boiler in the corner. Grade was loosening his collar when she came into a patch of light and looked up.

'Miss Ajlan?' he enquired. 'Grade. Daniel Grade . . . I phoned earlier.'

'Yes, Mr Grade,' she said, and she turned and busied herself with pouring a clear-pink liquid from a bottle into a measuring jug. 'I'm sorry, I'm not being rude, but your call spoke of urgency . . . and today I was scheduled to be here.'

Grade noticed first her long dark hair, but her face was still partly in shadow; his fleeting impression was of large, soulful eyes, an almost Madonna-like face. He wondered whether it was just the half-light.

'No, that's all right.' He hoped that the surprise hadn't showed in his voice.

'I help out, you see.'

'Yes, I see.'

They both looked at each other for a moment, as if inviting the other to speak first.

'It's not that I'm unsympathetic to the journalist's plight,' she smiled. 'I think you could still just about call me one.'

'Yes, I know.'

‘Ah, you’ve been doing your homework, Mr Grade,’ she wagged a finger at him, then beckoned and led him down the aisle. ‘Please let me show you something first.’

Grade watched her shape from behind as she made her way along. Out of the shadows, her beauty was almost startling. He had expected someone curt and matronly, with short hair. The surprise was pleasant.

‘There are almost two hundred patients in here now,’ she waved her hand. ‘In a hospital designed for just over a hundred. And of those, a good fifty will be released well before the prescribed time to make room for incoming cases. A sad fact we have to face.’

She took a long breath. ‘This is one of only five ICRC units which work in close conjunction with the Lebanese Red Cross, my own unit. The Palestinians have their own hospital in the city – the “red crescent”.’

‘So your unit represents the Christian element?’ asked Grade.

‘No, religion doesn’t come into it. The ICRC and the Lebanese Red Cross aid both Christians and Muslims alike. The Palestinians merely have their own units because their camps are set apart. I think they feel isolated by that factor.’

A doctor came over. ‘Your favourite boy’s awake. He’s been in and out of the anaesthetic for almost the last hour now.’

Leorah’s expression became intent, and she looked across sharply. With a brief nod, the doctor led the way.

The boy hardly acknowledged them as they approached; the *No solids* notice remained at the foot of his bed and he was still slightly dopey.

‘He was very good really,’ the doctor added. ‘We had to cut the leg, but we got all the infection out, and I think it will take quite well now.’

‘But I thought you said the leg would be all right.’ Leorah looked at him accusingly.

‘Yes, yes, we could save the leg, of course. But we had to cut out a cartilage. It was just too badly damaged, I’m afraid.’

Leorah looked down at the boy and stayed in silence for a moment. Then she reached out and stroked his forehead as he lightly slept.

He muttered, '*Ummhat*,' and opened his eyes; then they slowly fluttered shut again.

'He'll be able to walk perfectly well,' the doctor tried to reassure her. 'But I'm afraid most athletics will be out. He'll also experience a slight limp for a while, but a few months' physiotherapy should put that in order.'

'He probably won't even remember me,' she said quietly. She felt elated, but at the same time cheated. She had wanted more for him. So much more. She had a sudden picture of other children running and jumping and playing, and him just sitting watching them, quietly, thoughtful. She turned away as the tears came to her eyes.

Grade could sense the special tie between them.

'Someone you know?' he asked.

'No, it was a boy that I saved from Zalqua. From the ashes and rubble of Zalqua.' Her sorrow turned quickly to anger. She turned her back to hide her tears, but she knew that it had showed in the quavering of her voice. She spoke quickly over her shoulder. 'Thank you, doctor.' And led Grade away.

She didn't speak again until they had almost reached the far end of the room, back near the main entrance doors.

'I'm sorry, Mr Grade, I should be getting on with things. There'll obviously be a lot of information you'll be needing.'

'It's something more specific. An event that occurred at the beginning of the war.'

'Could *you* be more specific, Mr Grade?'

Grade looked around; it was busy by the doors. 'It's difficult to talk here.'

Leorah studied him carefully. On the phone, he'd spoken of *urgency*, but then she'd merely interpreted that as impatience. Even as she'd seen him walk in, he'd seemed to confirm that impression: squat, bullish and *impatient*. But as he'd walked closer, she realized that really he was quite tall, it was only his broad frame that had made him seem smaller.

And his blue eyes seemed quite frank and open. He had been prepared to let her go at her own pace, allow her the few minutes of indulgence with the boy, Rashid. She began to revise her opinion of Daniel Grade. She made a concession by walking a few paces away, towards a quieter corner.

'Can you at least give me some clue?'

Grade gave a heavy pause. 'It concerns the assassination of Al-Hakim and Khourem almost eighteen months ago, before the start of the war. You did a report on it for the *Yaumi Rassul* at the time. You were the first journalist on the scene, I believe.'

Leorah glanced around. 'How do you know this?'

'From a man called Anton Reiner. A banker in Switzerland – you spoke to him.'

Grade could see her searching back through her memory. 'Yes,' she said finally. 'I spoke to him once on the phone. Quite briefly. Over a month ago now.'

It was Grade's turn to show surprise. 'You mean he didn't come here personally? He didn't fill you in on what was happening, perhaps forewarn you of my visit?'

'Oh yes, he shared his thoughts with me briefly,' Leorah said. 'And he said someone might contact me, but not you specifically, Mr Grade. Quite honestly, I'd almost forgotten about it. He said simply that he got my name through my articles on the assassinations of Al-Hakim and Khourem, and since he suspected a possible Swiss connection was particularly interested in my own theories on *outside* involvement. If he sent someone to see me, might I care to expand on them. But he didn't ask me to expand on them there and then, as if he already knew what I might have to say. It seemed more a back-up call than anything else. I remember now thinking about it afterwards. I mean, how odd it was.'

They were less than two feet apart, and Grade could feel the questions multiplying in his mind. He looked around hastily.

'Look, when I said it would be difficult to talk here, I was thinking as much of you.'

Leorah smiled wryly. She wished she'd also given some earlier credence to his tact and discretion. 'You're right, Mr Grade.' She glanced at her watch and then asked for a bit of his notepaper and wrote something down. 'If you come about nine o'clock.'

Grade looked briefly at the address, then tucked it into his top pocket.

'Would you normally have eaten by then?'

'Well, er, yes,' Grade stumbled.

'Well, don't eat before you come along. In the Lebanon we eat late, and I have no wish to be eating alone while you ask me questions. Nothing could be more off-putting.' She turned with a half-smile and went back along the aisle, busying herself with moving some bandage rolls.

Grade went out and up into the foyer without looking back. It struck him that he had had enough of hospitals, especially since he felt uneasy in them at the best of times. In a hospital full of suffering humanity, that unease was almost overwhelming, stifling, and already, without even doing the ghoul's tour of the desecrated streets outside, he could feel the atmosphere of the war – the toll in blood, pain and anguish – permeating to his very bones.

He pushed the thought away and went through the double doors, not quite sure what to make of Leorah Ajlan. She was disarmingly beautiful, and her moods changed rapidly – in their short conversation, from offhand to near flirtation. But her expression as he'd mentioned Al-Hakim and Khourem overshadowed, as if the memory still pained her.

He would try and enjoy the evening before he asked her about that.

General Itzaak Pohlmann squinted through his binoculars.

Behind him was a unit of the third infantry division, brought down from the Golan Heights, complete with a tank, two field-guns and a half a dozen bazookas. There were thirty-four men in all, all of them with rifles, handguns and grenades – standard army equipment. Fourteen of them held Uzi machine-guns and Simi automatic rifles. Another unit from the sixth infantry division was on its way from just outside Tel Aviv.

General Pohlmann stood fully ten paces ahead. Somehow he seemed curiously apart from them, as if he was facing the tunnel and the vastness of the rock desert around him alone, defiant – and they were merely a backdrop.

He was a distinctive looking man. A small, greying goatee accentuated the prominence of his chin. What hair was left on his head was greyer still, but was now hidden by his cap – his only concession to pomp and uniform. It was much too hot for his jacket with its array of ribbons and medals, his only reminders of the Six Day War, Abri Housa and Gaza Strip. The memories themselves, through choice, had faded quickly. He stood now in khaki shirtsleeves. His eyes as he lowered the binoculars glinted the palest of blue.

'What time is the next communiqué due?'

His adviser, Major Gant, a sandy-haired, ruddy-complexioned man of forty-two stepped forward.

'In just over an hour, sir. At seven a.m.'

General Pohlmann remembered the time quite well. He wanted to establish the procedure again, for both of them.

The field telephone was another ten yards in front of both of them. A leather trader from Chamir had been first to come upon the far, blockaded end to the tunnel. Their end was clear, but the bus was deep inside and could not be viewed. A hundred yards from the tunnel was a barrier, and to one side was the field telephone.

It had taken five hours for the first army men to arrive from the nearest unit at Kounietra, relayed through the police and the Kiryat Chemone district authorities. And another two for the replacement unit from the Golan. General Pohlmann and Major Gant had arrived an hour later at almost 4 a.m. Major Gant had been the first person authorized to pick up the field telephone; Hasik had demanded that a high-ranking official negotiate, and Pohlmann had delegated the task to Gant. Gant had relayed what he could in the gaps to Pohlmann, who had stood close by throughout.

The sun was slowly rising now over the hills of Neveh Ativ, making the shadows there seem long.

'So, no demands as yet,' General Pohlmann confirmed. 'No ultimatum.'

'They want to wait until the media arrives. Until they are visible, at least.' Major Gant looked back at the long stretch of the deserted approach road.

They had not touched on the terrorists' preparations and capabilities in any depth as yet. Major Gant had been selected as his adviser due to his past experience of terrorist hijackings. In the early seventies he had been involved with two of the Dawson's Field hijackings, later to be known among the Israeli military as 'Revolution Airfield'. He could quote any number of statistics on 'location strength', ratios of hostage survival and varying terrorist groups' capabilities. General Pohlmann's strength was strategy; he had been quite happy just to observe, then had sunk quickly back into thought. Now he seemed more eager to discuss it.

'How many are they? Or do we have to guess?'

'We have to guess, I'm afraid. They haven't told us.' Major Gant pointed. 'But there is certainly a man on observation at each end of the tunnel, and earlier this morning, while it was still dark, one of the men with infra-red binoculars made out the movements of at least two others inside.'

'Do we have any idea who they are?'

'They say PLO, but that could cover a multitude of sins. Individually, we have no idea.'

'Yes. I remember you said PLO. I was hoping for something more specific.' General Pohlmann was pensive. 'You mentioned infra-red. Can we get identification through this? Some pictures perhaps?'

'That would be the only possible way. We will have to wait till tonight. In the daytime the tunnel is just an impenetrable coal hatch, even to infra-red. But I'm reluctant to risk another surveillance.'

'Why is that?'

'They also have Zeiss Dialyt nighttime binoculars, the

best. And the longest range infra-red rifle sights. If they so much as see us point a rifle at them, one of the children will be executed. We will have to be more discreet.'

General Pohlmann showed surprise. 'They told you this?'

Major Gant knew that he meant the technical information, not the threat.

'They have told us quite a lot. They think it pointless that we should be snooping around trying to find out their strength, wasting time, delaying deadlines perhaps . . . Or at least that is what they have said.' Major Gant paused significantly. 'More like they do not wish us to underestimate their power.'

General Pohlmann held the moment with another glance through the binoculars.

'What else did they pass on about their power.'

Major Gant found it hard to ignore Pohlmann's tone. It was as if merely by relaying the information he was in some way a collaborator.

'They have enough food for five days for the children, three weeks for just themselves. They have wired the bus with explosives – Loege-tannel plastique – all the doors and the emergency exit, and at intervals along its length. All wired back to a multi-detonator firing box. It's a professional job; it sounds as if they know exactly what they are talking about. They are heavily armed: automatic rifles, handguns, grenades, gas . . .' He held General Pohlmann's gaze. 'The last unspecified, I'm afraid. They have eight hundred rounds of ammunition, enough to hold off a fortress siege – again, unspecified calibres. And then, of course, they have what we can see for ourselves, what is obvious . . . the tunnel is partly blocked, they are in darkness, so we cannot pick out their movements, tell accurately how many they are. With the field telephone they have a closed link: nobody can listen in that they don't want to – or speak. They are surrounded by millions of tons of rock – there is no way in or out, except those routes that are already half-blocked and guarded . . .'

General Pohlmann had thought of stopping him earlier,

but didn't; he knew it was in part a retaliation, and momentarily regretted his previous tone.

Only two months beforehand he had sent a unit in to rescue a group of twelve children held in a school building near the Hebron Kibbutz by the PFLP. Everything had gone well, according to plan, but as a last action the three terrorists had set fire to the building. Two of the children had died. It had been proclaimed as a victory, but General Pohlmann had tasted that victory sour in his mouth as he'd witnessed the invective of grieving relatives in following news broadcasts.

And that had been an amateurish, unrehearsed action in comparison to this, Pohlmann reflected. He felt despondency grip him as Major Gant continued his diatribe. Still he asked the question.

'What's your overall view of the situation?'

'Impregnable. They have thought of every conceivable factor. We will have to accede to their demands when they come, or try and hold something on them from outside – perhaps we will know more about that possible element when their intentions become more clear. That would be our only chance. It certainly won't be in there.'

General Pohlmann allowed his defiance to resurface.

'We will see about that. We will see . . .'

The car was a silver Mercedes nine-seater. Its front windows, where the chauffeur sat, were clear, but the glass of its two rear sections was heavily tinted.

It drew up sleekly at the curbside on Zürich's See Strasse. A man slipped unobtrusively from the shadows of the trees bordering Reiter Park and into the back of the car.

He sat back in the plush seating and eased his breathing as the car pulled away from the kerb.

Facing him was a tinted glass screen separating him from the middle seat. Just below it and to one side was a small steel grille. The middle seat was turned towards him, but he could only just make out the shadow of the man inside. He looked expectantly towards the steel grille. After a moment it crackled.

'How did it go, Jaalgen? Do you think he took the bait?'

The man in the back settled quickly into the masquerade; the same masquerade they'd played for the last two years now. He addressed the grille as Herr Vruger, though he knew that to be as false as one of his own aliases: Herr Jaalgen and Francois Duffal amongst them. I've got you *marked*, he thought to himself.

'Quite a keen young boy, really. Longish-hair, tortoise-shell glasses. Typical budding Sorbonne intellectual – you know the type. If he got rid of some of his idealism, he could almost make a good terrorist. I don't think we'll have any problems there.'

'You're always looking for possible recruits to serve your causes for anarchy, aren't you?'

'Does it shock you?' Jaalgen asked flatly.

'No, I just find it amusing.' The voice sounded more distant and hollow through the grille now.

Jaalgen knew differently. He knew that it was just a messy detail to Vruger, something he'd rather keep apart from. His tinted glass screens, his anonymous meetings, insulated him from the smell, the blood of it all. Describing the boy had brought it too close.

'It has become quite a compulsion, hasn't it?' Jaalgen said, 'Al-Hakim, Khourem . . . With Reiner now, it will be *three*.'

'It's a necessity,' Vruger said flatly. He couldn't resist the rebuke. 'Anyway, we would now just merely be summing things up, not speculating, if it hadn't been for your escapade at Mürren.'

Jaalgen felt the muscles in his neck tighten. One small error in all of two years, the bastard. He wouldn't let him off easily now.

'You know, that package for Reiner is quite something,' Jaalgen said with faint pride. 'It's small, deceptively small – not the sort of thing you would expect a bomb could be in. But the plastique is a new compound – very powerful! It will probably take his shoulders off along with his head.'

There was a brief silence. 'I leave the details to you.'

'Yes, of course. But have you given a thought to where it might end. After Reiner – who next?' He laughed lightly. 'Perhaps you've got the taste for it now.'

'I've told you – it's a necessity. A necessity.' The voice became flustered.

'But what if this doesn't work with Reiner either?'

'You will have to make sure another way. That is what I am paying you for.'

'And if the journalist should get too close, despite Reiner being out of the way. What then?'

The silence was long this time. 'That will have to be taken care of, too.'

It amused Jaalgen, the way that Vruger avoided the word. 'Make sure another way . . . take care of . . . Why don't you just say what you mean? You want me to *kill* them.'

There was no response from the grille for several seconds. Jaalgen grinned almost triumphantly, then repeated, 'Why don't you just say it?'

From his side of the screen, Vruger could see through quite clearly. He mopped lightly at his brow with a handkerchief. He had disliked Jaalgen from the start, and their meetings since had done little to change that feeling. The only thing he gloried in was that for something as simple as money, this cold, sickening, killing machine would do his bidding. That sense of power and his loathing wrestled together inside him for control. He studied Jaalgen's face, the slicked-back light-brown hair, the thick, sensual lips curled up in a half-smile, and the eyes – the eyes were what always held his attention the most: cold blue and rounded, looking almost out of place, like a girl's.

He let the gibe pass. 'I think I can leave everything in your capable hands. I don't foresee any loose ends . . .'

'You seem to have forgotten one thing.'

'What is that?'

'The boy. The boy knows me now. He could identify me if things started heating up.'

Vruger faltered. 'But you used a disguise.'

'Oh, that's amusing. Very amusing. A wig, a blond wig! How long do you think it will take a policeman's pencil to draw that in?'

'Was the girl with him?'

'No, he was alone.'

Vruger considered. It had been his own idea initially to involve the girl indirectly, something that slotted neatly into place as a safeguard against possible future complications. Now he began to wonder.

'You should have brought this up in the first place. You must have realized. I paid you for Reiner, not for the boy.'

'Forget your precious money, Vruger, I will do it for myself – for my own self-preservation. And *yours*, if you troubled to think that far. From me, they will get to you.'

'I know, I know . . .'

'Of course, that is, *if* you have no objections.'

'My God,' Vruger spluttered. 'You don't exactly expect me to approve it.'

'No . . . let us just call it a *necessity*,' Jaalgen mocked.

There was a heavy pause. 'If you give me a bit of time to think. There might be a way of tying these new factors together, turning them to our advantage . . . But I need some time.'

'Time is your luxury, not mine,' Jaalgen echoed.

Vruger was tiring of the conversation. He flicked his microphone on to its other channel and directed the chauffeur, then came back on to Jaalgen.

'We are finished, I think. We will drop you off around the corner, on Limmat Quai.'

Jaalgen sat back with his own thoughts. Your elaborate car might have given you your privacy, but in the end it has *cost* you. He remembered his feelings of smugness when he had first traced the registration. So easy. Any problems, I've got you marked.

The car pulled up slowly just before Rathaus bridge and electronically the back door latch clicked faintly. Jaalgen let himself out.

'Thank you very much, Herr Vruger.' He had to be almost consciously careful not to say Schaarer.

In the Lebanon they call it a *maza*, similar to the Greek *meze*. The eight dishes almost filled the small table, leaving little room each side: two of rice with saffron and herbs, two with mixed olives, tomatoes and cheese; spiced lamb with almonds, spiced beef wrapped in a vine leaf; taramasalata, a fish paste; samboussac, a meat in light pastry, and pouched bread in slices.

Grade had brought two bottles of local table wine, one white and one red, so it wasn't necessary for Leorah to disturb her own modest stock. They set the bottles at each side of the table where they sat like markers. He was drinking red, she white.

It took her quite a while to bring up the subject of Al-Hakim and Khourem. She skirted it at first, talking lightly, generally. It seemed that she wanted to satisfy her immediate appetite first before she talked at any length. She put her fork down after a while.

'It's hard for me to talk about this, even now . . . and we are almost two years past the event. That is not just because of my journalistic interests or the impact of what happened, or for that matter what has developed since . . . some say as a result of *that*, I don't know . . .' She looked back to her discarded fork and scanned the food, as if searching for some inspiration. 'It is just that the men themselves meant so much. And I can't even begin to explain the many reasons why, Mr Grade. Politically, morally, emotionally to *me* as a Muslim . . . all of this.'

Grade let the silence ride before he asked. 'What was it, fate or coincidence, that you were first on the scene?'

'No, neither. My contact in the police department is a Muslim. He owes allegiance to me more than other journalists he knows. It's as simple as that.'

She picked up her fork again after a minute and started picking.

'Emotionally it was difficult. But I balanced that against the moral and political side. I realized quickly the advantage that I had. To write the piece from *my* viewpoint, someone who knew their careers and standing well. And because I was first, the story that would probably be read most widely.'

Grade wondered at the obvious strength of her opinion, whether it was a good thing in journalism. Whether it was even dangerous? He hadn't realized till then how much of a heartfelt issue it was to her, how close she'd been.

'You must have felt quite powerful.'

'*Yaumi Rassul* sales almost doubled that day,' she only half answered the comment.

Grade spooned some more rice and black olive salad onto his plate. They were silent as he poured more wine for both of them.

'Since you know what Reiner's claiming, he obviously told you something about his suspicions of SBECSA's involvement.'

'Yes, he did,' she said with an air of sour defeatism. 'Not in detail, but the essence.'

'And do you think he's right?'

She chewed the question over for a minute. 'I wish I *could* disagree with him; it would be so much simpler. But I'm afraid so many of the facts add up. In many ways, he was just putting substance to something I and many other people suspected. The rumours were quite strong, you know, and had been for quite a while.'

'Pertaining to Switzerland?'

'No, general. Just that there had been some outside interference: reaction to the Palestinian presence from the Syrian Saiquas, Syrian and Jordanian anti-Phalangist feeling, Israeli interference, even the vying of the superpowers. And then of course the money connection, because people recall all too well the Intra Bank closing in '68 through mainly political pressure. Everyone had their own ideas. Myself included, up until a week ago . . .' A shadow fell across her face as she leant away from the nearby table lamp. She lit a cigarette. 'What we have is an undeclared civil war – so there is no starting point that you can measure exactly in time or by events. It is true that there were other incidents before the assassinations – some small skirmishes, some Palestinians killed on a bus. Some say *that* was the start. There was retaliation. Some Phalangists were killed in a bar. But if there was any hope at that stage of a full conflict being avoided, it died with Al-Hakim and Khourem.'

'That was the turning point?'

'Yes, most definitely. The skirmishes themselves wouldn't have led to civil war. But after the assassinations, things escalated beyond belief. Within a few weeks, hundreds had been killed.'

'But was there anything that indicated Swiss involvement, or is that just Reiner's pet theory?'

Leorah drew long on her cigarette. 'As I said, up until a week ago, I might have thought differently. I spoke to Reiner a month ago now, and at the time I thought his theory was interesting – no more or less than the others, mind you. But he seemed to have something definite and, of course, he was on the inside of this organization – SBECSA, is it?' Grade nodded. 'So, that is why I attached more importance to it, or at least remembered it when this other information came through from my police contact.' Leorah's pause was heavy, deliberate.

'What was that?'

'A man gave himself in at the Mazzra station last week, asking for protection. They had dragged his friend's body out of the ocean only a few days before. His arms had been burned through with acid up to the elbow, cauterizing them at the same time. One of his eyes had been gouged out with a hot implement. Then they had shot him twice through the head. Unrecognizable. As a final gesture they carved a cross on his chest – the same as with Khourem.'

A shiver ran through Grade's body. 'They?'

'Nobody knows exactly who – but it was obviously someone previously aligned to Khourem. But that wasn't the main issue. This man – Reymenak – knew the victim, a certain Jubrahn Gahtlav, and knew that he *would* have talked. Now he feared that he would be next. The police would offer protection only if he provided them with information.'

Leorah ran a finger slowly around the edge of her glass. 'He was one of three men, all Phalangists, involved in the assassinations. He supplied names, too. Those of his colleagues aren't so important – one of course was Gahtlav, the man killed, and he'd lost track of the other. But he also gave the name of the man who'd supplied them with the details of Al-Hakim's movements that night – Al-Ben Salmad, an old banking friend of Al-Hakim's. He had fallen out with Al-Hakim over some deals in Khuwait. He was in the south of France for a while under an assumed name, and apparently is now in London. But the man who ordered the assassinations was Swiss – Reymenak overheard the name on the telephone one night. Kruger, Vruger . . . he wasn't sure. A Zürich meeting was mentioned. He could only pick out parts – it was in German – but he thought the man making the call at his end was Dutch or Belgian.'

'And who was he?'

Leorah held her hand up. 'I'm sorry, I'm going too fast. I should have mentioned that before. Kruger . . . Vruger's man, the one making the call, was from outside, a professional. *He* organized this Phalangist squad of three – and played a key part in it himself that night.'

'No name?'

'No, too careful. Good description, though – blue eyes, light-brown hair, forty, forty-five. Could fit a few million Northern Europeans.' She smiled briefly.

Kruger, Vruger? That shouldn't prove too hard to dig up. And if enquiries in Zürich should still prove a dead-end, he could approach from the other side: try and track Al-Ben Salmad. London? He could use Nabens or one of his assistants. He thought again of his feelings on that first night in the newsroom. Reiner a month ago; this information just last week! *It was all happening over eighteen months after the assassinations.*

Leorah was looking thoughtfully at the table. 'It bothers me still, you know, having to talk about their murders. The cold details express so little. They were such great men, I could tell you so much . . .' She let the sentence hang. 'Anyway, the rest of it, the war, everything . . . it's all history now.'

'I'd like to hear it. So far I've only heard the outside viewpoint – from our Middle Eastern correspondent. I'd like *your* view.'

Leorah studied Grade for a moment. He was holding up the bottle of white wine invitingly, and she found his faint smile quite endearing. It was hard to refuse. She let him fill her glass.

Then she started – delving back inside herself, through the pain, anguish and conflicting emotions of the past eighteen months. Much of it he had already read in her articles on microfiche the day before leaving London. She was obviously a cleverly persuasive journalist, putting across her left-wing views unobtrusively, yet within the bounds of the known facts of the war.

'I should try and explain this all more clearly, but it's a confusing war, one of ever-changing interests and allegiances. Taking it in simple stages, it started just with the left-wing Muslims and Palestinians against the Phalangists. Then Syria wanted to intervene – as a peace-keeping force they claimed.' Leorah started to mark the varying factions and stages with the plates on the table before them. 'Israel objected, because at that time Syria was their most formidable enemy, and the Israelis suspected this was more Syrian self-interest. The thought of the Syrian army just across the border was too much. They made *their* protests.' Leorah used the taramasalata to indicate the Israelis. 'Nevertheless, Syria comes in, in small pockets at first, in the form of Saiquas and PLA*. They *seem* to be upholding their peace-keeping strategy – or, at least, are not threatening the Israelis. The Israelis are quiet, but now the Muslim community and the Palestinians object to the Syrian

* Palestinian Liberation Army.

presence. More than that, they are split among themselves, with much in-fighting. Many of them formed pro-Syrian, anti-Syrian factions.' A laconic grin curled the corner of her mouth. 'It's so ridiculous, because now the Syrians and Israelis – previously dire enemies – have a partly common interest. And the Palestinians are in effect against each other – the PLA and Saiquas under Syrian control against the PLO supporting the Muslim community. Then there are the rebel, breakaway contingencies . . .' Leorah let the sentence hang, her faint grin turned sour, desperate. '. . . And there you have it. All the hatred, greed, lost honour and false pride which abounds in the Middle East has now come home to roost, and nurture and fester in my country!'

Grade was shocked into silence by the way she spat the last words out. He wanted to change the subject, the mood – but a comment of Nabens' stuck in his mind; he remembered a similarity to Northern Ireland.

'How did unequal representation affect things?'

'That has always been a factor behind tensions here. The 1943 covenant ensures a six-to-five ratio of Christians over Muslims in the cabinet. They are assured of political ascendancy, and to some extent this follows through in the business world. But there were other factors this time – the Palestinian presence, the constant Israeli raids on their camps, the right-wing reaction that resulted. This time it was different to '58.'

Her shoulders were hunched, her eyes distant, lost. Grade reached out to break her out of it. He touched her hand lightly.

'I'm sorry,' he said. Then, as she looked up, relaxed again, he felt awkward. He didn't know why he had said it. He took his hand away.

'That's alright.' She smiled, as though he could have kept it there. Her view of him was changing again. He was not only patient, but also intuitive, sensitive. She would tell him about Jamil one day, if she ever got to know him well enough for it to seem right.

'You were going to tell me more about Al-Hakim and

Khourem,' Grade prompted. 'Something of their background.'

'I was?' She was broken out of her thoughts. 'Oh yes . . . I was thinking of taking you to where it happened, on the coast road to Jounie. I could talk on the way. I thought it would be fitting.'

Grade thought it odd, except from the point of view of impact. First their lives, then the very place of their deaths! But out of respect for her obvious feelings for the two men, he agreed. They made arrangements for the following morning.

They finished the meal and, as Leorah cleared away, Daniel complimented her on it. Leorah made little of it.

'In a good Lebanese restaurant, a *maza* would contain anywhere from twenty to fifty different dishes.' She excused herself and brought in some grapes, fresh figs and halva from the kitchen.

Grade picked at them.

'I could also take you to the Aflak-Ham warehouse,' she said. 'That was where the shipment was meant to have come in from Securitee Maslegeisen.'

Grade looked up sharply. 'How did you know this?'

'From Reiner,' she stated with a hint of question. 'One of the few facts he gave me.'

Grade hid his surprise by looking back down at the table. He knew about Maslegeisen, but not about the warehouse. He wished now that his own meeting with Reiner had been more thorough. In London, they had hardly got through the 'feeling out' stage, then the second time had had that stupid argument. Even Schaarer's name had been provided as an afterthought. Just how much did anyone else know? Did Leorah know about *that*?

'Does the name Emil Schaarer mean anything to you?'

'Yes, of course. Co-chairman at the Geneva Peace Conference last year – and this one coming if I'm not mistaken. Is that right?'

'Yes . . . but nothing else?'

'No.' Leorah put a second halva cube in her mouth, aware

of Grade staring intently at her. 'Should there be?'

Grade thought for a moment of asking straight out, 'Anything from Reiner', but that would make it too obvious. He shrugged. 'It's just that Dr Schaarer was involved with SBECSA a year or so back. If this story broke, it could reflect badly on him, affect the peace talks.'

What was that in her face, Daniel thought: acceptance, surprise? He wasn't sure. She looked away after a second and suggested coffee. He nodded with a smile, and she went back into the kitchen.

Even with her out of the room, Daniel could sense the quiet tension of her mind at work; he could feel it even more when she came back in and stared at him levelly as she set the cups down, and so he wasn't too surprised when she came out with the question.

'Is Schaarer connected in some way?'

'No, not at all.' Grade said it simply, adamantly.

'Then why the question?'

'It's just that, with this investigation and the Peace Conference next month virtually coinciding, this past connection of Schaarer's with SBECSA seemed all the more poignant. I just wanted to see if you were aware of it.'

'Oh, come on, don't give me that . . . you know something.'

'I do . . . really?' he said caustically.

'Then why would you . . .' Leorah held herself in check. This wasn't getting anywhere – just making things awkward between them. Besides, she had already guessed half of it already; probably just another of those rumours that were rife. It wouldn't be the first time that a high-level official had been wrongfully accused, Arab or otherwise. People's imaginations ran riot with the mention of conspiracies. The thought of the implications if the rumour wasn't wrong began to worm away inside her, but she fought it back.

She took a grape for herself and offered one to Grade.

Over coffee they talked about work: the techniques of interviewing, the art of staying quiet at just the right moment. Leorah admitted that she missed the pure adrenalin working for *Yaumi Rassul* produced. Her work with the Croix Rouge was more worthwhile, more *necessary*, but she found no excitement in war; only pain, drudgery, sadness . . . And if there was ever excitement for her, it was through anger at what she saw. The flickering candles accentuated the fire in her eyes.

Grade felt like holding her hand again, but he stopped himself. He wondered why he felt awkward openly showing his emotions with her. Was it her beauty? Or the thought of Catherine? Or, more poignantly, the fact that he felt closer now towards Leorah than he had towards Catherine in a long while. He wondered whether that was just an embarrassing reminder of the weakness of his marriage, or just simple attraction. If it was the former, he didn't want to burden her with it.

She was holding up another grape for him. He took it.

The mood changed. Quickly, but so subtly that he wasn't aware of it immediately. An atmosphere thick with her enveloped him; her soulful brown eyes, the way her long hair wisped at times across her face, the olive texture of her skin glowing through the pure white of her blouse. There had been other moments during the evening – when they had first sat down and she had lit the candles, as he had held her hand – but now the mood was stronger. Perhaps it had been like that throughout the evening, only he had been too busy with his own thoughts to notice.

She offered another grape. This time he felt the soft play of her fingertips on his lips.

There was no mistaking the sensuality of her gesture. Or was he reading too much into it? He looked into her face, but she was looking down, away. He felt as if he was passing through some sort of barrier; the same barrier that had held him back all evening, that had made him feel slightly awkward. And now the grapes had become a symbol, a ritual of that.

'You know that you and I are similar in many ways, even aside from journalism,' he said. 'But our cultures, the very essence of our backgrounds couldn't be more different.' He thought, if they ever became too involved, how destructive they could be to each other, but left it unsaid.

'I know,' she said. And in her eyes now there was something else mixed with the sparkle and warmth; understanding or challenge, he wasn't quite sure which.

He took the last grape. He felt the barrier go down, ever so softly, behind him.

6

Julie was furious when Xavier told her about his meeting with Duffal.

'I told you I didn't approve. You must be mad!'

'Yes, but you spoke for yourself, for your *own* involvement,' he countered bitterly. 'You can't speak for me.'

She turned away so that he couldn't see the contempt she was sure was showing in her face. Her anger was more because he had gone his own way anyway, and then had sprung it upon her so casually. She felt he was deliberately making it clear her view didn't count. Now, faced with it, the possible repercussions of his action began to mount in her mind.

'I thought you were a rebel,' he hit out with – and she felt the blow. 'My father and I are the rebels of the family, quote, unquote. And now you're cowering over something as small and simple as a flash letter.'

Her mind debated whether to take the accusation or the minimization of the flash letter first. 'My rebelliousness, as you call it, doesn't stretch to doing something as pointless and mindless as this. College speeches, theses, yes, even demos . . . And by that I don't mean that circus at the weekend. I mean organized, purposeful, *legal* demos. *You* might want to get your head kicked in, see yourself as some sort of mini Che Guevara through your suffering – but not me.' She was pointing at him now. 'And as for my father –

when he was your age, his rebelliousness was taken out in the boxing ring, man to man, face to face across fifteen square feet of canvas. Now he takes it out in newsprint, his views laid bare where everyone can see them.' She shook her head. 'Never anything like this cowardly act. An anonymous package, sent under the wing of an equally anonymous organization.'

Xavier paced the room, looking for his cigarettes.

The two rebels! The expression made her laugh, half at its ridiculous simplicity: their bond was more a sharing of the spirit than anything else. She thought again of that worrisome letter from home – how to deal with it? She had never had that same bond with her mother. Oh yes, she was patient, understanding, warm. But that was half the problem. If Julie ever went to her with enthusiasm, she would just smile that patient and attentive smile. Nothing could be more dampening! With her father she could share her enthusiasm, her exuberance. Love could be shown, not just left unspoken. Julie often thought that if she was a different type of girl, plagued by all manner of problems, continually bombarding her mother with them, then her mother's quiet sympathy would surface, her best side would show. But Julie wasn't the sort of girl to air her problems; in that way, too, she took after her father.

Xavier lit a cigarette impatiently. He was scoffing. 'Ridiculous! You make too much of it.'

'Do I?' she glared at him. 'At the least, your precious flash letter will probably burn this man's fingers – that's actual bodily harm. Already you're talking about an eighteen-month or two-year sentence. With the spectre of 'terrorism' behind it – as the judge will no doubt scream – they'll probably up it to three or five. What's wrong? I don't see you laughing?' She grinned half-mockingly. 'And if you're really lucky, your man will have a weak heart, and you can tell me I'm making too much of murder. Murder, Xavier!'

Xavier started pacing back and forth. 'God, sometimes your dramatics make me sick. And the trouble is you almost have me believing it. You and your father . . . Huh! how could I have been so blind. Maybe that's what you want from me – to replace that father figure, be like him, act more like him. Is that it?' Her gaze was stony. 'God, you and he are more alike than I ever realized. No wonder he gets people to read all that shit he writes – fills it with the same phoney dramatics –'

Julie only half listened as he continued with his tirade, dragging up all the sour moments and misunderstandings of the eight-month relationship; she had switched off at the comment on her father. Xavier had admitted before that he liked Daniel's articles – apart that was, from their bourgeois undertone. So she knew he was striking out mainly through his own frustrations.

She scanned the room. The package was there where he had left it, among the books on the table by the bed which in the daytime doubled as a sofa. The room was small, no more than twelve-foot square, but she was seated on the other side of the bed; she would only need to roll across to reach it.

Her skin prickled faintly with anticipation. She started to move.

Xavier's speech and line of thought was interrupted by her growing distraction, then her sudden movement. The realization of what she was doing jolted him sharply. He took two long paces around the side of the bed.

Julie got there just before him. She lifted up the package as he came across to her, his hands grappling at her arms. She pushed him away and straightened up.

'For God's sake, Julie,' he hissed under his breath. 'Now you've gone *completely* mad.' His hands were at her arms, struggling to pull them down.

Xavier was taller, and she had to arch her body to keep him at bay. She could feel his heat and closeness, his breath on her face. He wasn't strong – more thin and gangly – but now his violent shaking and her bad balance threatened to loosen the package from her grip.

'Give it to me, give . . .' he grimaced. He tried one terrible wrench, and she felt it slip through the sweat now on her palms.

It fell back onto the bed, then bounced with a thud onto the floor on the far side.

He reached for it. She was too quick for him. She kicked it further away.

He grappled at her legs, catching at her jeans, but she pushed him aside as she went past, getting to it just before him; then he was at her arms again, clawing and pulling them low enough to get a hand on the parcel. She fought him hard.

For a second the parcel was tugged back and forth between them. Its wrapping began to tear.

Xavier's expression changed. Before it had been hard with intent and exasperation; now it held only consternation.

'Julie, please, please . . . be careful! We'll burn our hands if it goes off.' His voice was high and broken with the plea.

Disgust swept over Julie's face. She started to laugh, a throaty, chuckling laugh turning to a sneer. She let go of the package and turned away.

'So this is our heroic idealist? Our political purger of all that is bad in society?' She shook her head slightly. 'It's alright for your overripe industrialist Reiner to burn his fingers. But not our precious Xavier. Oh no, that would never do.'

The rebuke seemed to wash over him. He was still caught up in the heat and aftermath of their struggle; her laboured breath, the fall of her breasts against the loose checked shirt, the way her blonde hair had flown wildly, the sparkle in her grey-green eyes when she was annoyed. He moved close again and touched her lightly. She noted that he seemed excited by the struggle. 'While you're at it, you can put your thoughts in cold water as well.'

He looked faintly crestfallen. '*Your* fingers might have been burned too.'

Christ! He was such an adolescent at times. How could he appear so sophisticated, then just crumble to this? Was he just trying to lighten the issue? Certainly, his expression was earnest enough. She thought for a minute of crediting him with some sarcasm, but decided against it.

'Thank you for your concern, but I'm afraid it's misplaced. Almost as much as your principles.'

She walked out and slammed the door.

Someone upstairs was calling for the concierge as she made her way down the narrow flight of steps to the Rue Lemoine, but she was only half aware of it amongst the weight of her thoughts.

There would be other opportunities to remove the package; he had already told her the instructions were to deliver it early the next morning. She would try again that night. But be nice to him this time, she thought.

They were high up on the coast road, skirting the cliffs below the village of Nahr el Kelb, heading towards Jounie.

Leorah steered the Land-Rover, looking over towards Grade at intervals as she talked or changed gear. Today he looked more like one of the many foreign correspondents long established in Beirut. He was wearing a beige safari shirt and almost matching trousers. The day before, in response to the heat, he had merely taken off his jacket and rolled up the sleeves of his plain white shirt; very much what you'd expect from a newly arrived foreign newspaperman.

The night before, Leorah had sensed a closeness develop between them, and then suddenly he'd changed, become more apprehensive, as if he was unsure of his ground; the last thing she wanted was to make him feel awkward or embarrassed, and so she'd backed off. Then, only moments afterwards, she had wondered why she had felt attracted at all, what had made her warm towards him.

The same thoughts were back with her now as they sped along. They indulged in small talk, now feeling easier with each other. But that hadn't been a problem from the start, she reflected. What was it? His looks? His dress? His personality? His age? *God*, in age he could be her father, and his dress and looks were almost as bad. They were the two things which had initially made her see him in a bad light: bullish and boorish seemed to sum him up.

The note of the engine became deeper as they curved around into a steeper slope. Leorah changed gear.

She remembered from her childhood the Englishmen who used to visit her father's store – how they would pick their way along the neat rolls of cloth, treating her father offhandedly, almost disdainfully, showing little respect for either Arab customs or people. That had influenced her initial impression, she realized; he had reminded her of *them.*

But during their first meeting, and the night before, she began to notice the difference: he was courteous and patient, showing a respect that Arab men found hard to muster for their women. And when his male pride was apparent, it wasn't heavy handed. He would cushion it with sharp or witty remarks, or in the quick knowing-looks that so easily creased his face; something she found particularly endearing. He was broader and rougher than the Englishmen from her father's store, but his blue eyes and his countenance were softer. What before had made him look bullish, now made him look almost like one of Michelangelo's powerful sculptures. Now the sun had touched his face, he looked not hard and debauched, but healthy, his stone-grey curls contrasting well with his skin.

She liked him, but *more* than that – more than the two Arab boyfriends she currently went out with – he excited her; he was a challenge.

It took them less than another ten minutes to reach the promontory by the bay of Jounie. Leorah slowed the Land-Rover.

'Just a few hundred yards ahead – on the tip of the headland you can see there now,' she indicated. 'That is where it happened. Just as they came around the bend.'

Grade's anticipation took over from his first moment's relaxation since they had left. The drive had exhilarated him – it was a bright, sunny day – but he had begun to worry about both Leorah's speed and competence as they skirted sheer drops and he caught glimpses of surf breaking on the rocks far below. Now he was treated to a similar view as he got out of the vehicle and peered over the end of the promontory.

'About three hundred feet, straight down,' Leorah remarked.

'Yes,' Grade confirmed, feeling the cool whip of the wind swirl up from the bay beyond.

Leorah shuffled up alongside him, so that they were both close to the edge.

She felt a danger and excitement there that gave verve to her voice as she spoke about Khourem and Al-Hakim. She gave Grade the details of the attack which had been pieced together by the police – the limousine coming around the bend, the gunfire from the hillside – at points offering her own opinion and interpretation. When she had finished, she stared bleakly down towards the sea.

Grade waited a moment before he asked. 'And Al-Hakim? Was his body ever found?'

Leorah walked about ten yards to one side, and scraped the ground lightly with one foot. 'They think he went over here. Oh, it's all been cleaned up long ago now – but at the time they found quite a gout of his blood and some traces just over the edge. They found part of his *thobe* caught on some jagged rocks jutting out about eighty feet down.' Leorah pointed. 'It was obvious that the last bullet caught him here, pushing him over.'

Again they both looked at the sea for a moment.

'But what about down there?' Grade asked. 'Wouldn't his body have been found floating at some time, or washed up?'

'No, not necessarily. The coastline here is honeycombed with caves and rock cavities. It's quite common for things to get washed into them and get trapped. The prevailing current moves in their direction.' Leorah was thoughtful. 'They almost form their own vacuum, sucking objects in.' She smiled faintly after a second. 'I'm sorry, I'm not very good at explaining the technicalities of this. Fuamal, the police inspector would have been better. It was the first assumption he made – apparently he'd had a similar case just a few months beforehand. Unfortunately, the end result there was the same – the caves are too honeycombed, too much of a danger to divers, for them to make any real search. So there can never be any totally conclusive proof.'

As she turned towards the Land-Rover, she noted Grade's expression. 'Anyway, I don't know what else to think. If his body was here, or even if he *had* been able to move, he would have been picked up by someone passing. The next people from the Casino were less than ten minutes behind, the police estimated.'

Grade immersed himself in the atmosphere of the promontory a minute more, and tried to imagine the wildness of that night: the gun-fire, the limousine careening towards the edge, part of it hanging over . . . the two men mowed down . . . He tried to think beyond, to the next car arriving, discovering . . . picking up Al-Hakim's body? But no answers came.

'Who were they?' he asked Leorah.

'Who?'

'The people in that next car. Were they important? Perhaps connected with Al-Hakim or Khourem in some way?'

Leorah looked blank. 'No, just a couple, middle-aged, enjoying a night out at the Casino. Like anybody else.'

They were both silent with their own thoughts as they strolled back to the Land-Rover and headed off. Neither spoke again for another two miles, and then Leorah began filling in the background on Al-Hakim and Khourem. Grade picked the bones from it: Al-Hakim had been a trader and banker. Khourem had originally been a member of the Progressive Socialist Party, but then formed his own party, the Karim Sha'b – still predominantly Muslim, but with a more acceptable face to the Maronite Christians. Al-Hakim became his adviser in early 1973. Thereafter they grew from strength to strength. They were both formidable political campaigners. It was a widely held belief that if they had lived, the Karim Sha'b would have taken the June '75 election; a more 'middle-line' party in power would have had a calming effect, if not avoided conflict totally. It was all much the same as Nabens' analysis, Grade considered, except in more detail through Leorah's closer involvement.

At intervals, he was slightly distracted from what she was saying, to study the terrain. Now as he glanced fleetingly over his shoulder at the road behind, he felt a chill rise inside him. He had feared as much earlier, now it was confirmed. He looked into her eyes, but she hadn't noticed.

'But I felt sadder than just for the political loss,' Leorah added.

'You must have grown to like them very much.' Grade almost said 'love', but thought it too dramatic.

'Yes I did. I wrote almost a dozen articles on them through the years – during the formation of the new party. Al-Hakim's journey, the build up towards the election . . .' Leorah's eyelids lowered slightly. 'You might call it more of an affection. The way many American newsmen must have felt who followed John Kennedy's campaign – first a pride in his beliefs, in what he was trying to do, and then in the man himself . . . wishing that a brother or a son could be like him, wishing that *every* mother's son could be more like him, and then . . . and then . . .' Leorah's voice choked, and she stopped abruptly.

Grade noticed her eyes filling as she stared at the road ahead. He felt the way he had the night before, wanting to hold her hand, wanting to be close to her. At times her emotions were so strong that he felt she needed some type of buffer, of comforter, and he felt both guilty and frustrated that another part of him held him back, kept him in check. He felt so inadequate. He stared stonily ahead.

They snaked along the last stretch of the road that hugged the coast, passing by the village of Antelias, the bordering rock face now much lower, not so sheer. On the other side, the fall to the ocean was less than fifty feet.

They would be reaching the outskirts of Beirut soon. It would be best to tell her now.

'We're being followed,' he said.

Leorah studied him long and hard, then glanced into the

mirror. A message flickered in her eyes after a second. 'The green car?'

'Yes.'

'How long have you noticed it?'

'I was only sure a minute ago. You can only catch a glimpse of it at intervals on a flat stretch – but I also noticed it on the way up.'

Leorah looked back into the mirror. Her face paled slightly. 'What are we going to do?'

'I don't know yet.'

A plan was formulated as they weaved through the streets of Beirut: Avenue Charles Helou, Rue du Fleuve, Rue Pasteur . . . Rue Gouraud . . . Place des Martyrs.

The names reminded Grade of the past French influence on the city, and it could also be seen in the dress of some of the people they passed, particularly the women. But in the shops, the restaurants, the street cafes – what few weren't boarded up or derelict – the style was similar to that found in most parts of the Mediterranean.

They turned into Emir Bechir, then again into the Place de l'Etoile, and the mix became more apparent: the streets were narrow, the houses grouped tight on each side in white, straggling clusters, soiled by the stains of time, traffic and the war. Small domed roofs rose at intervals, and washing was strung across alleys, begging for what little sunlight filtered through.

The women here were different, too, from the few Grade noticed in the cramped doorways. These were dressed from head to toe in black or grey *thobes*, the veils of their head-dresses drawn across. The most one could see, if they were indiscreet, was part of a face, or an ankle.

As they reached the end of another small side-street, a long black limousine coasted sleekly by. The chauffeur wore a conventional uniform, but with a *khoufia* head-dress, and beside him sat an Arab in a white *thobe* and *khoufia*. The back windows were tinted, but the shapes of three women could be picked out inside. They were dressed the same as the women just passed, yet seemed different; whether because of the limousine, or their better-kept robes, or their gold and jewelled clasps, Grade wasn't sure. The double discretion of the tinted glass and their smarter dress gave the limousine a secretive, almost ominous aura.

Now the conflicts were total in Grade's mind – French: Arab. East: West. Muslim: Christian. Rich: poor. And some crossing the divides of others. He couldn't remember such a confusing yet cosmopolitan pot-pourri since Rio de Janeiro.

Leorah snapped him out of his contemplation. 'Any of these coming three streets on the left will do,' she pointed.

'Okay, take the second one.'

The Land-Rover swung into the turn, then accelerated hard up the short street. Grade didn't look around to see if the green car was following; he had caught a glimpse of it coming around the Place des Martyrs, and noticed also there was only one man inside.

This was a new game to Grade; he was used to following – not to being followed. But now he felt excited by it, anxious that they should lose their pursuer before the warehouse, yet intrigued. Exactly *who* was he following – himself or Leorah? And what was his purpose? Who had sent him?

Grade could now see the steps she had mentioned. They rose almost in a sheer wall – over fifty of them in all – to a small square. The three short streets ended at the steps, winding from the cul-de-sac back into each other. Leorah pulled up sharply at the base of the steps.

Grade got out, and she gunned the Land-Rover back down the third street. Grade risked a glance backwards as he was halfway up the steps.

The green car was coming up the second street, slowing by the steps, hesitating . . . then heading back down the third street. *Damn*, he either hadn't taken the bait or was following Leorah. A knot tightened in Grade's chest. But wait . . . *No!* The car was slowing again, stopping . . . reversing into a space. Grade felt his step a bit lighter as he made his way up the rest of the steps. He didn't look back again, but he knew that Leorah had already turned back into the main road, knew that the man would soon follow him up. So far, so good.

The square was cobbled, with a small mosque at one side, and palm trees dotted at intervals, shading stone benches. The opposite side to the mosque was blocked off by a high stone wall, and at the far end a set of similar steps led down to another street.

Grade walked across, his footsteps echoing faintly, and sat on one of the far stone benches. He was suddenly conscious of his own nervousness. He looked back.

The man had the sense not to appear openly in the square, but Daniel could hear the faint scuff of his footsteps making their way up the steps, then stopping. He knew that, similarly, the man could pick out his position if he moved. His palms grew moist as he waited out the seconds.

The roar of the vehicle's engine somehow seemed louder than it should have been – whether because of his own intense concentration or not, Grade wasn't sure. This wasn't the time for contemplation. He sat a minute longer, then started his run.

He had just reached the top of the steps close by when he heard the scuffing of footsteps pick up again on the far side – rapidly. He caught a glimpse of the man as he made his way down. The man appeared suddenly frantic when he realized what was happening. But that didn't matter now; Grade urged himself on . . . He was almost there – running blindly, taking the steps two and three at a time, half-stumbling. He reached the bottom a second after Leorah had pulled up with the Land-Rover. He got in quickly and they pulled away. A group of small streets formed a similar dead-end at that side of the square, and they headed back down one of them.

Grade caught a last sight of the man just before they reached the main road. His frantic expression had now turned to a mixture of fury and consternation. There would be no taxis that he could hail among the small side streets, and it would take him at least five minutes to get back to his car and bring it around. By that time they would be well away. Grade sat back and relaxed.

Leorah looked across at him with a slightly raised eyebrow. 'I suppose you're feeling rather pleased with yourself?'

'You could say that,' he said smugly.

It was dusk when they reached the Aflak-Ham warehouse.

Sebastian Aflak was a manager and partner at the warehouse. He was a fat, seedy-looking man of fifty-five, the product of a French-Lebanese mother and Syrian father. His hair was oiled slightly and his teeth showed the yellow staining of cheroot tobacco when he smiled. He was the sort of man that you wouldn't trust to go behind you in a market-place if your wallet was in your back pocket, Grade considered, staying in the background while Leorah did the talking.

They were at the end of the warehouse and their voices echoed slightly because most of its contents – in wooden crates and oversized cardboard boxes – had been stacked close to its entrance.

After quite a few acquiescent nods, Aflak went to his office and came back with a register. He opened it and turned it towards them on the workbench.

He had nothing to hide. The entries were all there.

He probably had another register for the underhand deals, Grade thought, but that wasn't important to them; from what Leorah had already translated, Aflak had admitted recalling a consignment of arms from a company called 'Securitee Maslegeisen'. Now it was a matter of picking it out in the ledger.

'And do you remember who the shipment went to,' Leorah enquired.

'The Maronite Christians,' Aflak said without hesitation.

'How do you know?'

'It was consigned to a company of which Pierre Femayen is a director. Need I tell you more?'

'No, no more. And it came through Al-Ben Salmad?'

'Yes, he acted as agent – but it was going to Femayen eventually.'

Leorah's look was brittle. She explained to Grade that Femayen was a high-ranking member in the al-Kata'eb, the main Phalangist party.

Aflak added that it had been easy to remember the name because of the shipment's size, but he had a bad memory for dates; he left them to it.

'*Wahid dahika.* I'll be in my office.'

They heard his footsteps retreat to one side, and silence settled quickly as they flicked the pages.

Grade felt mounting anticipation. Travelling three thousand miles for one line in a ledger might seem madness, but it was the only way it could have been done; to check Maslegeisen's records from the Swiss side would have given the game away immediately, prewarned whoever was involved, *even* if he had been allowed access to their records, which was highly unlikely. But now an essence of that madness added to his nerves and excitement. If it had been the reading room of the British Museum, perhaps it might have been different.

That feeling was heightened as they went through numbers and names with increasing rapidity in the scrawled columns. Leorah found it first.

'Here. Here it is: 7 February.' She looked up and called Aflak from his office. He peered out and asked the reference number.

'NX 5438.' He went back inside.

The seconds passed slowly. Some gunfire and mortar exchange were just audible, coming from a few miles away, on the eastern side of the city. Leorah looked up abstractedly at the ceiling, as if trying to judge its direction more precisely.

Suddenly, a clatter of gunfire came from close by. It was answered almost immediately by some even closer, and some booming, overhead mortars.

As they both still looked expectantly towards Aflak's office, all the lights went out. Grade sucked in his breath.

The mortars now sounded directly above them and he heard some ricochets whine and clatter on part of the corrugated-iron warehouse wall. One of the skylights shattered and, instinctively, he ducked. He was sweating heavily.

God, how could he have been so stupid! Aflak had probably betrayed them; he had known they were coming since the day before, plenty of time to plan this little scenario. Two people killed in some crossfire – just another day in the life of a city at war! A few lines on page fourteen of the local daily. He should have realized! Look at the easy way Aflak had provided them with information; he should have suspected from that alone.

Grade's second thought was that the man in the green car had somehow caught up with them, that this was part of his initiative. But he couldn't work out *how* – and he realized that now he was becoming frantic, clutching for explanations. He tried to calm himself, tried to judge shapes as his eyes adjusted to the thick darkness.

The exchange of fire became heavier, more imminent, with little gap in between the shots.

As Grade crouched down, he could hear and feel Leorah's breath. She was closer than he'd realized. He listened to her breathing for a few seconds . . . *a lifetime*, at the same time holding his own. Neither of them consciously reached out, but in that moment their hands were touching, then clasped together like the night before, but more desperately; and Grade felt suddenly assured, like a condemned man who chooses the last comforts of a woman, so that the portent of death doesn't seem quite so terrible. But this was ridiculous! He wasn't going to die! *They* weren't going to die. They would escape. Grade scanned across to the main entrance. His eyes had adjusted to what few rays of dusk light filtered through the high, oblong windows, and he could just make out the main swing-back door.

At that moment all the lights came back on. He realized only then that the gunfire had already stopped. There was silence from outside.

Aflak was by his office door. 'So sorry. If I have the lights on, sometimes they try and shoot them out.' He smiled his yellow-stained smile. 'If you wait a half-hour or so, it should be all clear and safe by then.'

He passed them the import papers on 'Securitee Maslegeisen'.

Julie Grade lay naked under the heavy sheets and blankets of Xavier's bed. The November chill of Paris had penetrated through to his small third-floor flat and she pulled the blankets further under her chin, protectively.

From somewhere outside on the street, an accordion sounded. Vite Dominic, Julie remembered Xavier calling him. He favoured that particular street because it was on a direct route from Notre Dame to the Museum D'Histoire. In the summertime he had a monkey which he would perch on the tourists' shoulders and catch with his camera, but in the winter he consoled himself just with playing the accordion. He was much better at playing the guitar, he had once confided to them, but the accordion – being such a classically French instrument – was a better money-spinner.

It was just past 6 a.m. There were other sounds of activity from the street, mostly people walking; probably housewives up early to catch the best produce from the *boulangeries* and *charcuteries.*

Julie looked slowly, thoughtfully around the room. They had made love the night before, and she could feel the salt sweat now dry and sticky on her skin. Somehow it accentuated the cold. She tugged at the blankets again.

She felt annoyed with herself. *Be nice to him*, she mocked herself, *then he'll see your point, will start to be swayed . . .* but not *that* nice. That had never been part of her plan.

But as she'd come up to his room the night before, she had softened more than she expected. She started to apologize, to get the ball rolling, calm the atmosphere. But he wasn't listening. All the time he was holding her, kissing her forehead, stroking her, toying with the buttons on her shirt, saying 'yes *chérie*, yes *chérie* . . .' but not really listening.

She should have been annoyed and frustrated, but in a way it made her mission that much easier; it seemed he had forgiven and forgotten already. And so in part she had surrendered to his touch. But something nagged at her mind, and that kept another part of her in reserve – and she didn't respond as fully, as normally as she would have as he unbuttoned her shirt, and lightly kissed her breasts. She was still mostly passive as he removed the rest of her clothes, and kissed and stroked her lower, and lower . . .

He seemed unmoved, unperturbed by her response, but slowly she felt a warmth growing inside her, and her intangible concerns vanished. He was already hard, she noticed. She reached for him, guided him then, making her first conscious movement.

But with the hard, persistent pounding of his body, and the intent look on his face, that ghost in her mind began to reawaken. He was treating her harder, rougher than usual, she thought, and he was obviously enjoying it more; he was almost leering. And then she remembered when she had seen that expression before – as they'd fought over the package! He had obviously enjoyed that, too; it had excited him, and now this was part fulfilment of the stirring of those sadistic impulses, part punishment.

Not with me you don't.

At that instant she turned cold. Turned off. It was something all women could do; some women were actually plagued with it permanently. Xavier felt the difference immediately. He looked at her with astonishment. She was still below him, her knees drawn up, her legs wide, but for all the response there was, he might as well be making love to cold mullet. He looked hurt.

Julie didn't say anything, but she looked at him defiantly. It was too late for him, he was in the final throes of his orgasm, although he looked now suddenly as if he didn't want to go through and finish – and the pain of that conflict showed in his face.

It had a disastrous effect.

As she rolled away abruptly and in silence, she heard him

start to cry. Then came the apology, the exorcism of his thoughts and desires. How he was sorry about their earlier agument, how it had preyed on his mind afterwards, how he had gone through the many ways of making it up to her. But, above it all, his desire had overwhelmed him; she had roused him. Not the argument, but *her*. And then he was annoyed even more at the disagreement – that it had put a barrier between them; between him and the beauty he saw in that blinding moment, between their *love* . . . He apologized again.

Julie had listened to his words. They were soppy and sloppy, but they made their mark. She had been too harsh. He was obviously obsessed by all this, more than she had realized, and now he was confused, distressed – split between his emotions for his ideals and those for love.

Later that evening she had made love to him again, but this time showing response, with passion and fervour; she gave as good as she got, and more. Now they were even.

But in the cold light of that morning, *her* feelings, too, were split. She knew that, despite Xavier's protests and apologies, he would still send the package. And she wondered whether, through loyalty alone, she should now side with him, however misinformed and misguided his ideals might be – or side with a man in Switzerland she had neither seen nor met: Anton Reiner.

Grade was back with Leorah, at her apartment.

The night before they had talked in general about the war, Al-Hakim and Khourem, her work, and how it touched on his investigation. Only now was he beginning to understand the core of her feelings about all of them; at the same time he was learning more of her background. First and foremost she was a Muslim, but she wasn't blind to the fanaticism – both political and religious – that often lost the Muslims sympathy from other groups.

To her own people, she herself was a dangerous yet somehow impotent figure: an opinionated Muslim woman in a culture that was male dominated. Whatever she had to say, their disapproval would largely prevent their hearing it. Her father had been a trader; her mother had been tied to the home. Her father died four years after the '58 war, and her mother had lived the life of a widow in black robes in southern Beirut ever since. She had some sympathy with the Palestinians – and that touched again on the current conflict. She spoke vehemently.

'It was the British. The British were the original cause of all the troubles, with their Balfour Declaration.'

'Our good old colonial friends,' Grade raised his glass. 'It nearly always comes back to them . . . or the French, or the Germans.'

'And "owning", as they did at the time, large chunks of the world,' Leorah continued unabated. 'They thought in their sublime pigheadedness that they had a right to give away a land that was never rightfully theirs. Stick a pin in a map . . . let's see where the Jews shall have their homeland.' Leorah shrugged, and turned to stare at him directly. 'And don't give me all that about nobody really owning the land, or them just being nomads, or where else would the Jews have gone? Or the Palestinians only want it back now that the Jews have done something with it. They were a *people* – nomads or farmers or fishermen or whatever – and they had a land. And whatever has happened since should never *ever* cloud the original issue.'

'You seem to have covered all the angles.' Grade sipped hard at the Arak-based liqueur she had poured him. He had a vision of an old East End lady he had once interviewed. A Jewish lady whose family had all been slaughtered in the death camps. She had lived on to be a hundred, and received the Queen's telegram; and he remembered thinking how brave she was, how unbearable those extra years must have been, living with the pain; how that had made the occasion all the more a triumph of her spirit and will. She had lived on, had survived and endured as a form of defiance, to show them that they hadn't won. Often, he thought of Israel in the same way.

'If you talk of the original issue, then you have to go back to how it was then,' Grade said. 'It wasn't so much a Palestinian problem, or a British one in particular; more a European one, and subsequently a world one: what to do with several million Jews? They had been batted from pillar to post, persecuted throughout history, and it was time for that to stop . . . time for them to have a haven. A "homeland" if you will.' Grade paused. 'Now I know that you'll say you shouldn't mix statistics with moral issues – but by then the whole thing had boiled itself down to a terribly simple question: whose rights were more important? Those of several million Jews or those of a few hundred thousand Palestinians? And you have to admit that – Bible references or not – Palestine *was* the most natural choice.'

'But it isn't only the original formation of Palestine – which I'm not for a moment saying I agree with you on – but since then. The Israelis have made little effort to calm the waters. They've been antagonistic, expansionist in their policies . . .'

'Because they're afraid, Leorah. They've been weak before, and have been crushed. They see safety only in strength; if the persecutions have taught them nothing else, it's taught them that. They see this now as their last hope – and they also see that they are surrounded by hostile neighbours. A desperate people can be pushed to do many things.'

Leorah rose from the table, fetched the bottle off the sideboard and topped up their glasses. She was thoughtful. However much she disagreed with his views, she couldn't but respect them, the way he presented them, and she wondered fleetingly how much that was due to her *other* feelings for him. But there was a flaw in his argument, one that her mind was already busy working on. After a moment she looked across.

'I think you're right, Daniel. I think the Jews have been persecuted and exiled long enough . . .' She noted the faint surprise on his face: *perfect.* 'But that is what upsets and confuses me most of all. They should have sympathy with the plight of the Palestinians, because they *too* have been exiled. They should understand more than anyone else on earth, because they should *identify* with them. Are the Palestinians now to roam the earth for two thousand years in the same way?'

Grade sipped at his liqueur, and thought: not bad – she had turned his own argument back on itself, hoisted him by his own petard. And he knew immediately that the irony was so strong that whatever he brought up to counter it would sound ineffectual, futile. Quite a woman.

'*Touché*,' he said softly.

She thought: a man that can accept defeat graciously, without resentment, now that was something different, too. Refreshing. She wondered how an Arab would have reacted. She was intrigued about Grade's background – he had stood up for the Israelis, and yet she was sure he wasn't Jewish. She decided to ask him.

No. He wasn't Jewish. She was relieved: that would have put too great a gap between them. There was a pause and then, as if he felt he should explain his feelings further, he started to tell her the story of the old Jewish lady. Leorah nodded slowly throughout. The strength of his words clawed deep inside her. He finished, on the point of the Jews' historical religious persecution, with a poignant rebuke.

'How would you feel, Leorah, if an outside group of people claimed that Allah had a son – not a messenger, but an actual son – and then because the Muslim race wasn't ready to accept it, cast them out from their own religion, branded them.'

She gripped his hand tentatively as he finished. All thoughts of contradiction had fled from her mind. She understood him now; they both wanted the same things from this world, only in different ways.

The following silence was long and awkward. Shadows flickered in her deep brown eyes. She felt suddenly afraid. The feeling towards him welling up inside her at that moment caught her by surprise. She tried to fend it of by distracting herself, pouring more liqueur. But as she leant across, that thin veil of pretence fell away. Impulsively, she kissed him lightly, lingeringly.

'If only it was that simple, Daniel, people seeing one another's view – there might be some meeting ground.'

Grade felt almost like a schoolboy: a curious mixture of warmth, confusion and embarrassment. This is silly, he thought; I haven't felt this way since, since . . . since the grapes last night, he finally recalled with some amusement.

Leorah wanted to know the rest of his background. Where he was born. About his school, his childhood, his early career. How he had filled those fifty-three years.

She asked each question hoping it sounded no more than casual interest, and began to build up a profile. Irish mother, Welsh father. Both in their seventies now, alive and well and living in Gloucestershire. She made a mental note to look at a map of England. Boxer . . . boxing journalist, finally investigative journalism. House in Surrey, cottage in Berkshire. Married for twenty-two years . . . *Married!* She started at that point. How stupid! She should have guessed that, at least. She hadn't realized till that moment how much she took for granted that their profession and marriage were bad partners. Leorah was only half listening as he talked of Julie and Pauline.

Grade stopped after a moment; this was getting too close to the present – *too close to Catherine.* It reminded him of his uneasiness the night before, brought back the guilt of leaving at a time when they had so many problems, guilt at the lost years during which they had germinated. His feelings towards Leorah made it all the more painful.

Already, in that short time, his views on her had coalesced: she was complex, unpredictable – aggressiveness and compassion at times jousting closely – and she was one of the most beautiful women he had ever known. Even more so because she wasn't overtly conscious of it. He had seen enough of that type of woman before; too busy thinking how beautiful they were to have room in their minds or hearts for much else. Leorah seemed equally unselfconscious about her own intelligence.

From her expression at the mention of his marriage, he sensed she might now dig deeper about it. He felt safer with the ball in her court.

'You're a red-blooded Muslim woman – if you'll excuse the expression – so what's your excuse for staying single?'

'It would never work for me to marry another Muslim, Daniel.' She was pensive, touching the rim of her glass. 'It comes back to what I said earlier. I am too opinionated, and in a position of too much influence in the media – these things are usually reserved for men. And even if I could divorce my home life from my work, *he* might not be able to divorce it in his own mind. I would be leading a double life just for him. Unless, of course, he was a public figure of such standing that my position didn't affect him – but then we would probably be too far apart; we would almost be living separate lives.' She hoped she did not betray it in her voice, but at the same time she was thinking: *we* might be from two different worlds, our views might be totally different, but with you it *could* work.

She had known for a long time that what little affinity she ever found with 'Western' men had been largely due to that one factor: a woman had a place in their world, could keep her individualism. But with Daniel now it was more than that; so much a mixture of things, she found it hard to assimilate.

'But, you know, the Muslim laws weren't originally so prejudicial to women,' she added ruefully. 'They have been rewritten through the years . . . Rewritten by our proud, chauvinistic despots and rulers through the centuries, to try and convince themselves that Mohammed blessed them with more power than he actually did.'

That was interesting, Grade thought: usually only men who were immature or insecure needed such reassurance.

'Where did you pick up your radicalism?' he asked.

'At the Beirut Arab University. The wild days.' She smiled slightly. 'The University was criticised for having too much of a "Western", free-thinking bent. But there were just as many who were very left-wing, and those again who were strict, old-school Muslim. Quite a pot-pourri.' She got up and fetched a framed photo from a shelf.

It showed three girls in jeans and loose shirts, with books and folders tucked under their arms. They were all very attractive, but after a few seconds Grade concentrated only on one.

'That's me,' Leorah pointed unnecessarily. 'I was twenty-one, then.'

Grade studied the picture more carefully, then looked across the table, as if, through it, magically piecing together the years in between.

'As beautiful as ever,' he bantered.

She took the photo and put it back. 'We were the best of friends then. The three of us kept quite close for a long while afterwards, but the war has split us up now.'

The awareness of lost times hung over them for a moment, and then Grade came back to an earlier point.

'Mentioning the Balfour Declaration and the Israelis, as you did, you obviously blame the current problems on the Palestinian situation more than I realized.'

Leorah's face clouded. 'It has had a backlash effect here, as in many parts of the Middle East. Perhaps more so because of the Palestinians' presence here for so long. Some of them were in Jordan for a while, and it created problems there too.' She remembered Arafat's 'two big lies' theory, but thought this might suggest the Palestinians were overstating their persecution as much as prove the point. 'It didn't trouble the majority of the Muslim community here at the beginning, but the Phalangists slowly grew antagonistic. As I said last night, their presence attracted a fair amount of Israeli raids, which quite frequently – though unintentionally – damaged Phalangist property too. *They* blamed the Palestinians – and soon it spread to other groups. But not everyone pointed their fingers in the same direction. There were those for, those against – as in everything here. Moderation was required – something our country has sorely lacked throughout history.'

They were back to Al-Hakim and Khourem. 'And without

it, you had the makings of a war,' Grade said resignedly.

Leorah knocked back her drink sharply. 'I don't even like the expression "war". It's so damn convenient.'

Grade wondered if it was really the mention of war that had jarred her, or the reminder of Al-Hakim and Khourem. He gazed at her quizzically.

Leorah's eyes implored him. 'Don't you see, Daniel? The word "war" covers so much, it allows so much that otherwise would be unthinkable.' She looked around the room as if searching for lost words. 'When you look at a crippled infant, or hold up the broken limb of a child, a child with one eye, or no arms – it seems so terribly out of place. And so they are called atrocities. They are isolated, and so they are labelled "atrocities", and the world is suitably shocked.' Leorah was gripped in the throes of her own spiralling thoughts. 'But when there are too many "atrocities", the world becomes overwhelmed, because their well of pity has already been sapped dry. And so a new label, a new name is required – *war.* Politicians and military leaders feel safer within the cocoon of that word, because it gives licence to mass genocide almost without shock . . . a hundred people killed last weekend . . . "Oh, yes, but there's a war going on there". Twenty children killed . . . "Well, that war has been going on a while now . . ." The politicians and soldiers would never be able to live with themselves without the cover of that single word.'

Grade was wrapped up in her words during those long seconds, lost in their depth of meaning. He felt almost overwhelmed, as if in their short time together he had sunk further and further, discovering new, surprising treasures with each second. Now she had surprised him yet again. And it occurred to him that some of her conflicting emotions went deeper even than she dared fathom herself. But her emotions were tempered by something else as well. *Softness?* No, more protectiveness. He remembered the young boy on that first day in the hospital, and now she was relating only children to 'atrocities'. Wetherall's news item played at the back of his mind. She would no doubt have heard it too.

'You feel something special for children, don't you?' he said softly. Her expression was still faintly questioning. 'So, obviously you think there's a limit to the actions of any group which may be condoned – however noble and worthy the cause?'

Leorah raised an eyebrow. 'In what way?'

'The bus hijacking that's going on in northern Israel right now.'

Leorah's expression became taut. She looked nervously down and brushed lightly at the table. 'Yes, I'm afraid you're right. I asked for that. And there's no way I can defend such an action. I could go on about all the Israeli raids, how they have killed so many of the Palestinian people, including children . . . but then I don't see things that way – tit for tat, an eye for an eye. To me, the children are the innocents in all this . . . Oh yes, sure, some of the "freedom fighters" say they are fighting for the children's future, but they have little compunction about using them, recruiting them for the Ashbel*. But children only see things in the present. They are either happy or unhappy – it's as simple as that. To try and burden them with the adult view of the "grand scale" of things is as cruel as it is unnatural. As far as the future is concerned, they will just be bitter and frustrated at having lost the joys of their childhood . . . joys that can never be replaced. They will remember only war, hatred, bloodshed!'

Of all the emotions she had revealed, Grade sensed that this was her strongest, most heartfelt. He felt almost guilty now for having pushed her to it.

Leorah's hands trembled slightly. She had been close. *So close.* But however much she had shared with Daniel Grade that night, and whatever might be between them in the future, she couldn't bring herself to mention Jamil.

Kent Ehnbridt sat in his car, half concealed behind a tree in the darkness of the Beirut street. From there, he could just see the light coming from Leorah Ajlan's third-floor

* PLO's children's army.

window, and he had a clear view of the main downstairs entrance. The heavy shadows accentuated the sallowness of his face, the hang-dog expression his drooping sandy moustache gave him.

He glanced at his watch. Two hours now. The night air was cold, and he hunched down further in his seat and huddled his coat up over his shoulders. Ehnbridt was annoyed; more annoyed that he'd been in a long while.

Only twice before had he been 'lost', and both times by professionals, people who knew that they were being followed and were wary. Not by two unprepared amateurs. Or were they just that?

Shortly after they'd lost him, he'd considered giving up the ghost. To the hospital, back to the hotel, to her flat, up the coast . . . to her flat again. They just didn't seem to do anything of consequence. But curiosity prevailed.

Ehnbridt had gone back to Grade's hotel. Grade returned just over three hours later. Three hours? What had they done in that time? Where had they been? The girl had picked him up at the hotel, so if they knew they had been followed, they must have also deduced that it had started from there. And yet now he was back!

A rustling sound came from one side. Ehnbridt's nerves bristled. He turned sharply. After a second, he could just pick out the shape of a cat pulling at a bag of rubbish. Its eyes held his defiantly for a moment, then it picked out a chicken carcass and scampered off into the blackness of a side alley. Ehnbridt's breathing relaxed.

He settled back into his thoughts. The answers had been clear at the time: they obviously weren't that concerned about losing him, except that for those three hours alone it *had* been important. Vitally important. He dwelled on that a moment more, but realized that such deliberation was wasteful: he had no way of knowing for sure. And Vruger was paying for facts, not guesswork. Even the possibility that Vruger might guess where they'd gone from what else Ehnbridt could disclose of their movements was out of the question; he knew he could never mention that he had lost them. It would reflect too badly on his professionalism. He could only keep up the vigilance – hope that something else might give him a clue.

He glanced back at the window. The light was still on. How much longer? *Gott*, this was going to be a long night. And probably afterwards Grade would just return to his hotel. Huh! But he couldn't take the risk of breaking his vigil. At any moment they might leave, go to a rendezvous that might be more enlightening.

The rustling noise was back again. That damn cat!

Ehnbridt turned and looked full-face into the barrel of a large gun on the other side of his window. Something cool washed his insides. Beyond the barrel, now more distinct, was the face of the girl. She was mouthing some words very purposefully.

'No sudden moves! Get out of the car very carefully.'

Ehnbridt complied. *Shit*, twice in one day. He climbed out and stood hesitantly beside the car. Though she hadn't ordered him to, he raised his hands slightly; it somehow seemed right. His shirt collar felt tight as he swallowed. He could see the man, standing just behind her. Ehnbridt tried not to show recognition, and cast his eyes down to the pavement.

'Why are you following us?' Leorah asked.

'Me . . . following?' His eyes shifted nervously. 'Why no – I am just waiting for a friend.'

'Okay, we'll skip that one. We know for sure you were following, so I'll save us both some precious time. Who has sent you?'

Ehnbridt remembered the name he had been passed if anything – heaven forbid – should go wrong. But it would seem too easy, too convenient, to come straight out with it. Vruger, he was sure, was a cover name, not traceable; but the name he had been told to impart was more obvious, more recognizable.

'Sent? Please . . . I don't understand.'

Leorah raised the gun in both hands and took a firmer stance. 'You know that there is a war going on – and, in a war, bullets have a habit of going astray . . .'

'Please . . .'

Grade stayed purposely in the background. It was an idea they'd worked out together. An exciting, almost childishly prankish scheme that had grown quickly out of the warmth and closeness of earlier. They knew almost for certain he would have followed – it was just a matter of scanning the cars in the street. There were only two; one Leorah already knew. From there, Leorah had done the planning: out the back entrance, through the side alley . . . into another street. The devilish fun of it all had grown as they went.

But now Grade began to wonder. The man was trembling, the sweat breaking out on his forehead, and Leorah's face was set with grim determination. This wasn't fun anymore. He had no doubt she could do it; she could pull the trigger and drop the man right where he stood. This was a new Leorah, one he hadn't seen before. Perhaps she had seen too much bloodshed – perhaps she assumed this man was somehow responsible for Al-Hakim and Khourem . . . The extenuations weren't important – Grade wanted no part of it.

Leorah started squeezing, taking up the slack in the trigger.

'For God in heaven's sake . . .' the man stammered.

Grade was about to intervene – it had gone far enough – when the man said another word, the name escaping softly, almost in an exhalation.

'Schaarer . . .'

The word cut deep inside Grade. Since first hearing it from Reiner, he had been hoping against hope that he was mistaken. Now, as that hope began to fade, its space was filled with dread of all the implications he had so far pushed away and refused to admit.

Leorah lowered her gun. She turned and gave Grade a half-smile.

Grade relaxed. So, it had been an act after all. But looking deeper into Leorah's eased expression, he could sense something else: a look that said 'You didn't tell me'.

Part Three

London Desk: Daniel Grade, Zürich

7

Danny. After your research in Lebanon, thought you might find this side-bar interesting when you come to write it all up. It was one I wrote recently, following the Syrian advance on the Litani River in southern Lebanon – *Rolf Nabens.*

CROSSROADS OF CONFLICTS

22 NOVEMBER 1976

With the advance of Syrian peace-keeping forces further into southern Lebanon, the multi-facets of the conflict become apparent. The threat of an Israeli counter-reaction and an all-out Israeli-Syrian confrontation is now a very real danger. Israel initially opposed the Syrian peace-keeping force presence, fearing that Syria had more nationalistic interests at heart – but in viewing that this presence was concentrated mainly around Beirut and with some degree of success, their fears were allayed. Now their concern is that Syrian forces will reopen corridors for Palestinian units to the border areas, and that border insurgence will resultantly increase.

More interesting still is that the other major protest to the Syrian presence has come from the Palestinian far-left, the very element which Israel now believes the Syrians will give ground to. Those with the least forceful comment on who should be present seem to be the Lebanese themselves. It is perhaps a sad reflection on the people's acceptance that their country is being used as a 'crossroads of conflicts', an arena in which the Syrians, Israelis, Palestinians and Jordanians vie for power against the background of an initial Muslim/Phalangist conflict, and many of the all so familiar issues of the Middle East are again played out.

Daily Post, London Desk

Six days left to the end of Golding's deadline. Grade was back in Zürich. There had been little he could do to affect the progress of events in Beirut, but now time passed in a whirlwind. He was back at the Bellerive au Lac hotel, and had made arrangements with the management to use one of their penthouse suites as his work centre. His first calls were to office equipment companies, and by early afternoon of the first day he had a hired telex machine and typewriter duly installed.

His next call was to Semleche and Bunt. They would send the files they had so far over by messenger. He made his other calls meanwhile.

He tried Rolf Nabens' direct line in London. He didn't want to speak to Wetherall or Golding as yet. Wetherall, he knew, would only ask about the implications of the shares dealings, and he wouldn't be able to comment on that until he'd seen the report from Semleche and Bunt. Golding would be interested mainly in conclusions, and he was even further away from that. After a moment a girl answered. 'No, I'm sorry, he's not in the office right now.'

Grade left a message and his number. The girl said Nabens would call back as soon as possible.

Grade dialled straight out again to the *Post*'s Middle East news agency. It was a direct-dialled international line, but it was engaged until the third try. He asked to be routed through to Chaim Halmater and asked for any articles on Al-Ben Salmad. He filled Halmater in on some of Salmad's background and stressed the urgency.

'It's a file-search job. Could take up most of the day,' Halmater commented. 'I doubt if I'll be able to come back to you until tomorrow.'

'It's alright, I can wait till then,' Grade said. But he wondered if he could. Six days would be narrowed down to five by then. Every minute would count.

He gave Halmater his telex code and asked hm to put it through on that.

Before leaving Beirut, he had established contact with Halmater and used him to get hold of articles on Al-Hakim and Khourem. He had gone through them all with interest on the plain to Zürich, but none so much as those written by Leorah. Hers had formed a good third of the available articles, and a lot of the other newspapers had been virtual copies of those originals. None of them had much to add to what he'd already learnt from Leorah direct, or from the few articles of hers he'd previously read on microfiche in London. But aside from giving added insight into her political views, it had brought the memory of her close again. *Damn her.* He wished his thoughts were more clear. Yes clear, that was it. *Clarity.* Get back to it: back to the main issues.

Clarity. There were two distinct camps: Beirut and Zürich. Grade forced himself to separate each in his mind, attach the people concerned to each camp.

Beirut: Al-Hakim and Khourem. Outside assassinations? Al-Ben Salmad was the main link, though that had only come to light recently through Reymenak, the man who had given himself up after his colleague, Gahtlav, had been acid-burnt and killed. So that accounted for two of the assassins; that left another Lebanese, then, the lead assassin and his paymaster: Kruger . . . Vruger? He pushed it aside; it belonged in Zürich. Reymenak himself didn't trouble him – he was in police custody and, besides, as with the other two Lebanese, he was small fry. So it came back to Al-Ben Salmad. He had found the name on Maslegeisen's arms shipment, but on its own it had been just another Arab name; now Leorah had linked it with Al-Hakim. Now the coincidences were too many. There was some substance.

Grade gave no more than a passing thought to the fact that Gahtlav had been the victim of an obvious revenge killing. Khourem's party, the Karim Sha'b, had been disbanded, but there were bound to be past supporters; it was but a small part of the bloody fanatacism that had sparked and spread so rapidly since the start of the war. Revenge political killings were common.

Zürich: Kruger . . . Vruger? The lead assassin, Dutch or Belgian . . . perhaps German? Could German-Swiss possibly fit? Then there were Schaarer, Reiner and Mendel, the three names that – through lack of alternatives as much as anything else – he had investigated.

Of course, it could be anyone outside of those three, and most probably was – but the shares records would spotlight them as well. He had instructed Semleche and Bunt to note *any* heavy trading over the last eighteen months.

Grade broke off. The telephone was on its third ring. It was Nabens.

After the preambles, Nabens said. 'David told me about Schaarer. It's even hotter than we expected.' Nabens quickly tempered his excitement. 'That is, if this can be believed.'

'At first, I doubted it as well.' Grade said. 'Originally it was only a suspicion of Reiner's, due to the timing of Schaarer leaving SBECSA and rumours circulating of a rift with management. But I'm afraid we can't ignore the possibility now . . .' Grade went on to describe their being followed in Beirut, and the confrontation with Ehnbridt.

Nabens' end of the line was quiet for a few seconds, then, 'I suppose there's no point in me stressing what the effects could be to Middle East peace.'

'No. Not necessary.' Grade's voice was subdued. The main implications of the investigation alone were bad enough; the added spectre of Schaarer took it beyond imagination.

'That's the trouble,' Nabens said reflectively. 'As newsmen, our duty to truth seems to cross so many other principles. We have to be the last to compromise, as if we're the final bastion of a free society. Shining examples! Our burden to bear.' Nabens laughed slightly. '*Print and be damned* should have been damned if we do, damned if we don't. We never really seem to have much choice.'

'Sometimes it does seem that way.'

'You know, on that first day we were discussing it in the newsroom, there was something troubling me about SBECSA – some small detail. Of course, it was the fact that Schaarer had been on their board!' Nabens half sighed. 'But even if I had remembered it, I would never have dreamt that *he* would actually be involved.'

'Look, Rolf, there's something else I phoned you for. Something important. Does the name Al-Ben Salmad ring a bell?'

'Vaguely,' Nabens ruminated. 'Financier, banker. Disappeared a few years ago, if I remember correctly.'

'That's right. Apparently he's in London now, under an assumed name. I want you to try and trace him.'

'That's easier said than done. There's a lot of people that would no doubt like to find him. What makes you think –'

'I can give you a head's start,' Grade cut in. He related all that Leorah had told him from Reymenak's confession and the connection with the arms shipment. He gave Nabens the last assumed name that Salmad had used in Cannes – Issam Ashonni.

Nabens' thoughts were still half on the early part of their conversation. 'Followed? My God, you do live an exciting life.' Nabens broke off for a second, and there was the sound of rustling paper. 'There was something else, Danny, while you're on. This bus hijacking in Northern Israel . . .'

The door-bell rang.

'I'm sorry, Rolf. I'll have to go. I'll get back to you later.'

'You were over there at the time . . .' Nabens faltered. 'Okay, it can wait. I'll catch you later.'

Grade rang off and opened the door. It was the report from Semleche and Bunt.

If nothing else, Semleche and Bunt were thorough. The report was thirty-two pages long.

All shares on the Zürich stock exchange were fed daily

into a large computer; listings came both from private buyers who had to deal centrally with the exchange, and from brokers. From this the daily board prices and issues and tradings were compiled. Condensed breakdowns were sent simultaneously to the main financial newspapers in the city for their daily listings, and back to brokers for their own records.

As a company specializing in 'searches', access to these lists had been no problem. It was in making some sense of the massive accumulation of listings over the past eighteen months that Semleche and Bunt's expertise came in. They had chosen listings at one-week intervals; on daily listings the movement was usually too insignificant. Weekly showed them the general trend.

Then it was a matter of identifying names behind that trend. Using a large stockbroker's as a 'front', they claimed they had a client who wished to purchase a sizeable option of stock. This was good and legitimate ground on which to obtain a stock report on SBECSA – and one which raised no eyebrows. Large buyers often required to know the full flow of trends in stocks, so as to avoid a possible conflict of interests: investing in a company in which a major competitor held a large amount of stock, or, worse, one in which a competitor was manoeuvring a take-over.

The easy part was over. Less than thirty per cent of the list were private names; the rest had been handled through brokers.

Brokers were reluctant to part with client information, but it was a pointless reluctance; because of Swiss tax laws they were required to disclose share ownerships, otherwise they themselves would become liable. For the most part it was a laborious, tedious telephone task. The final sway was enticement; a promise that the large buyer would purchase any SBECSA shares that became available through them.

All but three brokers took the bait. Their combined trading in SBECSA shares was small enough to be of little or no significance.

Details from the rest – along with the other private listings

– formed the substance of Semleche and Bunt's report. Where necessary, written explanations had been offered of the successions of figures, and special attention had been paid to two periods in that eighteen months that Grade had particularly specified. There was also short, additional text on the trading of Schaarer, Reiner and Mendel, and any other abnormal trading had been picked out; including that of any of the four major banking institutions. The figures combined with the explanatory text gave a very comprehensive picture.

SBECSA had a total of 780,560,000 shares, valued as of October, 1976 (last noted trading), at 14.20 SF each. Value as of 22 February 1975 (commencement of report), 12.70 SF. So they *were* up.

Grade flicked his way through quickly, scanning for the information he wanted first.

Although it had originally been the last thing he'd planned to look at, now his fingers sought it almost unconsciously, yet urgently – the pages relating to Mendel. As if he couldn't rest easy until that one bothersome, tiresome question was out of the way. Then he could turn his attention fully, untroubled, to the rest of the report. His fingers were hesitant as they ran down the page.

The first reference to Mendel was on page seven. Grade started reading . . . Simon Mendel, Chairman of the Sweizerische Institut (Swiss Banking Institute), a general 'watchdog' committee to the Swiss banking system, elected June 1968 . . . Unnecessary. He had told them half of that already. He scanned further down, and figures and dates started appearing.

Shares owned in SBECSA . . . 14,000 (nominal), as of 22 February 1975. Increases recorded on: 15 August of 1200 shares; 12 December of 500 shares; 6 March 1976 of 700 shares; 17 September of 400 shares. (All nominal.) No further increases recorded. Decreases in SBECSA stock held recorded: 12 January 1976 of 400 shares . . . Grade skimmed through the remainder of the decreasing shares held by Mendel, and then went back over the introductory text. He checked Mendel's name against any heavy trading in the other major banks. Nothing showed. As a final check, he studied the preceding photostats of the stock reports, to ensure that Semleche and Bunt had transferred all the entries. Nothing had been missed.

Grade lifted his eyes from the report. He stretched slightly. It had been half an hour since the messenger had handed him the report.

Whichever way he looked at it, it came back to the same thing. Mendel had started with 14,000 shares, and by October 1976 had 15,700. The total value was 222,940 SF. The dates showed normal trading patterns – buying on the ups, selling on the downs. None of it coincided with the two periods he had stipulated. All of it, if anything, was below the number of shares you might expect a man in his position to own. *All* of it was nominal trading. Simon Mendel had made approximately 35,000 Swiss Francs. Just over £10,000! His yearly salary alone was in excess of 300,000 SF, nearly £90,000. All of it added up to only one conclusion . . .

As with Mendel's own theories on Swiss involvement in Beirut – the one thing which went against Reiner's claims, and could have cast suspicion – there was no motive! And without motive?

Grade got up and walked to the window. His suite was on the front and the view was directly over Lake Zürich. He watched the movement of tugs and boats on the water. The sunlight was bright, casting silver dapples on the grey water, and clouds were distant and few.

The conclusion lingered pleasantly among his other thoughts – Mendel was clear.

Near-elation rose from his relief; he didn't realize till that moment how much it had troubled him. Then it was quickly overcome by calm planning again; of course, really, he had *known* from the start.

He turned from the window and back to the rest of the report.

*

It was almost 9 p.m. when Grade finally lifted his head. He had broken off only twice during the day.

He went to the window and looked out again. It was dark now, only a few solitary lights showing the boats that had remained in mid-channel; most of them were clustered along the shoreline, the lights merging with the streetlights reflected a good distance back on the water.

Deep inside he felt sick; sick from the overwork, *sick* from what he now feared.

He had smoked too much. The butts of seven Romeo and Juliet cigars were in the ashtray behind him. The Scotch hadn't helped much either. He'd had two early on, then when room service had brought up lunch, he'd asked them to leave a bottle. It was down one-third.

Despite the cigars, the room was fresh; small grilles below the windows sucked the air silently from the room and replenished it. The windows were thick glass, insulating him from the sounds outside. It was a sanitized, almost unreal atmosphere. But his thoughts were real, terribly *real*. He closed his eyes as if fighting to shut them out.

The sequence still played over.

He had specified two periods in that eighteen months to Semleche and Bunt for a purpose. He knew that anyone engineering the plot in Beirut would have purchased large blocks of shares just before or slightly after the war. The three months directly after the assassinations of Al-Hakim and Khourem had therefore formed the first period. Equally, that same person or persons – with knowledge of the current investigation and thoughts of the resultant effect on SBECSA – would wish to offload those same shares. The last month formed the second period.

Reiner, now that he had dispensed with suspicion of Mendel, was the only person he could say for certain knew. Schaarer, along with many of the other shares traders, would likely not know. So, in ignorance, they would probably still be holding their shares. But still some heavy trading was required within those first three months to cast suspicion. That had been the starting point.

The rest had been a matter of going through the report in much the same way as he had with Mendel. First Schaarer; then Reiner; then picking out any heavy traders both on SBECSA and the other major banks. Early on, he had thought of calling Semleche and Bunt for information on one of the *other* names; but quickly another name was added to it. He decided to make up a list and call them later on. The list slowly grew in length.

He finally made the call close to 2 p.m. Semleche and Bunt answered his queries on a number of them straightaway. '. . . *Rumoured take-over, never happened*' . . . '*Issued due to increased position and duties, quite normal*' . . . '*All advised by the same broker, if you'll notice – he's done the same with others previously.*' The others they phoned back on within the hour. '*Bought virtually the same stock last year.*' . . . '*Large buyer, has almost as much, if not more, in industrials and mining.*'

The list swiftly diminished. Only one partial query remained in Grade's mind: the broker who had bought on behalf of three clients. Individually they weren't large enough, but together? It brought to mind the possibility of other combines and cliques buying – but Semleche and Bunt, on delving deeper into trading patterns, discounted each one as he presented it. When he checked the buying and selling dates of the first broker, they didn't coincide with his two key periods.

So, after three hours, apart from some questionable small trading, it had come back to Schaarer and Reiner.

Schaarer had owned 4,500,000 shares as of the initial date, 22 February 1975. It was not an abnormal holding for a director; some of the other directors held up to ten million shares each. The last increase had been recorded almost two years beforehand, of 500,000 shares. Schaarer had offloaded 1,500,000 shares on 9 July 1976, only two days after his resignation. Again, standard procedure. Again, the dates didn't fall into the two key periods. On the face of it, Schaarer was clear.

But Reiner's was a totally different picture. He had bought

shares through four different brokers, all on the same date: 15 March 1975, only weeks after the assassinations. They totalled 220,000, an increase of 180,000 over his initial holding. Their combined value was in excess of 3,124,000 SF. And Reiner had sold out only weeks beforehand. He was left with only 10,000 shares. Grade calculated the profit: 315,000 SF.

Not vast considering the overall implications, but certainly a good coup taking into account Reiner's salary of 90,000 SF per annum. Over three year's earnings!

It was then that Grade had lifted his head from the report for the second time that day. He had called Semleche and Bunt again and asked them for a more thorough investigation of Anton Reiner. Now he wanted to know *everything*. They said they would see what they could pull up on files – driving licence, tax returns, mortgage and finance arrangements, car registration, past employment – in the course of the next day. Good enough.

Then the contradictions had started plaguing Grade. Surely Reiner hadn't paid assassins? Reiner with his steel-rimmed glasses, his close-trimmed brown hair, his almost mousy expression, his frailty. The image of Reiner paying blood money jarred. The added expense would also cut into the overall gain. Would it be worth it then? Surely not.

And yet the dates and the transactions were all there; it was hard to ignore.

And what about the attempt on Reiner's life at Murren? Could it have been faked? Could he possibly have paid someone for that as well? . . . It was the only answer that came to mind. Certainly, that one incident had gone a long way towards convincing him of the worth of Reiner's story, especially so soon after Mendel's contradiction.

Yet why the indictment of Schaarer? And why as well from Ehnbridt?

Grade relit a half-finished cigar, poured another Scotch, and started going back over the report. The pluses and minuses of Reiner's involvement kept fighting for control in his mind. He knew he wouldn't sleep much that night.

*

The chattering of the telex woke him at 6.50 a.m. He should have remembered that in Beirut it was already 8.50 a.m. *Shit*.

The print-out continued for almost fifteen minutes. Grade waited for it to spit to an end, then got out of bed and tore the paper from the machine. It was from the Halmater Agency.

Grade had a momentary inclination to put it to one side, unplug the machine and go back to bed, but by now he was fully awake. And curious. He started reading.

Semleche and Bunt's first 'files' information on Reiner came through just before 11 a.m.

For the first time since the start of the investigation, Grade felt in control. At last there was some direction. The small room with its telex and telephone, the links with Beirut and Tel Aviv and London and Zürich, and the news that had come through at regular intervals, had quickly built a picture. Grade felt as if he was at the centre of a web spun wide, some of its threads split again into parts by other people, out of his control; but gradually the main threads came back to him again, so that he could pull them in tight – a cohesive pattern beginning to form.

He'd already called Wetherall in London to get more feedback on the reports from Semleche and Bunt. Wetherall confirmed very much his own findings; that Reiner's heavy trading did look suspect, but from the other key tradings Grade related, there was nothing else that looked abnormal. Wetherall promised to call back if he had any more thoughts on it.

Then he called Simon Mendel. If anything, Mendel seemed more concerned with their last conversation. 'I'm sorry, but I probably made too hasty a judgement. I should have given it more thought. I fear now that I might have overstated the point of our currency protection measures deterring investors. We have many Arabs now investing here in dollars, it's just that with the introduction of the measures there was quite a fall-off of investors.'

When Grade told him of his findings to date, Mendel

commented, 'Well you seem to have got along quite well without me this time. Of course, I should have recognized the possibility of a ruse, and pointed the finger at Reiner myself – but I'm afraid my unreadiness to admit the possibility of Swiss involvement coloured my judgement. I'm sorry. I haven't been much use to you this time.'

Typical Mendel, Grade thought: apologetic and altruistic to the end. It didn't help his unease at having had Mendel checked out.

Grade looked at the pieces of the puzzle he already had.

The first piece had arrived with the telex from Halmater: Al-Ben Salmad had done business with Securitee Maslegeisen before, and one of his lesser-known activities apart from banking *was* as an arms dealer. He had acted as agent on almost nine previous arms deals. So, that shipment – the one link with SBECSA was nothing particularly suspect. As an import/export compay, Maslegeisen had taken the arms as part consignment under Salmad's signature. Their part had been purely as hauler, not supplier.

He turned to the assassinations: Leorah had already mentioned that Salmad had fallen out with Al-Hakim over some deals in Kuwait, so his turning traitor was perhaps not so unusual. Any one of the opposing political parties could have been responsible – and when he considered it more deeply, probed its many ramifications, the deduction that the assassinations were ordered by an opposed Lebanese faction had probably been the most logical right from the start. How could he have been so blind? Having an outside lead assassin and contact – Vruger? . . . Kruger – would have also been the most effective mask of their involvement!

Bit by bit he detached Al-Ben Salmad from the Swiss banking community, split the events in Beirut from Zürich.

It swept over him then that Reiner had probably merely stumbled on the SBECSA connection, then had selected and presented the facts in such a way that – on the surface, at least – only one conclusion was likely. But why?

Part of the answer was in the 'files' information from Semleche and Bunt. It took Grade only a few minutes to read it; minutes in which he felt his breath coming short, his hand unsteady as it ran down the page.

At its end he rubbed his eyes as if they were weary. He reread part of it:

> In early 1975, Anton Reiner was nominated for promotion to Managing Director of Banque du Martigny . . . On a final SBECSA board vote the promotion was reprised, and it was said that the director who vetoed it was Dr Emil Schaarer . . .

Now he had *motive*, but not in a way he would ever have previously suspected.

Other 'files' information arrived in the course of the day, each item tolling the bell more heavily for Anton Reiner.

> A man fitting Reiner's description was seen by a doorman at one of the leading Zürich hotels . . . the doorman remembered a car – a nine-seater Mercedes – which we don't have registered for Reiner. The car has been there before and so caught his attention. Usually the occupants couldn't be seen for tinted glass screens, and each time a passenger was let off. But on one occasion Reiner rolled his window down slightly . . .

> Re earlier report, passenger description: 5-5 to 5-6, brown hair, slightly balding, stocky, drooping moustache . . .

Ehnbridt! The final item came through at almost 4.30 p.m.

> On further checking, we discover the car is in fact registered falsely to Dr Emil Schaarer; that registration has been placed in Lausanne for two of the periods concerned, and the models don't quite match.

Now everything was clear.

Motive had been revenge against Schaarer from the start! The money had been a secondary issue. Reiner knew that the

Beirut war and the transfer of funds to Switzerland was in itself suspicious; all he needed were some links. He'd found one through Securitee Maslegeisen, yet another through Khourem's 'outside' assassin, Dutch or Belgian, the overheard mention of a Zürich meeting from Reymenak. It all too conveniently pointed to the Swiss camp. And, as Grade reminded himself painfully, for many newspapers that would have been enough: *Based on available information . . . reliable sources . . . elements that point to . . .* He knew the circumspect language of journalism all too well!

Then – when the investigation had obviously gone deeper than Reiner had first anticipated – *other* elements had been required. The faked attack at Murren. The connection between Schaarer and the car! *Reiner usually couldn't be seen because of tinted glass screens . . .* But that part had backfired; Reiner *had* been seen. Obviously the intention had been to link Ehnbridt with Schaarer. Then the coup de grace of Ehnbridt's indictment – after all, he had said that it was Schaarer who had hired him! What better proof?

God, he had been so close to believing it all, so close to writing it up. And how simple a coup for Reiner!

With the printing of the story, SBECSA shares would have fallen drastically. Of course, Reiner had no way of knowing that Schaarer would resign and offload some shares; but still the loss to Schaarer would have been catastrophic. Whereas Reiner himself would have already benefited from the rise in the eighteen months, and sold out before the story came to print. 315,000 Swiss Francs? Deduct say thirty or forty thousand for a few small-time imposters, the car hire and false registration. Revenge plus 275,000 Swiss Francs! Quite neat.

Grade started making a rough draft. David Wetherall's return call came through almost an hour later. Grade told him of his conclusions.

'So, the little man himself,' Wetherall commented. 'Quite a nice little number.'

'You don't seem that surprised?'

'Danny, you should remember just as well as me the

statistics for crimes committed by those who actually report them. Look in the home camp first.'

'I suppose so,' Grade said thoughtfully. 'Is that why you recommended the checks on Reiner and Mendel as well as Schaarer?'

'Partly. And, well, let's face it, the whole thing originally was reaching for it a bit. Large international bank involved in starting a war! Co-chairman of the peace conference at the head of it all . . .' Wetherall half chuckled. 'Reiner, revenge and money is a bit easier to swallow.'

'If I remember – you didn't have much to say on that score during the initial meeting?'

'Ah well, natural caution. Didn't like to be pessimistic in the face of all that refreshing optimism.'

'David, you're a regular pain in the ass.'

'Always glad to be of service,' Wetherall said. 'No, seriously, I often think that perhaps we hedge our judgements more than any other profession. We're observers where people don't want to be observed; reporters of facts where people would prefer that we had everything *but* the facts. And after all that, we're allowed the narrowest possible margins of truth and accuracy. It's no wonder we're cautious.'

'One "I told you so" forgiven,' Grade said light-heartedly. 'You know, when you try, you can be quite nice, David.'

Wetherall laughed. 'Always glad to be of service.'

'I'll get back to you again tomorrow. Tell Rolf and Uncle Bob I'll speak to them then. I want to get some of this typed up first. Oh, and before I forget, thanks for the advice.' Grade rang off.

Two days. Two days in the same room. The room was strewn with the debris of the conflict: telex print-outs, loose pages from Semleche and Bunt's reports, telephone notes . . . In some ways it had been simpler than he'd anticipated, and that faint sense of anticlimax tempered the elation he knew he'd normally feel.

It wasn't going to be the story of a giant corporation provoking a war, and the head-swirling statistics of monetary gain that would have accompanied it, nor of a champion of peace paying for the assassin's bullets; but of a dejected and embittered banker who sought a gainful and complex path of revenge against the man he blamed for his demise. Interesting nevertheless, if nothing more, for the pure cheek and scope of his chicanery. He would type up the rough draft first, then confront Reiner and perhaps get more input from his reaction, or lack of it! If Reiner had no comment, it went as is.

Depending on the weight of news on the day, it would probably get a page three or four placing. Another story of lost hope and wasteful folly among the many. Could have been worse.

Grade half filled his tumbler of Scotch and sat down at the typewriter.

8

General Pohlmann gripped the receiver of the field-telephone tight in one hand. He had stood silent for fully a minute, staring blankly ahead. The line was already dead, the communication ended. The demands of the terrorists had all been made.

Major Gant hazarded an interruption. 'General, I don't think we can keep the press away much longer. They will become even more curious and speculative as time goes on – and I'm sure that's the last thing we want.'

General Pohlmann blinked slowly and replaced the receiver.

His presence of mind began to return: in a preliminary communication with Hasik, Pohlmann had explained why he was still keeping the press out of earshot, suggesting that any publicity might negate the possibility of the demands being met. – 'If the press had already made an announcement, any following declarations or actions by the Knesset might seem pure folly.' Hasik accepted reluctantly, but with a firm proviso: a full announcement to be made to the press within twelve hours, the demands to be met within twenty-four.

Half an hour had been gained in moving the two mobile press units back, and now there were twelve hours in which to determine just how damaging media coverage would be.

But all thoughts of that advantage fled from General Pohlmann's mind as Hasik announced his demands. Pohlmann had wanted to ask immediately for a twenty-four-hour delay for the press, forty-eight to meet the demands, and would have settled for eighteen and thirty-six – but his mouth was suddenly dry and a numbing chill slowly suffused his body.

Hasik had clicked off abruptly.

Pohlmann remembered a dream from his childhood that would turn slowly into a nightmare: he was running along a white sand beach in Haifa, dodging the incoming waves – but when he looked down, there was concrete beneath his feet; he was on a dockside, decrepit and rundown, and the sky and sea became rapidly dark . . . Then rats were suddenly all around him, worrying at his feet, and still more coming from the darker corners. And he would suddenly want to get into the water to get away from them. He felt like that now; as if the rats had come and it was time to immerse himself.

Major Gant stepped closer.

'General, I must –'

'I know, I know,' Pohlmann cut in sharply. 'You don't have to remind me of anything, Major. I'm fully aware of what must be done.'

Pohlmann paced briskly away from the field-telephone and Major Gant fell in step behind. It was sunny, with only a few clouds, but the air was brisk. A mile or so behind were green valleys, but ahead the rock landscape became progressively harsher, rising to the peak of Mount Hermon. Their boots crunched on the rough shale and rock.

'I'll have to go to the sub-HQ at Tiberiade,' Pohlmann said over his shoulder. 'I'll be gone perhaps three hours in all. Meanwhile, you'll be in command here, Major.'

Gant tried to read some expression in the hard blue eyes fixed straight ahead, but there was none.

The journalists, held behind a front line of artillery, converged on them as they approached. The whirr of cameras started as microphones jostled for position.

'Are the children alright, General?'

'How many terrorists are there?'

'What hope do you see of rescue?'

'Is there any indication of how long it will last? How are the food supplies?'

'We've heard that it's PLO. Can you confirm this, General?'

Pohlmann walked through the crowd without comment until he was close to his jeep and the sun was behind him. He could see that many of the journalists were now squinting; he had learnt through his long career to play for small advantages.

'They claim to be PLO, but we can't be sure as yet,' Pohlmann said.

'Has any responsibility been announced by Arafat personally?'

'No. But then you'd probably get to know about that before I did.' Pohlmann smiled slightly. 'Still, we have yet to check our own sources.'

'Are the children safe?'

'As far as we can tell.'

Another microphone came close, hedging for room. 'What are their demands, General?'

'The usual – release of prisoners.'

'PLO?'

'Some, yes – but one, if I remember correctly, is an undeclared Palestinian Popular Front Liberation member.'

'And names?'

Pohlmann smiled again. 'Not yet, I'm afraid . . . an announcement will be made later . . .'

Pohlmann turned his back smartly and climbed up into the jeep. He directed his driver, and the questions and general babble died in the roar of its engine as they pulled away.

It had been the right moment to break things off with the press. Another small advantage. Pohlmann wiped his forehead. He hoped that his manner had hidden his concern. Too serious wasn't his style; they would fear the worst. Too casual and they would know it was put on, a smokescreen.

Hasik's demands seared once again through his mind as the drone of the jeep settled into monotony.

He felt somehow that he should be sad, but that emotion seemed far away as he surveyed the harsh rock and scrub landscape. He felt only fear. If he had been looking at the stone symmetry of Jerusalem or the vineyards and orange orchards of Jaffa, it might have been different; then an ache of sorrow might have welled up from deep inside, the tears held back behind non-seeing eyes. But he felt only fear of what was impending, fear of the loss of a nation he had loved and sweated and fought a lifetime for.

And fear for the children. For he knew that if the decision had to be made, if nothing else could be done to avoid meeting the demands, their lives would be lost, sacrificed to save the state of Israel. And *he* would be the general with the blood on his hands. Even talk of martyrdom would be quickly discarded; martyrs had a choice. Quite an end to his career, really.

He shook his head in disbelief. There was little chance of avoiding that inevitability, and Gant had been right all along – the tunnel *was* impenetrable. Each run-through of possible strategy, and its final rejection, and then the nature of the demands, had only served to underline the fact: he had sadly underestimated the terrorists.

There remained one slim hope, drawn from a hazy and now desperate corner of his mind: some weeks before there had been reports both in the HaMossad and Shin Bet of 'rumblings' within the PFLP. Rumours on which Hasik's demands were now based. At the time, Pohlmann had dismissed it as preposterous, but now he began to build upon that hope. If they had been able to discover exactly what extreme Palestinian elements were claiming against Israel, they might already have some contingency plan; or, at the least, some advice.

The only 'safe' radio link was at Tiberiade. Pohlmann looked at his watch: 3.18 p.m. They would be there in under an hour.

Golda Meir looked thoughtfully down at the table before her. The two men opposite sat silent in her presence, out of respect for both her age and the anguish and turmoil they knew would be at work in her mind.

It was an early Tuesday evening, and during midweek she was resident at her Tel Aviv bungalow. To one side was her kitchen, and on the stove a pot of coffee began to percolate more rapidly, as if keeping pace with their thoughts. Just beyond the kitchen doorway was a sergeant in the Mishma H'agvul, and another five men guarded the surrounds of the house itself.

Shimon Peres, Defence Minister during her past term of office, sat closest, leaning slightly across the table. The other man was Eli Samuelson, a legendary figure in the Shin Bet* who, among his many ventures, was most noted for masterminding the plan to spirit away 200 tons of uranium oxide from the cargo ship *Sheersberg* in 1968. He was now in his early fifties, a plump, balding man with sharp eyes and features that somehow warned you not to take him the least bit for granted.

The first call had come through to Prime Minister Rabin's office at almost 5 p.m. Pohlmann's call had been relayed from the military HQ at Tel Aviv to the Mossad centre less than a mile away. Samuelson, since the Shin Bet is as much military as it is secret service, was ideally placed as spokesman for any 'co-ordinated response'. Peres, in turn, acted as intermediary between Golda Meir and Samuelson.

Golda Meir was now but a shadow of the figure she had cut in her prime; age had softened her edges, but it had taken

*Israeli internal and military secret service.

its toll on her memory and powers of concentration. A few years ago, Peres would have been required for back-up advice only, not to explain and relay Samuelson's speech as he went along, and even at times formulate part of the answers.

Golda Meir was not embarrassed by Peres' presence, only grateful and slightly flattered, the way that any old woman might be that a younger man had paid her such a courtesy. Besides, Peres was her favourite. Not so long ago it had been Pohlmann; but Pohlmann had turned down the opportunity of a cabinet post during her office, and now he was in the middle of this mess.

In the half hour since the two men had been ushered into the house, they had outlined the situation – much of the time being taken up with Peres' explanations. They could tell that her mind was still grappling with parts of it; she bit her bottom lip lightly.

'What does Prime Minister Rabin have to say?' she asked.

'He is in Washington at present, as you know,' Peres said. 'And he is forestalling any decision until your comment on the situation.'

'And he wishes *me* to make a decision?'

'No, of course not. Just that on something of this magnitude he insisted that you be informed, as you might have some valuable input. And you have the benefit of being on the spot.'

'That's a polite way of putting it.' Golda Meir's mouth almost trembled into a smile. 'How long do we have now?'

'About nine hours to hold off the press,' Peres said.

A slight frown creased her forehead. 'I'm afraid you've lost me for a moment, gentlemen. News broadcasts have been on the radio for several hours now.'

'It's not that type of censorship,' Peres began to explain. He moved one hand on the table. 'The hijacking itself and the way it has been executed, the number of children held hostage, and exactly who the terrorists represent – that can all be broadcast. There's no danger in that. But it's broadcasting the demands we have to hold back on. Even without acceding to the demands' – Peres shrugged dismissively – 'which is obviously out of the question, the announcement in itself could cast sufficient doubt about our involvement. There would be too many questions. Embarrassing and perhaps dangerous questions, even if they *could* be satisfied.'

'And this is where your man comes in to this, Mr Samuelson?'

'Yes,' he confirmed.

'It's an unusual and very tense situation,' Peres remarked, coming to what he thought would be foremost in her mind. They were all well aware that terrorist demands were normally made through intermediaries: the press or radio, usually with PLO or at least Muslim sympathies. 'For some reason, on this occasion, they specifically wanted direct communication. I think they feel that their own media voices would be ignored or, at least, distrusted by much of the Western world. That's obviously where this blow of theirs is aimed.'

Golda Meir's eyes flickered. 'But these men – if they are inside the tunnel, they are cut off from outside radio contact. How will they know of any possible announcements?'

'They have men at either end, in the open, with radios,' Peres said. 'They have told us all of their intentions, and much about their preparations and equipment. Nothing has been held back. It seems they are very thorough, and wish us to know it.'

She sat back, looking faintly defeated. Her heavy hooded eyes flickered only slightly.

'This journalist – you feel that he might be the answer?'

'He's certainly ideally placed,' Samuelson offered. 'It would be pointless to make our own statement or use any of our own national journalists on an issue like this. We must remove even the thought of any possible bias.'

'He worked on a Swiss pharmaceutical fraud quite recently, exposing one of the large combines,' Peres supported. 'There's absolutely no doubt that he's equipped for this. *And* his voice will be trusted. In fact, his aid in an investigation to discover exactly *who* from outside was responsible had already been secured, but the hijacking caught us off guard.'

'And your contact with him is through this Swiss banker?'

'Yes, we've used the banker before,' Samuelson said. 'No problem there.'

Golda Meir sat silent for a moment, staring towards the kitchen. Both men had been very thorough, very convincing, but still the whole thing seemed to her somehow tenuous. There would be little point in airing that view, though; there were enough negative elements already. She lit a cigarette and drew on it anxiously, then reached for the message that had been sent by Pohlmann.

It was the second time that she had read it, but now it held some meaning. Before, she had read it with scepticism, in the almost sure knowledge that it wouldn't come to anything. It wasn't the first time that wild claims had been made against Israel. The manner in which Samuelson and Peres had summoned themselves to her home was the only hint at urgency. Certainly, she had heard the news, but Pohlmann was there, and in her eyes *victory*, *impossible* and *Pohlmann* – had become almost synonomous. So why the big worry?

Now the cold reality had seeped through. She picked up the message and scanned it again:

> 16.08 Tiberiade
> Demands made at Neveh Ativ. Group claiming PLO. No verification. Habash followers suspected. Press hold-back of 12hrs agreed. 24hrs for the demands which are as follows: announcement to be made from the Knesset – no other representation will be accepted – stating that Israel through its Shin Bet agency started the war in the Lebanon. Assassination of two prominent Muslim politicians cited as prime cause – full details of wording and statement to follow.

The words 'Israel started the war in the Lebanon' leapt out from the message like a fiery augur. She had to put the message down to stop her hand from shaking. *Habash*,

PFLP; they were names that on their own would have struck horror in her, their atrocities – Munich among them – reaching far beyond anything PLO-inspired. She remembered the New York of her childhood. A New York that neither she nor even her generation might have to go back to – but the next generation, and the generation after that? Nice enough though the memory had been, it just wasn't *home*. New York? London? Los Angeles? Munich? There were any number of places for the homeless!

She gathered her composure; she had long ago cried enough tears for this lifetime.

Samuelson had been perturbed at the meeting's beginning, but now his worry reached a peak. He had always looked at Golda Meir very much as Israel's mother, a 'Queen Victoria' figure, but more approachable, the edges somehow softer. In his eyes, nobody could be quite as mothering as a Jewish mother. And, more poignantly, Israel was new, a baby, not a burgeoning empire; a mother figure couldn't be more apt. But now Golda Meir's pained expression – each deep line etching its own sadness – cut him to the quick. It took a moment for her question to register.

'What is the name of your man in Switzerland –the Swiss banker?'

Peres didn't know the answer, and turned to him as well.

His voice faltered slightly. 'Reiner – Anton Reiner.'

'And now our main hope lies with him?'

'Yes, that's right,' he said. 'My man Swenkel is trying to contact him now.' But this time he couldn't bring himself to look into Golda Meir's face, and his eyes fell instead on her pale grey fingers still clutching Pohlmann's message.

Art Swenkel dialled out the eleven-digit number for the sixth time.

There was a pause of several seconds before it started ringing, a long persistent tone . . .

So, it had happened; but he wondered how many could have foreseen they might be held to ransom over the claim.

Though they had made all the preparations, in his heart of hearts he hadn't really thought that anything would happen; he was sure that others in the Mossad shared that inner belief. Reflecting deeper, the warning signals *had* been there: a week ago one of their main PFLP informers had been gunned down at a Jerusalem *falafal* bar. But the arguments for or against, or the manner in which it had happened, weren't important anymore – it was *timing*. In the end, that was what had caught them out; that was the enemy now.

Swenkel let the phone ring a moment more before replacing the receiver.

God in hell, where was he? He had tried Reiner's number the first time almost two hours ago now. Zürich was an hour behind, so at the time it would have been just after 6 p.m. there. Now his initial concern was edging towards paranoia. There had been nothing from their man to say that Reiner's schedule had changed, so he should be there. Early evening was usually a good time to get hold of *someone* in the family.

What if there'd been another cock-up? The memory of Reiner's ski-lift incident at Murren was too close and painful to ignore; that had been the main reason for them posting a more vigilant look-out. *Twice*? Surely not. They were wise to the 'Falcon' now – he wouldn't easily fool them again.

But other things troubled Swenkel also: the fact that Grade hadn't made contact again when Reiner thought he might, and that – as far as they knew – Grade hadn't as yet fully tracked the leads he'd been fed. Up until now they'd been patient – more to the point, they'd been able to be patient. But not any more. Time had run out.

Swenkel reached for the phone to try again.

Christmas was approaching.

A number of the shops in Zürich were already beginning to put out their displays. In another week the lights would be strung along the main thoroughfares, ready to be switched on on 16 December. The surrounding mountains were heavy with snow, and soon the level would drop to encompass the hillside houses and chalets, adding the final seasonal touch to the scene.

Children were already feeling the excitement, counting the days: just over a month to go now.

For the rest of the year the two Reiner children, Marc and Anna, had no interest in the arrival of mail to the house; but now, with Christmas approaching, it brought all sorts of mysterious promise, and they shared the opening of anything that looked 'unbusinesslike'. Parcels and small packages were grabbed first, followed by anything that looked obviously like a Christmas card. Brown envelopes, franked envelopes, and envelopes with windows were left aside. Dad would open *them*.

The bell rang at just after 8 a.m., and the two children bolted to the door at the same time, Anna just slightly behind.

'Not so fast,' Anton Reiner called after them. 'You might have an accident.'

He was seated opposite Piai at the breakfast table, and she had just set out coffee and croissants for all of them.

Piai could tell that something was troubling him. When they had come in the night before after taking the children to the cinema, the phone had been ringing. Since taking that call he'd been virtually in his own world . . . lost.

To some extent she had got used to his mood of preoccupation in the past weeks. The Murren incident had increased it, but now it had reached such intensity she found it almost unbearable. Murren had been frightening beyond belief, so what on earth could be *worse* than *that*?

She knew something of his dealings with Swenkel, but only superficially; the inner complexities were kept from her with offhand excuse that they were tiresome – '*not worth troubling yourself with*'. She accepted that; she was the first to admit she wasn't one to cope with complex problems; but at times like this she wished she *did* know more, so she could share some of the burden.

The children had seen to the postman and were scampering

back to the table with the mail. There were eight items that morning: two were parcels, the rest assorted envelopes. Marc had the largest parcel, Anna the other, and an envelope each; Anna passed Anton the remaining envelopes with a cute smile.

'Anything interesting?' Piai enquired.

Anton flicked through them. 'No, not really.'

'Wouldn't this be the forms for the insurance renewal on the car – the ones you've been waiting for?'

Anton looked absently back at one of the envelopes. 'Oh . . . Oh, yes. Probably.'

God, his mind was still buzzing with it all. How could it have happened so quickly? When Swenkel had first briefed him, he'd said at least a month, even if it did happen. He'd been concerned when Grade hadn't made contact again, but then he'd reassured himself. Why worry? There was time to spare. But not any more; Swenkel had made that all too clear with his call of the night before. Grade had to come through for them, and *fast*. But how?

Piai was looking at him thoughtfully. 'More coffee?'

'Yes . . . please.'

Marc had finished opening the large parcel, and Anna was halfway through hers. Marc held his up proudly; inside were four separate packages, each wrapped with bright blue paper and tied with orange ribbons. He looked at the accompanying card.

'It's from Uncle Dominic and Aunt Elsa!'

There was a letter inside the card, which Piai picked up and scanned.

'They're hoping to be with us on the twenty-seventh. 'They're going to Elsa's family in Lumbrein, but if the snow's too heavy in the passes they won't be able to make it – so they've sent these along now just in case.'

Perhaps he would try the Bellerive au Lac. Grade could be back there now. At least get some feedback.

'Anton . . .'

'Yes, fine.' He looked up briefly from opening his envelopes: insurance forms, electricity bill . . . circulars.

Nothing out of the ordinary. He laid the opened letters in a pile to one side and washed down a bite of croissant with some coffee.

'The twenty-seventh, you say?'

'Yes.' Piai controlled her impatience.

Anna was holding up her opened parcel.

'Look, Daddy!'

It was a rough wooden box of cigars. Anton peered inside: twenty large Havanas. Not bad. He recognized the accompanying note from a shipping agency that did a lot of business with Martigny. Very thoughtful. Shame they didn't bother to find out he was a non-smoker. That would teach him to politely drop hints that he had enough gold pens to fill a suitcase.

Grade smoked, he recalled. He would give them to him when he saw him next. Nothing like a small gift to increase confidence. He pushed the box to one side.

What a joke. With everything that lay in the balance, here he was worrying about gifts to sweeten the bait. Get back to basics! What had Swenkel stipulated? Twelve hours! There was no way that Grade could go to print within that period; the story would have to be wired to a Middle Eastern news agency whose voice the terrorists would trust. And that was presuming Grade had followed the threads the way they hoped he might. Even then it was unlikely Grade could come to a conclusion within the terrorists' deadline.

Anton felt a wave of hopelessness. Everything was turning bad, and he was at the centre of it all. Part of the blame would undoubtedly fall on him. *Why on earth had they chosen him*? Was there any end to that service to a homeland? He'd thought it was all over all those years ago. He suddenly felt frail, incapable. This sort of chicanery was too much for a middle-aged banker. They shouldn't have chosen him! He sipped uncertainly at his coffee.

In the last few years his life had begun to take on some purpose, some order. He should have told them that. After all, he was a family man now, he had *other* responsibilities.

He could sense Piai looking at him, but he didn't want to

meet her gaze directly, so he turned to Anna. She was struggling with a thick padded envelope.

He watched the movements blankly, unseeing for a moment, then it dawned on him that there was something out of the ordinary about the envelope: the stamps were French. The wrapping was brown, and obviously the children thought it large enough to be of interest. But Anton couldn't immediately think of anyone who would send them a present from France. The thought was still revolving in his mind as Anna ripped off the outer wrapper. He held out his hand.

'Wait a minute!'

Piai looked up. 'What's wrong?'

Anton took the envelope and turned it around, appraising it.

'It's from France. I just can't think who would be sending us a present from there.'

'Oh, I see,' Piai said, nonplussed.

'It could be business.' Anton commented. 'Martigny have their main sub-office in Paris. Sometimes they send things through.'

He hesitated a moment longer, then met Anna's hurt expression. He touched her head lightly.

'Don't worry, if it is a present, I'll let you have it back.'

Anna's returning smile was eclipsed by blinding white light as he ripped open the last of the wrapping. A loud buzzing built to a deafening roar inside his head as the room rushed away from him, and he was suddenly looking at the far corner of the ceiling . . . A shroud-like haze permeated the air, its dark edges washing slowly inwards.

The main force of the explosion had ripped through Anton's shoulder blade and one side of his face, throwing him back over five feet from the table. On its outer arc of devastation, it removed two of Anna's fingers and blew out a ragged three-foot section of the table, its remainder rising with the thrust, toppling Piai and Marc to one side.

A billowing sphere of displaced air picked up the shattered plates from the table in its rush towards the four walls, consuming in its path the glass and china from the sideboard and mirrors. The maelstrom rose irresistibly to the ceiling, its edges almost touching, then was sucked back into the remaining vacuum with even greater force, the loose fragments whipping through the air, scything cruelly, indiscriminately.

Piai tried to shut off her eyes and ears from the cataclysm. Only as it subsided did she realize that she was screaming.

9

Xavier Peton nodded worriedly, the telephone in one hand.

'Yes, yes . . . I see.'

He listened for fully a minute; his eyes clouded slightly as he looked towards Julie. 'Uh . . . I think so. Yes, should be no problem.'

'. . . In a half hour then . . . the café on the opposite corner to St Etienne.'

'. . . Yes. Okay . . . fine.'

He slowly replaced the receiver. Julie sat down and leafed through a magazine, trying to look preoccupied.

'Something I should know?'

'Not exactly.' He went to the wardrobe and took out his jacket and scarf. As he headed back across the room, conflict began to show in his face. The memory of their disagreement and their final coming together was still painfully vivid in his mind. Now that trust had been re-established, it somehow seemed foolish to damage it so quickly.

'If you must know, it was my "Marteau Rouge" contact again. He wants to meet with me now, *alone*.'

'Oh, that,' she said disdainfully.

'Yes, *that*, Julie,' he mimicked, lifting his eyes. 'And God knows you've already made it clear you don't want to get involved – so don't act hurt because I agreed to you being excluded.'

'I wasn't . . .' She stopped herself, turning back to the magazine. 'Anyway, my protests are by the way. He wanted to meet you alone the first time, as well. It seems that's the way he likes things.'

'Yes, well . . . okay.' A small nerve flickered in Xavier's face; he pushed his glasses further back on the bridge of his nose. 'Just that I never intended all this to upset you. I was hoping we'd be more together on it.'

He hesitated in the doorway for a few seconds, as if expecting an answer – then turned away. 'See you in a couple of hours.'

Outside it was dark; the last Sorbonne classes had finished over three hours before, and the only sounds now were from the dying rush hour.

It was an odd place for a meeting, Xavier thought.

When he had started talking with Duffal at the Brasserie Montpasse, Duffal had kept looking uneasily past him. Then he had abruptly announced, 'Let's go someplace else. I don't think it's suitable here.'

Once away from the café, Xavier had asked, 'What's wrong?'

'Somebody was looking us over, paying us too much attention. It could have been nothing, but I take no chances.'

Then, as they discussed the possibility of Xavier sending another 'flash letter', he had walked alongside Duffal without really noticing where they were going – until they came round the side of the Palais de la Mutualité, heading towards the Seine.

In daytime there was usually a crowd of people along the river bank, and in summer they remained till quite late in the evening; but in winter the numbers thinned as it grew dark, and now it was almost deserted. Winter chill gripped the Paris air, and it rose even colder off the river.

Xavier gave Duffal a questioning look.

'You don't like the river?' Duffal asked.

'It's cold here, that's all.'

'Yes, but it's quiet; that's the main thing – we won't be observed. And I can think of a few colder places,' Duffal added, glancing towards the far bank, partly obscured in mist. 'Your girlfriend will get you warm again when you get back.'

They continued walking – their footsteps echoing off the high front edifice of the Paris VI and VII University.

Now is the time, Duffal thought. He'd worked it all out since their last meeting. Reiner would have received the package either that morning – or tomorrow at latest – and the following day it would be in all the newspapers and on the radio. Then Xavier would know.

'This other package – when do you want it sent?'

'I'll give it to you when we part. But you should wait exactly three days before posting it.'

Xavier was thoughtful. 'I thought you were going to wait and see the results of the last one before anything further?'

'I have to go away for a few days, so plans have changed.' Duffal had half expected the question, but he was still slightly phased by it. 'That's why I'm giving you the package now. We'll know about Reiner in a day or two – and if anything's gone wrong you'll receive a call that everything's off. Then, of course, you shouldn't send the package. Anyway, the main part is over – you've posted Reiner's package, and that's all that matters. It's not your fault if it's intercepted.'

'You mean I've been accepted?' Xavier smiled crookedly.

'In essence, yes.'

Duffal looked away. He felt an odd compassion for Xavier: he looked so frail and pathetic that killing him seemed almost unfair – and unworthy of his own skill. Certainly, he had killed men before who seemed just as frail and pathetic – but they always had money, or position, or influence, so in real terms they had *power*, and were worthy adversaries.

Not so with Xavier. Even what little ego and intellect he possessed were sadly misguided. There wouldn't be that same adrenalin surge, that sense of pitting wits, of possibly changing history, ideologies . . . the fate of so many men with the removal of just one man. And so he would deal with him merely as the case dictated, as a means to an end – just another piece in the much larger, overall strategy. He would even forego the small pleasure of letting him know a moment before – of relishing that fleeting expression. He would kill him quickly, painlessly, without feeling. It was the least he could do.

'How far are we going?' Xavier enquired.

'Not far – I'll let you have the package under the parapets of the next bridge. We won't be seen there.'

After Xavier had left, Julie sat quietly thoughtful. She continued absently flicking the pages of the magazine. And her own words came back to mind: '*He wanted to meet you alone that first time, as well. It seems that's the way he likes things*'. She told herself she had no real interest in what they were doing – the whole thing was *mad*. And despite Xavier's desire to get her involved, this 'contact' of his would likely have gone against the idea. She could see the sense of a group like 'Le Marteau Rouge' having to be cautious, the enlistment of one recruit at any one time was probably risk enough. But it wasn't that which troubled her, and she sat there trying to put her finger on exactly what did.

She remembered back to when Pauline, her elder sister, was thirteen and she was nine. Pauline developed a habit of disappearing into her room for half an hour after school each day. Julie became curious as the habit continued, but Pauline would lock the door – which merely increased her curiosity. On the few occasions she did manage to sneak in just after the half-hour vigil – while Pauline was in the bathroom or making tea – she discovered nothing. Julie became daring, almost frantic in her occasional searches. Then finally, after this had continued almost three months and all but obsessed her, she discovered something: a collection of Elvis Presley photos and some love letters written to him – some crossed out and rewritten – all hidden in a brown envelope deep in a bottom drawer.

She recalled the feeling of anticlimax. If she'd discovered them originally, it would have excited and part amazed her – but the mystery had carried on for so long, the possible explanations mounting one upon the other in her mind, that really *anything* would have been a bit of a disappointment by that stage.

It was that which troubled her now with Xavier, she realized – not the immediate curiosity, but the thought of it growing with time. If Xavier kept up his association with 'Le Marteau Rouge', he would gradually develop a secret side – a part of his life would be hidden from her more and more with each successive meeting.

There were other factors, as well, too jumbled to assimilate immediately: his contact's impromptu arrangement of the meeting, the change in rendezvous from last time, Xavier's poorly concealed uneasiness after the first meeting, the fact that the contact had managed to exclude her without even making Xavier overtly aware – all of it contributed. She was suddenly curious to see what his contact looked like. If nothing else, to give her a mental image to cling to when Xavier said offhandedly he was going to another meeting, as would, no doubt, increasingly happen over the coming months.

The whole thing would hold less secrets for her then, less unknown elements.

She put down her magazine and glanced at her watch. If she went along now, they might still be in the café opposite St Etienne.

The parapets of the Pont de la Tournelle cast heavy shadows over the walkway bordering the river. Duffal slowed his step; they were less than fifty yards from it now. The embankment at that point was quite steep, the road above – into which the bridge merged – being raised by a good fifteen feet. Duffal could just make out the glow of passing cars, not direct headlights. It was impossible for anyone passing to view them directly. *Ideal.*

'Who is this flash letter to be sent to?' Xavier asked.

'Another rich industrialist,' Duffal invented spontaneously. 'He's very important to us. A Monsieur Heumenage, lives in Montepellier.'

'Never heard of him,' Xavier shook his head.

'He's not exactly a front-liner, so I wouldn't expect you to. You'll have to wait a bit longer for those, I fear. Be a bit more patient.'

'I didn't mean it like that,' Xavier added hastily, flushing slightly. 'I just thought I might recognize the name. I'm sorry.'

Duffal glanced towards the night sky, inhaling deeply. 'That's alright. No offence taken.'

They walked on in silence. A heavy truck thundered past on the bridge.

Xavier felt awkward: the atmosphere was somehow wrong. At their first meeting he had expected no less, while they were sounding each other out: the conversation had been stilted, reactions guarded. But somehow Duffal seemed to have closed up even more since then. Could something have gone wrong? Reiner's flash letter? Julie? Her father's right-wing articles? . . . The possibilities raced through his mind.

Duffal was speaking again. 'I'll give you the package up ahead.'

'What?'

'The flash letter for Mr Heumenage – I'll give it to you over there.' Duffal pointed.

'Oh, yes . . . of course.' Xavier was slightly disorientated.

Duffal eyed him thoughtfully. 'I hope I didn't cause you any problems with whoever you were with when I phoned.'

'No, no. It was my girlfriend.'

'You never know. It might have been someone you weren't able to trust.' Duffal paused. 'I would always ask to meet you alone as a matter of course.'

'I understand,' Xavier nodded slowly. 'No problem.'

Duffal studied him a moment longer. 'That's fine. Let's hope this will be one of many meetings in your new association with Le Marteau Rouge.'

Duffal smiled faintly. He sensed that Xavier's hesitation had died; he was now more at ease. Duffal started timing: too long a pause might give a warning, and that would make an accurate heart puncture difficult. They were slowing to a halt, the bridge now almost directly above. *Perfect*. Duffal let the stiletto slip firmly into his grip. He took out the padded letter with his other hand.

'If you'd like to put it inside your jacket where it won't be seen.' Duffal edged into half-darkness, the direct street light slanting across his waist.

'Yes . . .' Xavier opened his jacket, and the movement registered only as a faint flicker. Thinking for a moment that the letter had been thrown at him, Xavier brought his hands up protectively. He felt a pang of coldness, and Duffal's face became a bright blur as he leant into the beam of light. He was clutching at Duffal's sleeve, his hands seeming suddenly distant, dissociated . . . and at something else, damp . . . only he didn't know what.

Duffal let Xavier sink slowly to the ground as he eased out the stiletto. Xavier's glasses had come loose in the struggle, and Duffal was concerned now that the grappling had put off his aim. He leant the limp body back against the brick base of a parapet and opened the shirt-front, wiping away some of the blood. After a second he could make out the small hole to one side of the left breastbone, and he relaxed; the heart would have been punctured neatly. Xavier Peton had died on his feet.

Duffal wiped his hands on Xavier's jacket and tossed the stiletto into the river. He tucked the letter into Xavier's inside pocket, and took out a small bottle from his own. Opening the flap of the letter, he carefully squeezed a droplet out of the bottle onto one of the exposed wires. The letter was the same as the one sent to Reiner, except that acid would burn through to make the connection, rather than needing the opening of the flap.

Within three minutes the explosion would rip through Xavier's chest cavity, completely obliterating the small stiletto mark; the short time gap would also prevent the internal system from resting sufficiently for an autopsy to ascertain that he had died from anything other than the explosion.

Prompted by the photographs sent, the police would have little doubt that Xavier had sent the bomb to Reiner, and had now died carrying this with a faulty connection. The risks of 'terrorism'. Then they would pick up the girl.

Duffal smiled faintly. He couldn't help admiring parts of Vruger's strategy.

He double-checked everything, then brushed himself off as he turned away, his footsteps making a faint and desolate echo . . . He stopped suddenly.

There was a movement among the trees on the embankment.

Julie had caught up with them just as they were leaving the café.

She immediately thought it odd that they were leaving so soon; it couldn't have been more than five minutes since Xavier's arrival. She sank back into the shadows of the adjoining street, watching them cross the square in Ste Geneviève. Just as they began to disappear from view, she started to follow.

There were other people walking in the square, so she was sure she wouldn't be too conspicuous. As she started into Ste Geneviève, she had to be more cautious; it was quiet at that time of night, and Xavier and his contact could well be the only people in the street. Julie was silent and stealthy, almost consciously holding her breath, clinging to the shadows of doorways out of the direct beam of the street-lamps. Fifty yards along, she caught sight of them turning off again. She picked up pace, covering the rest of the street swiftly.

They were making their way down the side of the VI and VII University complex, she could now tell. As they started to cross the road in front of them, momentarily held up by a few passing cars, she realized with a sense of foreboding that they were heading for the river.

Julie was forced to remain where she was, at intervals peering cautiously round the corner of Fosses St Bernard, until they had disappeared. To enter into full view in the street, let alone try and cross the main Quai road, was too great a risk.

The question preyed on her mind in the passing seconds: why the river? She could understand the need for secrecy, but surely this was taking things too far? Virtually any street corner at that time of night would have served the same purpose. She pushed the thought away; it wasn't the realities of the situation, but more the darkness and desolation creating their own imaginary demons, she decided. It was unsettling.

A moment after they had disappeared from view, she edged out and scampered down the Fosses St Bernard, waiting for a break in the traffic before crossing to the wide pavement above the embankment. From there, the river bank and path were a good fifty yards away. It was pitch dark by the river, and it took Julie a moment to work out which way they had headed. As she followed, she was conscious that the lights along the promenade were quite stark, so she had to keep below their line of vision, only moving into the edge at intervals behind the cover of some equally-spaced elm trees. When no cars were passing, it was almost eerily silent.

Her feelings of foreboding returned as she slowly followed their progress; few words were spoken between them, and Xavier's contact appeared curiously detached, staring mostly straight ahead, as if he had his mind set on a particular rendezvous or purpose.

She wondered whether she should head back; after all, she had now seen what his contact looked like, and watching the rest of their meeting held little relevance or meaning – but something kept her following almost hypnotically. Perhaps her apprehension, perhaps hoping to view some fuller conversation so that she might gauge their relationship, she didn't know – but she was unable to wrench herself away.

The river mist was more noticeable now, most of it in mid-stream. It seemed almost two hundred yards that Xavier and his contact had walked, when they stopped suddenly, close to the parapets of the Pont de la Tournelle. Behind them, mist clung to the bridge supports.

At last, Julie thought, there might be some meaningful conversation between them, some clue to what was happening. Why the impromptu meeting? Why their sudden departure from the café?

Then the nightmare started.

She watched the sequence of actions with a mixture of sickness and horror, wanting to shout out or scream – but the sounds seemed to catch in her throat. She was conscious of her heart pounding, feeling it almost rise to constrict the sour dryness she tasted as she fought to swallow. The blood rushed to her head.

All their actions appeared somehow hazy, dissociated, as if part of some ghostly silent movie. She noticed Xavier's glasses fall to the ground in the struggle. Her last impression was how innocent and frail he looked. It was the first time she shed any tears for him.

Suddenly Julie snapped herself back to reality. She must have stoody immobile, watching for longer than she realized, and unconsciously edged out beyond the cover of the elm tree, for Xavier's killer had turned to look directly towards her – and instantly she could feel the cold intent in those distant eyes.

She remained frozen and numb only seconds longer. Then she started running.

Duffal didn't know why Vruger wanted the girl implicated in Reiner's death, and suddenly he didn't care. His own protection came first. The fact of the girl seeing him surely blew the whole thing, anyway. He cursed his bad luck.

Everything else had gone so well, and now he would have to kill her.

He was already breaking into pursuit, as he pulled out his gun, a twelve-loaded automatic. The chamber was already full, in case of problems with Xavier – but he had to unscrew the silencer. A silencer would cut down the impetus too much for long-distance shooting.

She had already disappeared from view before he could get off a clear shot, but he had seen which way she was heading. Once he reached the top of the embankment, he would know for sure.

A two-tone city bus coasted by as Duffal neared the top of the steps to the promenade, and he momentarily concealed his gun beneath his windcheater.

Julie caught a glimpse of the bus as she looked back, but she couldn't see Duffal. The shock of what she'd just witnessed had taken much of her breath away; although she had run only a few hundred yards, she felt exhausted. She realized that she'd been running blindly – not knowing, not caring in which direction. She looked up hastily at the upcoming street: Rue Mirbel. The name meant nothing to her.

In that instant an explosion made her hesitate in her stride. At first she thought it was a shot – but it was both too distant and booming. She pondered a second longer, then took the right-hand turning, only because it appeared brighter, less foreboding. *Try to think*, she spurred herself. Formulate some sort of plan, some purpose, some *direction*. The street was quiet, and she was suddenly conscious of her heels clattering as she ran.

Get back among a crowd, was the only message that came through: among people, traffic. There, the sound of her running wouldn't be so marked, and her pursuer would surely be loath to try anything among too many witnesses. But where? Which direction, for God's sake? *Think*! She checked her pace for a second, trying to pick up the distant sounds of traffic in front, trying to distinguish it from that behind on the Quai de la Tournelle.

Sudden frantic footsteps behind broke her thoughts.

Turn left at the end, instinct told her. As she came up to the turn, she heard footsteps at the far end of the street, almost halting – and then a shot whistled past in front of her, kicking up dust from a house wall a few yards away. The sound was deafeningly loud in the short street.

Her skin bristled and her legs felt weak – then quickly she was round the corner, out of sight. Defying her paralysing fear, she fought for extra speed. He could be upon her any minute.

A shutter opened without warning on a second floor further up the street, and an old man looked out, probably alerted by the shot. Julie said nothing, and the man watched silently as she ran past. Her mind registered fleetingly that she could have called for help, but Xavier's contact was much too close behind. She would have to run on anyway. By the time the old man could summon help she would be far away. It had been the right thing to do. Don't hesitate. *Think ahead.*

As she listened, trying to hear above the sounds of her own body, she thought she could hear traffic sounds at the end of the street branching off ahead. She headed that way.

Duffal was wary of the old man as he passed. He was all too conscious of how loud his shot had sounded, echoing off the walls of the closely encroaching terraced houses. Another window slowly opened behind him. He kept his gun hidden. A second shot among this network of narrow streets was too risky. The first had been too optimistic, but it was the only clear chance of a shot before she turned off. He watched her shadowy figure at the far end of the street.

Duffal recalled a man he had once killed in a Munich park. On the face of it, an easy contract: the man came to the park at the same time each morning to feed the pigeons. The problem was that that part of the park bordered one of Munich's main thoroughfares, and it was then during the rush hour. From lack of an alternative place or time, Duffal resigned himself to it, and in the end was surprised how much the situation had aided him. The shot was largely drowned out by the traffic noise, and people were much too preoccupied with their journeys to work to notice a figure slumping on the park bench and rolling to the ground.

At the end of the street he halted, momentarily confused. Which way? *Where*? In the direction she had headed there were two turnings off. He heard the sound of her heels before he caught sight of her movement.

He ran on into the street, and after thirty yards he could make out traffic and brighter lights at the end. *Good*, she was playing right into his hands. He pulled out his gun again, lining up the dark silhouette on her back.

The image of the wide avenue jolted in Julie's sweat-blurred vision. The lights seemed to spin, revolving slowly as she stumbled out into the road itself; a horn blared from somewhere and she wheeled round towards it, the headlamps washing brighter all around her, searing her eyes. A car bonnet loomed suddenly in front with a screech of tyres, and she had to jerk back and wend her way around it, half supporting herself against the bonnet. Another horn blasted.

At that instant a star-burst appeared on the windscreen of a car in the far lane – then the glass fell in, the car swerving to a halt. Christ, he *was* firing! The very thing she didn't think he'd do. She became frantic. The street was no sanctuary. She'd held out all her reserves of strength, just clinging on to make it here, convincing herself with each laboured stride that he wouldn't risk shooting among the crowds . . . just hold on, *just a few more yards*. And now?

She felt defeated, confused. She hadn't even heard the shot this time.

A man with his dog on the far side – one of the few people out walking – had stopped to view the confusion. Julie saw this as her only hope. She ran towards him.

'*Cet homme*,' she shouted as she approached, pointing back. '*Il me poursuit. Je vous en prie, aidez-moi*.'

The man looked puzzled. '*Quoi, ma jolie? Qu'est ce qui ne va pas*?' He was still preoccupied with the traffic mêlée.

Julie pointed more insistently. '*Cet homme – S'il vous plaît. Je suis en danger* . . . Please, help me,' she pleaded after a pause; her French was stunted even further by her excitement.

The Frenchman seemed only then to notice Duffal coming across the road, and looked uncertainly between him and Julie. But Julie felt suddenly unsure, from the confident way in which Duffal was approaching, whether it would make any difference – whether he wouldn't just shoot the old man as well. She turned again and fled, oblivious to the old man's protests. She headed into a short side street leading to another avenue.

Another plan began to formulate; she only prayed it would work. Her legs were trembling and her breath was coming in short gasps, rasping achingly in her throat. She knew that she couldn't run much further. She started unbuttoning her coat.

Duffal followed her into the short, dark street, immediately noting another avenue at its end. She hadn't learnt.

As Julie came into view in the avenue, her coat was fully undone. She ripped desperately at the front of her jumper, at the same time running to one side, keeping as close to the oncoming traffic as possible. The threads pulled away unevenly, and she quickly fumbled with the buttons of her blouse beneath. The cold night air hit her as her breasts were exposed. She frantically flagged down the traffic.

Two cars passed without stopping, one of the drivers noticing her but looking quickly away – and she began to voice her till then silent plea.

'Please, please . . . help me!'

A third car passed without faltering, but the fourth – a small bakery van – wavered and slowed slightly.

Duffal had a clean shot of her as the second car passed. He stopped and steadied his aim; her back was full in the sights.

A white van distracted him momentarily, slowing and stopping at her side – but it was of little importance, he was already squeezing off the shot.

She moved – scampering around to the side of the van. Duffal followed her around in the sights. It was clear again. Okay, *now*.

But at that instant the van edged forwards, blocking his view. And Duffal cursed: a moment's hesitation and the opportunity was gone. He watched helplessly as she scrambled up into the van.

As an afterthought, Duffal considered shooting them both, but there were too many cars passing nearby and he could hear some footsteps from somewhere behind. And by then the van had started to pull away.

Duffal dashed out into the road, trying to wave down a car, but the Parisian drivers were suitably unimpressed, some beeping their horns and cursing. For one clumsy moment he considered using his gun – but that would draw too much attention. Finally he stood at the edge of the traffic flow, exasperatedly watching the tail-lights of the van disappear.

Julie kept her eyes glued to the mirror until Duffal's figure had completely gone from view.

The van driver, a young, unshaven man of thirty, had been asking her what was wrong, but Julie was unable to answer immediately. Only now that her terror had subsided could she gather her wits, and pretend she had almost been raped. She could feel his eyes upon her as she spoke and wrapped her coat around her to cover her nakedness. She fumbled and hesitated on some of the words, her body beginning to shake – and then the wave of shock and confusion caught up with her and she burst into tears.

He looked ahead for a while, in silence.

'*Bien. Que faire*?' he asked finally. 'Where do you want to go?'

It was the first time Julie really considered this. She could have said the police – but it struck her that Xavier's involvement with 'Le Marteau Rouge' might prove awkward to explain. And she couldn't go back to her room, or to anyone else at the college; Xavier's contact would seek her out all too easily there.

Suddenly she felt very alone, as well as afraid, and her thoughts turned to the one person who she knew would help, who she could rely on: her father.

10

Art Swenkel heard of Anton Reiner's death in a frantic phone-call from his own man who had been keeping watch close to Reiner's home at the time.

Swenkel wasn't particularly superstitious, but this coming so soon after the directive relayed from Rabin and Golda Meir through Peres, he couldn't help thinking it an omen. He also felt a mixture of sadness and regret that he had recommended Reiner in the first place, against the advice of some of his colleagues, and indeed despite Reiner's uncertainty of his own worthiness for the task. The tragic image of the staid and efficient banker, meek and prim and strongly settled into family life, preyed heavily on his mind.

There wasn't even much they could say to his widow and children. To come out into the open at this stage would be far too dangerous, and it could drive whoever was behind the murder completely to ground. Their last chance would then be lost. Swenkel clenched one fist hard. All they could do was watch the police investigation with interest, and perhaps send through polite clues and messages, unofficially.

Swenkel checked his watch. The police would have arrived within an hour of his man calling. The newspapers would have it by evening.

His thoughts moved on abruptly. There was something much more vital to consider than mere superstition, or pity for Reiner or self-recrimination: which direction to take, who to contact now that Reiner was gone? More than anything, Reiner's death had compounded the problems of the last twenty-four hours. Only seven hours remained.

It took him only minutes to decide – though long, anxious minutes – for the number of options were small. But having made his decision, he delved once more into self-examination, turning the name of Daniel Grade over in his mind – at the same time wondering whether it was right for the fate of the children, if not of the nation as a whole, to be left in the hands of a man who had no connections, no allegiance to Israel.

Daniel Grade had learnt a lot about Dr Emil Schaarer, even though the investigation had steered strongly away from him being a suspect.

Between the numerous reports from Semleche and Bunt, he had requested from their local news agency any cuttings relating to Schaarer over the past eighteen months. As a bonus, they had got hold of a documentary video of one of the Geneva sessions, which Grade viewed with interest. Partly to gauge the man himself, and partly to view the arena which, by then, he felt firmly, would continue its proceedings unabated.

Switzerland was not a member of the United Nations. Although Schaarer had sat as Chairman of SBECSA, he was by birth, Austrian. He had started with UNESCO, but now most of his time was spent in New York, apart from the three-month annual sessions in Geneva. In appearance he looked older than the fifty-eight years mentioned in one of the news clippings: his hair was wavy and grey; only his trim beard and moustache showed remnants of the original light brown. His hazel eyes – when the camera moved in close – were the only feature that showed youth and vitality, piercing through steel-rimmed glasses at those with whom he was locked in debate. He gave an impression of intense seriousness, yet also calmness, understanding. From visual impression alone – if that could be relied on – he seemed the sort of man Daniel would immediately like and trust, if not admire. The accompanying news clippings bore out this impression.

At first, Daniel had not bothered to play the video tape, seeing no point in it after his findings. But after finishing the skeleton of his story on Reiner – then phoning Reiner that morning to arrange a meeting in which to confront him, only to find the line constantly engaged – he found himself with some spare time and nothing planned. So he decided to play the tape which had been sitting there from the day before. Intermittently he stopped it, and tried ringing Reiner's number again – but to no avail.

It was already 10.30 a.m., and the early morning bustle of Zürich's rush hour had abated slightly along the opposite lake-front.

Suddenly the telephone rang and Grade picked it up.

It was Rolf Nabens, which at first surprised him, for he had called the office only the night before and passed over his findings, speaking to Rolf and David Wetherall at the same time. Rolf's manner now increased his curiosity.

'Something's cropped up, Danny.'

Grade reached over and switched off the video. 'Something to do with what we discussed last night?'

'Not exactly.'

'Then what?'

There was a pause and Daniel pressed him, 'For Christ's sake, what is it?' Only then did Nabens begin to speak. Daniel said no more, just listened. It became instantly apparent why Anton Reiner's number was constantly engaged.

Daniel remained in cold shock for almost an hour over the news of Reiner's death.

As his mind finally started to clear, he stared blankly at the television screen, seeing only the reflection of his own stricken and thoughtful face.

He had been wrong all the time! But it wasn't the pages of worthless paperwork and the hours of wasted research that troubled him, more the feeling that he had betrayed a man who was now dead – and, more poignantly, had probably died as a result of the same business which Grade had him marked as perpetrator of, not the victim.

Reiner's words of warning and his fears after the Murren incident now clung desperately in Grade's mind. He should have known! Or, at least, tried to believe him, given him a bit of quarter – analysed the facts and figures on the Semleche and Bunt reports a bit deeper, searched for some alternative explanation.

Ironically, all the explanations of Reiner's suspicious shares dealings would probably have come out when confronting him anyway; but it was too late for that now. Whatever defence Reiner may have had, had died with him. The only legacy was his innocence – proved by the hard fact of his death. But it was a hell of a way to have to prove it! Grade cursed inwardly.

His mind worked back frantically through the few facts that Nabens had passed on: a bomb attack, probably terrorist connected, Reiner's daughter slightly injured as well. The police were there a good hour before any correspondents; as yet no further leads from them. The story would probably just make the Zürich evening papers, London by the next morning. Grade searched back again, trying to pick out any details that didn't quite fit, just one irregularity! There were none; the details were too slim as yet to come to any conclusion.

Grade looked down and noticed that he'd been rubbing his clasped hands together, working them ever tighter. He tried to relax, tried to clear his thoughts again – but it was hopeless. He got up, pacing restlessly for a moment, and finally decided to watch the rest of the video film.

The images washed blankly over him as he settled down again. He sat unseeing for almost fifteen minutes before the film flickered to an end and he heard the hiss of the blank tape coming up.

Still Grade sat there – the hiss seeming to grow ominously louder. Then, as if propelled, he jumped up and rewound the tape, hastily pressing the play button again. This time he watched intently, leaning forward in his chair, watching each movement, each nuance of Emil Schaarer's expression. He no longer viewed the film with the same easy acceptance as earlier; he struggled to look beyond the shield of Schaarer's calm expression, wondering with each passing second if he actually *could* be behind it all? Or alternatively, who could possibly hate him enough to indict him falsely, if it wasn't Reiner?

After a while he was satisfied and switched off the tape. What had fallen into place on his second viewing was a valid point: Schaarer was quite a distinctive figure, even at a distance – the colour of his hair and beard alone should pick him out amongst most crowds. If someone had gone to the trouble of falsifying a car registration in Schaarer's name, then why wouldn't they go the whole way and have him impersonated? With a hairpiece and beard of the right colouring, it could be effective at anything but the very closest of distances. Instead Reiner, or someone who looked like Reiner, had been identified. Unless someone deliberately wished to give the impression that it was Reiner trying to implicate Schaarer falsely, this appeared pointless. Only an assumption, but at least it was a start. The one inconsistency he had been looking for!

Grade picked up the phone and called Semleche and Bunt. He asked for a re-check on the shares dealings of Emil Schaarer.

'Wasn't the report we supplied the other day quite full in every respect, sir?' Herr Bunt enquired politely.

'No, it's not that. It's just that I have some new information, and I would like another check in case something was overlooked.'

A short silence indicated that Semleche and Bunt rarely, if ever, overlooked anything.

'Certainly, sir,' Bunt complied.

'And I'd also like a re-check on the general SBECSA shares dealings, to see if any other names might appear,' Grade said.

'As is your wish, Mr Grade. We will call you back sometime later today.' Bunt rang off.

The report on Schaarer came through by messenger within two hours. It was virtually a copy of the first report, except for an additional listing of shares purchased by Schaarer in two other banks and an industrial group not connected with SBECSA. The dates involved could have, on their own, cast possible suspicion, but the purchases were small, and neither bank was large enough to receive any significant gain from a shift of Arab funds. As for the industrial group, they produced mainly chemical fertilizers, and Grade couldn't see any possible connections. Nothing there.

The more general re-report arrived just after lunch, and it took Grade considerably longer to pick his way through it. Most of it was a list of major shares tradings in *all* Swiss banks, not just SBECSA. Grade picked out five names from the list. Two were the same as from the day before, and after another hour he'd discounted the other three, either because the shares dealings or the banks themselves weren't large enough, or the dates didn't coincide. Grade looked up finally to rest his eyes, and pushed the reports to one side.

He walked slowly over to the window and looked out across Lake Zürich towards the intersection of the Quai and the Banhof Strasse, the banking core. He felt confused, dejected. One week into the investigation and he was back to square one. A questionable motive and *no* suspect.

Except a totally unconnected name. *Vruger*? Throughout, the name hadn't appeared anywhere in the Zürich community; he was almost convinced now it didn't exist. But then, when negotiating with assassins, it was unlikely you'd use your real name.

Only a slim possibility remained; that Reiner *had* been involved, but purely as a front man, and as the investigation picked up pace, had to be removed. But, then, where did Ehnbridt fit in? Also the fact that Reiner had approached him in the first place, and the clumsy identification with a Schaarer registered car, pointed away from Reiner's involvement. But whatever the conclusion, *someone* else was at the head of it all. Someone who was probably using the name *Vruger* as a front.

But if that someone wasn't Schaarer, and shares dealings hadn't highlighted any other suspects, then for God's sake who?

The telephone rang in the Zürich office. It was picked up after only seconds.

The caller spoke straight away. 'There's been a problem.'

'I see,' Vruger commented blankly, without asking who was calling. 'What sort of problem?'

'The girl. The girl saw me.'

There was a short silence. 'How did it happen?'

'I met the boy first in a café – she must have followed us from there.'

'That was a bit careless. Why didn't you . . .'

'I didn't call to be admonished like a schoolboy,' the voice cut in sharply. 'It could have been arranged between them, or done of her own accord. It's part of the unavoidable risk of splitting one person from a couple or group. Either way, it *happened*. Now what do you want me to do?'

'I don't know. Let me think.'

'She'll have to be killed now. You realize that of course.'

'For Christ's sake let me think . . .' Vruger broke off, fighting to concentrate; the ticking of a clock on the far wall suddenly sounded maddeningly loud. 'Do you think she could recognize you again, Jaalgen?'

'Maybe. I chased her for a while afterwards – at points she was quite close. I was wearing a blond wig, but I don't think that will count for much.'

'What name were you using in Paris?'

'Duffal. François Duffal.'

'What a mess . . .' Vruger commented. 'Do you know where the girl is now?'

'No. She's not at the room she shared with the boy, or at the college. I was hoping you might be able to give me a new lead on that.'

'I've no idea. If you've looked there, then I don't know where you might find her.' Vruger lapsed again into thoughtful silence; a chill washed slowly through him. The events with Daniel Grade, and now with the girl, had brought things closer . . . *too close*. The decision would have had to be made in the end anyway, but he had hoped for more time. Now that the moment was upon him, he found his mouth suddenly dry.

'There is another way,' he said finally.

'Okay, lay it out.'

'The journalist. It's her father, Daniel Grade. He's getting too close, beginning to find out things he shouldn't. He'll have to be taken care of. Through him, you can get to her.'

'You didn't tell me this before.'

'Before, it wasn't necessary for you to know – now it is. It's as simple as that.'

'And now you want me to kill him?'

Vruger stammered. 'Yes, that's right.'

'I thought originally you were going to do it another way?'

'I was. But now with his progress and *this* problem, I'm not sure how effective it would be. I received the photographs you arranged just this morning. However, I will probably still go through with the plan as a back-up to your efforts.'

'You shouldn't worry so much,' Jaalgen said sarcastically. 'Mistakes are rare. Where do I find him?'

Vruger gave Jaalgen the Bellerive au Lac address. 'He was there yesterday, but if he's moved on, his newspaper should know his whereabouts.'

Jaalgen laughed mockingly. 'You know, you really are a card. First you act shocked at the thought of having the girl killed – and then you calmly tell me that you want me to kill her father as well.'

'It was never necessary that the girl be killed,' Vruger spluttered. 'With the journalist, in the end it *would* have been necessary. Your actions have merely brought it closer.'

'Killing is killing – the reasons behind it don't support it, one way or the other. One day you'll come to realize that, Herr *Vruger*.' Jaalgen rang off.

Vruger slowly replaced the receiver. His palms were sweating from the short encounter. He began to wonder whether Jaalgen's final derogatory emphasis meant that he had guessed his true identity.

Daniel Grade was on his way to dinner when the phone rang.

At first there was no answer from the other end, so after a second he repeated, 'Hello?'

'Dad, it's me . . . Julie,' a faint voice came finally.

'Well, this is quite a surprise. How on earth did you know I was here?'

'Your office . . . When I called, they gave me your number.'

'And you're in Paris now?'

'Yes. I'm calling long-distance.'

Daniel sensed the hesitancy in her voice.

'What's wrong, Julie? Something's wrong, isn't it?'

Silence from the other end.

'Tell me,' he said more urgently.

She broke finally in a wave.

'Oh Dad, oh God . . . I don't know. I don't know where to start. This man, he chased me because I saw them . . . I saw what happened. And Xavier, poor Xavier . . .' Her voice faded, becoming jumbled, incoherent.

'Julie, *please* . . . what is it?'

Silence again.

Daniel listened intently, and after a second he could just pick out the staccato breathing of gentle weeping and, in the background, the faint sounds of Paris traffic.

There was a noise like someone knocking on glass; then the line went dead.

Vruger spread the photographs and papers out on the desk top.

There were five photographs in all: Xavier coming out of his apartment building; Xavier posting a package; Xavier and Julie Grade together; Anton Reiner coming out with Daniel Grade from a meeting at a Stampfenback Plaza café;

a man who looked like Anton Reiner at the opened window of a nine-seater Mercedes.

The papers concerned Schaarer's false car registration; Reiner's shares transactions, and reports on information that Daniel Grade had compiled from other sources, including a video tape of Schaarer at the UN Geneva peace conference.

Only one element now remained; and if Jaalgen was successful, it wouldn't even be necessary.

Nighttime had settled on the desert.

Faint moonlight glowed eerily on the batteries of artillery and trucks around the tunnel. Quarters for the men had been made in large canvas tents. One of the smallest tents was that which General Pohlmann shared with Major Gant.

But Pohlmann found sleep difficult. It was too quiet. He was used to the nighttime movement of traffic, and the general hum of activity that went on past midnight in Tel-Aviv. He found the quiet hills unsettling; and, as he stared wide-eyed at the canvas roof, he wondered if it was just that which kept him awake, or what this area represented to him not only now, but also on past campaigns. He had known only fighting and bloodshed in the hills and deserts of Israel.

Please, don't let me be right. Not this time. The image was too clear, too harsh, and he closed his eyes and shook his head to dispel it. But in the darkness of his mind, it still played over . . . the shelling and bombardment of the artillery, the brave young soldiers and sabras who had lost life and limb. The faces of children, hazy and indistinct, superimposed on the bloodied bodies. He couldn't see the blood that was flowing, *only feel its clammy touch . . . the gun's firing . . . the tunnel, its depth and darkness . . . No . . . No! . . . God no!*

'What . . . ?'

Pohlmann sat bolt upright.

Somebody was tapping at the taut canvas. 'General, a call on the field telephone for you.'

Pohlmann hastened into his clothes and went out. He picked up the receiver.

'Pohlmann here.'

'I hope I haven't disturbed you,' Hasik said. 'It's just that I thought it strange you were all sleeping. You have only four hours to the deadline.'

'I know. I know!' Pohlmann found he was sweating. 'I am expecting a call from our Foreign Minister any minute. I thought this might be him.'

'Ah, Allon. Good. Hopefully you have made him aware of the situation – he will make the right decision. Sleep well, General.'

Part Four

Farid Mahblil, Beirut: United Arab World, Cairo

11

BIZARRE KILLINGS!

With the recent murder of Jubrahn Gahtlav, a Phalangist-inspired *assassin*, thoughts turn back to the previous similarly bizarre killing eighteen months ago of Al-Hakim and Amir Khourem. This is no coincidence as the three killings are linked, and Beirut police now believe that the cross markings are a revenge sign. One of Gahtlav's colleague's, Reymenak, is presently in police custody. A recent police bulletin names Al-Ben Salmad, arms dealer and financier, among those wanted for questioning. The war, however, hampers procedures in its usual way, and police are loath to push matters too heavily in what could be a major political issue. Especially on that side of the body politic.

Farid Mahblil, Beirut

The Cessna 150 battled through the night sky.

The haphazard sequence of events played over in Daniel's mind. He'd flown over, scheduled, from Zürich the night before, arriving in Paris Orly at 1.30 a.m. From there he'd headed straight to the all-night bar where he'd arranged to meet Julie. The name 'Bar Roussillon' meant nothing to Daniel, but the taxi driver seemed to know it.

It was a small run-down establishment near the Gare du Nord, full of shift workers from the station and street-cleaners having their early-morning brandies over games of cards and dominoes. Daniel took a seat with Julie in the far corner of the bar, away from the main bustle.

Julie's second call to Zürich had come through less than half an hour after the first. Someone had been waiting outside her booth during the previous call, and she'd been too distraught to continue anyway. On her return call she started to tell Daniel of her encounter with Duffal . . . enough to get him on the first available flight out of Zürich. The rest of the nightmare tale she imparted in the Bar Roussillon over bread rolls and *pastis*.

Daniel was jolted sharply by the mention of Xavier sending a 'flash' letter, his mind racing to cope with immediate suspicions, but he hadn't probed any deeper then or mentioned his fears – not knowing if they might be valid, or what Julie's reaction would be to everything being somehow connected with his investigation, if that was so. He just hoped his initial instinct was wrong.

Halfway through the story, Julie broke down again, and Daniel gave her one of his typically bearish hugs and held her close while she wept, until he felt all the grief and pain had finally worked itself through. The fear would stay for a while longer, he knew. An old, toothless man in the corner winked and smiled at Daniel as he stared blankly over her shoulder . . . obviously thinking the endearment too strong to be merely that between a father and daughter.

Daniel had kept his fears to himself until Julie finished her story, then had tentatively asked.

'This 'flash' letter – do you remember who it was sent to?'

Julie remembered only that it was going somewhere in Switzerland, and the name she thought was *Reinhardt* . . . But that was enough. Daniel ushered her out of the bar and booked them into a nearby hotel.

He'd found sleep difficult that night, and first thing in the morning had gone out to get hold of a first edition of *L'Express*. A story about Xavier was there and, in a smaller section, the bomb attack on Reiner – but nothing connecting the two. Daniel made the call that had been on his mind from the night before, to a golfing partner of his who was also a keen amateur aviator, Roy Aitkinson.

The early evening *Le Soir*, from what Daniel could make out with his limited French, carried the first hint of a connection between Xavier and Reiner. The name of the terrorist group that Julie had talked of, 'Le Marteau Rouge', was mentioned. Daniel made his second call. The airports were probably being watched already.

It was then that Daniel first aired his fears to Julie.

'You'll have to bear with me, Julie. But I believe that a lot of this is somehow connected with an investigation I'm now involved with. Don't ask me exactly how – because I don't know yet. But I don't want you staying here in Paris, where the police might pick you up and hold you. It could be a while until this mess is cleared up, and I want to know *exactly* what the score is before I let you answer inquiries. I want us to leave. I'm taking you home.'

These last words Julie clung to desperately – and it was as if the rest had washed over her without meaning. Her abject fear had thrown her suddenly back to her childhood; whenever there had been fear or doubt then, home had seemed the only sanctuary.

'Oh Dad,' she said simply, her eyes softly imploring him, and suddenly he was hugging her, comforting her again.

They'd met up with Roy Aitkinson at the Le Touquet airfield at 10 p.m. that night. Roy had already fuelled up, so they turned straight round for the return leg to Biggin Hill in Kent.

Only now, sitting in the Cessna 150 high over the English Channel, did Daniel turn his thoughts to the deeper implications of the events of the past twenty-four hours. Whoever was behind it all knew or had found out about Julie's movements. The entire scheme with Xavier had been too carefully planned for mere happenstance. But to what end? If killing Reiner had been the only objective, most certainly there would have been easier methods – so obviously involving Xavier and consequently Julie and himself was somehow important to the whole operation. But why? Discrediting his investigation, was that a possibility?

No, he decided at length. Or, at least, other pieces would

have to fall into place: no connection with Julie had been indicated in the newspapers as yet, let alone Daniel or his investigation with Reiner. He would have to keep track of developments, though – get Nabens to give him a direct line on any wire-service information. Keep one step ahead.

Distraction was the other possibility, and the more Daniel considered it, the more feasible it became; nothing could have served better to take his mind off Reiner and the main course of the investigaton than Julie's present plight. But then was Julie's attack faked? What were the odds against her being able to get away, if her pursuer was a professional? Or perhaps the whole affair was conceived purely to frighten him off.

Fear? It was odd, initially he had felt only bewilderment, and felt that fear would quickly and surely follow, but the emotion had never come; instead he felt a mixture of anger, determination and loathing. Determination to find out who was behind it all, *who* had caused his daughter's life to be threatened. Anger and loathing that someone could even conceive such a sheme.

Daniel bit his knuckles, forcing his mind back over the various possibilities – but, without any particular one taking prominence, his thoughts spiralled quickly into confusion.

An abrupt drop as the small aircraft encountered turbulence. He looked out of the window but the wing lights penetrated only a few yards into a thick swirl of mist.

'Is everything okay, Roy?'

'We've got some heavy gusts coming in from the east, and the ground boys report some heavy "sheer" below fifteen hundred feet,' Aitkinson said over his shoulder.

It was the first time Daniel had paid any attention to the faint, static, smeared messages coming in over the radio. Aitkinson's expression was more one of alertness than concern; but as the plane was struck again by a rapid succession of flurries, his face changed.

Daniel looked back out at the wildly flexing wing. Aitkinson had said initially that this could be a rough night for the flight, and perhaps another time would be better . . .

but Daniel had pushed him that bit more, stressing the urgency of the situation; and now he felt guilty. He had been so preoccupied with his own and Julie's problems, that it never occurred to him he could be putting them all in danger by his actions.

Aitkinson looked back. 'We've almost fifteen minutes to landing, but I'm going to try to get below the worst of it now.'

Daniel watched the dial needles on the dashboard drop as the plane tilted and began to descend.

'Hold on. This could be the worst part,' Aitkinson said.

After seconds, the entire frame of the small aircraft shuddered and jolted. To Daniel, the movements seemed far beyond mere turbulence. Reiner and the cable-car flashed fleetingly through his mind . . . but he couldn't imagine an occasion when anyone could possibly have tampered with the plane. *No*, his mind was just working overtime because of the build-up of events. Or was it? The dials appeared to be flickering unevenly. He tried to read Aitkinson's taut expression.

Julie gripped Daniel's hand as the small plane was buffeted by the invisible winds, lifting high then dropping sickeningly low. Julie was obviously exhausted, with this on top of everything else, and closing her eyes she rested her head against Daniel's shoulder.

Aitkinson wrestled with the joystick. He watched the gauges more than the cloud-dense sky ahead. He was just below four thousand feet, and wished to drop to three thousand, but any single air pocket could drop them dangerously low.

It seemed an eternity that they were caught in the tumult – but as they settled and levelled out again, Daniel was surprised to see from his watch that it had only been six minutes; they still had almost ten minutes to landing.

Julie slowly let go of his hand. She was thoughtful for a while.

'I haven't said this before – but I *am* frightened you know. And not just by what has happened with Xavier, and me being chased – but what the future holds.' She wrapped her arms around herself, as if she was shivering. 'And I'm confused as hell. Perhaps if I knew more it would help . . .'

Daniel gazed at her. Earlier Julie had asked him about the connection with his investigation, and he had promised he would tell her everything when she was more settled. At the time she had accepted his excuse, but now she was beginning to want more explanation. In one way, Daniel was pleased: obviously her fear was subsiding, giving way to natural curiosity.

'When we get home, Julie. I made that promise and I'll keep it.' Daniel met her lost expression, and added. 'It wouldn't help you to know right now. It would only confuse you further.'

Julie started to say something, but at that instant the 'sheer' hit them – a burst of downrushing air from a storm cloud travelling at over a hundred feet per second.

Again Aitkinson fought with the controls, lifting back, giving rise to the flaps and sending a surge of power through the throttle at the same time. The tops of some trees seemed perilously close at one point, before drifting below them out of sight as the engine tone increased, giving them lift once more. They stayed at that level for a while before dropping sharply again. Heavy rain slanted against the windows as they came through a final burst of mist, and then the runway lights were suddenly below them.

Aitkinson taxied in easily.

'I'm sorry about that,' he said. 'But that "sheer" can play hell with you. I've heard of guys being ripped apart by it; it can literally drop you a thousand feet in the blink of an eye. Which is no fun if you're only five hundred feet from the ground.' He smiled sheepishly. 'I don't mind telling you all this now that we're down.'

'You should have protested more, Roy. You know I wouldn't have forced your hand to that extent.' Daniel put a reassuring hand on Aitkinson's shoulder. 'I really do appreciate it though. Thanks.'

Aitkinson braked the small plane slowly to a halt.

As they unstrapped and stepped out, turning up their collars against the driving rain, Julie asked.

'What's Mum going to say?'

'I don't know,' Daniel said pensively. That was another thing he hadn't thought of.

Memories came from another age.

Liège, Belgium, thirty miles from the German border. He remembered a stocky, fair-haired man – his father – stiff with pride as he was led out to the makeshift gallows by the local resistance. And how the small bands of English soldiers had watched in the background with nonchalant acceptance, some laughing and lighting cigarettes for each other as the sickening ceremony was carried out.

The charge had been shooting a resistance member in the back; but even at that age, at eleven, he *knew* his father wouldn't have done that. He would have shot the man face-to-face or not at all.

A month later, his mother – a quiet, flaxen-haired, blue-eyed woman of thirty-eight – put a Luger gently and firmly into her mouth and pulled the trigger. His memories, from then, were of an older, sour-faced and loveless aunt. But the scars had stayed, had been fostered carefully.

The mental picture of his parents had faded, their habits and turns of phrase now disjointed, out of time. Only the memory of his father's allegiance to the Third Reich and resultant hatred of all semites had stayed with him, and at times he wondered why. Perhaps because it was the cause his father had died for. Perhaps because his father had dedicated himself so totally that family life had paled in comparison. That was the way of the world, he thought resignedly: causes and beliefs live on; people die. Those same beliefs had become his last tie with his father, and he clung to this now largely to blot out the bitterness and the terrible sense of waste. But a part he also relished, and through the years it had become almost an obsession.

Each contract was a fulfilment of his father's ambition, as

much as his own – in that moment he became an extension of his father's will and desire. Almost a part of him. It wouldn't always be the semites, or the 'dark gypsies of the world', as his father would call them; just as often it was those who defended their rights in this modern, crazy age: the liberals, the sympathizers. It all came down to the same thing.

Though now part of that obsession concerned him: it had led to that nightmare night on the motorway near Mannheim when he had narrowly escaped the *Polizei*, and now it had drawn him into a situation he had thought would end long ago. None of the current contracts had he relished like the one involving Al-Hakim and Khourem, but they were necessary, and so his professionalism took over. But with the recent turns of fate – first Reiner in the cable-car, then the girl in Paris – even that professionalism looked sadly lacking; and now only a grim determination to right his errors quelled his anger and indignation.

He coldly surveyed the two guns he had methodically cleaned and stripped earlier, then his eyes fell to the telephone.

The Paris hotel room was small and nondescript, with worn furniture in beige floral patterns. It was similar to so many where he had waited patient hours, and he had taken to reading in the spare time that otherwise would aggravate him. He had read everything from Jung to Rabelais to *Mein Kampf*, and had since taken an interest in political and philosophical works from outside France and Germany, whether he shared their views of not.

It was almost three hours before the call he was expecting finally came through. The streetlamps outside had come on. He folded over page 194 of Lyndon B. Johnson's *Memoirs* and picked up the receiver.

'There is one element we have overlooked,' the caller said. 'There is someone who could implicate us both if the journalist catches up with him. His name's Kent Ehnbridt. I'll tell you where he can be found.'

*

Catherine Grade was deathly pale when she sat down at the kitchen table. Slowly the colour came back to her cheeks.

'I won't bore you with stock remarks like "Tell me it isn't true, Danny". I'll accept it all, just as you've told me. But tell me *how* could it have happened? How on earth is it connected with this investigation of yours?'

Daniel noticed Catherine's hands clenched on the table, and turned slightly away. Her anguish was so real, so complete, that he suddenly felt inept in his explanation – inadequate.

'I don't know yet. I just don't know,' he said, the exasperation that had built up through the long hours showing through, despite his resolve to hide it.

'Okay, is there *anything* you might have overlooked?'

'No, that's it. I've told you everything.'

'Is there any way of finding out, then?'

Daniel considered. 'Well, only perhaps by looking into Reiner's background and finding out why someone might want to kill him. Apart from that there might be a traceable connection through a man called Ehnbridt in Zürich, or a certain Al-Ben Salmad from the Lebanon – but they're both slim hopes.'

'I don't mean in *that* way, Danny. Obviously you wouldn't want to stay involved now, not with all this. I mean through the police or something – proper channels.'

Daniel looked back pointedly. 'Well there's a couple of points there, Cathy. First of all I would have been continuing with the investigation anyway. Apart from this business with Julie, there's certain answers I just *must* have. Secondly, I can't possible involve the police until I know the full implications of Julie's connnection with this boyfriend and "Le Marteau Rouge".'

'You never learn, do you?' Catherine shook her head in disbelief. 'You know how I felt about you going on this one so close to Christmas. Well, maybe it wasn't just that making me feel uneasy. But now it's gone beyond mere foreboding . . . and you're actually trying to tell me you're willing to keep going? You're willing to toy with the life of our daughter?'

'I'm not *toying*, as you put it,' Daniel snapped. 'Why do you think I went over there and brought her back, for Christ's sake. She'll be safe here. I put *her* before anything else.'

'Oh, that's a good one,' Catherine mocked.

'If things hot up, I'll take her down to the cottage,' Daniel continued unabated.

'Then you admit that there's a risk.'

'I was thinking more of the police,' Daniel said with forced patience. 'They'd be the first to call for her here, if they make the connection with Reiner.'

Catherine was silent. She wasn't surprised at the mention of the Berkshire cottage: it had been their first home, and they had kept it after they moved. Since then it had been a place to go on quiet weekends, short holidays, or frequently Daniel would go alone for some writing solitude – most especially when there were problems and things were strained at home.

Daniel was trying to read Catherine's expression beyond the firm set of her jaw.

'And as for risk. Have you ever tried to look at it from the other side?' he asked. 'What if what Julie saw has really marked her, so that she must be dispensed with . . . at all costs. Because, believe me, all the police on earth wouldn't stop a man like this if he really wanted to get to her.' As Daniel said it, he stopped himself. What *did* he know about Julie's attacker? Julie's description had been too general for much use: blond or light-brown hair, tall, quite well-built, fawn windcheater. He had killed Xavier and Reiner and, if he was the same man Reymenak had described, Al-Hakim and Khourem. *Dutch or Belgian*? What exactly would stop a man like that?

'How the hell would we even go about asking for protection, with this Xavier incident and everything?' Daniel questioned. 'You can see how bad it looks. The only thing that will help is if I can find out who and why first. Those are the only answers that will matter.'

Catherine gnawed at the back of her hand, fighting back the tears.

'Oh, you've got all the answers, Danny. You've got all the answers, alright.'

Daniel walked away from the table towards the window. The view extended over the garden towards Wentworth's thirteenth green and fourteenth fairway. He lit a cigar as he watched a group assembling for the tee-off.

On some assignments it always seemed incongruous to him how the world outside, often so close at hand, went on as normal, seemingly oblivious to the dramas behind closed doors. Now the drama was in his own home, and the people on the fourteenth fairway were enjoying the crisp winter sunshine. He slowly exhaled the first puff of his cigar, turning back.

'Can't you see it at all, Cathy?' He gestured hopelessly. 'Or can't you at least try and see it from my side? If anything, the fact that Julie's involved makes it all the more vital that I continue. Before there was cause, yes, but mainly a journalistic one – and then of course the plight of this Swiss banker. But now it's *personal*. It's different. It's down to you and me – and Julie.' Daniel held her gaze, willing the message home.

'What I'm trying to say is that, well . . . earlier I could have given it up because it didn't mean that much to me, not with *everything* . . .' Daniel lapsed into momentary silence. He looked down at the table. 'In retrospect, I wish I'd taken your original advice; but it's too late for that now.'

Catherine wiped at her tears, and Daniel tentatively reached for her hand – but she pulled it away. The silence of unspoken thoughts hung in the air.

'What does Julie want?' she asked at length.

'She wants to know, too.'

'You always were closer to her,' Catherine remarked flatly. 'I suppose it's natural that she would follow your wishes.'

'No, I don't think so this time. It's more her natural curiosity.'

'Yes. She gets that from you, too.'

Daniel let the comment pass and tapped his cigar into the ashtray. 'Do you now understand better why?'

'Another lost cause, is that it?'

'What was that?' he snapped.

'It doesn't matter. Forget it.' Catherine appeared to apply more serious thought to his question, at the same time gathering her composure. 'Perhaps I understand only one thing. That you'll do what the hell you like anyway, regardless of what I say.'

She contemplated him coldly, and then they both looked around; there were sounds from the hallway.

Daniel had thought it best that Julie stay upstairs while he confronted her mother, but Julie had chosen to of her own accord. Now their raised voices had obviously drawn her downstairs. Neither of them was sure exactly how long she'd been standing here. Daniel was the first to break the silence.

'I suppose we'd better be going,' he said rather stiffly, standing up. 'I'll take Julie down to the cottage now. I might as well – it will save possible complications.'

'Complications' could have meant the police, Catherine thought, but with what had passed in their conversation she thought it more likely that Daniel was eager to get Julie away from her influence.

They stood in an awkward triangle for another moment before Daniel paced away. Julie stood looking at her mother, the words in her mind – except for a simple 'Goodbye' – suddenly lost. Then at length she followed.

It was the same every time lately, Daniel cursed inwardly: Catherine gave no concessions, apart from a few grudging agreements; each time they reached an impasse.

Julie didn't speak for the first half of their journey to the cottage at Peasemore.

Daniel talked superficially of minor things: where the frying pans were kept . . . the local shops if she ran out of anything . . . the nearest farms. He could tell that she was working her way round to saying something, but each small comment of his seemed to push the thought away.

When she did eventually get around to it, her voice held a simple finality that didn't seem to require an answer.

'She's lonely, you realize.'

Daniel was silent for a moment.

'How did you know?'

'I didn't know, exactly. It was more a case of guessing – of reading between the lines. Why? Was there any reason I should have known?'

'No, I suppose not.'

Julie looked ahead at the passing hedgerows and a group of cyclists they had to weave around.

'It was this letter she wrote. I guessed from that.'

'Yes, I knew she'd written.'

'But not that something was wrong?'

Daniel faltered, thinking for a moment. 'I suppose I *am* guilty on that score. I did know, but what with everything, there wasn't much I could do about it.'

'I'm sorry. I've touched a sore point.'

'No, no, it's alright. You'd have known in the end, anyway.' Daniel thought back to their heated breakfast conversation, eight days ago now, and was suddenly curious to know what had been in the letter. 'Did she hint at anything in particular — offer any explanation?'

'No, it wasn't that so much.' Julie's eyes roamed for a second, searching for the right words.' 'It was just the tone of the letter. It was so . . . so *lost*, is the only way I can describe it. On the surface it was just a pleasant chit-chat letter. But the undercurrent was so defeatist, almost hopelessly resigned.' Julie looked down slightly, then towards him. 'I might be wrong, Dad – and I'm sorry if I've put my foot in it – but I took it as a cry for help.'

They were entering the main square at Newbury, and the streets were busy with traffic and later-afternoon shoppers. They edged their way through them slowly. Daniel pondered on what Julie had said.

'I think you're right. That's half the trouble. Of late your mother has taken a dislike to my work – or rather, I should say, the hours that it dictates. In fact, she didn't want me to go on this assignment in the first place, so you can imagine where things stand now, after *this* turn-out.'

'I see,' Julie said blankly. 'What are you going to do about her?'

'I don't know. To be honest, since the whole thing came to the surface, I've been too preoccupied with this investigation. And right now I'm more concerned about you.'

Julie fell silent and looked away, as if suddenly the realization had come back to her.

Daniel felt a pang of guilt at what he'd just said. He knew all too well that he'd found plenty of time to think of one person . . . *Leorah.* But he pushed his thoughts abruptly back to current concerns. Julie's description of the killer by the river: blond hair, angular features, six foot plus, fawn windcheater. Was that enough to start a trace through the wire service? Or perhaps through their agencies, if police channels could be avoided? He looked towards her with a mixture of concern and reassurance, but she was still turned away – and it suddenly struck him how selfless she was, to even think of her mother at a time like this, when she was in so much danger.

During the drive back from the cottage, Daniel stopped at a phone-box near Reading to put a call through to Rolf Nabens. He'd already phoned early that morning, arranging to call back, so Nabens was expecting him.

'Anything yet?' Daniel enquired.

'Afraid so,' Nabels said. 'Came through almost an hour ago.'

Daniel took a pen and pad out of his inside pocket. 'Okay, fire away.'

'Well, they've made the connection between the boy Xavier and the bomb that killed Reiner: same plastic explosive, carbon markings, etcetera. Reiner's wife, Piai also remembers the package having a Paris postmark – so it's pretty conclusive. The police had all this a few hours ago, apparently, so when they released it, it came through with a pile of other stuff.'

'Anything about Julie?'

'Yes. You'd better hold tight, Danny – almost all of it. That was what I was getting to. As soon as the police went to the University, they made the connection between Xavier and Julie – and when they discovered she was missing, they put out a bulletin on her. At present, it seems their interest in her ranges between a 'helping us with our enquiries' line and a 'missing persons' enquiry. So it's hard to tell what they *really* think at this stage.'

'Who's involved? Just the Paris police?'

'No. Not at the fountainhead. It's been passed down to the Surété for the Paris end of things; but Interpol are running the show. The Swiss involvement alone would dictate that, but they're billing it as an 'international terrorist enquiry', so the early noises aren't good, Danny. They're going big on this one; we're getting more each time on the wire.

'When will it be in the papers?'

'Paris and provincial France probably tonight. We'll have it along with the rest of Europe in tomorrow's edition. But be careful, Danny. The police have got hold of a photo of Julie from the University records, and have been circulating copies of it. The story isn't prominent enough here yet to warrant a photo in any of our papers. In fact the whole thing will be lucky to get a quarter column on page nine. But I think in France it will be a different story.'

The background clatter of the newsroom became more prominent, and Nabens' voice faded slightly. 'Oh yes, okay, okay . . . I'll catch you later . . .' Then he came back. 'An Inspector Laboille is heading the investigation, if it's of any interest to you.' He paused. 'And there's something else you should think on as well, Danny. It might not be long before Scotland Yard have got hold of this, the way things are going. And if that happens, it will have more prominence in the papers here. Then you'll have to be doubly careful.'

'It's alright, I've already taken precautions. I've got Julie safe. But thanks for letting me in on it all, Rolf. I'll do the same for you some day.'

'Let's hope you don't have to.'

The reports came in mostly to the local Surété *gendarmeries*, and were routed to the Surété headquarters on Rue de Prony; then, in turn, to Inspector Laboille's Interpol office in St Cloud. He made a side report to the Police Judiciaire.

One of the first to arrive was from a patron of the Bar Roussillon who had reognized Julie from her photograph on page five of *L'Express*. It wasn't often that good-looking young girls came into the bar. On questioning, he described the man with her as of heavy build, fifty to fifty-five, with grey curly hair and wearing a large sheepskin coat. 'Could have been an older lover or a close friend,' he commented.

The taxi driver who had run Daniel and Julie the last lap to Le Touquet airfield also noticed the newspaper photograph. But he had only recently had a major rift with his wife over a supposed flirtation with one of his passengers, and the incident was still strong in his mind; the fact that he had even noticed this young, blonde English girl could only lead to problems. He laid the newspaper over on the seat and threaded back into the late evening traffic. He hoped that nothing else appeared about the story; then he could rest easy with the decision he had made.

12

Daniel Grade was still in London. His travels, traced on a map, looked like part of a spider's web: London to Zürich, then Beirut, Zürich again . . . then the sudden nighttime hop from France. He was trying to decide where to go next, which place offered him the most hope.

He separated the elements again, in the same way he had done only days before in Zürich.

Only two leads now remained: Al-Ben Salmad, the financier involved in the arms shipments who had likely betrayed Al-Hakim and Khourem; and Kent Ehnbridt, the shabby investigator who had followed and watched him in Beirut. Both could probably lead him to the source; but which would be the better bet? Or, more to the point, which would be more easily traced?

Then there was the killer who had chased Julie in Paris, but for him there was only a description, not a fixed identity, so he discarded the option of tracing him.

He suddenly remembered that with all the excitement he had forgotten to ask Nabens if there was anything yet on Al-Ben Salmad. He had asked for a trace on his last contact with Nabens from Zürich. He felt fairly sure that if there had been anything new, Nabens would have raised it without prompting, but all the same he should check.

It seemed ludicrous that he was even having to make this choice of destination – a choice on which could hinge the life of his daughter. *God*, if only he'd known – been able to foresee – before he'd become too involved. For once, Catherine had been right. But how *could* he have known? From an investigation which, until now, had only been unusual due to its size and lack of apparent answers?

Two days, and everything had changed. It was all like a bad dream. First Reiner, then Xavier . . . *now Julie*.

He recognized the change within himself. Before, he had been methodical, calm in his planning. But now his thoughts were fractured, confused – and at times he could feel the dangerous emotions of vengeance and fearful protectiveness taking control, pushing him towards an ill-judged action. So now, as in the wretched hours past, he fought against them, willing his mind back to the issue at hand: a decision.

Al-Ben Salmad or Kent Ehnbridt?

Without doubt, if there was no further information on Al-Ben Salmad, then Ehnbridt – as a registered Zürich investigator – would be easier to trace. Beyond that, nothing else came to him immediately.

He would phone Nabens back and let the outcome guide his decision: whether he stayed in London – where Salmad had last been reported – or booked a flight to Zürich.

'You can pick him up on the train. At Feldkirch.'

'Okay. Anything else?'

'No. Only Ehnbridt. You should see to it that . . .'

'We've already discussed that,' Jaalgen interrupted harshly. 'My plans are already laid.'

'I see. Then that is all.'

Jaalgen put the phone down without saying goodbye, and started packing.

Kent Ehnbridt wasn't the easiest person to trace. By necessity, investigators form one of the most secretive professional cliques. Each one seems protective towards the other, whether they work within the same agency or not. A bond of non-related, distant cousins.

Daniel Grade had been in Zürich for over five hours. At first he'd thought it a good idea: he would simply pick the name of an investigative agency at random from the yellow pages, phone, and ask for Kent Ehnbridt. If Ehnbridt didn't work there, they might know which agency he did work for. If there was no luck there, try another. There was almost a page and a half of them. He'd tried Semleche and Bunt first, because of his already established contact with them, but they'd been unable to help.

Grade was on his seventeenth agency. The responses were varied: most were vague, some were defensive and questioning, and a few were plain hostile and rude, but only one so far had slammed down the receiver mid-sentence. Grade's limited German obviously didn't help, but in some cases people would sense his awkwardness and quickly switch to English.

The eighteenth call bore fruit; the girl at the other end

mentioned the name of the agency Ehnbridt worked for – Lanenkreil – before she asked who was calling.

Grade said something about an English relative.

'I didn't know he had any English relatives.'

'No. You probably wouldn't.'

Grade put the phone down. He had neither the time nor patience to bow himself out with niceties.

But he would have to be more patient and convincing on the next call.

Grade looked up the number and dialled it. A man's voice answered 'Lanenkreil', and asked who was calling.

Grade ignored this. 'Hello. I'd like to speak to Herr Ehnbridt, please.'

'*Who* is calling please?' The voice was more insistent.

'He is working on a private contract for me, and my name was never disclosed, so will mean nothing to him. Everything was handled through my lawyers –' Grade was running his hand down the *Advocats* column in the yellow pages – 'Becker and Freunleitz.'

There was a short silence.

'I would like to speak to him *now*, if I may,' Grade pressed.

'I'm sorry . . .' the voice stumbled slightly. 'Herr Ehnbridt is out of the city right now.'

'Could you tell me then where I could locate him? This is a matter of some urgency.'

There was another silence, then the turning of papers and the conferring of background voices.

After a moment. 'He is on an assignment, you know.' But it was a lame protest; very obviously he was split between giving information to an unknown caller and upsetting a major client who had come through one of the city's largest law firms.

Grade didn't answer, and the unsettling silence made the decision for the man. He gave Grade the address where Ehnbridt could be found – in Villach, Austria.

Grade wrote it down. He made a last concession to politeness. 'I'll try not to drag him away from his assignment too long. Thank you.'

He rang off and looked at the map of Switzerland at the front of the directory, split into coding areas and showing its border with Austria. The main Austrian towns were marked. Villach? What was the best way of getting there?

Three telephone calls later he had the answer. By train. There was no direct flight service.

The express left at 10.20 and at 16.42, and stopped at Feldkirch, Innsbruck and Mallnitz.

The nightmare was in motion – fragmented.

A wheel was turning and someone was shaking him, saying, 'Julie is dead. *Dead*!' And he started to cry and run and try to find her – but no sounds came from his crying or his footsteps on the dark lonely streets that extended like caverns around him. He chose one and ran into it. He saw her blonde hair straight away . . . it moved towards him quickly from the end of the street, and he was over her, looking at the back of her hair, turning her body over to face him . . .

But as he touched her, he felt the warmth and life tingle through his fingers, and he knew that she was alive – *alive*. But there was something wrong. The eyes! The eyes weren't Julie's, they were Leorah's. The *face* was Leorah's. And the hair wasn't blonde but dark brown, almost black, hanging to her waist . . . and she was reaching for him, whispering '*Lover*' . . . and clutching him in warmth and wetness that burnt through his loins to his very stomach.

He was sinking, *sinking* into that warmth . . . that fiery pit. Her eyes were red. 'Oh, lover'. He was inside and yet beyond her, mingling . . . their spirits wrestling in the dark cavern. *No*, it was a street. Then it was the clear, azure air; they were floating; but the darkness returned quickly, surrounding him, warm then searingly hot. Her arms were wrapped around him, and her legs were so high that he felt his whole body arching through her, as if into a liquid and bottomless lake full of treasures. Golden treasures. Glinting in the sun.

But a man was hoarding the treasure and yet another was

running towards him, faceless and wearing a fawn wind-cheater . . . And he struggled to look into that face, to recognize it – but knew that he never could.

The other had his back towards him, grappling and struggling with the treasures, and he looked at him, willing him to turn around . . . and in that instant the sun caught the glint of the man's spectacles. The man was looking directly towards him without having moved. The glint died and he saw the colour of the eyes . . . the *face* . . . it was Schaarer.

The eyes held him transfixed – first with their soulfulness, then their malevolence . . . and he didn't notice the object of treasure held high by Schaarer – a golden arc with a face on it – until it cleaved down swiftly, scything through their naked, coupled bodies.

Daniel Grade woke up with a jolt. He was sweating.

It took him a moment to clear his mind and assimilate where he was. He sat up and looked out the window. He cupped one hand against the glass both to steady himself against the rocking of the train and to cut down the reflected interior light. Thick-grouped forest firs flashed by, followed by a succession of fields in neat oblongs. Nothing to pinpoint where they were.

The compartment was empty. There had been an elderly woman opposite before he'd fallen asleep, but now she was gone. Probably for a drink, or to a sleeper. Daniel rubbed his eyes.

Whether it was because of the dream or not, he didn't know, but he found himself thinking of another element. Perhaps Schaarer somehow knew that the evidence would finally point to him, so had created a ruse with Reiner and a falsely registered car to make it look as if he was being wrongly indicated. But what about the shares tradings? They had pointed away from Schaarer. That had been the main link, his only indicator all along . . . His chain of thought faltered: what if it was something else? Another motive would throw a completely different light on it all. *Then* it could be Schaarer – probably was.

He would confront Ehnbridt, and Ehnbridt would look at

him stupidly, and say, 'But I've already told you. It's Schaarer.'

Another motive?

The motive of a shift of banking funds had been with him from the start, since that first day with Reiner – and he had applied so much thought and planning to it that it seemed inconceivable now that it could possibly be anything else.

He stared blankly at some distant, passing lights. He felt suddenly lost, like a man who has walked a certain path and only then discovered that it might be the wrong one – but had already invested so much time and energy that he doesn't know if he can manage the new route. Even if he *could* turn back.

Or was it just that? Was it perhaps that he'd have as little assurance of success with a new motive, even if he did pinpoint it? He didn't know. Only that his inner instinct kept urging him on that same path. One failure he could afford. But two? He would need *time* for two, failure or success. *Time* which he didn't have. Perhaps that was it.

The same thoughts stayed in his mind for a while – until he was suddenly aware of the changing tone of the train's ricketing progress. He looked up.

The lights outside were slowing gradually, some of them bright and very close to the train. Then the train jerked slightly before the final braking.

It was one of the three stops, but the board announcing it stood at the far end of the platform. From the size of the town, he felt sure it was Innsbruck.

Jaalgen was alone in his compartment. He drew the blinds nearly all the way down and switched on one of the small reading lights.

The corridor outside had been busy during the dinner period, but now for nearly half an hour it had been quiet. The quartz on Jaalgen's watch glowed in the semi-darkness: 10.12 p.m. He started making the final preparations. They had just stopped at Innsbruck, and would be reaching the high passes of the Hohe Tauern within minutes.

Vruger's stipulation that it appear an accident had proved the worst obstacle of all. If it wasn't for that, he could have stepped briskly into Grade's compartment with a silenced gun and finished the job almost at any time since he had boarded the train. The waiting annoyed him, but at the same time steeled his nerves for action.

Grade's compartment was two away – but the one between was empty and, with the comparative silence of the last hour, he could pick out the slightest sound: pacing, coughing, the door or shutters being opened . . . He would know if Grade left the carriage again, or started walking about.

An hour and a half before, he had been checking through the same compartment. He had waited till Grade went to dinner, double-checked by looking into the dining car – then he had gone to work. It was a standard seating compartment, with the blinds drawn to leave only a few inches at the bottom. He drew them completely shut. He'd worked out that he should have at least a safe twenty minutes: it had taken two minutes to rifle through Grade's small overnight suitcase; he'd found a notebook. There was too much in it to take stock of quickly, but he'd written down the address inside the cover. Probably Grade's home. It would be the most obvious place to look for the girl. Another six minutes was taken up getting the right mix of putty in the door latch: enough to hold it steady, though anything more than the slightest weight would send the door swinging open. He fixed the blinds in their original position before he left.

Now it was just a matter of finding the right moment. He wanted to be able to push Grade easily, catching him off balance, so it would have to be done while he was standing up or pacing about. Any one of the high passes would ensure a fatal fall. If he encountered resistance, he would try for a heart or lung puncture with his stiletto, and hope that the fall would disguise the mark.

The train slowed slightly as it negotiated the curved approaches to the bridge parapets. Jaalgen looked out of the window. It was rare that he travelled on a train. He remembered being on a train once with his father, in 1943, just after the occupation. The train was full of local peasants, and he recalled how his father pointed out the few German soldiers on board, remarking how fine they looked in their uniforms; how much it put them above the masses. Although his father was a sympathizer, he could never wear a uniform; it was too dangerous because of the strength of the local resistance, and this had rankled with him. He wanted badly to wear a uniform. The emotion seemed laughable now, but at the time he could understand it: that need to belong, to feel special, apart from the masses. In his own way, he was now doing the same. Though that had never been totally his own choice: by design and fate, the world had set him apart long ago – even if he had wanted to turn back.

Jaalgen's attention returned quickly to the alert: there was some movement, the jangling of keys as someone passed, then the door of Grade's compartment slid open. But there was no sound of him moving out into the corridor. Jaalgen sat very still for a moment. He would wait till he heard the door close again, then make his move.

Grade opened the compartment window slightly to let out some of his cigar smoke. The window gave easily, and he was about to look out when the jangling of keys in the corridor caught his attention. If it was one of the stewards, he could ask if the bar was still open. He could do with a Scotch.

Grade slid open the door and looked out. It was only a passenger – an elderly man jangling the change in his pocket as he passed. He looked round briefly as Grade's door opened, before disappearing through the communicating door to the next carriage.

Grade slid his door shut.

A split second, and the door slid wildly open again. Grade had already half turned – and looked back to see a dark figure rushing towards him. He felt the air leave his body in a gasp as the solid weight hit him before he could think what was happening – and he was thrown backwards, his feet shuffling wildly for balance.

He managed to steady himself partially, and was relying on the outer door close behind to support him completely. But he felt only a slight jolt as he connected, then the door swung free and he was falling out into the night . . .

He felt the rush of air around him, and glimpsed part of the bridge framework swinging above him, or was it to one side? And then something hard cut into his chest.

His eyes closed involuntarily in terror, then opened to see another bridge support pass him in a flash. Another motion, and he found himself looking straight at the wheels and the underside of the train. His stomach churned, but it wasn't the same sensation as falling.

Electrical sparks flashed out at him, and the thundering of wheels and the hiss of steam was deafening.

Then he realized what had happened. Because he had half turned, he had been caught sideways in the half-open window, sliding it the rest of the way down, its rim cutting into his chest, as the door burst open. Now his weight was supported on the door as it swung wildly out towards the parapets – at times pulling slightly in as it was buffeted by the airstream of the train and the wind rushing up from the valley passes far below. He clung desperately to the window frame and the cool metal of the outside door panel.

He looked back up. The dark figure filled the door frame, silhouetted against the interior light. Its head was covered by a ski-mask; he could see only the eyes and mouth. The trousers were black and it was wearing a windcheater . . . *a fawn windcheater*!

Grade noticed then that one of his ankles was still on the stepping board, and the figure was leaning out, trying to kick it away.

Grade knew immediately that if his attacker succeeded, he was lost; he could sense that his present balance partly depended on that ankle. With his bulky weight, he could hold on only seconds without that support.

He fought to swing back in on the door, levering on his

ankle and hoping that the airstream buffeting him didn't wrench him back out again. Some of the steel bridge frames passed perilously close as the train rocked. The dark void of the valley below swayed sickeningly.

Jaalgen saw immediately what Grade was trying to do. He was cursing now, impatient to finish things. This stocky, overweight Englishman should have been an easy target. He leaned over and grappled the leg with one hand, trying to push it out and away . . . and saw his mistake too late. The other foot rose swiftly, striking him in the face. He fell back – his nose bleeding under the mask.

It was a calculated risk. Grade now feared that this action might push him even further out – but now his ankle was released. He hooked it around the door frame and started to pull himself in. He prayed that he had the time and space to make it.

Jaalgen was quickly back on his feet. He lunged at Grade's body as it swung back into the compartment on the door.

Grade didn't trust himself to stand, knowing that he'd make an easy target, and fell to a kneeling position as Jaalgen came at him again. He felt a foot strike him in the chest, but managed to keep his balance. In response he head-butted forward and felt it connect just below the man's groin.

The figure fell back slightly – and Grade knew then that he had the advantage in weight.

Jaalgen pulled out his stiletto. It flashed in an arc.

Grade parried Jaalgen's arm, but felt the blade slice his shoulder. He struck out with his other fist and caught the man a glancing blow to the chin. The blade retracted; Grade saw blood on its tip. He knew then that he'd been wounded, but dared not look to see how badly. His eyes locked on his opponent . . *those cold blue eyes*. He searched for the messages there: how they corresponded to the movement of the knife arm.

The man was fast, obviously a good athlete, but in this enclosed space Grade sensed that his own weight and his fighting prowess must count for something. *Age takes the steam out of your footwork, not your punches*, he recalled from his old trainer.

The blade flashed in again. Grade ducked down and back. The sound of rushing air came from behind. He realized he was very close to the open door again. He gripped the door frame to steady himself.

Jaalgen sensed an advantage. He came in close, gripping one hand under Grade's chin, forcing his head back. He swung the knife in with his other hand.

Grade saw the blade coming low, but was trapped against the door frame, his upper body half out of the train. He brought one leg up in protection, the only action left to him. He felt the blade bounce off the bone of his knee, breaking skin and grazing along his thigh.

'Cunt,' he hissed, Jaalgen's grip under his chin forcing the exclamation through clenched teeth.

The swaying image of the parapets and the valley floor lay below him again; they were now at the mid-section of the bridge, the highest point, and the lights of a small village twinkled like stars below.

Jaalgen's blade came in a blur. Grade felt it slice across one of his fingers gripping the frame. He slipped back a bit, his feet almost losing their grip. He knew that if the blade caught him again, he couldn't hang on.

He struck out with a right-hand punch and felt it connect with the solid bone of Jaalgen's cheek. Visible shock showed in Jaalgen's eyes. Grade recovered his balance in that moment.

Jaalgen shook his head slightly, then leapt forwards again, aiming the stiletto at Grade's face. Grade parried cleanly and countered with a low body punch. Jaalgen heaved slightly as it connected, staggering to one side. One hand held his stomach as he came forward again.

Grade parried again, but he felt the blade snag his jacket. Jaalgen gripped onto his arm, and for a moment they were locked, the blade inching closer. Then, without warning, Jaalgen wrenched free, snaking the blade in under the arm.

Grade weaved, dodging it by only a fraction, and got in another good body punch.

Jaalgen's eyes were bloodshot. His step was uncertain as he wheeled back round.

Grade hit him full on the nose. He felt the bone crack, and the figure swayed slightly. The stiletto was held loosely at waist level. Grade swung up quickly with an uppercut, then stepped aside.

Jaalgen tottered by the open doorway.

For a moment, Grade was undecided.

There was the question of information, but he sensed things had already gone too far for that. Besides the knowledge that this was almost certainly the same man that had killed Reiner and Xavier and had threatened Julie's life made him suddenly thirsty for vengeance. Yet Grade had never been known for a 'killer instinct' in fights – that ability to take out opponents when already half-finished . . .

Jaalgen made one final, hopeful lunge with the stiletto – and made the decision for him.

'Cunt,' Grade spat again, and before the arc of the blade reached him, he brought his fist full and hard into Jaalgen's face, sending him spinning out of the open doorway and into the night.

He saw the body clear the parapets and start spiralling down, swallowed within seconds by the darkness of the void below.

13

Villach is a picturesque old Austrian town, but like many towns it has an industrial section. In Villach it straggles along the river Drau, much of it comprising timber yards and related industries.

Daniel was directed to this area after showing Ehnbridt's address to his hotel porter. He felt faintly sick in the back of the taxi heading there – though unsure if it was the Bratwurst and sausage sandwich he'd grabbed before hailing his taxi, or the horrific events earlier.

At the station he had dived into the men's room to tend to his injuries. The shoulder wound was superficial; the cut on his finger more serious. It would need some stitches when he had the time. He put a thick wad of toilet paper on his shoulder and wrapped some more around his finger.

It was late, almost midnight, but Grade had the feeling that he couldn't afford to waste any time. He had to get to Ehnbridt at soon as possible – though now he wasn't sure any more exactly what was driving him on.

Now the main threat had gone – but he just didn't feel the surge of relief that he should. Or was it that the urge to know the truth had been strongest all the time – and he was only now realizing it? The journalist's lifeblood – the one thing that he had vowed to keep apart from the other portions of his life – had finally taken control. Had Catherine been right all along? *No – not with Julie in danger. Never Julie*. He shook his head.

He was still in a daze from it all – finding it impossible to focus. Everything had happened so quickly.

Earlier, it had struck him that his assailant on the train might have left some clue to his identity. He had studied the compartments nearby – discarding those occupied – and had come upon a small hold-all two doors away. Inside was a change of clothes and a washbag. No passport, no papers, and no wallet. He threw it out the window. He'd already removed the putty from his door lock; till he decided whether or not to report the incident to the police, it was best if no evidence remained. He still wasn't sure where things stood regarding Julie. Besides, the investigation and questioning would hold him up unnecessarily.

The taxi had now slowed, and Daniel became aware that the driver was speaking.

'*Hier ist es*. Kralsenbruck apartments.'

Grade looked out. The taxi had halted in front of a dull, greying building backing onto the river.

'Oh, yes. Okay.' He got out and paid, then made his way across.

The street was quiet after the taxi had pulled away, except for the pounding of a paper mill a few hundred yards downstream.

It was a large block of small self-catering apartments. The company that had hired Ehnbridt probably owned or kept one at their disposal. From the front parking lot, Grade judged that most were used by companies for their representatives and long-distance delivery drivers travelling through.

In the lobby, Grade turned on the lights for the stairwell, which operated on a time-switch. He judged that *408* was on the fourth floor, and made his way up. The lights went out again as he passed the third floor. Some half-light filtered from the skylight of a flat below, and Grade groped his way along to the next switch. A row of dome-covered bulbs came on. He started counting his way along . . . *408* was fifth in from the stairwell.

Grade pressed the bell. No answer. After a minute, he rapped hard on the door, and waited. The sound of the pounding mill came back to him through a window behind. Still no answer.

He leant closer to the door; there was no movement discernible inside.

It was then that he noticed something odd about the door: part of the wood around the lock was split. The lights went out, so he pressed the time-switch again.

Grade turned back to the lock. Delicately, he pushed the area around it. It started to give way. Putting his shoulder against the door, he pushed more firmly – and the door opened. He held it a foot ajar and looked in. The room was dark, except for some faint orange light filtering through from a street-lamp outside.

He didn't want to turn on the light, which might alert any neighbours who knew of Ehnbridt's movements, so he edged cautiously through the near-darkness. After a moment, he could make out a low table and a bed by the far wall.

It struck him that someone had made an earlier, uninvited

visit – but not immediately why. He started looking for signs of disturbance: ransacked drawers, upset clothes or papers? There were none. Everything looked neat, in its place. Except the bed; the sheets and blankets were in disarray, parts of them trailing onto the floor. Grade moved further into the room.

The light from the hallway picked out a shape on the bed, under the sheets – quite large. Grade froze. There was someone in the bed. A part of the face showed above the sheet, pressed hard into the pillow. It was Ehnbridt! Ehnbridt was asleep. No. Grade noticed the uncomfortable angles of the legs and arms, and a chill touched him. Tentatively he reached out and drew the sheet back.

Ehnbridt's body looked unmarked. He shook the shoulder gently, but Ehnbridt lay limp. Grade heaved the body over. The mark was small, almost unnoticeable – a puncture in the side of the neck, from which a thin trail of blood flowed into his collar and onto the pillow.

Grade drew the sheet back over the face and turned away. He shut his eyes to blot out the image. He was too late again – the man on the train *had* got there before him. But what of the time factor? He looked again at the wound. Ehnbridt's blood looked only recently to have coagulated – he must have been dead only a few hours. How could the man have made it back to catch that train?

A sound came from inside the room. Grade stood very still. His mind raced to grasp what it could be, and in that frantic moment the only thing that occurred to him was that Ehnbridt wasn't quite dead. He looked back, but the body lay still.

Somebody else was in the room.

Another sound came, then some movement. It was still indistinct, but Grade pinned it down to the darker part of the room, just beyond the faint orange pool of light from the window. He concentrated hard: the sound of his own breathing and heartbeat came back to him, and the pounding mill outside seemed louder – but nothing more.

The silence persisted, and Grade coughed slightly to

relieve his nerves. Then, without warning, there was a rapid shuffling as something flew at him from out of the darkness. A flash of gleaming silver, turning to orange . . . *a stiletto.*

Grade side-stepped, and in that instant saw the face behind the thin knife in the orange beam: a small man, middle-aged, his face heavily cragged. Grade stepped back a pace, trying to draw him into the harsher light coming in from the corridor.

Grade suddenly realized how stupid he'd been. He should have thought of it: the man on the train had an accomplice. That explained the timing: his own attack and the one on Ehnbridt had been dealt with separately.

The small man leapt forward surprisingly fast. Grade saw him clearly . . . The corridor lights went out; he was lost again in shadow. The stiletto flashed in the darkness.

Grade dodged, and punched out with his right – but it connected only with air. Another flash. Grade saw it at the last second, weaving swiftly and striking out again, and he hit something solid – with the feel of stiff material covering. He'd probably caught the man on the shoulder or arm.

Grade recognized his own terrible disadvantage. The small man had been sitting in the darkness for some while, and his eyes were accustomed to it. Whereas he himself had been there only minutes, and it was fearfully disconcerting striking out blindly at an opponent who you knew could probably see you quite clearly.

The blade flickered in, and Grade parried; then it came in from the other side, and he side-stepped and swung out at the air again. Grade felt defeated. He *had* to get to the light switch.

The thin blade came in a straight lunge, and Grade backed up and used the extra yard to swing around and try for the open door and the switch . . . And in the split-instant that he reached out and took his eyes off the small man, the blade reached him, going deep into his arm. The blade was pulled out smartly, rising above him again.

But Grade was suddenly curious . . . curious to see who his killer was . . . and he reached out the last inch and switched on the light . . . And he wondered vaguely why the small man didn't finish it – get it over and done with.

The numbness in his arm was spreading through his body, and he felt something burning at the back of his eyes and noticed in the harsh light that it no longer looked like a knife, but more like a needle. And he thought: *Julie*! I must warn Julie. Then the small man's face came closer, his eyes staring intently, and the line of corridor lights swayed lazily down into a dark and hollow horizon . . .

The Arab man in the *thobe* looked thoughtfully at the two men before him.

'I am now satisfied that this British journalist, Daniel Grade, is acting in our interests.'

One of the men nodded, although he understood little of the reasoning behind this conclusion.

'Al-Ben Salmad is now our main concern. Has he been located?'

'Yes. He is in London.'

'You have an address, or know of his movements?'

'Yes.'

The man in the *thobe* looked down briefly. 'Then there is little else to discuss. Report to me as soon as possible.'

Both men nodded slightly, lowering their eyes in respect and accord as they stood up. They made their way to the door.

Outside, one of them – the newest recruit – turned to the other and asked why the man inside never left his chair. In all of their visits, he had never seen him move or walk about, or found him in any other part of the rambling villa.

'It is a long story,' his colleague answered. 'In part, it is why we are here now, doing what we are doing. I will tell you . . .'

A tap was dripping somewhere behind him.

The room was large: a pantry-style kitchen with rough-hewn cabinets and worktops. A heavy wooden trestle table stood at its centre, and the floor was of rough flagstone with a tile surround. Daniel rested his elbows on the table and shook his head wearily. He sipped at the cup of steaming coffee before him.

The first surprise had come half an hour before – to realize, awakening, that he was still alive. The second was to find the small man sitting opposite the bench he'd been laid on, smiling in a friendly manner, with a touch of concern, and pouring some coffee for him.

Further surprises had come as the small man introduced himself and began to speak. His name was Art Swenkel of the Ha Mossad, the Israeli secret service. The Ha Mossad had been aware of Grade's activities and movements since his first contact with Reiner. Swenkel had guessed that Grade was trying to track Ehnbridt, and had himself hoped to reach Ehnbridt before Jaalgen. He was sorry about the unorthodox approach, but had a favour to ask.

Jaalgen? . . . The man on the train? The rest of it was still vague though, almost ridiculous . . . *Israeli secret service*? Perhaps he was still dreaming. He was sure he would have made some sharp comment if his head didn't feel so heavy – but, apart from his outward amiability, Swenkel didn't look the sort to appreciate oblique humour.

'Where are we?'

'Near Vienna. It was the closest safe-house.'

'Oh . . . I see.' Daniel looked around thoughtfully for a moment. 'Why the attack, then?'

'I'm sorry. I couldn't be fully sure who you were in the dark. The only photo we have of you is from years back. You look much fatter now.'

'Thank you.' Daniel forced a smile. He looked over at the guilty needle laying on the far worktop.

'Don't worry,' said Swenkel. 'I knew what I was doing. I was a medic in the Israeli army for almost four years. There's just a trace of pethidine mixed with hyoscine in the syringe – a common anaesthetic.'

Daniel rubbed his arm. 'That's reassuring.'

'While you were under, I also took the opportunity of stitching your finger.'

Daniel almost laughed, but Swenkel looked serious. 'Thanks,' Daniel said. He was unsure whether Swenkel hadn't recognized him, or had merely used the needle to save himself being on the wrong end of a left hook. It didn't seem to matter now – but for a moment he stared Swenkel out, for the satisfaction of making him feel awkward. The hard brown eyes gave nothing away. The face itself was hard and craggy . . . *well lived in*. But there was something about the way the mouth curled up at the corners in an almost constant smile which was endearing; you couldn't help liking the man. Daniel looked away. The whole thing was getting more ridiculous . . . *Syringes*? *Safe-houses*? *Israeli agents* . . .

'Look, why have you brought me here? You mentioned Reiner . . . That you knew about my movements since my first contact with Reiner. And a favour?'

Swenkel looked troubled. He drew hard on his cigarette. 'About your daughter . . . Julie.'

'What about her?'

'We knew about Jaalgen's attack on her – and killing her boyfriend. It all came to the surface after Reiner's death – but I'm afraid we were always one step behind. There was nothing we could do to stop it. I'm sorry.'

Swenkel watched the effect on Grade and gloated inwardly; the emotion never showed on his face. Another part of him felt guilty, but it had been necessary. Now he had Grade's attention, and partly his trust.

'By the way,' Swenkel asked, 'what happened to Jaalgen? I know I couldn't have been far behind him in Villach. And I knew also that he would be trying to intercept you. What happened? Didn't he make the connection?'

'Oh, he made the connection alright.' Daniel sipped at his coffee and looked across, his eyes still slightly glazed from the drug. There were a number of ways of saying it: a slight pause, a tone of gravity – but he didn't feel either remorse or guilt – he was still too numbed. 'I killed him,' he said softly, and he watched the shock register on Swenkel's face.

'You what?'

Daniel drew breath and began to explain what had happened on the train, making it little more than a factual account. Halfway through, Swenkel whistled slowly and stood up and started pacing about. He looked anxious, his eyes darting to different points in the room as if he felt suddenly claustrophobic.

As Daniel finished, he was conscious of Swenkel eyeing him curiously.

'I don't think he knew about my past boxing experience,' Daniel said.

Swenkel smiled wryly. 'Looks like he found out the hard way.' He held his stare for a moment longer. He should tell Grade *now*. The ice had mostly broken. Swenkel moved closer to the table, fumbling with his cigarette.

'There's something you should know about Reiner,' Swenkel said. 'It goes a lot deeper than our merely following your activities since your first contact with him. You see, we engineered the whole thing from the start.'

Swenkel leaned over and laid one hand flat on the table. 'Oh no, not Zürich and the war and everything – though that's what a lot of our enemies have ended up claiming. But Reiner's involvement – and, more to the point, *your* involvement. It was all planned from day one.'

Grade was incredulous. 'Who? . . . Why? For what purpose?'

Swenkel's face clouded, as if with the new weight of his thoughts. In the silence, he walked over and turned off the dripping tap behind them.

'For the answer to that, you'd have to go back almost thirty years, to just after the war – 1948. In the same year that marked the formation of the State of Israel, Anton Reiner became a Ha Mossad agent.'

Swenkel's expression became more distant as he delved into Anton Reiner's background. Reiner's father had been a goldsmith. By religion his father was Jewish, an Italian Jew, and his mother was a Catholic. The family lived in Udine, near the Yugoslav border. With the German persecution of Jews, Anton's father, Rami, was taken to Eivari and was never seen again – presumed dead. Swenkel explained how – unlike most other religions – the Jewish religion passes through the mother, not the father, so Anton was not Jewish. Even though the Germans had their own ways of determining whether someone was of Jewish race or not, it had been enough to confuse the issue. Anton stayed in Udine. His mother died a few years later.

'That same year, 1948, Anton Reiner joined the Ha Mossad. He was only seventeen years old.'

Swenkel's eyes roamed. 'The Nazis hadn't taken one thing into account: how strong Anton's tie with his father had been. Though he wasn't Jewish, his love for his father had been such that he wished he *had* been. Perhaps he felt doubly robbed and wished to compensate. I don't know. But in the early days, he was a good agent.'

Swenkel flinched slightly at his own words. How many times had that phrase been used to describe his own career? And how different the paths that their lives had finally taken? A Boston-born son of a German Jewish father and Syrian Jewish mother, who was accepted as Syrian and rose to become Syrian Foreign Minister before returning to the fold. He had become one of the élite of the Ha Mossad, and Reiner had become a meek and mild banker, and now he had died as a result of his one major show of service. It somehow seemed unfair.

Swenkel reached out for the coffee pot and offered some to Grade.

'No thanks.'

Swenkel topped up his own cup. 'Before his father's death, Reiner had already been helping out in his goldsmith's business, and he took over the running of it afterwards – before selling out and going into banking when he left college at eighteen.' Swenkel paused. 'He had a good knowledge of finance *and* the gold industry. In this capacity, he was of use to us.

'After the war, millions of pounds' worth of Nazi gold made its way into Swiss vaults – much of it pulled from the teeth of Jews in concentration camps. You know the story – it's been well documented. I don't need to elaborate.'

Grade nodded, in silence.

'Reiner was helped as much as possible with his progress in banking circles. The right papers were produced at the right times. He got his first transfer to a Swiss bank at the age of twenty-one. We were almost there: a man on the inside – what we had always wanted. But from there it was downhill. The constitution of Swiss banking law rapidly tightened – particularly those facets relating to secrecy. Information became sporadic. We had the best of it out within the first few years, up until '57. There's been little of value since.' Swenkel tapped the ash off his cigarette into a saucer.

'So Reiner has stayed there through the years, becoming more and more immersed in the Swiss banking system, and keeping a watchful eye on our interests.' Swenkel met Grade's quizzical expression and made a dismissive motion with one hand. 'Oh, we have other people like that in various capacities, in various parts of the world, who either serve us directly or who we can use. People who wait until we call on them; *if* we ever do. Sometimes that's not necessary. With Reiner, we *did* have reason to call on his services again.'

Swenkel shook his head slowly. 'I now regret that decision. If only there'd been some other choice. Too many years had passed – he was so much a banker, so much into family life; he had a stable reputation within the community. His edge had gone.'

Swenkel was looking down at the table – and it was the first time Daniel sensed the depth of feeling in the man, some emotion behind those dark brown eyes.

'Reiner – you mentioned using him again?' Daniel prompted.

'Yes. You'll probably remember a few days ago there was a hijacking of an Israeli school bus.'

Grade had been expecting Swenkel to return to Reiner and

Zürich banking, and this threw him slightly. He looked blank for a moment.

'It was in the news.'

'Yes, yes, of course.' Daniel said quickly. He remembered now talking briefly with Leorah about it; and Nabens had mentioned it in one of his calls. How totally other things had occupied his mind.

'Well, we have a man sufficiently close to get information out of the PFLP – Habash's lot. Several weeks ago we started getting reports that the PFLP believed Israel had sparked off the war in the Lebanon through the assassination of two Muslim politicians. The assassin Gahtlav who was killed had talked carelessly to a brother. Unbeknown, that brother had a Palestinian mistress; part of her family were still in Shattilla camp. We think that's why Gahtlav was killed; the leftists caught up with him. Eventually the story worked itself back to the PFLP, but Gahtlav's mention of an 'outside' assassin led them to suspect an Israeli involvement. At the same time, we were aware of what our own intelligence was supplying – through the Maslegeisen, Al-Ben Salmad link – which implied Swiss-backed involvement.

'So we were put in the position of having to prove this Swiss rumour, in order to kill speculation as to our own involvement. That's why we contacted Reiner.' Swenkel looked directly at Grade. '*You* were selected because of your last case in Switzerland, the pharmaceutical fraud; and Leorah Ajlan because she's a left-wing Muslim and the PFLP would accept what she had to say. In addition, she's also one of the most balanced of all of them . . . if that's an appropriate word – and should, in turn, accept your views. If it came directly from us, it would be no good.' Swenkel looked down slightly, as if he was still partly in doubt about the decision.

'It was the only way around everything we could see. But we were pipped at the post by the bus hijacking. Our intelligence never predicted that.'

Daniel was still in a daze from it all. 'So . . . right from the start, you used us all?'

'Yes. I'm sorry about the involvement of your daughter, if that could have been foreseen . . . but, then again, we never expected to lose Reiner either.'

Daniel hadn't been thinking of that; but more the way they had all been woven into an intricate net. Leorah had come as the biggest surprise of all – perhaps because she seemed so independent and uncoercible, he wasn't sure.

'But Israel started the war . . . Why? For what reason?'

'There's a story of a Habash lieutenant, a man more used to riding camels than Cadillacs, jumping into his car and driving it at speed into a tree, killing himself. It was reported that *we* put a bomb in his car, because they were too proud to admit that a brave fighting man died driving like an idiot.' Swenkel waved his arm. 'Okay, that's an extreme example – but the point is they'd blame us for anything and everything if they could. Air attack in south Lebanon, it *must* be Israel. Arab minister shot, it's down to Israel. This time, though, there's some substance behind it.

'Before the Lebanese war – as the Habash story goes – Israel was alone, fighting on all its borders with hostile neighbours. But with the advent of the war, the arena moved to the Lebanon, and the war was no longer a purely Arab-Israeli conflict, but a Phalangist-Muslim one. Okay – we are still harassed by Palestinian rebels from across the border. But it's a matter of choice: it's better to have them the other side of the doorstep than within the door. Now Arab is fighting Arab, religiously and politically, and the focus of attention has shifted somewhat from Israel. A *united* Arab front against Israel no longer exists. And they have a good point . . . if only it was true.'

Swenkel clenched a fist on the table. 'That's why we've approached it the way we have. It's the sort of claim that could all too easily take hold, be accepted in the Arab world – not to mention the possible effect on world opinion if anyone in the Western alliance got hold of it. Any hope of future peace would be destroyed!' Swenkel drew a slow breath. 'And now we're up against a deadline to disclaim it, with the lives of a busload of school children at stake.'

'That was their demand – that you claim responsibility?'

'Yes,' Swenkel said flatly.

Grade thought it was a like a giant jigsaw that he'd been working on for days, without success; and suddenly Swenkel had come along and said, 'Here. Here's how it should be', and rearranged it and laid it all out in minutes. But a few pieces still didn't quite fit into place.

'What about Schaarer? Why did Reiner indict him? Surely that would only further damage the peace initiative?'

'You'll recall that Reiner didn't give you that straight away. Only when you pressed him. You see, already in Reiner's enquiries Schaarer's name had come up – but Reiner believed it to be a false accusation. But when, after a while, you'd come up with nothing, he thought he should give it to you. Because at least then you might discover who was falsely indicting Schaarer – if that *was* the case. Either way, it should lead you to whoever was behind it all.'

'Is it possible that it actually could be Schaarer?'

'Yes, I'm afraid so.'

'There was something else that doesn't quite add up.' Daniel cast his mind back to Semleche and Bunt's report. 'Reiner bought quite a large batch of SBECSA shares and then re-sold them. Why was that?'

'Reiner expected a promotion. It's normal procedure, once you become a director, to increase your share stake in the company. The promotion didn't come through, and so he re-sold them. It's as simple as that.'

As simple as that, Daniel thought ironically. It had almost led to him indicting Reiner falsely. 'And involving Xavier and Julie through the letter bomb – where does that fit in?'

'We can't be sure . . . but it looks as if whoever is behind it all is afraid of what you might find out – or have already found out – and wants to discredit you. Your credibility as a journalist – at least on this case – could be on a short time-fuse.'

'I thought it might be that,' Daniel said emptily.

'I've seen some of the French newspaper stories on your daughter,' Swenkel said. 'It doesn't look good.'

'I know.'

Now the puzzle was complete . . . Reiner, Schaarer, Xavier, Leorah Ajlan . . . *everything*. Except *who*? Daniel knocked back the last of his coffee and looked thoughtfully into the empty cup.

'At least Jaalgen's now out of the way,' Swenkel remarked. 'That's one factor we no longer have to worry about. Your daughter is safe.'

'Yes,' Grade agreed vacantly. Now that Swenkel had mentioned it, perhaps the wave of relief would finally hit him. But he felt nothing. 'What was his part in all this?'

'We know of a few things: that he killed the two Muslims Al-Hakim and Khourem eighteen months ago, and that he was hired out of Zürich. But we don't know the vital point – who hired him.' Swenkel sighed. 'Outside of that, we have a dossier on him this thick. He's half-German, half-Belgian, and works freelance, but nearly always on contracts for extreme rightist groups – fascists, anti-semites, and the like. Internationally, he's known as the 'Falcon'. He had a close scrape once in Mannheim, Germany, and a hotel employer overheard one of his colleagues call him Jaalgen. Apparently it's very close to the German for falcon, and since then the name stuck.'

Swenkel's brow creased. 'Our good friend had a rather peculiar quirk, rather old-fashioned really – although a lot of my colleagues assure me there's been a rebirth of this in parts of Western Europe. Our preoccupation with the left-wing has made us ignore the new right. As that may be . . . Jaalgen believed in the original prejudices as laid down in *Mein Kampf*: Negroes, gypsies, Slavs and, of course, semites. And that includes the Arabs – not just the Jews, as many came to believe in later years. It was just our misfortune that *we* were in Germany and eastern Europe at the time – not hoards of Arabs.' Swenkel smiled sourly, but the effort showed the lines of his face more pronounced in the harsh light.

'The German *Polizei* believe that he was badly injured in the incident at Mannheim, and for a few years an identikit was circulated to agencies in which the 'Falcon' was shown with quite a distinctive scar on one cheek.' Swenkel ran an imaginary line with his finger. 'Reports have it that things hotted up for him. The scar could identify him too readily, so he had plastic surgery. Probably about two years after the Mannheim incident.'

They were silent for a moment.

Swenkel's personal opinion of the 'Falcon' was obvious from the tone of his voice, Daniel thought. No point in probing any deeper into a shared loathing.

'Our only lead on who was controlling the Falcon is the name Vruger,' Swenkel said. 'But we believe it's a front – the name doesn't check out with anyone recognizable in Zürich. I suppose you found the same.'

'Yes, pretty much. It came up through Leorah Ajlan.' So Swenkel had confirmed it: *Vruger*? Now that the rest of the puzzle was complete, if he could just find out who was behind that name, he would have that final all-important piece. 'One of Khourem's assassins, Reymenak, remembered the name – Kruger or Vruger – being used by the Falcon in a telephone conversation. But nothing like it showed up on the shares check.'

The extent of the scheme came back to Daniel, just as on that first day in the *Daily Post* boardroom . . . with slight variations. And now it was no longer so obscure, so intangible. If the key *was* Schaarer, then there was still the forthcoming peace conference to consider, but the hijacked children posed a more immediate, more poignant threat, and – as Swenkel had described it – a more easily calculable threat to Middle East peace. He would have liked a reaction from Nabens on it all; though he knew that ethically and morally – or whatever other word described endangering the lives of thirty schoolchildren – he just couldn't say anything. Not yet. He knew some journalists who would, however, and it suddenly occurred to him the tremendous risk Swenkel had taken. It must have taken a lot of trust on Swenkel's part. Or lack of choice.

Swenkel was speaking. '. . . I'd hoped you would keep helping us . . .' He paused significantly. 'I know that you may not have any particular bond with Israel. But knowing what you know now, I thought that as a journalist you might feel a certain dedication to the truth.'

Grade didn't answer this directly. 'How long do you have left with the hijacking?'

'It's difficult to say. We've already pushed the deadline back, and used up all but five hours of that. I don't even know if we can push it back again.'

'And you want me to try and convince Leorah Ajlan into talking with the terrorists? To make them aware of the Swiss involvement.'

'Yes. But you won't find her in Beirut now. She's on a short visit to Zellaq in Bahrain.'

That would be the hardest part, Daniel thought. Leorah would rather spit blood than help the Israelis, and here he was talking so casually about it. But then there was the fate of all those children? Surely that would help persuade her?

'So you'll help us,' Swenkel pressed.

'I haven't said that yet,' Daniel said sharply; then he rubbed his arm and smiled crookedly. 'I'm still not sure if I've forgiven you for sticking that needle in my arm.'

Swenkel smiled back; not at the comment, but because he now knew what the answer would be.

14

The sea was a clear azure blue. It was mid-afternoon.

Daniel felt the sun on his back as he turned his head where he lay and squinted along Zellaq's white sandy beach.

One or two of the distant chalets were fairly large, but most were small like Leorah's: one bedroom, a lounge, kitchen and bathroom. They were spaced quite widely, all of them white, one-storey, with pointed windows to remind you that you were in the *Fatah*-lands. A thin line of palm trees and shrubs separated the flat monotony of the desert behind from the sea. It was a Thursday and the beach was almost deserted; the nearest people were over fifty yards away.

He felt strangely guilty lying in the sun, acutely aware of time ticking against him. But it had seemed somehow wrong to arrive and immediately blurt out, 'Leorah, I want you to help the Israelis,' so he'd bided his time the last two hours. When the moment's right, I'll know, he thought.

He had told Leorah about Reiner and Ehnbridt and Julie, carefully neglecting any details relating to Swenkel. She'd listened attentively, without saying much, her expression becoming graver as he explained about Julie. She'd touched him gently and said, 'I'm sorry,' then had fallen silent and stared straight out to sea. She stayed like that for several minutes, then asked him some straightforward, practical questions which seemed merely to fill the gaps since their last meeting and set everything straight in her mind. Afterwards, she looked ahead again, as if searching for an answer in the sea and the horizon beyond, then said abruptly, 'I'm going for a swim.'

When Daniel had reached agreement with Swenkel to undertake this meeting, he had mentioned that another obstacle could be the increasing investigation of a certain Inspector Laboille of Interpol. Swenkel remarked wryly, 'Don't worry, I'll be your guardian angel.' It was a reassuring thought, but Daniel wasn't sure if he still believed in guardian angels.

The other small problem had been that it would take him away from his main investigation for a couple of days, and – what with Julie and the police – it had seemed that he would be neglecting one element just to satisfy another. So he'd called Simon Mendel and asked for his assistance, to see if Mendel could come up with anything concrete connected with Reiner's death, the link between Maslegeisen and Al-Ben Salmad, or perhaps something on Schaarer. Mendel was in a better position to overview things in Zürich and had helped him in a similar way over the pharmaceutical investigation. But Daniel had still been pleasantly surprised and relieved when Mendel complied. He hadn't been sure at first if Mendel would even have the time. Daniel related to him the progress of the case since their last meeting, skirting any details relating to Swenkel and, more carefully, that he had had a file search done on Mendel himself. He looked upon that now as a temporary mental aberration on his and David Wetherall's part, and still felt faintly guilty about it. He left Mendel with the Halmater agency number.

Helping Israel? It still felt unreal, an unusual role for him to play. But as soon as Swenkel had started talking about it, he knew what his answer would be. Was it just the fate of all those hijacked children, or the deeper implications for peace? Or was it, as Swenkel had suggested, the journalists' dedication to the truth? Or, cleaving closer to the bone, after having accused Reiner virtually upon his death, his need to fulfil Reiner's purpose in order to expiate his own guilt. He could still see Reiner's face at times . . .

He looked up. Something cold had touched his back.

Leorah stood over him, smiling, dripping wet from the sea.

'What were you thinking about?'

'Oh, nothing. This sun makes me sleepy.' He squinted up at her. She was wearing an orange bikini, little more than string at her hips, and it blended well with the smooth coffee tone of her skin. She knelt beside him.

'I was so sad to hear about Julie. I know how you must feel.' She reached out and brushed some of the hair from his forehead. 'You look tired, my poor, noble philosopher. Somehow now you don't look so much a pragmatist.'

Only the sounds of the lapping waves and some distant gulls could be heard for a moment.

'What made you say that?'

'I don't know.' She stood up. 'Perhaps just the look on your face.'

The white sand had stuck to her knees, contrasting with the darker tones of her thighs and flat belly. Only the backs of her legs and the insides of her arms held any semblance of her normal olive colour.

Daniel thought that if he was younger he would have put

her over his shoulder and run with her, half-naked as now, screaming and protesting into the sea. But even the image of him doing it somehow seemed wrong.

'If you're fishing for a further compliment, forget it.' Leorah smiled and started drying her hair.

'I'm going for a swim,' said Daniel.

She was still standing, drying her hair, when he looked back before plunging into the water. It was very clear, the white sand beneath ridged with its ripples. He waded in up to waist level, then dived under and swam out briskly, stopping about eighty yards from the shore and turning over to float lazily on his back.

He felt he understood now what Nabens meant about the 'sense of the region', so often referred to in his articles: that you actually had to be in the Middle East to really understand the conflict. Certainly he could feel it now looking back at the thin line of domed white chalets and palms, and the desert beyond. Peaceful as it was, he was reminded all too painfully of the conflict taking place a few hundred miles north, perhaps in a similar desert region . . . had a sense of all the conflicts and blood that had been spilled through the centuries in this cradle of civilization. And here he was in the middle of it all, a gentile doing the bidding of a Jew to a Muslim, and not even knowing how to broach the first word . . . *God*, he wished she didn't make him feel the way he did.

The chalet was in near darkness as he walked in; the shutters were half-closed. The heat outside was unbearable, but inside it remained relatively cool.

Daniel listened for the sounds – light rustling movement – and after a moment he realized Leorah was in the bathroom. He proceeded into the bedroom and dried himself. Sounds of running water and gentle humming filtered through the door.

Thinking about Nabens reminded him that when he'd phoned London from Vienna, Nabens had mentioned finally tracing a solid lead on Al-Ben Salmad – but after Swenkel's information, it just didn't seem to have any relevance any more. He wondered if that would be the pattern of things: events would fall into place, but *always* too late. He would convince Leorah to help, but the terrorists would have already taken their action . . . *the bus would be running with blood.* He shook the image away.

The humming behind the door had stopped. Daniel finished his drying. He was just slipping on a robe when Leorah walked in, naked.

He was startled and stared at her openly, then turned to make his way out.

'I'm sorry . . . I should have realized.'

'You don't have to go,' she said.

He hesitated, and he heard her chuckle.

'You know, you shouldn't be so embarrassed. If the beach was as quiet as today, normally I'd go topless. If there was nobody around, I'd go naked.'

She walked closer. The half-darkness accentuated her curves and delicate shadows. Her figure was statuesque, her legs tapering, her breasts large, sloping lazily to bell-like firmness.

'Muslim women,' she remarked, 'are usually head to toe in black, their faces half covered. Doesn't the image fit? I'm sorry if I've upset you.' She hung her head coyly, her wet hair still in tangles around her face and shoulders.

'Or perhaps it's not that at all. Perhaps it's the thought of what you might do to me – or feel like doing to me – this wanton, liberated lady.' She laughed again. 'And, of course, the knowledge that you have a wife. Perhaps that's why you're embarrassed?'

Daniel didn't answer.

Leorah perched on the bed before him. As she crooked a leg, he caught a glimpse of pink, like some exotic petal among her thick and dark pubic hair.

'Please . . . Leorah.'

She reached for him and touched him gently on the arm. He was trembling.

'I'm sorry, Daniel. I shouldn't have said that. It was wrong of me.'

'I'm not even sure if it's that,' he said emptily. 'I'm not sure of much these days.'

She looked to one side. 'I understand.'

They were silent.

'It's not your fault,' he said.

'Yes, it is – in a way,' she said. Her awkwardness was now apparent. She looked at Daniel for a moment, then smiled and shook her head slightly. Then she leaned forward and kissed him lightly on the forehead. She frowned in near disbelief.

'Didn't you really know this might happen, Daniel . . . Deep down, didn't you prepare yourself at all? Not even the possibility? I thought you knew . . . or might at least guess how I felt about you.' She kissed his forehead again, as if in benediction. 'Since that last time, I thought I wouldn't see you again, that I'd forget about you, that it was just passing fate . . .' She'd started as if incredulous, but now she sounded faintly despairing. 'My feelings were mixed at first . . . but then I began to miss you, to think about you more . . . Quite a surprise for a liberated woman, really . . .'

'Leorah, please . . . don't.'

'And then when I saw you again this time, I knew. It all became more clear, it confirmed my feelings of earlier . . . and I thought, no *sensed* that you felt the same way about me. I'd had that feeling right from the very start, even that first day in the hospital.' She gripped his arm tighter. 'And I suppose I read too much into that, misjudged – or perhaps wished to ignore the possible complications. If I'd known how you really felt, how awkward it might be . . . If I'd guessed, I would have never, *never* . . .'

She stopped, then.

Daniel had laid one finger firmly on her lips. He looked hard into her eyes, thinking: *No. It was me as much as you. I wanted this, too*. He slowly dropped the hand and traced it lightly across her breasts.

As he gently laid her back, she noticed he had stopped trembling.

For a while all he remembered was her breathing matching the lapping of the waves outside.

But there was a faint picture flickering through his mind: the stark beam of sunlight slanting through the small dome window and flickering with her movements across her breasts and stomach and thighs. Her ankles and feet were in darkness – as was her face – but he could tell where her face was from her breathing, the warmth and closeness of it . . .

Then she was turning over, the beam of sunlight breaking down the curve of her back, down the strongly indented hollow of her spine, and she was reaching for him, guiding him into her from behind. Her thighs were spread wide, her back arching.

At one point he remembered the sound of small gasping screams . . . but his mind was distant in place and time, almost apart from him, *floating* . . . and the sound became that of the gulls outside. For a moment he was with them, their silver wings catching the sunlight . . . Then there was the feeling of sinking, but slowly . . . the light breaking in became stronger, then blindingly bright . . . and he could see her face. She was staring at him, at some point deep inside of her. Her eyes were moist. He gently wiped the dampness from her cheeks with the back of one finger, and she kissed the end of his nose in thanks.

They lay there for a while. The sound of the lapping waves outside soothed their afterglow.

Daniel had never felt quite like he did at that moment. There had been moments with Catherine, oh yes . . . but not recently; and Leorah's lovemaking had a ferocity and passion to it that was hard to compare with anything else. Or was it just his memory playing tricks? Perhaps it *had* been like that with Catherine at one time . . . and he felt a sudden pang for the lost years.

It never does to analyse love, he thought; like all the strong emotions – hate, jealousy, revenge – it often creeps up on you without warning. He knew that if it hadn't been for her sudden declaration of her feelings, this probably never would have happened. They would have gone on as before, his desire for her carefully shielded or shrugged off with delicate teasing, and with their absorption in their shared profession. It had come as something of a shock to him – and he'd realized then that what had held him back all along was not just the guilt, but the fear of making an advance and being rejected – of making a rather clumsy, middle-aged fool of himself.

That had been a fear too: that the age gap would tell, that she would make him feel old. But that feeling hadn't come; if anything, he felt younger. But throughout his life, he had always distrusted emotions like that in other people, and it made him slightly uneasy.

The nights drew in cold early in Zellaq. By 6 p.m. the sun had set, and the heat built up during the day rose quickly from the desert floor.

Leorah had lit a small log fire in the lounge of the chalet. Only a small lamp in the corner was turned on, and the light of the flames flickered on their faces as they sat close.

The room was adobe style, with seating moulded in white plaster over which was scattered brightly covered cushions. On two walls, small Persian rugs had been hung. They sipped at some white wine Daniel had poured.

'Do you feel guilty?' she asked.

'No. I don't think so. I'm not quite sure what I feel.'

Leorah grimaced. 'I've got a cheek asking you that, after virtually pushing you into it in the first place. Perhaps it's because *I* feel guilty.'

'You shouldn't. I played cat and mouse as much as you.'

'That's one of the more objectionable throwbacks of having suffered Muslim male domination, I suppose,' she said. 'The desire to reverse the trend. I should have restrained myself. Reminded myself more forcefully that you were married.'

'How could you hope to remember,' he said wearily. 'When I hardly act married. I've been home three days in as many weeks.'

Leorah looked hard into his face. Its lines were etched deeply by the glow of the fire.

'I sensed that you had some problems,' she said. 'Apart from those now involving Julie.'

'Does it show?' he asked bleakly. 'Like one of those badges you wear on your sleeve?'

'No, not too much. You just seemed a bit lonely. A bit lost, perhaps.'

They were silent. The fire crackled.

Leorah leaned over and kissed him on the cheek. As he turned, she slid her tongue gently into his mouth. She reached inside his robe and started stroking him. They clung together for a while before breaking apart.

Their earlier conversation had been mellow and relaxed, filling the gaps of each other's lives left out on their first two meetings. Small comments passed back and forth about their families, the trials and tribulations of life in general, and the lessons learned from them. As the conversation developed, Leorah had the feeling that it was somewhat one-sided. Daniel had a full family as well as his parents and a younger brother and sister to talk about, whereas she had only her parents – her father now dead, and her mother living the traditional, stoical life of a widow in the southern outskirts of Beirut. Whether it was that, or the fact that he had opened his heart to her about Julie, or what they had shared in the past few hours, she wasn't sure – but she finally told him about Jamil; about the war of '58 and what the loss had meant to her. Her voice was choked with emotion as she finished, her eyes misty and distant, and Daniel had held her close, as if trying to take on the burden of some of the pain.

It all made sense to him then: her love for children, her desire to help them in this war, her closeness to that young boy on his first visit to the hospital.

He only hoped that she was able to separate them in her mind, that she wasn't just expressing her lost love for Jamil through them; otherwise it could end disastrously. She could one day wake up to the fact that it was a poor substitute, and the sense of loss would hit her all the harder. Thinking about *children* reminded him . . .

Leorah was speaking '. . . Shall I put another log on the fire?'

'Yes. Yes, okay.'

Daniel watched the sparks fly as it went on; and Leorah sat back, nestling her head against his shoulder.

'You know, I was trying to analyse why I feel the way I do about you,' she said dreamily. 'One thing I came upon was that you're not like any other Englishman I've known. Maybe it's because my memories of the English are mostly from when I was a young child, just after the British occupation of Palestine. They used to pass through Beirut for the trade – colonial types, stiff and formal. And since then my experiences have been chiefly with Arab men . . . who defy description. You're not like that. You're very relaxed, unassuming. Not pompous.'

'And I'm also a lot older than you.'

'You see what I mean?' She sat up slightly. 'Most men would gloss over that fact, not wanting to admit it even to themselves, hoping that it might be overlooked – or would go away. But not you. I should correct myself and say you're different from *all* other men that I've met – not just Englishmen.' Leorah smiled. 'Perhaps if you have a fault, it's that you're a bit too honest for your own good.'

Daniel chuckled. 'The good journalist's Achilles' heel. You've probably got it too.'

He fell silent abruptly. With the mention of honesty, he couldn't help feeling guilty about the purpose of his visit. He sipped anxiously at his wine.

'What's wrong?' Leorah asked.

The moment still wasn't right, but Daniel already felt a mixture of annoyance and guilt at the hours he'd so far delayed. For some subjects, the moment might *never* seem right.

He stared blankly ahead for a second longer, then he started . . . Slowly unravelling the tale Swenkel had imparted in the early hours of that morning, piece by piece filling in the details he had so carefully left out earlier. It seemed that he talked for a long time. Leorah stayed unnaturally still and silent throughout, and his voice sounded to him somehow distant and hollow, coming back to him from all corners of the room. He poured another glass of wine as he finished.

'Is that it?' she asked.

'Yes.' He smiled awkwardly. 'No more tricks up my sleeve.'

Leorah was wide-eyed, with an almost hunted look he'd noticed take over at the first mention of Israel. He'd brought that out early, not wanting to trick her further by milking her emotions over the attack on the train, only to crush them immediately afterwards.

'You certainly plan your timing.' She looked frantic. 'Is that why you waited till now, till after . . .'

'I *couldn't* tell you straight away,' he said. 'Can't you see that? It's an awkward enough subject as it is. I wanted a yes, not a blank refusal.'

'So you thought you'd soften me up a bit first.'

'*No*, that was never my idea . . . As you said, that part of it *you* pushed more than I did.'

'Yes. Yes. How right you are!' She glared at him for a moment before looking away, and lightly bit her lip.

'I wanted to talk about the other things first, so that when I did mention this proposal, it would fall into perspective with everything else. Otherwise, none of it would make sense.' Daniel's expression was gloomy. 'I must admit to delaying for another reason, too – probably the most valid. I was afraid. Afraid of what your reaction would be; afraid of the best way to approach it; afraid that if I didn't put it to you right, and you said no, I'd have only myself to blame.'

Leorah softened slightly. 'But it *was* the reason for your visit?'

'Yes,' Daniel said frailly. 'But I'd be fooling myself and

lying to you if I told you that I hadn't looked forward to seeing you again for other reasons.'

'Okay . . .' Leorah's eyes lifted. She played nervously with her hair. 'I suppose we've covered that ground enough. It's probably a woman's strongest paranoia . . . being used.'

Leorah exhaled slowly. She asked a few questions about his meeting with Swenkel – to get some final points clear in her mind – then commented: 'You know, it's odd really. You mentioned the bus hijacking the last time.'

'Yes, I remember.' Though it had only been four days ago, it seemed longer to Daniel. So much else had happened.

'We were talking about children at the time, too,' Leorah said. Her expression darkened, and she ran one finger around the rim of her glass. 'I know something about this Hasik. He's a Habash man. Bad type.'

'I think we know that from what he's done. How does that affect things?'

Leorah met Daniel's expression. 'It means that with someone like Hasik, it would be difficult. If not impossible.'

'Impossible? Isn't that overstating it a bit? Come on?'

'Please, Daniel . . . This is hard enough for me . . . I just don't think I can do it.'

'Can't . . . or *won't*? Let's be sure about your convictions.'

Leorah's voice was heavy. 'Don't test me out with words, Daniel. The whole scheme just won't work. I can't do it. It's as simple as that.'

Daniel stood up and leant against the mantelpiece. He looked down for a while. 'I thought that if and when you said no, you'd at least think up a decent excuse. God knows, I know how you feel about Israel, so you've got enough excuses there. But putting it all down to this feeble-minded Arab is beyond me.' Daniel turned to face her. 'And what about the children? I thought you had something there, Leorah . . . perhaps my only hope of swaying you. I thought you felt something *special* for kids?'

Leorah glared back at him. 'Don't use that on me, Daniel.'

'What the hell else can I use . . .' Daniel waved his arm in a helpless gesture. 'The lives of thirty-odd schoolchildren at stake, and you tell me that you won't help because one rebel Arab is *awkward*.'

'It's not as simple as that . . .' Leorah shook her head, as if to rid herself of some inner thought.

'No, it's not,' Daniel said flatly. 'It never is when you have to put one principle before another.'

Leorah stood up sharply, and slapped his face, hard. Her eyes were aflame, hostile, but Daniel sensed an uncertainty beneath, a need to be understood. He held her furious gaze for a moment, then turned away.

God, he thought, an hour ago they were sharing love and now they were ripping each other's throats out. At least the mood now matched the circumstances. He only hoped he hadn't built up Swenkel's hopes too high. It looked as if offering to do his bidding had been an impotent gesture. The image was back with him . . . *The bus was running with blood*!

'I'm sorry,' Leorah said.

'For what?'

'I'm sorry about your ordeal on the train. You mentioned it along with so much else that it seems to have got buried.' She lowered her eyes. 'I know how you must feel to have risked your life only for me to come up with a refusal. And to slap your face into the bargain.' She tried to smile but it came out wrong. Her eyes were moist as she looked up. 'Daniel . . . why do we have to punish each other like this?' She leant against him, tracing a finger thoughtfully along the lapel of his robe. 'I know the things that must have gone through your mind before you came here – the points you must have laboured over to try and convince me. But please, don't use all your weapons on me at once.'

She pulled away slightly. 'You see, my view of Israel doesn't really come into it. It's Hasik's view that counts.' Leorah noted Daniel's expression but went on before he could make any comment. 'When you started talking of this, don't think I didn't weigh everything up, because I did. All of it ran wildly through my mind: my feelings about the safety of those children, how much even an act like Hasik's alienates the causes of more moderate Palestinians. And I reached a quick conclusion: I wanted to help.'

This reversal threw Daniel – but he kept silent, not wanting to spoil the mood or pace of her thoughts.

Leorah paced slowly in front of the fire. 'But people like Hasik are hardliners, Daniel. They set themselves apart from moderates – if the situation calls for it, even Arafat himself. In fact, they distrust the motives of anyone who starts talking of negotiations with Israel. Very quickly *they* become the enemy too. And believe me, if anything their hatred for Arab "turncoats and traitors" is stronger than for the Israelis. They have a word for it . . . *Khayin.* If I went to Hasik with these proposals, he would spit in my face. It would achieve nothing.'

'I see,' Daniel said hollowly. Now he understood her thinking. 'Is there any way round it?'

'I don't know. But at present nearly all your information has come from a Mossad agent and a banker who, as you put it, they "used" in Zürich. You can see how it would look.'

'Yes, I can.' Daniel paced to one side. He wasn't sure how strong Leorah's desire to help really was – or whether it was just guilt after what he'd said earlier – but he thought he should make use of the advantage. 'So if the situation had been different, you'd have done it?'

'Yes.'

The plan grew stronger in his mind. 'If the information came from the Arabs, for instance?'

Leorah noted the change from past to present tense and realized he was thinking of something specific. Thoughts and images replayed in her mind: Hasik and the children; hardline or moderate, the *fear* of 'selling out'. 'Yes . . . but it would depend.'

'A prominent Muslim who was close to it all,' Daniel pressed the point. 'You could quote him exclusively; the Mossad or any possible connection with Israel wouldn't come into it.'

Leorah's eyes darted nervously. *Jamil had been killed by*

Phalangist bombs . . . children she tended each day were killed and maimed by Israelis . . . but, then, children were children! 'Yes, then I suppose it would be different.'

'*Then* you'd do it?'

Leorah stared into the fire for a moment. The flickering revealed the pain and uncertainty in her face . . . *They were the innocents! Did the sides really matter any more*? 'If it was a Muslim Arab whose voice they would trust. Yes. Then I'd do it.'

'Leorah, you're beautiful,' Daniel beamed, and he hugged her close and kissed her on the cheek.

She smiled ruefully, not quite sure if she was more bewildered by his outburst or the decision she had finally made. 'Why? What were you thinking of?'

'I'm not sure yet.' Daniel's exuberance faded slightly. 'Can I use your phone?'

'Yes, of course,' she said, and turned away so that he wouldn't notice the trembling in her voice. Forgive me, Jamil, she thought: I've looked upon you as a child first and an Arab second. I hope I haven't betrayed you.

The Concorde flew high over the Adriatic sea. Its machometer had been steady between 1.96 and 2.03 for the last fifteen minutes. The two Arabs a few rows back from the front watched it with little interest now.

They looked somehow out of place in their suits, as if they were not used to wearing them. Both men were dark-skinned, one with a trim beard and moustache and the other with a slightly unshaven look. The man who had sent them on this errand had told them that they should consider themselves privileged; he himself had wanted to fly on Concorde since its inaugural flight on that route earlier that year, but was unable to. Knowing what the unshaven man, Ibrahim, had told his new colleague, they both now understood why.

The girl across the aisle from them was a typical Arab beauty with dark hair and wide, slanting eyes. Ibrahim had found it hard to take his eyes off her legs for much of the journey. It seemed a shame that she had to be used in this.

'Rolf – it's Danny.'

'Where are you?'

'In Bahrain . . . but that's not important right now. How close are you to finding Al-Ben Salmad?'

'Pretty close. Apparently he's been a bit of a naughty boy lately in his love life. He left his wife high and dry in the south of France recently, and an investigative firm hired by her think they've now located him again and are hoping to get a few pictures of him *in flagrante delicto*. I was in touch with one of their boys the other day.'

'I want you to find him as quickly as possible.'

'When we talked earlier, I got the impression you weren't . . .'

'That's all changed. I can't tell you *why* right now – there's a lot involved. Just trust me that it will make a good story at the end of the day. Now, if and when you find him, there are some specific questions I want you to ask him . . .'

Nabens took his pad from the end of the desk and made some notes.

'Anything else?'

'No. That's it.' Daniel gave Nabens the number he could be reached on. '*Every* minute counts though, Rolf – I can't stress that enough.'

'Okay. Got the message. I'll phone them back right now.'

'Hasik! General Pohlmann speaking. Major Gant has tried to explain the situation to you . . .'

'Yes, I told him – and now I tell you! No deal. No more delays!'

'Then there is nothing I can do to help you,' Pohlmann said flatly.

'Help – *help*?' Hasik laughed hollowly. '*You* are the one who needs the help, General.'

'What I'm talking about is more important to you than to me. If you take action without paying heed to it, you will be making an historic error. You will only damage your cause and that of your fellows.'

'You talk of causes and history! Words that should not easily pass your lips, my friend. Be more specific!'

Pohlmann fell silent. He knew that he was walking a thin line. He didn't want to lay all their cards on the table for fear of refusal. If they were faced with that same refusal at the end of the day, then so be it – at least by then they would have gained vital hours. 'We have a journalist who wishes to speak to you. You probably know her well – Leorah Ajlan. She wrote for the *Yaumi Rassul*, and now works with the Red Cross. She has some information that will drastically change your situation.'

'What information?' Hasik asked coldly.

A ridge of sweat broke out along Pohlmann's spine. 'She is still gathering part of it . . . She wishes to speak to you personally. We need another twenty-four hours.'

'This is another trick!' Hasik hissed. 'Just another ruse to cause further delay. You are lying to me! I asked you a question. Don't try and side-step me! What information?'

'I don't know it all. Even if I did . . .'

'I say lies! Lies! You will tell me *now*. In another second I will break this communication and that will be the end of it!' Hasik sensed some of the children's eyes on him as his voice rose. These little ones are sensitive, he thought. They know they are about to die.

'She has evidence . . .' Pohlmann offered frantically. 'I can't show you that, or speak for that . . . Even if I told you what little I know, you wouldn't believe me.'

'At last, a truth.'

'The fact that she is even stepping in on our behalf must indicate something to you?'

Hasik didn't answer.

'Part of the bargain was that she would only speak to you directly – so I am sworn to secrecy by that alone. She has also made you a promise, Hasik. If you make a wrong move on this, you will never get support from Arafat, and even your good friend and mentor Habash won't be too pleased with you. You will have set the Palestinian cause back ten years.' It was a brave move – too brave perhaps, Pohlmann feared. There was silence at the other end.

The waiting had been the hardest part, Hasik considered. Their food supplies were good and they were firmly entrenched, but some of his men, particularly Jahlib, had begun to get edgy. The initial nineteen hours before the arrival of Pohlmann . . . then the first deadline of twenty four hours; then a delay of eighteen hours, in the end stretching to nearly thirty eight hours . . . now a request for a further twenty four hours! He had watched the infantry and tanks and equipment outside slowly grow in numbers. Now the passing hours and minutes in the isolation of the dark tunnel had begun to nibble at part of his mind too.

What exactly was Pohlmann implying? *Habash*! It had been almost two years now since his break from Habash's PFLP and the formation of the Palestinian Liberation Fighters. He had been a lieutenant, a right-hand man to Habash, but had left because he felt there wasn't room for two decision-makers. The time had come when he felt *he* was ready to make the decisions. There had also been the question of wider acceptance. Habash had alienated nearly all of the Palestinian moderates; Arafat disassociated himself from Habash actions almost as a matter of course. Whereas a *new* organization, though perhaps just as extreme, would be given more of a hearing. When the Israelis made their announcement, Arafat would have little choice but to support him, otherwise he would be missing out on the coup of the decade! Yet now Pohlmann was saying that even Habash would consider it extreme. *Ridiculous*!

But how could he be sure about this new situation, until he'd seen this Ajlan woman? If in fact her offer of mediation was even true! Pohlmann was probably bluffing. Though what if he wasn't?

'All right, General. But not twenty-four hours. *Twelve hours*! For each hour after that we will kill an Israeli child.'

*

'How long have we got?'

'Twelve hours. But that was two hours ago,' Swenkel said. 'We're left with ten.'

'I'll get back to you,' Daniel said.

'Okay. I'll be here. I'm not moving from the phone.'

Part Five

Reuters Paris: Reuters London

15

PARIS: 14.02

BRITISH GIRL SOUGHT BY FRENCH POLICE!

The Paris Surété have today announced that they have had no success in tracing an English girl, Julie Grade, missing for the last 36 hrs: Miss Grade was sought for questioning after the death of her boyfriend, Xavier Peton, a suspected member of the French terrorist group, 'Le Marteau Rouge'. It is now suspected that Miss Grade is no longer in Paris. The Surété have passed their information on to Scotland Yard.

Reuters

'Westmoreland Enquiry Agency'.

Nabens waited for the girl to put him through. 'Hello. Bill Morsen? Rolf Nabens calling. I spoke to you the other day . . .'

'Oh yes.'

'I was wondering – have you actually pinned Salmad down yet?'

'Well, he's been sighted in the Mayfair area – been frequenting some of the hotels there, apparently. But so far nothing more than that. We've narrowed it down to five or six hotels. From there it's just a matter of staking them out from time to time.'

'Something new's cropped up, you see. It's very urgent that I contact him now.'

'You *and* a few others.'

'Yes, I know.'

Morsen fell silent for a second. 'Well look, it might not be quite your cup of tea, but I'll be heading out on another look-see in a short while. If you like, if you want to meet up with me at the Hilton, you could tag along. It's up to you.'

'I'll see you there.' Nabens was already reaching for his jacket.

The Rolls Royce Corniche glided along Piccadilly. It took a left turn into Berkeley Street, then left again towards Curzon Street. As it approached Shepherd Market, it slowed, and Al-Ben Salmad peered through its side window at the back. Among the few people on the pavement, he spotted a girl with blonde hair.

'I think that is her,' he directed the chauffeur, who pulled the Corniche into the kerb.

Al-Ben Salmad's thick moustache twitched with anticipation as the girl came into clearer view.

Her legs were slim and tan, with graceful, tapering ankles. Her dress was fawn cheesecloth, quite short, with a small slit at one side to accentuate the length of her legs. Her breasts were firm, and he could see tantalizing glimpses of them between the laces that tied the top of her dress.

Al-Ben Salmad pressed the electric window down and smiled at her. 'Please?' He was overweight and had a constantly beaming countenance, so it was hard to tell when he was smiling genuinely.

She faltered for only a second, then walked towards the car. Salmad noted how her silver-blonde hair, hanging almost to her waist, swung in delicate, bouncing curves with each movement of her hips. He wasn't sure if he would be able to contain himself much longer. He opened the door and she nestled in alongside him; the car pulled away with a gliding swish. Her hand delicately tugged at his white *thobe* and ran high up his leg.

Salmad licked his lips slightly. 'You are welcome, my child.'

Exile was at last beginning to have its advantages, he

thought. He sweated when he thought of how he had run the gauntlet the past eighteen months. Especially when he'd heard about Gahtlav and the others, the acid burnings and killings!

At times he wondered what had attracted him to the scheme in the first place. He had enough wealth, surely: banking, arms deals and shipping had made him one of the wealthiest men in the Gulf apart from the sheikhs. Perhaps it was just greed: the same greed in his blood as the effendis and sheikhs who had subjugated the fellaheen and controlled the unequal destiny of Islam for a thousand years. But then the scheme had been so audacious! He couldn't help smiling about it, even now. He had also felt proud to be such a kingpin in the scheme; the choice of Al-Hakim and Khourem had been his; he had been the only one close enough to Arab affairs to decide which action would create the desired atmosphere of instability. He had been as much at the hub of it all as the man in Switzerland. The rest were merely investors.

The hand on his leg was getting higher.

'Yes . . . that is nice. That is nice.'

Another element of his exile now also pleased him: for the past year he had taken it into his mind to have several wives, as permitted by his religion. But he had made the mistake eight years ago of marrying his English first wife in a Christian church, and she was opposed to the idea. Ridiculous! What say did she have in the matter? If this was the civilized world, he would have told her three times that he renounced her and that would have been the end of the matter; but this was a new and strange world of lawyers and writs and matrimonial rights and laughable demands. Let them try and find him! He had already changed his name once; to take on another identity was but a small detail. Women were such fools.

Salmad gazed at the girl beside him. Except in pleasure, he thought. They were designed in such a way, and their instinct to please a man was so natural; how could anyone think they were destined for anything else.

'You are very beautiful,' he said thickly, and his fat fingers reached out and stroked her hair. It was so smooth, its colour so shiny and lustrous that he trembled at the feel of it.

Part of her face was in shadow, and his gaze travelled down, studying and relishing each of her features. Her dress had ridden high, its slit falling open, and he was treated to a view of much of her thigh. He followed its smooth expanse across the curve of her hips and up to the swell of her breasts. The cheesecloth was thin and faintly transparent, and he could discern their perfectly rounded shape and see the rich dark nipples at their centres. He mopped his brow lightly with a handkerchief clutched in one hand. The girls were getting more perfect each time! Her neck had long, graceful lines, her chin and nose were chiselled symmetry. Her mouth was rich and wide, the full lips slightly parted with just a hint of even white teeth, over which at moments, would lazily run a pale pink tongue. Salmad mopped again. The bone structure was high and proud . . . and the eyes. *The eyes*! Salmad's heart froze. He stared more intently. The light from outside now enabled him to see the colour of her eyes clearly . . . *They were brown*! He clutched the handkerchief tighter. He had specified *blue*! How could they have made such a mistake? He always specified blue! But in almost every other way she was perfect. Undoubtedly the best they had so far provided. The conflict worked itself deeper in his mind. His mouth twitched. After a moment he realized she might sense something was wrong, and he forced a smile.

He felt her fingers work their way higher and find him under the *thobe*. He relaxed himself into their gentle stroking emotion. It was no use. It was too late now to turn back. He wanted her. Badly.

He ran his hand slowly up her legs. They parted slightly, and he felt the smooth satin of her knickers. Her legs parted more widely. He slid his hand in deeper, probing with one finger, and felt the coarseness of her pubic hair. Oh yes, she was wearing split French knickers, as he'd requested. At least that part was correct. He probed deeper, feeling the warmth and moistness between. She was warmer there than any woman he'd known. The outer lips were thick and luscious and moist, and as he probed the inner lips, he felt them grip his finger like a mouth.

Oh yes . . . She is the best. Without a doubt she is the best. But as he admired her again, slowly and longingly, he was careful to avoid her eyes.

Bill Morsen had quickly agreed with Rolf Nabens that two of them searching was more efficient than one; so they had split up and staked out a few hotels each. They would spend fifteen minutes at each, then phone at predesignated times to check on each other's progress.

Morsen had put in his time at each hotel so far without anything turning up, and was just heading along Hertford Street when he saw Al-Ben Salmad's Corniche heading the other way, towards him.

He was in shock for a second, and then pulled in. He watched the Corniche go past – caught a shadow of figures in the back seat – then backed into a nearby driveway. He had to wait for some passing traffic before he could pull out again. There were two cars between him and the Corniche. He watched it indicate right into Old Park Lane and then eventually pull into the forecourt of a large hotel.

Morsen drove a short way past, and pulled up on the opposite kerb.

After a second a blonde girl got out, followed by what looked like Salmad. Morsen took an envelope from his inside pocket and rustled among its contents. He picked out a photo of Salmad taken a few years ago, shaking hands with Kuwait's foreign minister. He studied the man across the road again. That was him – no doubt about it.

Morsen reached into the back seat for his camera. He was a champion of dark back streets and hiding in the shadows by the tenements and boltholes of illicit lovers, so daylight in Park Lane was refreshing by contrast.

He clicked off a few photos with the standard 50mm lens

as Salmad and the girl began walking away from the car, then he snapped on a 100mm-300mm zoom lens. He got two or three clear ones of them as they turned briefly, and Salmad gave instructions to the chauffeur . . . That's it . . . good . . . *good.* Then a few close-ups just before the entrance.

'Great!' Morsen took a last couple of shots of the blonde's legs for his own private album and put the camera down.

Now he had what he wanted, he should phone Nabens. He looked at his watch: the next contact time arranged was seven minutes away.

Al-Ben Salmad always felt undressing was the most awkward part. He drew the curtains. He wondered whether it was because he was overweight. Certainly in his father's time being overweight was a sign of opulence. But he was aware that in the modern age it had lost some of its attraction.

The blonde came over and helped him with the last part of his *thobe*. Her eyes appeared to be half closed in pleasure as she removed what remained of his clothing. She makes it all so easy, this one, he thought. He lay down flat on the bed and watched as she removed her earrings.

'Wait!' He said. He pointed. 'Turn on the lamp there. I want to see you.'

She flicked it on. It cast a pale orange pool of light.

Salmad began tapping his fingers on his stomach in expectation.

The girl unlaced the top of her dress. The dress was very tight, little more than a sheath, and it slid off in one motion. Underneath she wore a red and black garter belt to match her French knickers, but no stockings. She went to unhook the garter belt.

'No, no! Leave it on,' Salmad directed.

Her breasts were high and firm, and moved only slightly as she walked towards the bed. She knelt on its edge. He noticed the lips of her sex pouting through the open crotch of her knickers. They were thick and bright red. She had rouged them with lipstick, as he had instructed. Oh, yes. Roger really had excelled himself this time. This was marvellous, *marvellous.*

The girl's blonde hair hung almost to her waist, covering part of her breasts. She leaned over and started slowly stroking Salmad's legs, moving higher, then planting small kisses where her hands had already travelled. Salmad closed his eyes, and the sensation was like delicate bird's wings fluttering over his skin. She kissed higher, then started licking . . . her motions becoming increasingly lascivious until she engulfed him completely in her mouth.

Oh yes . . . yes . . . marvellous.

The muted sounds of London traffic rose up to the room, but Salmad was already in a different world . . . a world of blinding white sand and flashing scimitars. There was a bedouin feast. The firelight flickered. His father sat in its glow telling him a story . . . it was a pleasant story, of opulence, of wealth, of bold and noble Islamic traditions. A whole sheep roasted on a spit to their side, turning slowly.

He felt himself growing in her mouth, his pleasure rising.

Some women danced to one side, the coins of their yashmaks jangling lightly. His father was pointing to them, smiling smugly. I want many wives, too, father. I have been cheated.

Oh yes . . . oh yes . . . the sensations were becoming more intense.

The women were dancing wilder and faster. A light wind whistled through the dunes, picking up the finer sand. The fire crackled more intensely. His father's expression was suddenly grave.

The sensations were building to a pitch . . . too soon . . . too soon! But he felt powerless to stop them.

His father was speaking, issuing a warning, his face aflame . . . but he couldn't hear the words. He leant closer . . . 'The brown eyes are the devils . . . they will . . .' But he couldn't hear any more. It had faded again.

The sensations died suddenly.

'What?' Salmad's eyes snapped open.

The rope was already around his neck.

He looked down to see what had killed his pleasure so suddenly. She had bitten him; he could see her teeth marks clearly.

'*Yalla*! Oh God . . . *God*!'

The shadow of the man behind fell across him. The girl had stood up, and now watched him coolly from the far end of the room. Her eyes were dark and intent. As the rope tightened around his neck, she pulled off the blonde wig and shook loose her long dark hair.

'Is that his car?'

'Yes.'

'Okay.'

Nabens got out and dodged his way through the traffic towards the hotel. Morsen followed.

Nabens confronted the male receptionist.

'You have a Mr Al-Ben Salmad staying here. Could you connect me with his room please?'

The receptionist turned to the card indexes behind him. He leafed through them for a moment.

'No. I'm sorry. Nobody by that name, I'm afraid.'

Nabens' brow creased. He turned to Morsen.

'What name did he use in the south of France?'

'Ashonni. Issam Ashonni. But I don't think you'll find him under that either. That's the last name his wife knew him under.'

'Okay.' Nabens looked back to the desk. 'This gentleman came in here about ten minutes ago: An Arab in a white robe, overweight, thick moustache. Very distinctive figure; you couldn't miss him. He was with a very attractive blonde girl.'

The receptionist looked bemused. 'Look, sir, we do have the discretion of our guests to consider. I don't think I can . . .'

'The message I have for Mr Salmad is very urgent,' Nabens said tersely. 'Now, his car's outside, and I can wait for him there. But if he's annoyed at the delay, I'll let him know that it was you who personally obstructed me.'

The desk clerk grimaced uncomfortably. 'The best I can do is phone up to his room. If you'll give me your name, I'll find out if he'll see you.'

Nabens handed over his press card. The clerk dialled out and let it ring for almost a minute. He wore a concilatory but faintly smug expression as he handed back the card.

'Sorry, sir. No answer.'

Nabens paced away, looking dismayed. 'I suppose we'll just have to sit it out. He'll probably be up there half the day.'

'I think I know which number the clerk dialled,' Morsen commented as they got out of earshot of the desk.

'You're joking?'

'It's one of those things you pick up in this game. You can tell by the timing of the dial spinning back; with just three numbers, it wasn't so difficult. As I see it, we've got four choices . . .'

Al-Ben Salmad could now see the other man in the room. For quite a few minutes he had sat in a darker corner and merely fired questions at him. Now he came into the light, walking across to the side of the bed. He leaned over and scraped a large curved knife gently on its flat side across the skin of Salmad's stomach. The man behind him kept a tight grip on the rope around Salmad's neck.

'You will give us the name of the man in Switzerland . . .'

The questions were becoming repetitive; Salmad had been vague so far. Fear had broken out beads of sweat on his skin.

'What would be the point? You will kill me anyway.'

'Yes, but it can either be slow and extremely painful – or quick and merciful.'

Al-Ben Salmad's eyes blinked. This was a new choice. He had hoped to bargain for his life.

'But if I give you his name, you will have bigger fish to fry. Why kill me?'

'That's not open to negotiation,' Ibrahim said flatly. 'We have offered you your choice.'

'But it is a worthless choice! What does it matter to me if . . .' Salmad's voice faded with nervous apprehension.

Ibrahim had gripped his left hand. Ibrahim took out a knife and sliced off Salmad's little finger. Salmad let out a scream, muffled quickly to a bellowing wail as Ibrahim stuffed a pillow into his face. Tears ran down Salmad's cheeks.

Ibrahim let the finger gush blood for a few seconds, then ripped at the bedsheets and tied a rough bandage around it. He surveyed Salmad coldly.

'You say a worthless choice. You have several other fingers and toes. Your eyes would be plucked out last – otherwise you wouldn't be able to see and appreciate what had preceded.'

'*Ajab! Rahmi!* Please . . .' Salmad blubbered. 'I beg of you. Mercy!'

'You say mercy?' Ibrahim gripped the same hand.

Al-Ben Salmad started talking.

He wailed and cried his way through the ordeal as Ibrahim asked his questions. He cursed his misfortune at ever getting involved with the evil men he described, he spoke of how that had never been his intention . . . but he had been offered little choice. He again bargained for his life. He swore on the grave of his mother and the life of his sister that he didn't know that they had planned to kill Al-Hakim and Khourem. When he saw that this made little impression on Ibrahim, he offered him untold wealth if he would let him go.

Ibrahim ignored it. 'Why? Why was this scheme perpetrated?'

Despite his anguish, Salmad realized that if he explained why, it would go against his claim of ignorance about Al-Hakim and Khourem. 'I'm afraid this I don't know.'

Ibrahim gripped his hand again.

'*Ajab!* Please . . . I am telling you the truth.'

Ibrahim sliced off Salmad's index finger.

Al-Ben Salmad fainted.

Ibrahim looked worriedly at his colleague. 'I'm not sure if we have the time to wait for him to come around.'

'Come on . . . *come on*,' Nabens muttered under his breath.

The lift had stopped twice on its way from the ground to the ninth floor, to let people off.

Morsen had explained that the last digits on a dial were always hardest to discern, because of the longer spinning back, so it had either been 0 and 9 for the first number; he also wasn't sure between 4 or 5 for the second. They had already checked 043 and 053.

The lift doors opened. They walked swiftly along the corridor until they confronted 943.

Nabens rang the bell. He waited for a moment then rang again. Still no answer. He leant closer to the door: he could just discern some faint movement from inside. He spun around on Morsen.

'See if you can grab a room boy!'

Morsen sprinted off and came back in a couple of minutes with a blue-suited valet.

'Could you open this door, please?' Nabens requested.

The valet frowned slightly. 'I'm sorry, sir. Is there a problem?'

'Yes. I have a friend in here, and he's not answering. I'm afraid something might be wrong.'

The valet glanced at the Do Not Disturb sign.

'Well, sir. He has asked not to be disturbed. This is a bit irregular.'

'For God's sake. I haven't time to stand here and argue!' Nabens took out a five-pound note and stuffed it brusquely into the valet's hand. 'My friend has a heart condition – he could be dangerously ill in there!'

'Yes, yes . . . of course.' Partly flustered, the valet fumbled with his masterkeys and opened the door.

The scene of carnage inside held Nabens where he was.

It took a moment for him to realize that there was actually

a body in the welter of blood on and around the bed. He stepped forward uncertainly. There was nobody else in the room.

'Oh Christ . . . *Christ*!' he whispered under his breath.

Morsen and the valet stayed in the doorway. The valet looked sick.

Nabens tried to shut out the terrible image of carnage and pick apart piece by piece exactly what had happened. Some fingers had been removed, but he couldn't tell how many; the neck was blue-black, indicating strangulation; the chest and stomach had been cut into. Moving closer, he could make out the rough shape of a cross.

Grade's description of the deaths of Al-Hakim and Khourem and Gahtlav came back to him. He tried to assemble the pattern in his mind, but couldn't; perhaps Daniel would be able to make more of it. On the bedside a note had been left. It was in Arabic, so Nabens could understand only a few words of it.

A flapping noise to one side. Nabens looked across sharply. The curtains were blowing in the wind; the window behind had been cut open neatly. It was obviously the noise he'd heard from outside. He went across and looked through the hole: there was another room's balcony close by on that side. They'd obviously used that as their way in and out. He ran back into the corridor and knocked on the room next-door; then asked the valet to open the door.

It was empty. Nabens started hastily down the corridor.

'You phone the police,' he said over his shoulder to Morsen. 'I've got another call to make.'

16

'You tricked me, Pohlmann. As I thought earlier, it *is* just another delay.'

'No . . . no, I promise you. The girl is coming. She is on her way now.'

'You have been delaying right from the start. I will have no more of this!'

'You have my word, I . . .'

'Your word . . . your word is worthless!' Hasik hissed. 'The deadline is now past, and you are trying my patience too far. Soon, one of the children on this bus will be killed! Is that what you wish? Is that what is necessary to make my case clear to you?'

General Pohlmann's voice grew solemn. 'If you do that, I think you know where Israel would then stand on this issue. We would refuse to negotiate with you further.'

'And you, General, will then be clear how *we*, the PLF, stand on this issue. The day will not end until every child on this bus is dead – and *you* will have sealed their fate!'

Pohlmann felt a mixture of fear and cold rage possess him.

'You're a madman, Hasik,' he said.

'No madder than you will be, General, when you later try to balance your conscience. I have warned you repeatedly, but you have not listened! Now I must take some action.'

'Wait! Wait . . .'

The line went dead.

Inside the bus Beni watched and listened to El-Hasik more intently than the others did. Ever since hiding the gun in his satchel, he'd had forebodings. Just the thought of the gun so close made him nervous, and he was sure it would show. Hasik would single him out and find the gun, and he would be the first to be killed.

What made matters worse was that he had been chosen as spokesman. So far it had only entailed speaking once through the field telephone shortly after General Pohlmann's arrival, and assuring him plainly and simply that they were all unharmed. It hadn't been an easy task, since the atmosphere created by the death of the boy Hasik had now hidden at the back still hung over the bus. Hasik had seemed pleased with his twenty-second performance. Perhaps that would combat any suspicions Hasik might have towards him. Beni hoped so.

Over three days had now passed, but you could only tell when it was daytime from a faint light filtering off the walls at the end of the tunnel. The cold and darkness was frighteningly desolate, especially at night. At intervals, gentle, muffled weeping could be heard, quickly stifled by a cough as one of the guards became alert. Most of the children slept sporadic, irregular hours.

But Beni had hardly slept at all. The message kept growing stronger in his mind. *You are all going to die . . . you are all going to die . . .* The soldiers would then come aboard and pick their way among the bodies, and discover the gun. '*This one could have saved them all!*' . . . '*Yes, but he was probably –*' But in his nightmare he could never hear that final word. No, no . . . I'm not *afraid*! I *will* do it.

There had been only minor opportunities so far, while Hasik was talking on the field telephone or one of the guards was sleeping. But even one of those moments looked good, if the alternative was that they would all go like lambs to the slaughter. At least they would die fighting. Not like the old ghetto Jews his father had talked of, but more like sabras!

He watched Hasik make his way down the aisle. Now that Hasik was going to single one of them out to kill, it could offer an ideal distraction. Perhaps the last real opportunity. Beni realized that he was sweating more than he should, and looked away, fighting to relax. He closed his eyes slightly.

'*So David proved the victor with his sling and stone; he struck Goliath down and gave him a mortal wound, though he had no sword.*'

The words played over in his mind, the words that his father used to read him from the Bible, almost as a fairy tale, when he was younger. He wondered how David had conquered his fear. He tried to put himself in David's position.

As El-Hasik came closer, harshly surveying each of the children, Beni clutched his satchel closer to his side.

*

Daniel Grade was still at Leorah Ajlan's chalet in Zellaq. He had received Rolf Nabens' call about Salmad over two hours ago. Leorah had gone off to the centre of town, saying she'd be away only an hour or so; but it was almost four hours since she'd left.

The hardest part for Daniel was having to tell Swenkel. Afterwards, with Leorah still not returned, Daniel felt badly in need of a drink. He raked around in Leorah's drinks cabinet but couldn't find any scotch. He settled finally for a bottle of white rum.

An hour later the bottle was half empty, and his mood grew fouler with it.

Daniel caught his reflection in a mirror and raised his glass to it. You really did it this time, Danny! You should have listened to Catherine. Half the police of France chasing Julie . . . Reiner and Xavier and Salmad dead . . . and the death toll still rising. Soon you can add a busload of schoolchildren!

He knocked back another shot. You might as well admit it, Danny, you're out of your depth this time – *in over your head*, as your dear Welsh father would say. Even Nabens, after the news of Salmad, was beginning to get cold feet. 'We're meant to report the news, not make it', he'd said. 'Bob's not too pleased, Danny. Things with your daughter are hotting up further with the French police, I'm afraid . . . Look, you've done enough. Nobody could ever say otherwise. Why don't you call it a day?'

Call it a day? Perhaps he should. At the time he said he'd call Bob Golding later to discuss things, but the last thing on his mind had been actually doing so. But then what more could he achieve here now? He still had little more than some unconnected facts, and his two main leads, Ehnbridt and Salmad, were both dead. All that remained was a link between Salmad's murder and those of Gahtlav, Al-Hakim and Khourem. *Crosses carved on their chests*! It seemed so bizarre, almost out of place in the modern world. An Egyptian journalist on the scene had claimed he could connect it all to one organization. Nabens had promised to send through a copy report, along with some photographs from the investigator he had been with at the time. It seemed odd that on the one hand Nabens could urge a pull-out, yet on the other send through more information. Or was Nabens politely hinting that things had already gone above both of them; that as with many large stories, the decision to continue now lay between Bob Golding and the *Post*'s directors.

The thought of the paper pulling out their backing made him feel suddenly alone and empty. At least you won't be alone in deserting me, Leorah. Here's to you. Clash of cultures and beauty and all! He poured another tumblerful of rum.

The bottle was almost finished when Leorah finally walked in. Daniel's mood was so dark that he didn't trust himself to speak.

Leorah went straight into the kitchen, without a word. She came back sipping a cool drink. She looked at Daniel thoughtfully.

'I'm sorry. I know I'm late.'

'That's an understatement!'

'You look troubled.'

'I should do.'

'Please, Daniel, don't play games with me. What's happened? Did something go wrong?'

'What, apart from you being late?'

'You know what I mean. Did you receive your call?'

'Yes. Salmad is dead.' Daniel's tone was flat.

'I see.' Leorah looked away with a pained expression. She took a seat.

'Not that it would have made much difference, anyway,' Daniel said cuttingly. 'Did you realize you've been away so long that the deadline has already passed. Where the hell have you been?'

Leorah didn't answer.

Daniel noticed that he was clenching and unclenching his fists, and he laid them flat on his knees. He let out a long sigh.

'Our dear Palestinian freedom fighter, Hasik, has promised to kill a child for each hour past the deadline. If we go along now, you'll just be in time to count the bodies. You've had some experience of that with the Red Cross, no doubt?' Daniel glared at her and knocked back the last of his tumbler. 'Yes, yes, come along. You'll be invaluable.'

Daniel saw Leorah flinch. Shadows deepened in her eyes, and her expression changed; but he couldn't read anything there.

It had gone far enough now, Leorah thought; she couldn't bear the tension, the barrier between them any longer. The moment would never be righter.

'Could we bluff it?' she asked.

'Bluff what?'

'I mean the hijackers.' She looked up meaningfully. 'Does it really matter that Salmad is dead. Hasik and his men are not to know that. Or even if they do, how are they to know that Salmad didn't pass on information before his death?'

Daniel shook his head in disbelief. 'You amaze me. The whole point of getting information from Salmad was to satisfy you. Not anyone else.'

'Yes. Because I couldn't see myself convincing Hasik without that. If a single piece of information came via an Israeli source, that would have been the end of it! Hasik would have stonewalled us.'

'So how has that changed?'

Leorah went over to the window. She looked out, keeping her back to Daniel.

'I went out earlier because I had to think. I had to have some time to myself, Daniel. Your proposition came so suddenly, I felt forced into a corner.' Leorah paused. The sound of the sea outside came to them. 'I don't think you really understand what it meant to me. I was being asked to decide for or against a lifetime's principles within minutes. While I was out, several things came to me. First, that I was betraying one principle with another. Did it really matter that the children were Israeli, not Muslim? And what difference did it make that I was taking the word of an Israeli agent, if it meant that I would be saving their lives? A life is a life, and I suddenly realized that I had been guilty of categorizing. Would I have asked for the same qualifications and proof if they were Muslim? I don't think so. And who am I to decide who is important, who should be saved? I left that to our beloved generals and leaders long ago. Otherwise my service to the Red Cross would become false, an hypocrisy.'

Daniel sat back. What a fool he had been. He had prejudged the situation and had got drunk not only to numb his senses, but also – he now realized – to quell that terrible sense of being let down by Leorah. His mind fought to clear itself and grasp the full meaning of what she was saying.

Leorah had turned back from the window. 'The only question then was how to satisfy Hasik and the PLF. And I realized they would never know! If I said that the information from the Israelis had come from Salmad, they would never know differently. And it would probably never occur to them that, of all people, I – a strong left-wing Muslim – might lie for the Israelis.' Leorah came over and sat next to Daniel. She traced one finger lightly along his cheek and into his hair; her expression was one of deep concern. A smile flowered hesitantly at the corner of her mouth.

'But then what's a few lies against the lives of these children? I owe no allegiance to Hasik's brand of extremism.'

Daniel thought: it was like a microcosm of East-West differences at play between just the two of them. In the space of a few days they had made love or argued or berated each other almost constantly. Just when he thought he had Leorah summed up, she would surprise him. The strength of her Muslim convictions, in particular how she was able to balance those against her people's more extremist elements, had been her one major flaw. Now she had tempered that as well. It was a gesture he found hard to come to terms with.

'Look, Leorah, you don't have to do this just because I want you to – because of what's happened between us.'

She gave him a cynical look. 'I'd never dream of it, I'm doing it for the children.'

'Drunken oversight – sorry.' Daniel watched Leorah smile. He ran one hand unevenly through his hair. 'No, really, it's not that I wouldn't be flattered to carry the can – it's just that some things are worth selling yourself out for, some aren't. As you well know, I want you to do this, and badly. But I also want *no* regrets. There's no turning back from this point in.'

Leorah nodded solemnly. She realized he wasn't as drunk as she had first thought. His eyes held hers a moment longer.

'I just hope we're not too late.' Daniel started timing things in his mind.

'We certainly won't find out sitting here.'

Daniel snapped himself out of his contemplation and smiled for the first time since her arrival. 'You know, I still don't understand you.'

Leorah leaned over and kissed the end of his nose. 'How could you hope to? We come from totally different cultures.'

The night before had been the hardest, Jaalgen thought. Each detail of it was replayed vividly in his dreams; or was he now awake?

The ledge was about twelve feet above him.

He had been contemplating it for a while. Only one train had passed in that time, but it would have been hopeless to wave or make any movement to attract attention.

Although his clothes were dark against the white snow, with the number of fir trees on the hillside, he would be difficult to pick out. The bridge was at least eighty feet above him. Besides, a sudden movement could dislodge him from his position.

Jaalgen looked below.

Another smaller ledge jutted out beyond the lip of the gently sloping one he lay on – but it didn't look wide enough to hold him if he slipped. Beyond that, apart from a few jagged promontories, it was a sheer fall to the ravine floor.

Jaalgen couldn't make out the bottom. It was too dark. Some village lights twinkled further out, but it was difficult for him to judge distance by them; viewed from that height, they could be anything from three to ten miles away.

The wind was cruel when it cut into the ravine.

For a while he had been dreaming, and he had woken up shivering – and realized that it was the sound of the biting cold wind that had disturbed him. Even during the dream, he knew that he hadn't died. He'd blacked out immediately he'd hit the slope, then had come to only minutes later, suffocating deep in the thick snow. He'd clawed and twisted his way out, then blacked out again – and the dream had started.

. . . He was still falling, and falling . . . and the bottom never came. He couldn't tell which was more frightening, the dream or the reality or, after a while, which was which. He started screaming . . . and the broad face of the man with curly grey hair glared at him, then the impish face of his daughter. He tried to reach out to grasp them, both in anger and in desperation . . . but he fell past and below them, and their smiles became a laugh – then a howl which grew rapidly louder and drowned out the sound of his own screaming.

He had woken up. The wind was gusting through the ravine, making hollow cooing noises against the rock.

How long had he been unconscious? Three hours, maybe four. It was still dark.

Looking up, he tried to reconstruct in his mind what had happened. With the speed of the train, he had probably fallen at an angle and then met the slope as it shelved steeply inward. The snow was thickest on the shelves, so it wasn't just pure chance that his fall had been broken. The snow had also stopped him from slipping too much further once he'd hit the slope. He guessed that he'd landed a few yards above the lip of the slope above, then rolled down.

Was anything broken? His legs and arms moved easily, but one shoulder ached – probably dislocated – and his back felt stiff. He'd twisted to one side to see if it was just a sprain; he felt a sharp twinge, but could move. It wasn't broken.

It was then that he'd started to study the shelf above. If he could make it over the lip, then he had a chance of survival. A long, arduous trudge perhaps, but the main danger would then be exposure or exhaustion. Already he felt that his skin, badly bruised from the fall, had been burnt raw by the cold air.

Another few hours and the question of whether he'd make it over the lip or not would be immaterial.

That Hobson's choice was little comfort in the long, painful hours ahead as he finally made his way over and trudged down into a small valley, which rose quickly to another peak. Towards its top he faced another ledge.

He shook his head slightly as he studied it, then looked back down to the floor of the ravine.

This one looked altogether too formidable – but the inner voice was surging ever stronger . . . *You have to make it*! And not just for Vruger. Now you have your own scores to settle.

He started to claw his way slowly upward.

17

The helicopter whirred in from the north of Neveh Ativ.

There was no direct flight between Bahrain and Israel, so Daniel and Leorah had flown to Beirut, then taken a bus down to Sidon, where Swenkel had picked them up by helicopter.

Swenkel sat next to the pilot. He looked over his shoulder as they started to descend.

'Quite a show, isn't it,' he grimaced. 'Nobody can suggest to General Pohlmann, though, that he might be overdoing things. "Psychological tactics". Whatever happens to the children, it must be clear to Hasik that he'll *never* get out of here.'

Daniel looked below. It was probably the best view of the area they'd get. He counted four tanks and the same number of field guns, and at least a dozen jeeps and large transporters. The artillery and tanks made up the front line, and a number of tents had been erected behind. At one side of the makeshift encampment stood two helicopters and four small ground-to-ground missile-firers.

Swenkel studied Daniel's expression and looked concernedly between him and Leorah.

'Let's just hope for all of our sakes we don't have to use any of this.'

The entrance to the tunnel became visible as they levelled out for the final descent.

'How deep is it?' Daniel asked.

'Eighty yards plus. They're closer to the rear – not visible even in the best daylight. We've got almost half the show of strength again on the other side.'

The noise of the rotors became almost deafening as they hovered downwards for the last fifty feet. The engine cut as soon as they touched ground.

As the door was opened by a soldier outside, Swenkel touched Leorah's hand lightly.

'Perhaps I might not get another chance to say this – but whatever the outcome, we appreciate what you're doing. You can't know how much.' Swenkel smiled wistfully. 'My uncle used to tell me that Israel had Arab friends like you once – but that was a long time ago.'

Daniel noticed Leorah flinch slightly at the 'Arab friends', but she didn't protest that she was only doing it for the children, as he thought she might. She merely smiled. He began to wonder what else was going on in her mind.

El-Hasik paced the front of the bus like a caged lion.

When he had threatened to kill a child, it had been in haste and anger. He knew that Pohlmann was right: if he did kill a child, further bargaining would become difficult, if not impossible. But now that he had made the threat, the apparent weakness if he didn't carry it through could be equally damaging.

He thought of the boy that Jahleb had killed by accident, and had been hidden under a tarpaulin, tucked behind the back seat of the bus. In a way, they had already crossed the hurdle of a killing. Would one more make such a difference? Or was it just the Israelis *knowing* that made the difference.

Perhaps they could claim that as their one killing, the enactment of their threat.

Five days! At the outset he would never have believed it possible. Five days in this stinking tunnel! He felt as if his brains were frying. It was running stronger and faster each time . . . *I can't take it much longer*, an inner voice told him. But another voice kept returning – *You have to. . . The others are weaker than you . . . If you don't, it will all fall apart – to no purpose!*

Hasik looked around keenly. Perhaps he *should* kill one, a fresh one. Perhaps only that would exorcise what had been building up inside him. Then he would be free, his thoughts clear. *Oh yes!* Please, let my mind be free of this. He held one hand to his head; thoughts seared his skull like red-hot pokers. *Please . . . Bi'aunillâh!* The second *sourate*, one of the five main Koran prayers, began to recite in his mind. He edged forwards, his eyes seeking haphazardly. *Pohlmann!* If I do this, let it be on your head. You have pushed me to it!

The burning tension continued pounding in his brain as he paced purposefully down the aisle. Some of the children looked up at him as he passed, but most averted their gaze.

Hasik's eyes were red with pent-up emotion as they locked onto a boy nine rows down.

'You!' he screamed. 'Stand up! What is your name?'

The boy got to his feet uncertainly. He was no more than ten, with curly reddish-blond hair.

'Paul,' he said.

'Move into the aisle!' shouted Hasik.

The boy edged across. Hasik held his gun out at arm's length, inches from the boy's face. The boy turned his face to one side, tears running unashamedly down his cheeks.

'Be brave, my boy,' Hasik uttered. 'You are dying for a cause which you don't yet understand, but is much greater than you or I.'

The bus hushed into a dread silence.

Beni, a few rows ahead, tried to make his mind up in that split-second. He had the gun out of his satchel and hidden to one side. He could have a clear shot at Hasik's back. But the men at each end of the bus looked too alert. He wasn't sure if he'd be given the time to turn and fire.

At that moment a click sounded, and Beni thought Hasik might have pulled the trigger and hit an empty chamber. But Hasik had turned wildly around, looking towards the front of the bus.

Following the click came a hiss, then a garbled voice over the field telephone. Hasik lowered his gun and ran over and gripped the receiver.

'Aman here,' came the voice. 'A helicopter has just arrived.'

'More soldiers?'

'No. I don't think so. The pilot's in uniform, but the other three are in civilian dress. One's a girl with long dark hair.'

After Swenkel's introduction, General Pohlmann had spent ten minutes with Daniel and Leorah outlining the situation to date.

'I'm afraid we don't know at this stage if Hasik has harmed any of the children.'

'Don't know?' Leorah bridled. 'I thought it was an Israeli prerequisite not to deal under those circumstances, not to be blackmailed.'

'Yes, that is true,' Pohlmann shrugged. 'But on this occasion we have the lives of so many –'

'I fully appreciate that, General,' Leorah cut in. 'I want to save those children, and *badly*. But if Hasik has already harmed any of them, then that severely weakens my bargaining position. I must know for sure before I go in.'

Leorah strode resolutely to a position just behind the front line of artillery, and studied the tunnel entrance ahead.

General Pohlmann threw Daniel a puzzled look; it was obvious that he was unused to this reaction from an Arab to what was a standard form of blackmail for the more extreme Palestinian groups. He wasn't sure whether to be agreeably surprised or mistrust her behaviour completely.

Pohlmann checked his watch: 5.08. Dusk was approaching; there was a quiet, unsettled atmosphere among the surrounding hills, as if they were holding their breath for the sunset.

Pohlmann glanced back to where Swenkel was standing, resting against a jeep by the edge of the main camp. Swenkel was lighting a cigarette; fixed on his face was the laconic grimace that was so much his trademark.

God help us all if your intelligence isn't correct, Pohlmann thought. He went over and rang out on the field telephone. It answered almost immediately.

'El-Hasik!'

'Hasik. General Pohlmann speaking. I have Miss Ajlan . . .'

'I know, I know! One of my men has seen her. Cut the formalities and put her on.'

Pohlmann waved Leorah across. He put one hand firmly across the mouthpiece. 'I have El-Hasik here. He wishes to speak to you. If you would like to have some further conference, I can delay him.'

'No. It's alright. That won't be necessary.'

Leorah gently gripped the receiver to her ear. Her hand was sweating. She stayed silent for a second, trying to sense the presence at the other end. 'El-Hasik?'

'Ah, Miss Ajlan. *Salam*. This is a pleasure. I have a few questions for you first, if you don't mind.'

'Go ahead.'

'You covered the assassinations of Al-Hakim and Khourem, I believe. What was Khourem's popular party slogan?'

'*Il rubat Ilsha'b* . . . To the shackled people of Islam shall come the freedom and brotherhood of the Karim Sha'b.'

'Khourem's half-brother is also involved in politics – which few people are aware of. What is his capacity, and who does he advise?'

'Yes, he is – but not in Lebanese politics,' Leorah snubbed the catch. 'He is a permanent secretary in the Syrian cabinet, advising Abdel Halim Khaddam, Foreign Minister.'

'Yes. Very good.' Hasik's voice was slow, deliberate. 'Did Khourem have any identifying marks?'

'A scar on the left side of his abdomen – from an operation four years before his death.'

Hasik stayed silent.

Leorah felt the sudden return of her nervousness; she started racking her brain for something she might have forgotten, something she should add.

'Put me back to Pohlmann,' Hasik said.

No indication in his voice, Leorah thought. There was nothing she could say now that wouldn't sound pretentious. The moment had gone.

Leorah held the receiver out.

'How did it go?' Pohlmann asked concernedly.

Leorah covered the mouthpiece. 'I don't know.' She shook her head. 'I just couldn't tell. He wants to speak to you again.'

Pohlmann took the receiver tentatively. 'Yes?'

Silence returned.

'Yes?' Pohlmann repeated. '. . . For God's sake Hasik, this is no time for your games.'

'You have kept me waiting quite some while, General. Now *I* will decide the time and the conditions.' Hasik drew a long breath. 'The girl is accurate, she seems genuine. But I need proof. We know her by name, but not by sight – she could so easily be a well-trained plant. I will deal with her only face to face, with identification.'

'What sort of identification?'

'Her passport, a press card perhaps. She would surely carry these as a matter of course.'

'Yes. I suppose so.' Pohlmann was hesitant. 'But I don't know. I must discuss it with her.'

'Call me back immediately!' Hasik said. 'In two minutes I will disconnect this line and she will have to come here to the bus, whatever you decide.'

'Hasik, before we talk on this, we want to know if you have killed any of the children?'

'No. We have not killed any of the children – *yet*.'

The line went dead.

Pohlmann felt an instinct rise quickly: Hasik had hardly faltered, but then perhaps he, Itzaak Pohlmann, had been lied to by too many Arabs not to know. But if he voiced this instinct of not believing Hasik, would the girl still deal? He turned slowly to face Leorah.

'It's not good, I'm afraid. He wants to see you in person with some identification. I don't like the idea of you going inside the bus – but then I don't see much option.'

Leorah looked towards the tunnel again, as if weighing up the proposition.

'You understand that if you do this, we can offer you precious little protection,' Pohlmann added.

Daniel stepped forward. 'I don't like it. If he doesn't take the bait, Leorah's life could be in danger – with us practically powerless.'

'I won't underestimate the danger to you,' Pohlmann said, 'however much I now depend on your help. It's no secret that in Hasik's circles traitors are often treated more harshly than enemies. You knew the risks and the stakes before you came. *Now* you know the limitations of the aid we can offer.'

Leorah touched Daniel's arm lightly. 'It's alright, Daniel. I think I can handle it.'

Pohlmann was thoughtful. A light wind played around them; it felt as if a *Hamseen* was on its way. 'There are ways of minimizing the risks. In less than an hour it will be dark – about the only time that we're anywhere near equal on viewing. And this is the only end from which we'll get a view at all – they've blocked the far end with a rock fall. We've got a couple of starlight scopes and we'll be able to pick you out. My men have already been watching movement inside the bus. The only hope then is that Hasik doesn't put the headlamps on and blind the sights.'

'How do we play for that hour?' asked Leorah.

Pohlmann lapsed deeper into thought. One of his hands clenched nervously. 'We can say that you left your luggage at the main camp at Tiberiade – that would kill about an hour or so by helicopter. You've got some identification with you?'

'Yes. My Croix Rouge card – it has my picture.' Leorah bit at her lip. 'Do you think he'll go for it?'

'I hope so.'

Daniel still looked unsettled. 'And there's *no* other way of handling it?'

Pohlmann stared hard at Daniel. 'I wish there was, for *all* our sakes.'

They were silent for a second. The flap of a canvas tent nearby started to move with the wind.

'You asked about the children,' Leorah said. 'Are any of them harmed?'

'He says not.'

Pohlmann turned away after a second and walked over to consult with Major Gant. It *was* the best way of handling it, he felt sure. Let her decide for herself whether she trusts the word of one of her own kind.

It was cool and dark inside the tunnel. The heat outside, now dying fast after sunset had hardly penetrated its thick stone confines.

A powerful searchlight on top of one of the jeeps had picked out the first twenty yards, but now it seemed little more than a pale opalescence as Leorah looked back. Ahead was pitch darkness.

Leorah was counting her paces: thirty-five . . . thirty-six . . . The paces were becoming shorter, she realized, she was starting to almost shuffle her way along. Come on, Hasik . . . *Come on!* The arrangement was that you would turn on the headlamps to guide the way after the signal, then turn them off again to indicate that I'd reached the bus. The first two flashes had gone out sixteen paces ago; now Leorah could tell by the beam behind dying at split intervals that they were flashing again. She looked ahead: nothing. Only darkness.

She listened, trying to pick out sound and movement.

Some faint scurrying came to her; perhaps a lizard or a rat.

Suddenly she jumped. Her skin prickled. She had come up against something. She put out her hand; it was the side wall, its cool stone slightly moist. She had obviously been shuffling forward at an angle. She started to move again, touching the wall at her side as her guide.

A faint click sounded – and then the twin beam of the bus headlamps came on ahead. Leorah held one arm up to shield her eyes. The light was blinding after the darkness. The bus was about twenty yards ahead, she guessed.

She paced more confidently now, and for the first time was conscious of the echo of her own footsteps. Getting closer, she could make out some of the faces inside the bus.

It was easy to pick out Hasik and his men, since all the hostages were children. Two men stood at the front of the bus – one of them probably Hasik himself – and she could just make out a vague figure in combat dress deeper down the central aisle. On her way in she had passed one of the men above the tunnel entrance, and, from what Pohlmann had told her, there was another at the far end, too.

A man with a beard was making a waving motion, but she ignored him and took her time for the last few yards. The bus door was open.

The man with the beard stared intently at her as she came up the steps. He smiled slightly.

'You are the new breed of Arab woman, I understand, Miss Ajlan. But you should heed that there is an Islamic revolution in the wind – a return to the old ways and traditions. Which forebodes ill for you and your kind.'

'And I suppose the future belongs to you and *your* kind. God help us.'

Hasik's smile faded. He looked unsure whether to take this seriously or just as banter. 'You surprise me, Miss Ajlan. I thought that you believed in our cause.'

'I do.' Leorah stepped onto the main platform of the bus, a yard away from Hasik. She slowly surveyed the children. 'But not in *this* way. This can only damage our people's cause.'

'What other way are we to fight? We have merely learnt our lessons from the past. The Israelis give no quarter; they are ruthless, unbending. We are obliged to answer in the same way.'

'Has it ever occurred to you that actions like this only harden the Israelis even more? You both believe in the same laws of tit for tat, an eye for an eye. What end can there be if neither side will give ground?'

Hasik looked down. 'It's difficult to tell which side you speak for. If someone is to give ground, you should look to the side which committed the first wrong.'

'The first wrong?' Leorah shook her head incredulously. 'You talk as if this was still Biblical times.'

Hasik slowly lifted his red and weary eyes. 'You look out there into that never-ending desert, when the sun is rising, Miss Ajlan – or when a herdsman in his striped *thobe* is tending his goats, and *then* tell me that this is not still Biblical times.'

Leorah looked out through the tunnel in the direction of the desert. She took Hasik's point, but to concede it could give him an advantage; if his beliefs were endorsed in any way, it would be that much harder to prise him away from his intended course of action.

'Look, I haven't come here to discuss traditions or politics,' she said. 'Just to tell you simply that you are making an error, El-Hasik. A great error.' She stopped suddenly – something came to the forefront of her mind. *The lights!* 'You haven't switched off the lights yet,' she said.

'Is it so important?'

'Just that it was part of the arrangement. Otherwise Pohlmann will think something has happened to me.'

'Perhaps I should leave them on until I decide whether anything should happen to you.' Hasik smiled slowly and Leorah felt a shiver up her spine.

Hasik's automatic handgun was holstered, but the man at his side and the other further down the aisle both held machine-guns, poised and ready. She recognized them as AK-47s.

She had faced hostile situations with armed men before, but hadn't felt quite this way about it. The confinement and darkness of the tunnel, and the quietly mumbling, sometimes whimpering children added to the tension. Was it fear for herself, or for the children? Or could she only feel afraid for herself through them?

She sensed that Hasik was bluffing, and she was grateful that she had so quickly gained the measure of him. But another aspect worried her: if he could move so quickly from serious discussions into sly teasing, then it could be just as easily into rage and blood-letting.

Hasik made a small signal. Jahleb leaned over and switched off the lights.

Leorah looked away towards the children again, hoping he hadn't read anything into her mention of the lights.

'I'd like to speak to some of them.'

Hasik was silent for a second. 'You said this was an error?'

'Yes.' Leorah cast her eyes along, row by row. 'You claim that none of them has been harmed.' She turned and started pacing down the aisle. She felt safer, more confident now with the lights out. She could almost imagine the illuminated cross-sights on Hasik's back, the slightest hair touch that would trigger a bullet.

'That is correct.' Hasik flushed slightly. He wasn't sure if he was more put off by her ignoring his comment or by the overall arrogance of her determination. 'You have forgotten one thing, though, Miss Ajlan.'

'What?'

'You've forgotten who is master here. *I* will decide if and when you shall talk with the children. Before that you will show me your identification. And then you will explain this *error* to me – slowly and very carefully.'

Leorah met Hasik's stare defiantly. The sniper would have him clear now. *Yes*, go on, squeeze the trigger. I think I hate him enough already.

Hasik unfastened his gun, but didn't lift it from its holster. He waved his arm to one side. 'Please. We shall sit and talk for a few minutes first.'

*

An Israeli army Sergeant called Salkin looked through the starlight scope of his M14 rifle.

From the front he was half hidden under a canvas sheet, so that Hasik's look-out couldn't see the tell-tale beam of the scope. Directly behind him stood General Pohlmann and Major Gant.

Pohlmann noticed the concerned expression on Salkin's face.

'Is something wrong? Any sighting yet?'

'No. The headlamps are still on.'

Pohlmann checked his watch. 'Christ! She should be there by now.'

'They were late going on,' Salkin remarked. 'It looked as though she kept moving – but it was slow at points. Almost a standstill.'

Daniel and Art Swenkel stood about ten yards further back. Pohlmann hadn't given them a second glance in all of fifteen minutes; his eyes, like theirs, had been fixed steadfastly on the tunnel ahead.

'Hold it!' Salkin muttered. 'The lights have just gone out.'

'Can you pick out anything?' Pohlmann asked anxiously.

'No. Not yet. Though . . . wait a minute . . . I'm just focusing on something.' Salkin lapsed into silence for a minute. 'A man's profile . . . now his back. There's another man to one side – a yard or so away.'

'And the girl?'

'Nothing yet. Just panning deeper . . . Here we go . . . *Yes!* She's just turned away from the first man. Now she's walking down the aisle towards the back.'

'Where's the third man?'

'I've only got an outline at present – I think he's deeper still. Let's see . . . Yeah . . . Got him now. About ten feet from the back.'

Pohlmann ran over the strategy in his mind. The plastic explosive inside the bus had been one of the main problems. Because one of Hasik's look-out men at either end of the tunnel could be holding the detonator, he had detailed two other snipers with starlight scopes. Their jobs were easier: they had to concentrate on only one man each. One sniper was thirty yards to their side, and required only a hand signal; for the other contact was by walkie-talkie. Co-ordinating their actions would be the key.

'What's positioning like – are they all relatively clear?'

'Not bad. All the children are sitting – but the girl's half blocking the man at the back for the moment. Wait a minute! Something's happening,' Salkin hissed. 'The girl has turned. Looks like some heated words with one of them . . . The man has just unclipped his gun.'

'What do you think?'

'It doesn't look good.'

Pohlmann's nerves set rigid. He realized that he was hesitating more than he should.

'Is the man at the back still partly obscured?'

'Yes!'

'Look, I can't make the decision totally for you. But if you make a move, make sure you can get them all. And let me know the second you squeeze off that first shot.'

El-Hasik shook his head in disbelief.

'It is incredible. I know that you were close enough to Al-Hakim and Khourem to know this, that you did the main articles after their deaths – but still I find it hard to accept.'

Hasik looked out of the side window into the blanketing darkness of the tunnel. Condensation had formed on the glass and was beginning to run in droplets. The tears of Palestine, he thought ironically – from the breath of Israeli children.

It had never occurred to him that he might be wrong. The single-mindedness of an Ashbel! When that had been impressed upon them by the camp instructors, it had been as a strength, not a disadvantage.

It seemed so long ago now: the field marches barefoot over

rugged terrain, the snakes coiled around necks to induce fearlessness. All young men together! Hasik had joined at thirteen, quite old for an Ashbel recruit. His father had died two years earlier in the 'Kawujki' assaults of the early fifties, and his mother rapidly became too feeble-minded to wield any influence over him.

He remembered saying to her the day he joined that he was fighting for her freedom, the same freedom that his father had fought and died for. She was still – twenty years later – living in a hovel in a refugee camp, though she had moved after the sacking of Damour to Beirut's Shattilla, and he was *still* fighting. This time though that freedom had seemed at last close at hand. Was it all to come to nothing?

'And this came from Al-Ben Salmad? It was he who betrayed Al-Hakim and Khourem?'

'Yes.'

El-Hasik held his head in his hands. He had listened to Leorah talk for over half an hour, and there was little more to ask now except to confirm some of the points.

'A Swiss banker? Who would have thought?'

Leorah didn't answer; Hasik's disbelief had a note of acceptance about it, but she wanted to be totally sure.

'What you have said has some interesting factors – but then so did my scheme.' Hasik studied Leorah carefully. 'I think you know that well, don't you? Since the start of the war, we have other enemies besides the Israelis – the Saiquas, the Phalangists. We are no longer fighting on Israeli territory, but one day even the thought of us so close across the border will irritate them – and then they will not be happy until they have driven us into the sea. So how will my acceptance of what you've said now benefit my people?'

Leorah shook her head. 'The cause is right – but the issue you stood on is wrong. You were not to know.'

'But now that I have the advantage – why should I not play it? There are other issues at stake – release of many of my fellows among them.'

Leorah looked down at one of Hasik's hands clasping the seat in front. 'That is up to you.'

'Of course, that is so, even if I was to believe you.'

An awkward silence fell. The murmuring of some of the children came to them.

'Well, do you believe me?' Leorah asked at length.

Hasik's hand clasped tighter. The turmoil of his thoughts during the past scant hour showed in his face. 'Yes,' he said tautly. 'But I wish that I didn't. It is hard to stop clinging to a dream that has been with you for so long.'

Leorah looked into Hasik's eyes. They were weary and bloodshot, but now the fire had gone out of them; there was a hint of defeat. But still she couldn't be sure of his acceptance; she reminded herself how suddenly his mood had changed earlier – and, then again, it could just as easily be a bluff.

'So what do you want me to tell the Israelis?'

'I want you to tell them that I accept what you have said, and accordingly my demands have changed. I wish now only for release of prisoners. I will contact Pohlmann on the field telephone and discuss the full details with him when you have returned.'

Leorah felt relieved that Hasik had accepted her story, but annoyance that her main aim – the children's release – had been frustrated.

'I think you should get yourself another messenger for that, Hasik. I came here primarily to save these children – regardless of their nationality – and I only agreed to do the Israelis' bidding because of that, and because I felt you were making a mistake. It's bad enough that you might have killed some of these children, but can you imagine what it would be like to do so for the wrong reasons – not even *indirect* blame would have fallen on the Israelis for not saving them. Public sympathy would have been fully with them from every corner of the earth. You would have made martyrs out of those children. And don't forget that every ounce of sympathy gained for them is sympathy lost for the Palestinian cause – as some of your fellow madmen found out to their cost at Munich and Dawson's Field.'

'So now I am holding them for the *right* reasons. And I

thank you for your advice.' Hasik got to his feet. 'But now you will do *my* bidding.'

Leorah glared at him. 'I don't think so.'

Hasik moved close to her. He was sweating heavily. She could smell the rankness of five days of confinement on his body.

She was afraid, but at the same time she hesitated to provoke him further. His gun was still unlatched from its holster, and she felt sure that if he lifted it the marksman outside would make his move. She tried to measure up positioning: it would be close. Perhaps *too* close.

Without warning, Hasik burst into laughter, almost bellowing in her face. Then just as suddenly he stopped, and gripped a small boy by the hair, yanking him up so hard that the child screamed. Hasik's expression was frantic. He took out his gun and pressed it against the child's face.

'Still you don't understand how pathetic your little show of defiance is! You wish me to kill this one for you? You wish to be personally responsible for his death?'

Leorah froze. She expected to hear the whistle of the sniper's bullet at any second. But it didn't come. She looked past Hasik. The man at the front was now alert, and standing in the aisle – probably part blocking vision. *For God's sake move!*

Hasik started to squeeze the trigger.

'No, *please* . . . let him go. There is no need!'

'Then you will do as I ask?'

Leorah was counting the seconds as she watched the man behind: he had moved slightly, but obviously not enough. She closed her eyes finally in resignation.

'Yes. I will do as you ask.'

Hasik slowly released the boy and re-holstered his gun.

'You see, it is not I who will cause the death of any of these children – but you, or the Israelis proving unreasonable. In all these things there must be some balance. I have given much ground – now it is up to the Israelis.' Hasik held his gaze on Leorah. 'So we have an understanding?'

'Yes.' After a moment Leorah looked away awkwardly.

'May I speak with some of the children now?'

Hasik let out his breath. 'If you must. But only for a minute.' He waved his arm dismissively and sat down again.

Leorah steeled herself as she started down the aisle. The normally bright eyes of children were dull with fear and exhaustion, a look she knew well. She felt like screaming in anguish and frustration – because she knew now with certainty that there was little chance of reasoning with someone like Hasik. Unless you played it very clever. Very cautious. She stopped first a few rows down.

'*Shalom*. What is your name?'

'Kathleen.'

The girl was about eleven, Leorah guessed. She stroked the child's forehead gently. 'Be brave, Kathleen. It won't be long now before you are all out of here.' She looked one row behind. 'And what is *your* name?'

'Beni.'

'You look like one of the older boys here. You must try and set an example . . .'

Leorah's voice faded into the background as Hasik sat with his own thoughts. Half an hour of conversation and the entire path of the last year's planning had changed. Did he really believe her? Surely she had been too close, too devoted to Al-Hakim and Khourem to lie. Besides which every single fact she'd provided had fitted into place, and even filled some of the gaps in his own scheme. But, then, if the Israelis were to create a ruse, it would have to be a complete one, one which covered every angle. Certainly, they'd had enough time to plan it – *five days*.

He dwelled for a while on that, but returned again to the realization that she was simply too pro-Muslim to side with the Israelis. When he'd had that same thought earlier, with each passing minute of their conversation he'd found himself searching deep in her eyes for telltale signs of betrayal. He looked towards her as she moved about at the rear of the bus.

He realized he had agreed at the time only because the facts were simply too comprehensive for him to disagree and still save face. But perhaps it was best that the Israelis thought he agreed for now, even if later he chose to renegue on the deal.

Hasik suddenly jumped to his feet. The rear of the bus! *The dead boy!*

'Miss Ajlan!' he called out. 'I think you have had enough time now, please.'

The man at that end moved across and stood blocking the aisle to the final three rows.

'What is behind here?' Leorah enquired.

'Some explosives and such like. That's why we have to be careful.' Hasik walked a few steps towards her, trying to control his agitation. 'I trust you are satisfied?'

Leorah took one last glance. 'Yes. Okay.' She turned away.

The image didn't imprint itself fully on her mind until she was a few paces away. If she hadn't seen so many similar sights in working for the Croix Rouge, she would probably never have noticed – the shape of a hand and part of an arm beneath a canvas sheet. And then the smell suddenly made sense to her. It wasn't just the smell of so many closed in captivity; she should have picked out the difference! They had probably salted the body to stop putrification, but still it came through. She suddenly realized that she had paused in mid step.

'Is everything alright, Miss Ajlan?' asked Hasik.

'Yes . . . fine.' She forced a smile.

The blood pounded through her head as she paced up the aisle. He tricked me! Lied to me! He *has* killed a child. How can I possibly vouch for him now? The Israeli reaction aside, just from my own conscience! But a voice of fear also joined in. Did my expression give me away? God, I hope he didn't notice. Just another minute and I'll be out of here.

'So, you have everything clear, Miss Ajlan.' Hasik sat sideways in the driver's seat. 'I will call Pohlmann in twenty minutes, which should give you plenty of time to explain the situation to him.'

'Twenty minutes then.' Leorah looked hard into Hasik's eyes just before she turned away. She felt relief as she went down the steps of the bus: she sensed no change in Hasik.

Jahleb switched on the headlights as she started to walk away.

El-Hasik stood silently watching her. He waited until she was a full ten yards away, then he addressed Jahleb quietly.

'She noticed the boy. She will betray us to the Israelis. Kill her!'

18

Swenkel studied Daniel's anxious expression as he drew hard on his cigarette.

'You like her, don't you?'

'Yes. And I've only just found her. I don't want to lose her.'

Saying it out loud made him suddenly aware how strong his emotions were, and he felt faintly embarrassed.

'She's a brave girl,' Swenkel remarked. 'Unusual too. There aren't many Arabs that would help us like this. There was a time when that wasn't so – but that was a while ago now.' Swenkel ruefully studied the ground for a moment. 'It's probably even more difficult for her than for most Arabs. After all, she's openly proclaimed her Arab views in print.'

'Yes. She *is* rather special.'

They stood in silence for a moment – and the first shots rang out from the tunnel as Swenkel was about to speak again. For a second they were both stunned – then Daniel started forwards.

'*Christ's* sake!'

Swenkel came quickly alongside and gripped his arm firmly. 'Whatever it is, you can't help!'

Daniel tried to wrestle him off, his eyes fixed frantically on the tunnel entrance – then slowly he relaxed in acceptance. His body started trembling, and Swenkel released his arm.

Fifty yards ahead, they heard Pohlmann shout. 'Get the lights! The *lights*!'

Salkin focused in on the two bright orbs. They merged together in almost an oval, dazzling, yet hazy and indistinct around the edges. He had to concentrate hard to try and locate the centre of each light source. He split the oval into two segments and set the crosshairs at the rough centre of one. He fired at one-second intervals to allow the light to die in order to indicate a hit. On the third shot, one side of the oval faded and left a circle. He panned across; two further shots and he'd hit the other lamp.

The bus and the figures inside began to take shape again. He could pick out two of the men, but not the third. He started firing.

Leorah wasn't sure what instinct had made her glance back – perhaps the uncanny silence – but in that moment, above the glare of the lights, she saw Jahleb standing with his gun raised, and she threw herself forward spontaneously.

A bullet whistled close by in a rush of air, almost before the explosion sounded. A second bullet came, and she felt an impact like a kick in the back and found herself suddenly on the ground. She scrambled forward desperately, almost clawing at the rough tarmac. Only one of her legs moved easily.

Shots were still coming, Leorah could sense them passing close, striking the tarmac and kicking up fragments of rock from the side wall. She struggled to move again. The area of pain was widening. She couldn't tell whether she'd been hit in the thigh – or low in the spine so that paralysis had frozen her leg.

Another volley of shots sounded, and Leorah closed her eyes, expecting the bullets to strike at any second; she knew she was powerless to escape.

Events reeled haphazardly through her mind: Daniel, the Croix Rouge, the past year of war and bloodshed, the *Yaumi Rassul*, Al-Hakim and Khourem, her mother and her father

. . . all the family together in her father's store. She was touching the fabric of a rich satin, feeling it cool against her face . . . and her mother was sewing at the back. But there was something wrong! She couldn't see Jamil, and yet Jamil had been there at the time. Her mind searched harder and deeper, but still she couldn't picture him there. *Please*, Jamil – don't be lost to me, not now!

She started to cry, a sob that turned slowly to an insane laugh. Perhaps she *had* betrayed him. It seemed unjust and somehow ironic that she, of all people, should die in a welter of Palestinian bullets while trying to help the Israelis. Perhaps that was her punishment.

She opened her eyes. The sounds of the shots were different now – they had been for a short while, without her being fully conscious of them. She registered the whining of metal being struck and looked round to see one of the bus headlamps shatter.

A wave of relief hit her; suddenly Pohlmann's directive to keep close to the side walls made sense. Israeli snipers were shooting out the lamps! But what had happened to Hasik's accomplice who had been firing at her?

The second headlamp shattered. Darkness fell, so total that it made no difference if her eyes were open or shut.

Leorah knew that the darkness should protect her, yet for some reason her fear now felt even more intense. Only gunfire punctuated the sounds of her heartbeat and breathing. Her sweat was cold.

Which was the way out? She scrambled over and touched the side wall, and decided to follow it along. She had only crawled a few yards when the gunfire ceased. She halted and listened for a second in the silence, then continued – aware only of the faint sounds of her own movement echoing off the tunnel walls. Suddenly she stopped again. The sounds of other movement came to her. She listened more intently – and after a moment it became clearer; a light scuffing of footsteps from behind. Her heart froze. Somebody had followed her out of the bus.

*

The passing hours had taken their toll on Beni's nerves. Like all the other children, he had been kept sitting throughout all five days, except for the times when they had been taken out to stretch their legs or relieve themselves towards the back end of the tunnel blocked by rock fall.

In that time, only two real opportunities had arisen when he could have used the gun, but they'd passed quickly and he'd settled once again into weary watchfulness.

When the girl had arrived, it had been the first sign of hope that they might be freed, and he wouldn't have to use the gun. He'd felt oddly touched when she'd stopped to talk to him. From listening to Hasik and his men, he knew already that she was an Arab, and at first it seemed strange to him, the role she was playing. She was one of Hasik's kind, so why should she side with the children? His father had taught him that all Arabs were the enemy of Israel, that they had clanned together ever stronger as the years passed, and now *none* was to trusted.

He had been immediately thrown by her looks, and after her early exchange with Hasik, his attitude to her had softened. By the time she had finished with Hasik, and walked up the aisle and talked to him, he had melted almost completely. Some of his favourite pin-ups inside his bedroom cupboard looked like her, and if he was older she was the sort of girl he would like to be seen with. God forbid that his father would even guess that he'd had such a thought. Beni was still blushing slightly as she walked away.

She moved about the rows at the rear for a while. Then Hasik called out and made his way down towards her. There seemed to be some heated words, although Beni couldn't make them out exactly. He turned to look round as they walked back up the aisle, and from their expressions he tried to judge what had been agreed. They were both cordial but tense, and he judged from that that negotiations were still in progress. Leorah nodded curtly and left.

There was an unusual silence inside the bus as Hasik and Jahleb watched her walk away. Beni noticed Hasik mumble something to the other man, Jahleb, but what happened next stunned him to the core.

All the moments that he had thought of using the gun – and now when it was needed more than ever, he was totally unprepared! He felt shame and fear and uncertainty in equal proportions.

The seconds ticked away as a pounding in his chest. He was aware that the man behind him was on the alert, but the man at the front was already firing – and he couldn't let that happen! She had tried to help them – perhaps still was the only one who could. This was all wrong. She was too beautiful to die! He fancied he could still feel the tingle on his cheek where she had touched him.

Everything seemed somehow distant – and the shots sounded oddly hollow inside his head. He was almost unaware that he had snatched the gun from his satchel and raised it slightly to fire.

The recoil from his first shot jolted him back sharply, and he had to steady himself for the second and third. His nerves were raised to such a pitch that he had to grit his teeth to stop himself from shivering. He saw one of the bullets hit Jahleb – with a gout of blood in the back. Then something hit him from behind, and the seat rail in front rushed up towards him. There was a blur, then everything went dark.

Hasik crouched at the front of the bus as bullets whistled through the windscreen above his head. His eyes roamed frantically as he tried to take stock of what had happened.

He was sure the girl had been hit – or had she? Was his mind playing tricks on him? Perhaps it was the darkness and shadows of the tunnel. Before the lights went out, he was sure she had moved. So if she had been hit, it hadn't stopped her.

He couldn't remember which came first: the lights being blown out, or the shots from behind; they had come so close together.

He'd ducked down as the final headlamp had smashed and at the same time seen the boy firing at Jahleb. He was already clutching his own gun, but Fayek at the rear beat him to it, letting loose a short burst on his AK-47. The boy fell only an instant before Hasik saw the sniper's bullets find Fayek; one through the neck, then another to the chest, almost lifting him off his feet.

Hasik tried to calm his breathing. *Israeli snipers!* His mind was on fire. The girl had already betrayed them, the dead boy hadn't even come into it! How blind he had been! No true Arab could ever associate with the Israelis; he should have given more credence to that initial instinct.

His mind began to dwell on everything she had said – on how much she could have fabricated. He may have been right in his cause all along, and she had destroyed it within minutes! The sheer audacity of the dupe made him tremble with hate. Saliva was thick on his lips. She was a traitor of the worst kind! He would repay her for this! *But how?* The options were fast diminishing. Israeli fire was probably heavy on his outside positions, and troopers would doubtless be storming the tunnel at any minute.

His plan began to crystallize: the girl had been injured, she couldn't have gone far. His blood-red eyes surveyed the bus for a second; he wondered whether to shoot as many children as he could before he left, in order to repay the Israelis more savagely. But if he stood up, the sniper would pick him off. Suddenly he thought of a way of covering both options. Let them all go together!

He only hoped that Aman's position was still intact. He scrambled across and rang out on the field telephone.

It took a moment to receive an answer.

'Aman!'

'*Madah!* Thank God! How are things?'

'Heavy mortar, and some small fire – but I'm well dug in.' Aman sounded short of breath. 'I think I can hold for a while.'

'Are the lines still intact?'

'As far as I can see.'

'Good. Give me two minutes, then detonate.' Hasik rang off and faced the children; the murmuring among them had become more agitated. 'Any of you that go near this door, I will shoot.'

With the amount of plastique in the bus, the explosion would be considerable. He'd have just over a minute to find the girl; any more than that would be cutting it too fine to get clear. He checked his gun and made his way out into the darkness.

They were singing *Shir Hahehalutz*. It was in the school at Ma'alot Torchiha; Beni recognized it from the pale blue walls and the portrait of Ben-Gurion beside the flag. The voices were high-pitched . . . *Bamenuha lehagea, umargoa lealeh, layla iver mistarea, bisdot emek Yisrael* . . . It was almost a chant. But the tune was somehow different; as if it had been turned into a dirge. He recognized some of the faces as he looked around the hall, many belonged to those with him on the bus. Somehow he could pick out their voices from the others; then he realized they were talking all around him.

The last of his delirium lifted in a haze like a muslin shroud, but things were still blurred as he lifted his head from the floor. He focused first on the few rows in front – barely discernible in the darkness.

He heard Hasik's voice addressing them, although he didn't immediately comprehend all the words.

Couldn't go near the doors? *Why?*

Hasik was making his way out. What for? What was out there except Israeli troopers? It took a moment for the answer to come. *The girl.* Hasik was going after the girl!

Beni struggled to move. His shoulder ached numbly, but there was movement in his legs. The gun had fallen a yard to one side. Scrambling, he reached for it.

A faint light now glowed ahead. Leorah estimated that she'd crawled another ten yards since the lights went out.

The darkness had been impenetrable; she'd guided herself by feeling her way along the side of the tunnel, accompanied only by the sound of her own breathing, the scurrying of rats and insects – and now those faint, ominous footsteps from behind.

The light up ahead had appeared only in the last few seconds. The Israeli searchlights were back on, she speculated. It was still intensely dark, but the distant light was enough to judge direction.

She stopped and listened. The footsteps were getting closer!

If only she could move faster. She crawled furiously – but then it struck her that while the Israelis might see her more easily then, so could the person behind!

Who would get to her first? She wasn't sure she was bold enough to play the odds. Or capable. Her body was numb from the waist down, and behind she could just see the dark smear of her own blood.

The footsteps shuffled to a halt. The person behind was listening.

Then the footsteps moved slowly forward again. Who was it? Hasik? Jahleb?

Her pulse raced. She consciously curbed her breathing, keeping it shallow, silent.

Each time he stopped, she knew she had to stop too. It seemed an odd game to play in the darkness – hide-and-seek, with death as the forfeit. One advantage sacrificed against another: distance against discovery. With her legs paralysed, she knew she couldn't win on distance, so she might as well play discovery as best she could. Use the darkness as a shield. A sanctuary. Leorah kept very still. The slightest movement could pinpoint her position.

She heard an intake of breath, a sigh. She could almost *feel* his presence; little more than ten yards away, she estimated. The sound of footsteps picked up.

She paused until she felt they were loud enough to cover her own movements, and then started scrambling forward. She now felt slightly faint. As much as she struggled to control herself, she knew she was panicking. The loss of blood wouldn't help either. The faster she moved, the more excitable she became, the swifter her heart pumped her blood away. She'd learnt that much in the Croix Rouge. *Oh God!* Don't think. Don't think about it. *Just keep moving.*

The footsteps suddenly stopped again. Leorah halted. The echo of her own movement came back to her. She held her breath, but in that instant she sensed she had been too late. Only a fraction, but enough. He had heard her.

A slight shuffle, then a pause. The footsteps started again, slowly at first – then picked up pace, rapidly.

All pretence was over, Leorah thought – and she dragged her body forward as fast as she could. She could hear the footsteps behind at almost a sprint. Their pounding became ominously loud . . . And breathing – rapid, tortured. Her own, or his? The light at the end looked closer, but not brighter. She focused on it, and it appeared to fade. *No! No! Please.* Don't turn it off! I'll be alone in the dark. *Alone.* A child again. Jamil had been there then. Jamil. *Jamil* . . . you'll stay with me in the darkness, won't you? You won't leave me. But *still* she couldn't picture him; only a dark faceless figure came to her. She started to open her eyes . . . but discovered they were already open! *Daniel* . . . help me! I don't want to lose him forever. Please bring him to me. *Please explain* . . .

The world seemed to slip without her moving – and as the spinning darkness cleared, she saw Hasik's face.

She had fallen onto her back, and he was standing almost directly above her. She thought he was smiling – but she couldn't be sure in the half-light. It took a moment for her thoughts to focus.

'You tried to make a fool of me,' he said almost in a hiss, as if people unseen in the darkness might be listening. 'I could make quite a speech about how you've betrayed Islam, how your own people would spit on you – but I won't.' Hasik drew a tired breath. 'It was a nice little trick you played with the Israelis. It's a shame it didn't work out for all of you. What has been destroyed though, I cannot make light of. In comparison, my killing you is but a small atonement.'

Leorah's spirits sagged desperately. Diplomacy would now be wasted. Hasik had come for only one thing. The best she could hope was that the Israelis would storm the tunnel in time. Then she remembered: fire with fire was what Hasik responded to best.

'Don't try and make your killing me more significant than it is,' she mocked. 'The same as that child you killed, as your threat against all those children, it's an empty gesture – from a half-crazed idiot who thinks he's the representative of the people.'

Hasik somehow controlled his voice. 'I do represent a section of Palestinian thought, whether the rest believe in that now or not is of no matter – in the end they will see that Habash and I are right. Abu Ammar will finally have no choice but to lead them in that direction.'

'Do you really believe Arafat would support an action like this? So soon after he's cast off the shadow of Munich and gained recognition in the UN?'

'Yes, yes. Of course. It would be the greatest thing for the Palestinian people – a blow that Israel would probably never recover from. They would lose all their support, including the Americans!' Hasik only became aware of the desperation in his voice as it echoed back to him from the walls.

'And you can completely ignore any sympathy for those children?' Leorah asked disbelievingly.

'If any sympathy is spent, it should be for *my* people.' But Hasik's thoughts were suddenly fractured. *The children*. How long did he have left? Fifty seconds, forty? He'd lost track. 'But I don't have time for this now.'

The faint light broke unevenly across Hasik's face. Leorah could make out his chin and part of his cheek. Sweat had beaded on his beard. She listened hard: gunfire and mortar sounded outside, but there was no sign of anyone near the entrance.

'No, I suppose not,' she said. 'Like every coward you have to do your deed and make an exit.'

'You wish me to kill you in anger, so that you may gloat you had the final say.' A smile flowered on Hasik's lips, quelling the trembling in his voice. He judged they were little more than forty feet from the bus. Falling rocks could still easily claim them. Aman could be detonating at any second. He would have to finish things quickly! 'But that is not to be the way. *This* is the last image I wish imprinted on your mind.'

Hasik raised his gun.

Leorah felt empty. The last minutes of fear and tension had drained her; she had no more reserves. She glanced once more towards the entrance: *nothing*. If she was about to die, she might at least have the pleasure . . .

'You're an animal Hasik! Your father must have fucked a camel to produce you.'

Hasik's smile grew taut. His eyes glared.

The gun chamber clicked – but Leorah turned away and closed her eyes before the explosion came.

Pohlmann's mind was working at white heat.

He tried to take stock of the situation. Since the lights had gone out, Salkin had picked off two of the men, but not the third. There had also been other gunfire inside the tunnel. God alone knew how many children had been hit! *Or* what had happened to the girl!

The encampment around him looked ghostly in the darkness, with only a few of its lights glowing – like some enormous metal monster lurking in sleepy readiness. The babble of conversation in the background was subdued and hesitant. Only seconds before, a call on his walkie-talkie had announced that they'd taken out the man on watch at the far end of the tunnel. But there still remained the problem of the man at *this* end. Pohlmann had watched with growing frustration as sniper and mortar fire had rained on the position without success. One of the snipers had thought he'd made a hit, but it was probably just a flesh wound – a flicker of movement was perceived soon afterwards above the four-foot rock entrenchment. Deciding finally that it was a near impossible position to usurp from the ground, Pohlmann sent up a helicopter.

He studied the helicopter now through infra-red binoculars

as it winged across – carrying a sniper facing sideways, with his feet still on the landing rail. Pohlmann gripped the walkie-talkie in his other hand unnecessarily hard. They still weren't sure which of them had the detonator, but they would have alerted him with their ground actions anyway.

He lowered the binoculars and raised the walkie-talkie. 'How does it look?'

'The shelve is concave. Still not easy, even from this angle.'

'Anything else?'

A slight pause. The whir of the rotors came through. 'Yes. As you thought, some wires visible coming out. And some movement down there.'

'You *must* get that position. And fast.'

Pohlmann was still staring at the walkie-talkie as he released the speak button. The pulse in his neck pumped a small tick in his cheek. He couldn't even begin to contemplate the catastrophe if the detonator was activated. The fate of the children; his assurances to Peres; Rabin's and Golda Meir's mention of 'wider implications'; Hasik's raving – all the things which had given him three sleepless nights flashed through his mind in that moment, and gelled.

He fought to free his mind for his next action. Major Gant was looking at him expectantly.

They both heard the first shots of the helicopter sniper, and looked up at the tracers.

On the ledge, Aman was just over twenty seconds from detonation when a sniper's bullet found his right shoulder, throwing him back and to one side. He lay in shock for a moment, then began to scramble back to his position.

Less than a yard from the detonator, he heard the whirr of the blades in the darkness above, and the helicopter sniper's bullets started kicking up the rock around him. It might be close, but he was still sure that he could reach the detonator.

The walkie-talkie in Pohlmann's grasp stayed infuriatingly silent.

The decision would *have* to be made, he thought; whether there was one man still alive inside or not. The other way, they stood to lose everything. Now he was balancing the body count, he upbraided himself – what was a few more dead against total loss? One way or the other, on every battleground he had ever stood on, his role came down to much the same thing – deciding who should live and who should die.

As the tic in his cheek increased, his eyes darted. As in many campaigns past, his fear and self-examination began to transform themselves into a useful adrenalin. Fear alone made him impulsive, self-examination made him cautious. It was the ideal balance which had largely gained him his reputation for incisive judgement through the years. He steeled himself to a staccato flow of messages. His blue eyes glinted faintly. *The timing had to be right.*

He waited another second for a response from the helicopter, then made a small signal to Major Gant. Gant, in turn, signalled to six paratroopers with Uzis and stun grenades, who had already been briefed and were crouched fifty yards ahead of them. They sprang into action.

Pohlmann counted off twenty yards of their advance, then instructed the unit at the far end of the tunnel. Within seconds, both units would be at the tunnel entrances.

At another small signal from Pohlmann, two support jeeps rolled forward, lights glaring.

Pohlmann's walkie-talkie crackled. It was the helicopter.

'I've got him. Two in the back, lung shots!'

Pohlmann felt relief rising.

'. . . But *wait!* He's moved slightly again! He's reaching out . . . I'm trying for a . . .' The mouthpiece was dropped abruptly.

The relief froze, twisting in Pohlmann's gut. The muscles of his jaw and neck tightened. All he could do was start a silent prayer.

Leorah opened her eyes.

It couldn't be true! *What had happened?*

Shadows and blackness and redness merged, then finally cleared; the sound of the shot still reverberated inside her head. Hasik was looming towards her, red glistening like an open pomegranate on the front of his camouflage jacket.

The message slowly sank home: the bullet had come from behind! But how?

Another shot sounded, and Hasik was propelled forwards, almost on top of her, floundering to his knees. She felt some of his blood warm on her hands. Surprise flooded the fury from his eyes, becoming almost a plea as he toppled over.

The image of his face stayed before her for a moment in the darkness. She thought he had tried to say something, but she couldn't be sure. She stared wide-eyed at his body, face-down. Her thoughts felt entombed. She shook her head, her ears still ringing. The whole scenario felt distant, surreal.

Footsteps broke the spell. As the shock subsided, she began to shiver.

She saw the boy's face loom in the darkness – one of the boys she had spoken to on the bus. She wanted to whisper his name in thankfulness, but she couldn't remember it. Her tongue felt trapped. As the shivers ran deeper, she felt the emotions well up inside her: hopelessly jumbled emotions of sorrow, anguish and happiness. She fought against them – but as the boy came closer, she couldn't hold back any longer. Her body's trembling dissolved in convulsive, heart-rending sobs. Her tears flowed freely.

Then she realized that the boy was crying too. She could pick out a dark stain of blood by his shoulder. And she felt suddenly ashamed: *she* should be the one who was comforting, who was in control. Her instinctive role resurged.

She jerked back her tears as she crawled forward to meet the boy. She hugged him hard, their two figures feeling curiously alone in the darkness, yet somehow bonded by their shared injuries and the fate of the moment. Something seemed right, almost preordained about the boy having saved her, but she couldn't quite define it. For it occurred to her that his strength and spirit had belied normal boyhood innocence, the quality that drew her most strongly towards children, that made her feel they needed her protection. The same dauntless spirit of Israel which her people so feared –

lest it would eventually prove their downfall – had now been her own saving. It seemed odd, out of place: yet another of those pieces which refused to fit in the giant puzzle of East-West theories on the Middle East she had played with Daniel. *Daniel?* Oh God, he would be outside watching, waiting, not knowing what was happening. The gentle shaking of the boy's body broke off her thoughts.

'*Shalom*. You're alright now. You've been very brave. Only a little longer now . . .'

Another voice suddenly broke in, startling them. It boomed from the end of the tunnel.

'*Ti'tzeh!* Clear the bus! Explosives have been set. Out of the bus now. Clear the tunnel. Quickly!'

The beam from a torch washed the tunnel walls, sweeping swiftly from side to side. Another light then joined it.

The realization hit Beni first – in her mind's turmoil, Leorah had forgotten the explosives. She let go of him as he turned and yelled to his companions.

'*Bo!* Come on. Hurry. Get out of the bus.' He started back towards it – but a paratrooper was already alongside – another two virtually at his heels. Their voices grew more urgent.

'*Ti'tzeh*. Quickly!'

The first paratrooper played his torch fleetingly over Hasik's body, then over Leorah, as he passed.

'All clear here! Last man's dead. Only the children now.'

They were fifteen yards from the bus as the first children started filing out.

'Okay. *Come on!*'

The paratroopers formed themselves into a line at ten-yard intervals, stretching back through the tunnel, to guide the way with their torches. Instructions flew back and forth above the babbling children. The place was suddenly filled with growing pandemonium and flickering lights.

'Let's get it moving faster, *faster*!'

The progress of the children along the tunnel had become almost a sprint by the time the bus was half-emptied. The sense of danger, the full awareness of their predicament, spread fast, soon approaching panic – as if the days of captivity had fostered a stupor only now dispelled by the paratroopers' increasingly insistent instructions. The crowd trying to get down the steps was bunching dangerously, and screams could be heard.

'Okay, keep it calm. Fast – but calm.' The paratrooper checked his watch . . . almost thirty seconds since Pohlmann's go ahead. How much time left? He was sweating now, as he watched mechanically the procession of children continue past him. It seemed a lifetime since he'd entered the tunnel.

'Yes, yes . . . keep moving. That's it.'

The charge might go off at any time; each extra second was a reprieve. Borrowed time.

The soldier wiped his forehead with his cuff, and snapped himself out of it. The last of the children were now filing from the bus. Nearly everyone else was clear.

'Okay. That's it. Let's go now.'

He started to turn, backing up the last few stragglers – and at that instant the blinding white heat erupted so swiftly that he didn't even hear the explosion.

The explosion was deafening, even from where Pohlmann stood. He waited tensely until its ominous rumblings and after-echoes had died, then commenced fresh signals and instructions.

His mind was now beyond extremes of fear or apprehension. He had seen the first children emerge from the tunnel just before the explosion, and now they were coming out in a steady stream. His chief concern was how many got clear before the charge went off.

At his signal, a fire vehicle roared up first to dampen down the dust and fumes inside the tunnel and quell any remaining fire; it was followed by three open-back truck transporters. As the fire truck came alongside the children massing outside, it fired a plume of water above those still exiting.

Inside, a fine mist fell from the high jet, making all the

more hazy the beams of torchlights already struggling to penetrate the dust. Two jeeps with powerful searchlights stood at each side of the entrance, but their beams penetrated no more than ten yards.

Leorah and those behind her – she guessed at least ten children and two paratroopers – were still beyond the sphere of light. Only the pale torchlight of the paratrooper helping her along lit the way for a few yards ahead of them.

The explosion – its air-rush wickedly funnelled by the tunnel – had carried the two of them almost four yards forwards. She'd felt something twist in her arm as she landed, and her breath was momentarily taken away, but nothing more. The paratrooper was unharmed. Those facing the explosion weren't so lucky: the air-rush had damaged or completely collapsed their lungs.

The others seemed almost unimportant to her in that moment; all she could think of was the boy that had saved her. Was he alright? Where was he? God, *please* let him be safe.

He had been somewhere behind her, she knew – but looking back, she could pick out nothing in the dust and smoke. The plastique had spewed out a billowing jet of red and white flame, consuming the petrol tank almost immediately, and scattering inflammable portions of the bus so wide that the residual fire was minimal, lasting only seconds. Now only darkness remained. Rockfall from the tunnel walls and roof had been heavy close to the explosion, but now even the clatter of smaller stones had subsided.

Only the shuffle of footsteps could be heard; but *whose* she could only guess.

The paratrooper sensed her looking back, and urged her on.

'Come on. Keep going now. I've got to get you to a stretcher.'

Gradually – like sunlight breaking through patchy mist – things became clearer ahead. But another darkness started rising, blotting out the confusion of lights and figures, and the last thing she remembered, before surrendering to the darkness completely, was water falling in a fine mist around her body, almost like the rain among the cedars in the Becharre mountains.

When she opened her eyes again, there was a bright floodlight close by, and still other lights more distant. And she spotted Daniel's face among the ring of army medics carrying her stretcher. The voices all around were fast and excited, rising about the revving of jeeps and trucks shunting back and forth.

Daniel's expression was so intensely anxious that Leorah thought his attempts at smiling reassurance faintly comical. She tried to laugh, but couldn't – and then she feared the tears were coming close again; and probably, in the end, her smile was just as painful as his. She gripped Daniel's hand as he reached out.

'Well, at least I tried,' she muttered.

'Tried to get yourself killed, more like.' Daniel squeezed Leorah's hand playfully. 'You're going to be okay – but you shouldn't talk.'

Then it struck her again: *the boy?* She leant up slightly on the stretcher, her eyes roaming anxiously.

'Where is he? The boy who saved me. What happened to him?'

'Leorah, *please*, you must relax.' Daniel cradled her head, soothing her brow with one hand. 'Don't worry, they'll find out. It'll be okay, you'll see . . . you'll see.' He let it become a benediction, a whisper. Leorah gradually sank back, but her eyes still held their fearfulness.

Supervising the medic team a few yards away, Major Gant overheard her. He moved over to where General Pohlmann was still receiving casualty details from the command sergeant of the paratroopers.

'I'm sorry to interrupt you, General, but Miss Ajlan has come round, and she's asking about some boy that was with her inside the tunnel.'

Pohlmann shook his head, but the command sergeant interceded.

'There was a boy with her when we went in – one of our

men noticed. They got split up in all the confusion. She must mean him.'

'How is he?' asked Gant.

'Injured, but alive.' The command sergeant pointed. 'You should have him over there, with your medics. I saw him coming out on a stretcher. One of the older boys – twelve or thirteen, dark hair.'

Gant could only remember three stretcher cases among the injured, so it fell into place quickly.

'Oh, that would be Beni.' Gant took out his list and ran his finger down. 'Benjamin . . . Benjamin. Here we are. Benjamin Achelson.'

Achelson? A flicker crossed Pohlmann's face. At first he hadn't attached any importance to the name; after all, the boy was just one of thirty-eight – and the message itself had been just one of the increasingly paranoid memos from Tel Aviv over the last forty-eight hours. But, now, the fact that he was the son of a border-posted colonel noted for the vigour of his attacks on PLO encampments could put a completely different complexion on the whole thing.

'Major –' he started. He looked around, still searching for the right words. 'If Miss Ajlan asks the name of this boy who helped her, please don't let her know it. She might repeat it in some future article she writes, thereby making him a target for any PLF or Habash men seeking retribution for this day. Is that quite clear?'

'Yes, of course.' Gant hesitated only slightly. His expression lifted as he tucked the list back in his top pocket. 'How did we fare overall?'

'Five children dead – one of them killed by one of Hasik's men before the explosion. And one paratrooper.' Pohlmann's voice was almost a monotone. 'You have six injured with you, I believe, Major Gant?'

'Yes.' Gant surveyed the activity around them. The hills beyond appeared even more eerily silent against the present confusion. 'I know the aim is always *no* losses. And I suppose there'll be criticisms that we should never have even entered into bargaining. But personally I don't think you have any call to reproach yourself, sir. I don't mind saying now that I – and most of my men – honestly thought this one impossible. In the light of that, what we have salvaged is a near miracle. I'm sure that overall it will be viewed as a success in Tel Aviv.'

Pohlmann stared at him long and hard. 'I'm quite sure it will – *to them*. Now if you'll excuse me.'

Pohlmann stalked off unceremoniously. He was already cringing at the thought of the dinner-party conversations he'd have to sit through revolving around the whole affair; the innocuous questions and toasts and backslapping. Belonging to a nation which revelled so wholeheartedly in its victories had its drawbacks, too.

Gant watched Pohlmann's departing back for a moment, thinking how typical it was of the General to accept victory so modestly, though some mistook it for coldness, and then went back to tell Leorah about the boy.

Leorah smiled at the news, looking up into Daniel's eyes as she listened.

'That's marvellous, Daniel. You won't believe what that boy did to help me. Wait till I tell you.'

'Okay, okay. You've got a date.' And for the first time that day Daniel sensed some joy and relief in her eyes. The hunted look had gone. He squeezed her hand again.

The feeling of relief washed over Leorah; suddenly she realized why it had seemed so right that the boy had saved her. Jamil had been the same age when she'd tried to save him from Phalangist shells – and failed. The books had been balanced, her own personal account settled on that score! She found the beauty of the irony irresistible – with all its conflicting patterns woven so swiftly in her mind. It was surely fate.

But was it really possible that she had harboured such misdirected hatred all those years? And then – as her stretcher slid home and the doors began to close – she remembered why she had helped the Israelis in the first place, and fear gripped her again.

Part Six

Halmater Tel Aviv: Reuters London

19

Tel Aviv: 9.08
A Safed radio station announced early this morning that the hostage incident at Neveh Ativ in which thirty-eight Israeli schoolchildren were held by members of the PLF has been concluded in a successful army operation. Full details along with an official announcement are expected from the Knesset later today.

Halmater Agency

The lights of Ferleiten flickered in the distance.

It looked a small village – perhaps too small, in that his appearance there might cause a stir, thought Jaalgen. But, then, he was in no position to be choosy.

The day so far had been a nightmare.

The sun had been setting by the time he'd negotiated the second high ridge. It had been an arduous climb, the view downwards stomach-churning from a few of the ledges jutting out. Reaching the top, he'd thought the worst was over – but as he looked over the panorama beyond, his spirits sagged. The slope fell to yet another deep valley ringed by mountains. It was at least four miles from where he stood to the top of the ridge opposite, he judged. And not a single house or sign of life anywhere between; just snow and fir trees – and bare jagged rock where it was too steep for either snow or firs to cling.

He'd sat on the top of the ridge for a long while, looking out. Under different circumstances, he might have admired the sunset in such a setting.

At that time he'd thought of giving up; even if he continued, the chances of succeeding were slim. It was a habit born of his profession, balancing odds. After his fall from the train, he'd blacked out twice; and while he had blacked out briefly only one since, he couldn't be sure that he'd merely been concussed and was now pulling out of it. Each second of the climb he'd feared another blackout. And even if his mind stayed lucid, how much more could his body take? Skin had been scraped from his hands in grappling with rocks, and the tender flesh beneath was burnt raw by the cold. He could feel the bone-scraping tingles of frostbite cutting deeper. The thought of moving even a few hundred yards was agonizing. But what other choice was there? It would be a lonely, slow, deliberate death sitting and waiting for the hypothermia to finally seize his heart. And the spur of defeatism required to throw himself off one of the ledges, he just couldn't muster; perhaps it simply wasn't in his character.

The images resurged: the journalist Grade standing in the compartment as he himself had plummeted backwards into the void; and the daughter escaping slyly through the streets of Paris. Jaalgen's mood of vengeance had increased with each punishing step. He felt it urging him on now. *Yes*, why not? If he had made it so far, then why not the rest? He was over half way there already.

That resolve had been almost lost on the way, though. As he started up the far slope, he blacked out yet again. When he came around, his mind was gripped by a mild delirium. Only the images remained to keep him going.

Darkness had fallen five hours ago but now he had at last reached the top of the slope and glimpsed Ferleiten.

He raised himself to his feet from a near crawl as he stared in disbelief at the village lights. He felt like laughing out loud – but his lips were too dry and cracked, and he feared that laughing might break his last grip on sanity. He might slip once again into delirium, and fall right where he was, to die within sight of the village. He had gone too far now to be robbed by some pathetic irony. He trudged on relentlessly.

Suddenly he remembered his ski mask. He'd kept it on deliberately to help protect his face from frostbite. Now he realized it would make his appearance needlessly sinister. He started tugging at it – but it was adhered in parts to his face with his coagulated blood and the frost. He tugged harder; it *had* to come off. Thankfully the cold had numbed his nerves to the peeling flesh as it finally came loose.

He started taking stock as he entered the village: he was approaching some small chalets, spread widely. He picked up pace until he reached an area of more closely grouped houses, and started looking for a hotel or bar.

It was quiet. Though he had selected the street with the most lights, and it was probably not yet 11.00 p.m., there was little traffic. He walked in the road itself, avoiding the snow banked on the pavements. A hundred yards further along he spotted a Weizern Perle sign over a doorway. He paused for a second – almost in a daze that he had made it – then headed in.

To the few people in the bar he made a terrifying sight. His face was a mottled maroon and black from snow burns and dried blood, and fresh blood had been drawn on one cheek where the ski-mask was ripped free. He held his hands in front of him like a praying mantis, and he staggered as if about to fall at any second.

The barman, who was normally absorbed in the gossip of his regulars, found this one stranger he couldn't ignore. Most of his customers had already turned to stare.

'*Himmel!* I think you have the wrong place,' the barman exclaimed. 'You should be at the hospital. Somebody give him a hand.'

A stocky, middle-aged man rose and helped Jaalgen to a seat by the bar.

'What happened, my good friend?' he asked. 'Skiing, was it?'

The barman poured a large brandy in front of Jaalgen.

Jaalgen thought: he knew too little about the surrounding terrain to lie about a skiing accident. He might as well stick close to the truth.

'I fell from the train.' His voice was almost a whisper through lips cracked with frost. 'A door I leant againt – the latch was faulty.'

A man behind whistled slightly.

'Where was this?' The barman asked intently.

'I don't know. One of the passes. Seven miles or so away.'

The barman muttered knowingly to a man on one side, then reached over and poured Jaalgen a large glass of mineral water, placing it next to the brandy.

'You're very lucky to be alive, you know.'

Jaalgen tried to force a grin, but couldn't. He sipped at the brandy, finding it hard to keep hold of the glass. The spirit cut a pleasant knife of warmth from his chest to his stomach. He washed it down with the water, then alternated between the two.

The regulars around watched in sympathetic awe. The barman smiled welcomingly.

Jaalgen felt his senses clearing, and he began to remember his purpose – what he would need, what would be the order of things. The sequence playing over in his mind now absorbed him totally, merging slowly like a haze: he was climbing and falling, and the fir trees were like sentries, the snow like a deathly white blanket laid over a body, his *father's* body. Faces were leering now, and he was reaching for them, feeling satisfaction rise as he heard them scream in fear – but then it became his *own* fear, and the sound was the wind gusting around him on a high ledge, *howling . . .*

'Are you okay, my friend?'

'Yes . . . yes, fine.' Jaalgen noticed that he was shaking so badly he had spilt some of his water. His eyes were bleary as he looked up at the barman. 'Look, I have to arrange for someone . . . for some of my things, you understand. Can I use your phone?'

He saw the barman's lips move in answer, but couldn't hear the words. And then the shivering wormed itself deeper, and gripped him totally, dragging him back once more into the darkness.

*

Daniel was staying at the Commodore Hotel in Tel Aviv. He gazed out of the window of his room onto Dizengoff Square – for Tel Aviv what Times Square was to New York, and Piccadilly Circus to London. A number of stone benches circled the square, on which, Swenkel had remarked when booking him into the hotel, gleeful supporters would dance and sing if the home team won the football match on Sunday. Looking down at the people milling about, Daniel thought: if they really knew the full implications of the release of those children, if they realized just how close they had come – they would be singing and dancing on those benches right now.

Leorah had spent thirty-six hours at the Magen David Adon, the Red Cross emergency hospital less than a mile away. They'd operated within an hour of her admission, and she'd rested all through a day and a night before being transferred that morning back to Beirut. By the next day she would be resting at home, a situation dictated by the city's desperate shortage of hospital beds.

Daniel had gone to see her early that morning, before her transfer – the first opportunity he'd been allowed a visit. They'd had a pleasant but tense parting, full of promises to meet again which they both knew might never materialize given the demanding and varied schedules of their lives. Even if that was sensible for two people caught in the rift between emotions and practicality. They'd spoken at some length, but none of it the words they really deep down wanted to voice. Although her concern for the Israeli boy was obviously very real, he couldn't help feeling that she welcomed talking about him simply to shield the awkwardness of the moment.

He should have known that such a time would eventually come, and prepared himself for it more. The differences had been exciting at first, and perhaps all along he had been unwilling to admit that for just that reason their relationship could never last. The differences: on his side his work, his well-established home life; and on hers, her youth and her strongly ingrained Muslim culture – these would have become an insurmountable barrier between them. But they had both seen that early on, and accepted it, and had found it exciting rather than threatening, solely because neither of them had been pushed to its brink. Perhaps it was best that way, thought Daniel. One of those marvellous periods that only remains sacred, untarnished, if not repeated or prolonged. Frozen in a time frame.

He looked out towards Ib'n Gvirol, the road leading to the hospital. He wasn't sure if he'd really convinced himself. Certainly there were few differences between himself and Catherine – though Catherine was a bit more middle-class originally, and with a convent school upbringing – yet that relationship hadn't been working either over the past months. So what was the answer?

Daniel turned from the window. Was it that a part of him now perversely wanted to shatter his own theories just to satisfy his still strong desire to see Leorah again, or would the thought of Catherine having partly contributed make him feel any better for what had happened? What *did* he want? Reconciliation and pardoning – or continuation of this relationship with Leorah?

In that instant he thought of Julie – Julie still hidden away in the Berskshire cottage because of the events of the past week. What Julie would think if there was a serious rift between him and her mother – let alone if she learnt it was because of an affair with another woman.

With that thought – etching itself deeper at the back of his mind with each passing hour – there was only one possible answer. Part of it would depend on Catherine though.

Daniel turned away. The phone was ringing.

The international operator was on the line. This could be one of two people, he remembered. Rolf Nabens or Simon Mendel. He'd phoned them both earlier without success, and so had left his number. Both of their reports, re-routed through the Halmater agency – Mendel's on possible banking motives, and Nabens' a summary of events surrounding Al-Ben Salmad's murder – lay on the table before him. Both reports contained the seed of a possible cross-connection which Daniel was eager to establish firmly or disprove – one way or the other.

It was Mendel.

'Daniel, I got your call. Nice to hear from you. You got my report, I trust?'

'Yes, fine. Thanks a lot.' Daniel paused; key passages started coming back to him: *Due to the absence of an obvious banking motive within the Zürich or Geneva communities, my thoughts turned to other banking centres* . . . 'It rather threw me though, I must say. Bahrain. It was a possibility I'd never considered.'

'But possibility is *still* the operative words. You must understand that, Daniel. All I've done is to build upon some likely assumptions, and perhaps just a few indisputable facts. The list of names are mere likelihoods. Exactly who or how many might be involved is pure guesswork. What gave me the original clue was some investors who had moved their accounts from here to Bahrain. And quite sizeable, I might add.'

Al-Ben Salmad had been among them, Daniel recalled.

'And you did a thorough Swiss banking shares check?'

'Yes, well of course much of that I already had readily available on file here at the Institute, so it wasn't too difficult.'

Daniel hadn't mentioned the extent of his own shares check, not wishing to strike off the chance that Mendel might uncover something he'd overlooked.

'And nothing?'

'No. Same applies to Liechtenstein and Euro and bearer bond deposits with the majors in New York and London. Kuwait – well *some* movement, but not really large enough for what you're after.' Mendel let out a slow sigh. 'But Bahrain was a different picture: some very sizeable banking shares purchases before the first date you gave me, and frequent sales since. The list comprised mainly people who invested with Beirut banks, but some, as I say, were also account-holders here in Zürich. Some still retain accounts here.'

Daniel reached out for the list and started looking through it again: fourteen names in total, all Arabic. From these names, three Christian Arabs; perhaps those were the three to be discarded, leaving a totally Muslim Arab conspiracy. A footnote added that Al-Hakim had been among those investing heavily on the first date, but: *'Because he could not likely predict or wish to profit from his own assassination, his name had not been entered.'* Strange, all the same. Yet one of those small details that made it all the more credible. Possibly Al-Hakim had been involved initially, too, and had fallen foul of the scheme in the same way as Al-Ben Salmad; the original intention could have been to remove only Khourem.

'Look, Simon, I accept it all, just as you've laid it out, possibilities or assumptions or whatever. One thing bothers me, though. I'm still stuck with this lingering question of a contact in Switzerland.'

'Well' – Mendel cleared his throat slightly – 'I suppose the only thing to be drawn from that is that the assassin was hired out of Switzerland. Obviously a contact or someone would be required for that. But I don't think there's any basis to assume the conspiracy was actually centred *here* among the banking community.'

Daniel considered again the possibility of Mendel's understandable protectiveness – but the weight of evidence of his own earlier investigation almost totally supported Mendel's findings. 'No. True. I came to much the same conclusion.' Daniel reached for his cigars and lit one.

'Do you have any names as yet?' Mendel asked.

'Not traceable to anyone recognizable, at least – although I tried through one of the city's best investigative agencies. That's why I didn't bother you with it. The assassin, Jaalgen, is now dead, so he's no longer important.' Daniel blew out his first smoke as if dispelling the last lingering memories of the nightmare along with it. 'His contact I'm not completely sure of – sounds something like Kruger or Vruger.'

There was no response at the other end of the line. Daniel could hear the rustling of papers, and more distant background traffic noises.

'Rings no bells, I suppose?' he continued.

'No, Daniel. As you say, nothing immediately recognizable. Not familiar at all. But I was just checking through a card index I have here.' The flicking continued for a moment. 'But no, I'm afraid not. There is a Kreugal – but he's only a pensions manager at the Schweizerische Kreditanstalt. He doesn't have enough shares to blow his nose on. Not really in the league you're looking for.'

'No.' Daniel drew harder on his cigar. With Jaalgen dead, the name *Kruger*, *Vruger* had begun to obsess him. He had funnelled his hate, firmly believing that this was the man in control, manipulating everyone and everything else like a puppeteer; the one responsible for Xavier, for Reiner . . . *for Julie*. Now Mendel's findings suggested he was no more than a henchman to a cabal of Arabs in Bahrain. It seemed strange to have to change his thinking so drastically; as earlier he had found it hard to shift mentally the entire scenario from Zürich to Bahrain. Only after two hours of careful re-reading and deliberation, and going back over his own notes – and time and again facing that high barrier wall that no traceable banking plot existed in Switzerland – had he finally accepted it. *No plot!* Even if there had been, Mendel's theory carried as much weight: the expansion of the Bahrain banking community at the expense of the Beirut market. And probably a good deal more workable, since the Bahrain market was newly formed. Swiss banks were in many ways too staid for rapid infiltration.

Then it hit him like a wave just how much that one Swiss connection, *Vruger*, could have misled them: the Mossad, Reiner, and in turn himself and Leorah; all except Hasik and the PFLP, who would have pointed the finger at Israel, whatever the rumour circulating. But then, perhaps, if you'd engineered a plot in Bahrain, that is the way you'd want it. People pointing the finger everywhere *except* Bahrain.

'Look, Daniel . . . If I come up with anything on that name, I'll let you know.'

Daniel snapped out of his contemplation. 'Yes. Sorry. This man in Switzerland – I'm still getting used to the idea of him being just a contact, rather than the man in control.'

'Well, of course, he still *could* be. He's probably a financier that at least one of those on the list has had dealings with before. But while he might be better informed than they are, monetarily he just wouldn't wield anything like the same power.' Mendel's voice rose, almost sighing. 'Four of those men are among the world's richest. Given that, I think it unlikely they would allow him control.' He paused for a moment. 'But, as I say, I'll keep looking, see if anything shows up.'

Daniel tapped his cigar thoughtfully into the ashtray. Nothing else to discuss, that he could think of. He would need to go through the report again before his thoughts became more cohesive, he realized.

'Simon, thanks a lot for what you've done. If there's anything else can I get back to you later?'

'Certainly. Don't hesitate.'

'And I don't want this to be just an invoice job. This is twice now – I almost feel embarrassed. I owe you a lunch, so next time I'm in town – okay? Your home turf, so you choose the restaurant.'

'I'll look forward to it.'

Daniel waited for the click at Mendel's end, then pressed the cradle buttons at his end the customary ten seconds to clear an International line, and asked the operator for David Wetherall's number in London. While his thoughts were still fresh, he wanted to bounce them straight over.

Jaalgen opened his eyes. His mind was still clouded. Where was he?

The room was dark. He started to pick out shapes from the faint streetlight filtering through a side window: a long dresser; a side table the opposite side of the bed; an armchair at its foot; a tall glass cabinet against the far wall. He listened. The street outside was quiet. No noises discernible either beyond the door to his left.

He sat up. His head felt heavy, and his eyes lost focus for a few seconds. Something felt tight on his face. He reached up and felt bandages across his nose and part of one cheek.

The events that had brought him to the bed seemed from another time, another place. How long had it been since he'd fallen from the train, little more than seven miles away? Thirty-six hours, forty-eight? The sequence of images started revolving again – but he fought hard against it this time, holding it in check. His senses had balanced enough now to appreciate the clarity of thought he would require if he were to succeed. He consciously shut out the past, looked to the future. Money? Passport? A weapon? Contact with *Vruger*?

Standing up, he was pleasantly surprised to find his legs taking the weight. He started pacing. His joints were stiff and almost his whole body ached, particularly his left shoulder-blade, but he was able to move.

The items in the glass cabinet were clearer now: books on the top shelf, some drinking glasses and ornaments on the one below, but on the two bottom shelves were rows of small labelled bottles and jars: Atropine sulphate, anhydrous . . diprofiline . . . the names started stirring a part of his memory. A medical cabinet! He remembered now the fat barman mentioning a doctor. He was probably in some annexe to a doctor's surgery.

The cabinet sparked off an idea in his mind. He started rifling rapidly through its lower drawers – but couldn't find what he was after. Only masses of papers, pamphlets.

Jaalgen looked around sharply. There was no light showing beneath the door. He went over and tried the handle; the door moved. It wasn't locked. He opened it slowly and stepped outside. It was pitch dark. After a moment his eyes adjusted to a long corridor with two doors on one side, one on the other. No light visible beneath any of them. He stood almost unnaturally still. Nor any sounds of movement or talking. Pacing along, he found the corridor widened out into a square vestibule. Some stairs rose up at the far end, and to one side was a half-open door. He headed for it. The shadows of the corridor seemed to merge, and for a moment he was back on the mountainside in the dead of night, among the tall dark fir trees with the wind whistling through them.

Jaalgen started. A sound! He wheeled round – but it was only the clicking and winding on of a chime clock. Stroking the goose bumps from his skin, he found it strangely odd, alien to feel frightened; but then usually everything was pre-planned, mapped out to the last detail. Here he was dealing with the unknown.

He glanced up the stairs. No sound or light from there either. If anyone was in the house, they were probably asleep; and with that thought Jaalgen made his way through the half-open door, deftly easing it shut behind him. He switched on the light.

It was a small surgery. The strip-lights overhead were very bright.

Jaalgen noticed the telephone straight away, and, on a side bench, he saw what he had hoped to find in the annexe: a rolled cloth of instruments. He unfurled the cloth and picked out the largest scalpel, tucking it into the belt of his trousers. If he really got lucky, he might even find some money. Enough to get to Vienna, at least.

Jaalgen went over to the telephone. He remembered the number off by heart, but the trick would be getting the code right from Austria.

On the fourth attempt he got the number ringing.

Within two minutes, the International operator had called Daniel back.

'Looks like much the same set-up we had cited for Zürich,' David Wetherall commented, when Daniel had finished explaining Mendel's findings. 'Just swap the locations.'

'Any other thoughts? Feasibility?'

'Let's see. New and fast-expanding market. Lot of people

juggling for control. More flexibility, more loopholes for possible irregular movement, easier to shield or cover up; those are the plus points of Bahrain over Zürich.' Wetherall half sighed. 'And I suppose given the aura of respectability of the Swiss market, it's a bit easier to swallow that a bunch of Arabs have been busy shafting each other. But on the other side of the coin you have a much smaller gain: one, one and a half billion tops. Zürich would have been three or four times that. So – easier to work, smaller gain.'

Daniel was thinking: was one and a half billion enough to motivate four of the world's richest men? But then that could be merely pointing him to the others on the list.

'How about looking to the future. When we looked at the Swiss side, I remember you mentioning that investments could increase.'

'Yes, slightly different picture then. With a war or any disturbance like this, money tends to move away from the Middle East in general, then with time it starts gradually filtering back. Four or five years could double or treble that initial shift to Bahrain.'

So either those farsighted enough among the four, Daniel thought – or else look to the rest of the list.

'I was looking to prove a point,' Daniel said. 'Something sparked off in my mind by Rolf's piece on Al-Ben Salmad's killing, combined with Mendel's report.'

'Well, for my part, I can only talk about the financial side; and not even that too much without having Mendel's report in front of me, and going through some of my own files. But, as I see it, you've got a couple of strong things going for you there, Danny. Firstly, everything you had going for you in Switzerland – admittedly on a smaller scale, but then, on the other hand, more workable. And secondly, and more importantly, with those share movements, the one thing you were never actually able to come up with in Zürich: *motive*.'

Hearing it from Wetherall somehow cemented it. Was that why he had called Wetherall – purely for confirmation? Was he already that convinced?

Wetherall was speaking. 'Why don't I pass you over to Rolf for now, Danny. I'll have a fuller look at those reports when you're next in town. Any idea when that will be?'

'Tomorrow some time, probably quite late. Thanks, David.'

A click and a buzz heralded a girl's voice, and then Nabens came on. Daniel gave him a condensation of Mendel's findings and his conversation with Wetherall. 'Before we start, though, Rolf, there's one thing I must know. This Laboille – how's his investigation going?'

If Nabens hadn't already been all too well aware of Grade's concern over Julie, he would have read it clearly now in his tone.

He chose his words carefully. 'Some whispers at Scotland Yard have it that it's definitely been passed on – but it's at a sort of interim stage. Laboille feels that she's in England – but there'll be no firm commitment of men from the Yard until there's something more definite.'

Again the thought hit Daniel of what would be needed to clear Julie: either prove Xavier's connection with Jaalgen himself, or hope that someone might come forward who had seen them together. The prospect felt somehow distant – and not only because he himself couldn't think of any immediate practical plan of action.

'How's Uncle Bob now?'

'Lucky, there. He talked to the directors – and this joint story of ours on the hijacking seems to have given you a bit of a reprieve. Part of the worry was the growing involvement of Julie – but I think Bob also found it difficult to defend you, because increasingly he couldn't see a story emerging out of the whole mess. The hijacking changed that.'

'Well that's something, at least.' That feeling of isolation lifted slightly. The message was clear: could he complete his investigation, or clear Julie, before anything on her connection with Xavier and Reiner became too prominent with the British press or police; for then it would become too sensitive an issue for him to continue.

'. . . And by the way, from me on the hijacking – thanks,

Danny. We were well ahead of the game on that one.'

A *game*. Chasing sources, meeting deadlines, beating competitors, getting the lead story. A week ago, Daniel supposed he would have agreed – an apt description. Now it felt anything but a game, and suddenly it felt strangely overwhelming how the order of his life had changed in that short time.

Nabens described the *Daily Post*'s spread and layout of the hijacking story, in the knowledge that airmail newspapers often took two days to reach Tel Aviv. Then he came back to the subject of Mendel's report, asking a few questions before he commented on the coincidence of its timing with his own report.

'That might not be the only coincidence,' said Daniel. 'This organization mentioned in your report – the Hilal – tell me more.'

'Do you have the photos I sent in front of you?'

'Yes.' Daniel flipped open the folder and leafed through: four were of a blonde girl approaching the Inn on the Park entrance; two of Salmad's Corniche outside; three of Salmad in the south of France, from another agency; and two – which Daniel still found difficult to examine too closely – of Salmad dead, taken just before the ambulance's arrival.

'They're as good a place to start as any. First off, the blonde's an Arab, Nalini Abou-Shami. She's what gave the lead to the whole thing.' Nabens cleared his voice. 'An Egyptian journalist, Farid Mahblil, had already connected the girl with a Hilal member seen with Gahtlav shortly before his death. He'd been tracking her, linking her with other suspected Hilal members, all old associates of Khourem and Al-Hakim. And then she meets up with Al-Ben Salmad. Same girl and two almost identically executed murders put together the final threads for him.'

'How long's he been working on it?'

'Since about five months after Khourem's and Al-Hakim's assassinations. Just over a year now.'

'And does he know anything about the possible financial implications of it, or any connections there?'

'No, as you can see from the report, he tags the whole thing as a revenge plot by a clique of associates previously close to Al-Hakim and Khourem against their assassins and, as he puts it, the assassins' paymasters.'

With the flow and pattern of Nabens' words and where he sensed them heading, Daniel could feel tension growing like a coil in his stomach. He was likely the only one in a position to have put together the two elements.

'A cross carved on the chest is a symbol of Muslim betrayal,' Nabens continued. 'Employed falsely on Al-Hakim and Khourem, Mahblil believes. But on Salmad and Gahtlav it was meant both to demonstrate clearly the revenge motive and show its correct use. As you can see, the notes pinned to the bodies, too, are poignant and to the point.'

Daniel ran his fingers through the report until he came to Mahblil's translation: '*Il Khayins min* . . . To the betrayers of Islam shall come the vengeance of the Hilal.' Like a cold snake, the coil in his stomach tightened further. 'Nice people.'

'Yes.'

Daniel purposefully closed the cover of the report. 'But I think Mahblil has got it only partly right. I believe that these associates – this Hilal – plotted against Al-Hakim and Khourem right from the start to boost their own investments on the Bahrain market. Al-Hakim could have even been involved with them too at the outset, with Khourem as the sole target. The chain of killings – Gahtlav, Salmad, possibly Al-Hakim – were likely for those betraying or threatening to betray the scheme, pulling out too easily, knowing more than they should. Any number of reasons on something as large and tightly knit.'

'You're not serious?' Nabens fell silent for a second. 'So no Swiss connection at all?'

'If it ties in to what Mendel has given me, only through the hiring of the lead assassin. Did Mahblil give you any names?'

'Only the names of the assassins and the girl, which you've already got. But you mean those in control – the "paymasters"?'

Daniel mumbled a confirmation. He poured himself a glass of Perrier and started sipping it.

'Well, only a few possibles. He says it will take a month or so before he puts it all together firmly. That's why I didn't enter them in the report.'

'That's alright. Give me them anyway,' Daniel urged.

A faint rustling of paper, then Nabens started reading: three names in all.

Daniel reached out for Mendel's list. A tingle crept through him: Jubran Arayssi and Salah Fadel Al-Bitar. Two of the names matched.

London, Zürich, Beirut, Tel Aviv: he'd come so far – the course of the investigation changing so rapidly, so often, with all its deaths, its growing involvement and danger – that even though he'd sensed a conclusion within his grasp before speaking to Nabens, he found it hard now to beat down sensations of excitement and exhilaration. And now that it had come in such a sudden, offhand manner, at a time he'd expected least, a part of him still felt overwhelmed and numbed.

'I think we've cracked it, Rolf,' he said almost breathlessly. 'This organization – the Hilal. What exactly does it mean?'

'*Hilal* is a Muslim symbol. To them what the Star of David is to a Jew, a Cross to a Christian. In Arabic, the *Hilal* means the Crescents of the Moon.'

20

The line to Zürich was faint. Jaalgen had to talk louder than he wished to. As he listened, Vruger's reaction ranged from shock through incomprehension to, finally, annoyance.

When Jaalgen came to announce his plans, Vruger interceded.

'I don't think you should trouble yourself. What guarantee do I have of success after this exhibition? As you are well aware, I do have my own plan of action – much of it already well cultivated. Perhaps I should look more to that now.'

'You don't understand . . . after what I've been through, it's not just down to you anymore, down to contracts, fulfilments. Now it's *personal*.'

'I thought men in your profession couldn't afford personal issues.'

Jaalgen fell silent. From all his previous sparring with Vruger, he should have known he would jump on the first weak point. To fall into such a trap, his nerves must be more jaded than he realized.

'I'm a professional – it's personal to me to complete *every* contract,' Jaalgen said hastily. 'I have a reputation to protect, one of almost total success. Fulfilment is still a key issue, but now it's as important to me as it is to you. Wouldn't you agree?'

'I'm trying to tell you that now I don't think it will be necessary.' Vruger's tone carried impatience and annoyance.

Jaalgen laughed. 'A few photos and a few files. How long do you think that will work? Oh yes, it will be very effective for a while. But they will still be around to talk – and in time someone will listen to them and *believe* them. And then you'll come running back to me, or someone like me, with your blood money, begging for help. If you're not already too late.'

The line crackled. Its interference seemed to increase, and Jaalgen listened more intently. At length, Vruger spoke quietly.

'What is it you will need?'

Jaalgen allowed himself a moment's inner satisfaction. 'I have a passport in a safety-deposit box in Zürich, near the Kunstgewerbe Museum.' He read out the full address and box number and told Vruger where he could get hold of the key. 'If you enclose some money with the passport, I can take care of getting a gun myself. Send it care of the Vienna main rail station. I can find enough money to get to Vienna.'

'How much shall I send?'

'Make it forty thousand Francs – you can deduct it from the final payment.'

A slight pause showed Vruger's still lingering apprehension. 'Okay. I'll have it sent through a courier service. You should have it . . .'

Jaalgen suddenly went rigid. He had heard a faint click. Turning, he saw the door handle moving behind him.

'Be quiet,' he hissed.

'. . . late tomorrow morning, if everything . . .'

'I said, *shut up*!'

The door opened slowly. Jaalgen put down the receiver. An old man with curly, red-sand hair stood in the doorway in his pyjamas. His eyes blinked slowly.

'Aah. So you are up and about.' He started to smile – but his expression froze as he noticed Jaalgen's hand reach down and produce the scalpel. His next action was so swift that the old man had time for neither thought nor comment. In two strides, Jaalgen was on him and had twisted him around, holding his neck in a vice-like grip. The old man could feel the cool of the scalpel blade tight against his throat.

'Where do you keep your money?'

'I don't keep money in the house or surgery,' the old man muttered uncertainly.

'Don't be foolish. I don't mean a lot of money – just enough for my fare out of here. You must have something.'

The old man's eyes were blinking more rapidly. Jaalgen could feel the pulse in his neck quickening, his muscle cords already tight with fear.

'Third drawer to the left of the desk over there,' he said finally.

'Do I need a key?'

'No. The drawer is open. The money's in an old tea caddy. Just some petty cash, eight hundred schillings at most.'

Jaalgen was undecided. Identification wasn't the question, the people in the bar had seen him anyway, and would know where he was staying. But just how long had the doctor been standing outside the door, how much of his conversation had he overheard? Still in doubt, Jaalgen drew the scalpel deftly across the side of the old man's neck, severing the carotid artery. Clamping one hand across the old man's mouth, he sank slowly with him to the ground as the life ebbed from his body. Take *no* chances was always the golden rule.

Tel Aviv was an odd place for everything to fall into place on a story largely played out between Zürich and Beirut, Daniel reflected. But, then, that had been the way of things so far, offbeat timing and involvement – Reiner and Swenkel, Xavier and Le Marteau Rouge – so why not the locations as well? A week ago it would have been insane to think of Julie holed up in the Berkshire cottage for safety, and Reiner and Xavier both dead. Let alone Reiner acting as a Mossad agent, and Leorah helping the Israelis! After that, he wouldn't be surprised to look out into Dizengoff Square and see rabbis performing the dance of the seven veils.

It was curious how each event, perhaps monumental on its own, numbed you, broke down your resistance to the next. But then, one thing upon the other, it started to grow inside you as a whole, stretching your resilience to its limit. Just how long could he hold out? Daniel could feel it now, pulling and needling away, even though for the first time he was probably on top of the situation. His nerves felt raw after the nightmare of the last week.

Hastily he lit a cigar and sat down at the bureau, taking a fresh piece of headed paper from its top drawer. He started writing:

Al Hakim and Khourem's assassination. Plotted by the Hilal, a Bahrain-based group of oil-wealthy investors and bankers. Motive: expansion of key Bahrain banks by affecting the Beirut market. Stages: assassin hired in Switzerland through Vruger. Gahtlav and Al-Ben Salmad (and Al-Hakim, if originally involved) murdered to cover traces. As a result of the Swiss connection, rumours start growing in the Middle East (possibly purposely fuelled by the Hilal) of a Swiss plot against the Beirut market. Hasik and the PFLP believe the Israelis are responsible. The Israelis, in turn, contact a 'sleeper' agent, Anton Reiner, and set out to prove Swiss involvement in order to clear their own slate. Reiner contacts Leorah and myself.

Daniel looked quickly back over it. Two minutes for a thumbnail sketch of what had happened. Perhaps that would clear his thoughts. Anything he'd left out? He added at the bottom:

Xavier and Le Marteau Rouge. Distraction or discrediting? Past suspects: Schaarer, then Reiner.

Daniel lifted his head. Ehnbridt had been seen in Schaarer's registered car. But it had carried a false plate; the actual car to match it – only a standard six-seater Mercedes – was garaged at Schaarer's winter home at Lausanne at the time. Reiner, or a Reiner look-alike, had also been seen – by accident – inside the car by a vigilant doorman. But Daniel didn't quite believe in *accidents*; the intention had obviously been to make it look like Reiner trying to falsely indict Schaarer. Xavier and Reiner's letter-bomb had been equally as elaborate. Whoever Vruger was, whether just a contact or something more, he was obviously very clever. Very dangerous.

Daniel balled a fist tight. At each stage he had been thwarted: Reiner's death, Ehnbridt's killing before he could give any information, the timing of Xavier's death, and, on the Bahrain side, Gahtlav and Al-Ben Salmad. Not for the first time, the extent of what he was up against numbed and overwhelmed him, filling him with a mixture of fear and awe. He shook his head to break the spell.

Now, at last, they had something. He would pass the two names matching with Mendel's list on to Halmater, and see what they could come up with on them.

Daniel stood up and walked over to the coffee table. He was about to close the covers of the files lying there – but something stayed his hand. Aimlessly he flicked once again through the photos Nabens had sent. *The girl*. There was something familiar about the blonde girl, which had struck him at first sight. But he had pushed this to the back of his mind as probably due to a resemblance to some face from the past – or perhaps he had seen her picture in passing on a Tel Aviv news stand. The Salmad killing *had* been an international story.

Neither conclusion had really satisfied him, but other things had been more immediately important. Now it was back haunting him again. Where? When? He turned away, starting to pace.

Images flashed disjointed through his mind, then settled. The *wig*. Trying to picture her without the wig was the key. Daniel flicked through the photos again, picking out the closest to a front facial shot. It was just over a half profile, as she had glanced towards the doorman. She was certainly a beautiful girl. Not quite as beautiful as Leorah, but with the same dark attractive look, the olive skin tone, large eyes and . . .

He stopped. *Leorah!* The association jolting his memory, he looked back at the picture, following closer the line of the mouth and chin, going inch by agonizing inch over the nose and eyes, trying to imagine her face turned towards him. After a moment he was satisfied.

He exhaled his cigar smoke slowly, with a contemplative sigh. The photograph he had seen her in before was probably now nine years old, but, like Leorah, she had kept her looks. There was no longer any doubt: the picture on Leorah's mantelpiece, that first night. It was one of Leorah's two girlfriends from her days at the Arab university in Beirut.

It seemed hours later that he finally lifted his head. At first, he tried to answer it innocently in his own mind: they had probably drifted apart, lived totally unconnected lives;

perhaps she was already a radical, which Leorah knew of but never got involved with. Friendship didn't necessarily mean involvement – at least, not after nine years.

But then, combatting those thoughts, other things started creeping from the recesses of his mind . . .

Il rubat ilsha'b . . . the slogan of Khourem's old political party: 'To the shackled people of Islam shall come the freedom and brotherhood of the Karim Sha'b.' Just insert the words 'betrayers' and 'vengeance' and you had the words of the note pinned to Al-Ben Salmad's chest: 'To the betrayers of Islam shall come the vengeance of the Hilal.'

The wording was so uncomfortably close that Daniel found it impossible to ignore, however much he tried – or desperately needed – to detach Leorah from the Hilal and this girl in the photograph. Leorah's past close journalistic relationship with the Karim Sha'b stirred in his memory.

Small phrases she had used suddenly haunted him as possible lies, and the memory of their lovemaking and traded emotions began to turn sour in his mouth. Thoughts of betrayal and conflicting actions – like her helping the Israelis – became so intensely jumbled in his mind, that he didn't dare try to fathom them but merely to defend.

No, Leorah, it couldn't be, not after all that had happened. Sweet smiling Leorah, impassioned yet sincere in her thoughts, surely not. It just wasn't possible that she was involved with anything like the Hilal. Her action with the Israelis alone showed the extent of her Muslim indoctrination, her stance as a hard-liner. Compassion and generosity so instinctive that it stretched even to her enemy's children! And then how was it possible to explain the killing of Khourem, so much her political mentor?

The thoughts just didn't go together.

Yet each time he fought to reject her possible involvement, something else would come to the forefront. *Christ*, she had been in Bahrain that time he'd called on her to help Swenkel. Was that just another coincidence?

Wearily he laid his head in his hands and closed his eyes. There was only one way he could know for sure.

*

Vruger carefully sealed the large envelope and wrote on it: Paris Interpol, Rue d'Alsace, St Cloud, Paris, France.

He sat back smugly. The photographs combined with the information gave a very comprehensive picture. His wording at the end of the letter summed it all up neatly . . . 'It appears, as you can see from the foregoing information, that Daniel Grade wished to use Mr Reiner in order to fabricate a news story against the Swiss community, a story that would have greatly increased his journalistic standing. An agreement had been reached with Mr Reiner to split the money gained on the rights to an 'inside' story once the main story had been printed – but Mr Reiner on later learning the full implications of the story wished to pull out, and Daniel Grade's career was threatened. Through his daughter, he arranged for a letter-bomb to be sent under the guise of 'Le Marteau Rouge' . . .

'. . . I write this letter anonymously solely to protect my own delicate position, but with the interest of the Swiss community at heart and with the sincere and express hope that it will be put to correct use.'

The photographs spoke for themselves. But it was each snippet of information, so carefully engineered as most of it had been right from the start, that he found particularly apposite! Schaarer's false car registration, looking desperately like someone trying to fabricate an involvement; Semleche and Bunt who would no doubt verify when the Sureté contacted them that Mr Grade 'was indeed eager to prove a Swiss conspiracy'; the various meetings with Reiner; the connection through his daughter to the letter-bomb; and lastly the murder of Kent Ehnbridt – the hapless investigator who had stumbled upon his plot. Grade was a distinctive figure; one watchful ticket-collector, porter or train guard would place him in Villach the day of Ehnbridt's death. A forensic expert would sow the final, damning seed. Grade's fingerprints were probably all over Ehnbridt's room.

Vruger almost laughed out loud at the audaciousness of it, the sheer poetry of his planning. Machiavelli himself would have had to tip his hat. How pathetic Jaalgen's actions looked in comparison, driven mainly by rage and revenge as he now was. Almost out of control.

Control. Control was the key, but how few people truly knew his position, how separate he had kept each element. Jaalgen, he was sure, considered him mostly a pathetic intellectual, frightened by overt or unnecessary violence. But when that too had served its purpose, had stopped Jaalgen wondering too deeply about his true identity. To each, in turn, he had presented a different picture.

Little doubt remained in Vruger's mind that Jaalgen's actions would come as little more than back-up, insurance should the Interpol investigation start cutting too deep.

Almost reverently, Vruger handled the envelope once more before gently pushing it to one side. At the least, Grade's credibility and reputation as a journalist would be ruined, lingering even long after the many weeks or months it would take to clear himself, if he was actually able to. Meanwhile he would be hunted like a common criminal. Who would get to him first, Jaalgen or the police? It didn't really matter.

The twenty-six billion US dollars they had made so far – more than the stock asset values of General Motors and the five major Swiss banks combined – would have increased probably another eight to ten per cent by then. Vruger glanced reflectively at the *Zürich AGEFI* laid open on the stock-market page beside him. But after a moment only one small detail held his eye: that morning's gold prices, circled in ink.

Over a salami and stale bread sandwich at Vienna rail station, Jaalgen contemplated the next leg of his journey. The money from Vruger should arrive later that day, and then he could book his flight to Paris. He had a gun stashed in safe-keeping in Paris. From there, he could take the boat train to London. It was probably the best route to take anyway; gun checks were almost non-existent at the English docks.

Jaalgen glanced out of the station café window into the wide taxi circle and the street beyond. A light snow had begun to fall, and a sign on a store window opposite proclaimed '*Taüfen nun!* . . . eight shopping days to Christmas.'

Christmas 1940 had been the best one, he remembered. His father had bought him a toy fire truck, as bright red as the fire that reflected in his joyous eyes, the fire they had roasted chestnuts on.

After that, Belgium was overrun by the war, and his memories of Christmases had died, as much as his memory of fire took on a different meaning – of buildings bombed and burned out, of people screaming and running in panic, of distant glares and wailing sirens on dark stormy nights. 'Awaiting the victors,' his father had commented the year before his death. 'A new era will arrive soon, you will see.'

Christmases now had a different meaning – of nights spent in the beer halls and whorehouses of Hamburg, faceless among the crowds but revelling all the same; mad hours of gorging and beering and laughing – but always just as an observer – and sweaty, frantic humping that would hopefully free his mind for at least some while into the new year.

But even that small pleasure would probably be lost to him this year. Only one thing would free his mind this Christmas, he thought. As he looked out the café window again, the sky had darkened slightly and his reflection in the glass stood out against the street outside: his eyes red-rimmed, the main bandages removed to leave only a large plaster, his skin still raw and bruised in parts. The overall impression was of a man dragged low and now desperate. But feeling sorry for himself was as alien to him as this new heated craving for revenge which had replaced the cool impersonality of his usual contracts. He couldn't afford both emotions.

21

No point in denying it, no point in lying or deceiving any more, Leorah considered. The game was over; the day which she feared would have to come surprisingly filled her only with a mixture of confusion and relief – as a sinner at the confessional after a long absence – now that it was upon her. Daniel's words blazed in her mind: the similarity of the Karim Sha'b's slogan to the Hilal death notes, her own past journalistic connection with the party, her recent visit to Bahrain, and then the final inescapable link: the pictures of Nalini at the scene of Salmad's murder.

She listened, without interrupting, all the while Daniel was speaking; obviously he was deeply upset and at moments close to a tirade. As he finished, she was staring out onto Rue Maamari, her back to him.

She had been convalescing at home when he called, but now she didn't feel like clinging to the excuses of weariness or sickness that might have been her privilege. *No*, it was time that it all finished. The injuries would heal, but living a double life seemed to hurt more with each passing day, a sickness of the soul. Perhaps it would not have been so bad if she hadn't been so stupid as to fall in love with him – but that was another story.

Her eyes were moist as she turned to face him. 'I'm afraid I can't give you the answer you probably want – for me to deny it all. I just don't think I have the strength left for that.' Her voice quavered. 'All I can say is that in many ways they deserved what was coming to them for the deeds they had perpetrated. That isn't to say that I condoned it – just that I played my part.'

Daniel stood and stared at her, his eyes widening in shock. 'How can you possibly say that? Reiner and Xavier and

Ehnbridt all deserved to die? And the money gain to Bahrain, for Christ's sake!'

Leorah's brow knitted with confusion. 'Reiner and Xavier – what do they have to do with this? And the money . . . well, Al-Hakim was wise enough to sense the air of foreboding and move many of his own interests and assets to Bahrain, and to advise some close colleagues likewise, that is all.'

'Don't play dumb with me, Leorah. That's the last ploy I thought you'd use. What was the admission and acceptance for – to get my defences down before you did your turn-around?'

Leorah's expression stayed blank.

Daniel was caught up in the flow of his rage. '*God*, you don't know how all this has plagued me, turned over and over in my mind on my way here. And first you just calmly admit it, as if you were a boy scout caught stealing apples – then you start treating me like some idiot.' Daniel's voice rose to a near scream. 'I'm talking about the murders of Reiner and Ehnbridt, and Xavier, and the threat against my daughter's life – not to mention my own! And God knows how many billions of dollars gained at the expense of a city's welfare – built on the blood and bones of the people of Beirut, your *own* people. Those poor, defenceless old people that you're always telling me about. Those children that you treat every day, that you feel *especially* attached to.' Daniel moved close, looking intently into her eyes. 'How, Leorah, just tell me that. *How?*'

Leorah felt each word like a high-voltage shock. Her eyes darted furiously as the message sank home. She started to speak, but the sounds caught in her throat and came out almost as a guttural wail. 'No, *no* . . . Reiner and Xavier nor your daughter! The war here, and the banking . . . the Hilal had nothing to do with *that*. How could you think it?' She shook her head, her body shuddering. 'It was just the opposite, don't you see? Revenge for what started the war here against that traitor Salmad, and Khourem's assassins. You've got it all wrong!'

'Please, Leorah, don't do this to me. *Don't* do it. I've got the reports, the files, everything from *two* separate sources. And they both tie together. The Hilal's been behind it from the start, and you damn well know it!'

Leorah stared at Daniel intensely, hopelessly. Then, as if propelled, she flew at him with flailing arms aimed at his face and chest. Daniel gripped and held her after the first blows, mostly deflected painlessly – and then, as her body sank into sagging weakness and defeat, she was overcome by sudden and racking sobs, her tears flowing freely and frighteningly. Daniel made no move to hug or comfort her, just let her head rest against his chest, and he let go of her arms as the last of her strength dissipated. It seemed a long while that they stood that way.

Leorah wiped back her tears as she finally lifted her head. '*Oh God*, if only you could see . . . You said yourself how hard it was for you, on your way here, with everything revolving in your mind.' Her voice cracked with emotion. 'So please Daniel, can't you see how hard it is for me to admit this now, after all that's gone between us. Without you adding accusations that have *nothing* to do with me, or the Hilal. Accusations that I feel pierce my very soul.'

Daniel was about to speak, but Leorah continued, her tone cutting.

'When you arrived today, I gave you the benefit of speaking without interruption. Now I ask the same, that is all. No more, no less. *Then* indict me in any way you see fit.' Her gaze was constant, almost glaring.

Daniel remained silent. After a moment he lowered his eyes and nodded.

Leorah softened her tone, as if in weariness. 'I think I should start by telling you that Al-Hakim is still alive . . .'

'That night, when they were attacked on the coast road from the Casino, he fell close to the edge, not over it – and he was still alive. A herdsman higher up the hillside saw it all. He came down to Al-Hakim's assistance and carried him to his small cottage before the next people happened by on their way from the Casino. There the herdsman tended him, and when Al-Hakim became conscious again, he gave the herdsman the name of a doctor who could be trusted. Al-Hakim swore the herdsman to silence with a generous payment, and from that moment on *secrecy* forged the pattern of Al-Hakim's new existence. Miraculously, he was saved, but one bullet had shattered his spinal column – he was crippled for life.'

Leorah studied Daniel briefly. Daniel's absorption in what she was saying was complete.

'The next night, a cousin of Al-Hakim's went back to the scene and planted a small piece of Al-Hakim's *thobe* over the edge of the steep cliffside, clinging to a rock. It was discovered during the diver's search, and the evidence for Al-Hakim having gone over the edge was complete. Al-Hakim was convinced that if he emerged alive his enemies would try to kill him again, and the next time probably succeed. It served his purpose to be aware of his enemies' movements while they remained oblivious to his own. Only when vengeance had been exacted from those behind Khourem's death would he make his existence known, and it was this objective that largely formed the basis for the Hilal. Al-Hakim gathered around him close trusted friends, cousins, and political and banking associates – many of them oil wealthy – and some of those he had already advised to move funds to Bahrain, sensing the increasingly explosive atmosphere in the Lebanon. It had only partly occurred to him that Khourem's death and his own might be the ignition of that fuse.

'These people became bonded and entrusted to his secret, and his initial purpose was carried out reverently, some would say extremely. It was felt that if he were to reappear after having taken vengeance on his enemies, it would be seen as a great triumph, almost a rising from the dead.' Leorah smiled enigmatically. 'At last, the Lebanon would have a true, respected and acceptable leader; one who would endure and bond the bitter factions of the nation. It was a noble, if not slightly distant dream, you might agree?'

Daniel didn't answer; his shock was subsiding into puzzlement, his mind turning back through dates and events, trying desperately to tie in what Leorah was saying to what he already knew.

Leorah's eyes took on a fresh gleam. 'But after a while, it began to look as if that distant dream might actually be feasible, in a form that even I, with my usual scepticism, could accept. With the growing civil war, the present leaders began to look more and more extreme, unacceptable to the opposition. Karami, Hoss, Gemayel . . . all of them had by then made moves of lasting historical damage by both their allegiances and actions. It became very apparent that someone like Al-Hakim, strong yet as middle-line as you can hope for in a Muslim, would be right to strike the correct balance. Furthermore, he was – and would continue to be – absent during the period of fighting in which so many of those damaging allegiances were made, enemies gained.

'A sign was devised to mark the revenge killings, that of a Christian cross – and with the notes left on the victims the name Hilal became known, but not those behind it. It was felt that a particular aura of fear would be built up that way. Those responsible would start running scared, and perhaps betray each other by making errors. They would then be that much easier to track down and deal with. Also that aura – almost infallibility – would help when Al-Hakim chose to re-emerge and make his bid for power.'

Daniel had taken a seat now, and he rested his tousled grey head in one hand. The city was quiet of the sounds of war that afternoon; all that came to them in the small room was the faint rumble of cars and trucks carrying out what little normal commerce remained in the city.

'You mentioned earlier *your part*,' Daniel remarked jadedly. 'What exactly was your part in all this?'

'To direct information, *liaison* for want of a better word. My past journalistic support of Khourem was well known. I think my articles after his death sealed their decision to contact me. It was my task to help support the notion that Al-Hakim had died, and to monitor those journalists who might believe otherwise, or perhaps start coming close to the truth. I was in an ideal position for that.'

'Yes, you were,' Daniel said curtly. 'And what happened if a journalist, say *me* for instance, did stumble on the truth?'

Leorah's expression clouded. 'It didn't happen, so what's the point in talking about it?'

'Don't try and humour me, Leorah! God knows, those murders were *barbaric*. You don't need to be a Mensa to work out what would have happened.'

'Though barbaric in their revenge, you must understand what Salmad and the others did, Daniel.' Leorah leaned forward intently. 'No wrong would have been committed by your finding out; it would have just been unfortunate, that's all. We would have covered up by passing you some false information – that was all part of my job.'

Daniel ran one hand brusquely through his hair. 'God, I don't know . . . I don't know. What a mess. And where did your friend Nalini come into it?'

'I'm afraid it was I who introduced her to the Hilal. It became necessary to the plan for Salmad.' Leorah's voice took on a distant, saddened timbre. 'Nalini failed her exams at the Arab University and went to London to enter a teaching college. But she got involved in modelling and the teaching soon slipped – then a woman approached her, in the same way that many models are approached. This woman ran a high-class service.' Leorah glanced down. 'Nalini said many times that she wanted to return to modelling or to teacher training, but by then she was trapped by the money, and the lifestyle it afforded. The Hilal could have chosen any woman of that type, but they needed somebody they could trust.'

Daniel felt hollow and sickened inside. He'd felt only relief to hear that Leorah wasn't involved with the deaths of Reiner and Xavier, or the threat to his daughter – but still, from what she had admitted, he couldn't bite back the terrible sense of being used, cheated. The macabre killings of Gahtlav and Salmad came to mind again – then suddenly the image of Leorah gloating, urging on the assassins. No, surely he couldn't have been that blind all along? How could she have harboured all those different personalities, all those facets? The lover, the nurse, the child-carer, the philosopher . . . *the murderess!* And there still remained a chink of uncertainty that the Hilal wasn't behind the whole plot, that Leorah wasn't just admitting a lesser evil now that she'd been found out. He lifted his eyes slowly, his forehead heavy with sweat.

'*Christ*, how can I believe you after all this? How do I know this isn't another ruse just like all the others?' Leorah didn't answer. 'Perhaps if you'd told me earlier, before I confronted you with it, before *everything* . . . perhaps then, yes, it would have been different. But now?' Daniel was on the edge of his seat, clenching a hand against one knee. He stood up and paced about. 'I've got a problem, you see, Leorah. All along, the course of the investigation has been changing, the pieces never quite fitting . . . But with the files and reports I've just received, for the first time everything *did* come together. Two of the names from each report matched. Things were at last clear: the Hilal conspiring to secure a financial coup for the Bahrain market, Vruger as their contact and adviser in Switzerland . . . *everything*. Now you're telling me this, which puts me back to where I was at the beginning: *no* traceable plot. So which am I more likely to believe?'

'No, no, you've got it all wrong. Vruger, the man in Switzerland, *he's* the one in control.'

'That's what I thought originally – and that's what threw me. There's nothing traceable in Switzerland, not one damn stock of share movement worthy of note. *Nothing*.'

Leorah came close and gripped Daniel by the wrists, pleading with her eyes. 'What do I have to do to make you believe me? The Hilal didn't catch up with Gahtlav and Salmad just to kill them – information and names were gained at each stage, the pieces slotted together. Already we understand much of what happened . . . and what you are saying just doesn't make sense.' Leorah glanced to one side, as if seeking an answer there. 'These reports and files you keep mentioning, which tell you different. Who gave them to you?'

Daniel shrugged. 'Rolf Nabens, our Middle East correspondent gave me one; the other came from an old contact of mine in the Swiss Institute – Simon Mendel.'

Leorah slowly let go. Her eyes shifted uneasily, and then looked faintly lost. 'This Simon Mendel – has he been close to you long on this investigation?'

'Fairly. Why?'

'Then you are in more danger than I realized, Daniel,' Leorah almost whispered. Shadows on her face from the fading afternoon light now became more pronounced. 'His was the name Al-Ben Salmad muttered on his deathbed. Vruger *is* Mendel.'

Inspector Laboille was a fat, somewhat morose man, often considered slothful – but it was an appearance that disguised his more profound thoughts.

Inspector Searle had presented the main obstacle to him, but, in a way, Laboille had to admit Searle was right – there had been no actual evidence that the girl was in England, only suspicion. Until the night before.

A taxi driver had called into the Porte Maillot police station in Paris and described how he had run the girl to Le Touquet airfield along with – what seemed from the description – her father. Laboille had telephoned the information through to Scotland Yard within the hour. So, Searle had at last agreed to mobilize the British police. Laboille allowed himself a trace of satisfaction.

This had developed into quite an important case, with its heady mixture of terrorism and high finance; and Laboille had become increasingly determined to solve it. Thankfully, with the almost totally international implications, involvement by the Surété and the Judiciaire had been minimal; now he had a free hand, which was how he liked it. He'd had his eye on the assistant commissioner's desk for some while, but nothing had come along yet to particularly bring him to the notice of the upper corridors. This could be the one.

Especially with the envelope that had arrived that morning. At first Laboille was sure it was a hoax; it was too detailed, far beyond the sketchy clues they normally received thus. It was odd that someone would go to such trouble. To what purpose? But his doubts were soon put to rest as the accusations started bearing fruit: first, the connection with Reiner and with Grade's news story, Schaarer's false car registration, then the death of Ehnbridt – and the fact that Grade *was* sighted in Villach that same day.

Laboille had then become excited for the first time. *The implications!* A prominent journalist, a double murder, and a false news story involving the assistant Secretary-General of the UN and the movement of countless millions of international funds. It could be the case of the decade, and his own name would be at the forefront.

When he had the final detail, he would pass it all on to Searle. With Daniel Grade's distinctive appearance, there was little doubt he would be that much easier to trace than the girl. All he was waiting on now was the forensic report from Villach.

Mendel! At first, the accusation struck an icy chord inside Daniel. The feeling suffused slowly through his body, touching every nerve. The same thought kept resounding in his head, no motive . . . *no motive!* Parts of what Leorah had said made sense, but yet other parts were unacceptable, faintly ludicrous – and as they bit deeper, the incredibility of it all built to such a level that, along with his pent-up nervous energy, he almost felt like laughing out loud.

'*Mendel* . . . Hell knows how you expect me to believe that,' he blurted out finally. 'I mean it's so damn convenient, isn't it? I mention Mendel's name, and then you indict him.'

'You're wrong. It's not like that . . .'

'I suppose you think that wraps it all up neatly – explains away why he'd compile the report he did. I suppose your blessed Hilal didn't happen to find out *why* – a motive.'

'No. Salmad passed out before they could get that.'

'Yes, he would,' Daniel agreed tartly. He forced a wan smile. 'No motive, no explanation . . . just a name dropped casually.'

'But Zürich – the banking connection, the money transfers?'

'How many times . . . There's no traceable connection in Zürich! I checked every aspect of Swiss banking: stock assets, short and long term deposits, bearer bonds, broker trading, equitable funds . . . and nothing! As for Mendel, he traded even less than a number of others I could name. His yearly salary alone would have been four times what he'd have gained.'

'But there must be *something*,' Leorah remarked, and lapsed into silence, her eyes searching distantly. Then she continued, 'At least with Mendel it would explain why everything has been kept so neatly from your view, why you've been thwarted so effectively at each stage. And the involvement with your daughter and her boyfriend. He would know those things.'

Daniel didn't have an answer for that, and joined Leorah briefly in her mood of contemplation. It was uncomfortably true, he realized – despite all the other elements still against it. He studied Leorah's face. The way her eyes were searching so desperately, the way she had implored him – it seemed she was telling the truth. But then other memories came to him: the grapes and her fingertips on that first night, her plea for the Lebanon and a Palestinian homeland, their lovemaking, her helping the Israelis . . . her feelings for the young Israeli boy who had saved her life. All of those had seemed equally heartfelt, and yet she had been deceiving him all along. Could he really believe her now? He scanned back in his mind through the other factors.

'Surely Salmad could have been lying just to save his own skin,' he conjectured.

'I don't think so. At the time his quick release from suffering depended very much on him telling the truth.'

'Or this Hilal. Possibly all along they were responsible

through this Bahrain plot, as I suggested, but have been holding information back from you, only telling you so much?'

'No, almost definitely not. I would have known. Besides, if you knew Al-Hakim as I do, how fiercely nationalistic he is, the idea of him plunging his own country into war is unthinkable.'

It was a strong point, Daniel considered. Previously when he had pictured the Hilal, it had been as a group of Bahrain-based businessmen, non-partisan to the Lebanese. Al-Hakim being alive put a totally different aspect on it. But the thought of Mendel still jarred.

'Simon Mendel . . .' Daniel shrugged awkwardly. 'You don't realize how close that man has become to me, Leorah. I've worked with him twice now, and found him very forthcoming and absolutely scrupulous on both occasions. Even my family knows all about him – he sent them small presents during our last investigation together. You don't know what you're suggesting.'

Leorah didn't answer at first, and hearing his own voice Daniel realized how desperately he was fighting acceptance. Then she spoke.

'But still you had sufficient doubt to check him out at some stage.'

Daniel flushed. With that, he began to question himself: was it just unreasonable loyalty, or was part of him still finding it difficult – despite his much larger fears – to accept Leorah's admissions and accusations. One had come so close after the other. His mind was still wrestling to unscramble it all. Parts were at odds, just didn't fit together.

'How could you help the Israelis the way you did, yet still be a part of this Hilal. How can you possibly balance that in your conscience?'

'I can't, now,' she said quietly. 'You'll remember from the time in Bahrain that at first I refused.'

'Yes.'

'Well, in the meantime I went to see Al-Hakim. They'd caught up with Salmad in London and had the information from him. We were sure then that it was a Swiss-inspired plot.'

'So the children had nothing to do with it?'

'Yes, of course – partly. But at the time I couldn't think of going to their aid with even the slimmest doubt that Hasik was right, that the Israelis were behind everything.'

Disappointment showed deeper on Daniel's face. So, that action hadn't been as altruistic and selfless as he'd initially thought. His sense of being cheated reached a new peak.

'My thoughts changed a lot though during the investigation,' Leorah continued. 'I suddenly realized how wrong I had been to base my thoughts on such a political bias. *All* children – Israeli, Palestinian, Muslim, Christian – all are the victims. There really is no difference. Caught up and bred into a world of violence, with sides and differences which are often more futile than their own childhood games – which they don't understand, and when they do, they are already part of . . . and it's too late. We never learn . . .' Tears brimmed in her eyes. 'When that boy . . . with what he *did* . . . if you had any idea how I felt. Disgust, inadequacy, foolishness – all those emotions we adults try so hard to shield. Yet is there one of us not guilty at some time?' Leorah put one finger to her cheek, wiping gently across. 'You are a great man, Daniel, because you can admit you are wrong. You are open in your emotions, you have compassion, you are *simpatico* . . . *shafaka*. I am slower in learning, I'm afraid; each day comes a new, harsh lesson. But you . . . I saw this in you from the start, from that first real discussion we had. I think that's why I fell in love with you.'

Daniel shuddered like a man possessed. 'Christ, I wish you hadn't brought that up. I was trying hard not to remember. How can you mix love with *this*. How can you be in love with me yet betray and cheat me at the same time?'

'The Hilal didn't *order* me to fall in love with you, Daniel. That wasn't part of their scheme. I did that freely – though perhaps foolishly – of my own accord.'

'But having fallen in love, with all that went between us,

with all those *words* . . . to still keep up the masquerade. I just don't understand.'

With the tangled emotions and the accusation, the constant defending and explaining, Leorah finally snapped.

'Don't ever ask a Muslim woman to put her love before her beliefs! Don't *ever* expect that, Daniel.'

Daniel felt the words like a slap in the face. His rising fury and confusion deflated, it was suddenly all clear to him: how all those families, those mothers of the Lebanon could sacrifice their own – some with token resignation, some readily – to fighting, to death . . . *Beliefs before love!* Perhaps in the past century, at Waterloo, during the American Civil War, such jingoism and belief in ideals and country were also put before close family, loved ones, friends. But not now. But perhaps that's where it all really belonged, in some distant, chivalrous age. Perhaps that was a measure of where the Middle East historically lay, the outward image just a cloak demanded by the values and technology of the twentieth century. Beneath, through yanking itself so rapidly from Bible days, from Bedouin tents and mosques, the mentality of its people lay trapped somewhere between. Now it all made more sense.

While still in Beirut, Daniel had arranged to keep in contact through the Halmater Agency. So when he arrived back at his hotel, he called them, and received a message to ring Rolf Nabens. Lines were bad out of Beirut, and it took almost half an hour for the operator to get him through.

'What's up Rolf?'

'I've a message here from your Israeli friend Swenkel. He says there's been a sighting of someone called Jaalgen in Paris.'

Daniel's mind was still wrapped up in Leorah's words and it took another moment to detach himself. 'That's not possible!'

'I only pass on the messages, Danny . . . I'll read it if you like: "Sighting of Jaalgen in Paris. Contact usually reliable.

Followed from Boulevard Voltaire to Gare du Nord. Jaalgen at that point apparently suspicious of a tail, and unfortunately lost. Could you confirm in more detail events on the train – Art Swenkel".'

A cold feeling rose inside Daniel at the possibility of Swenkel being right. The Gare du Nord, he remembered, was the station for trains to London.

'Is it something to do with the attempt on your daughter? I seem to remember you mentioning that name.'

'Yes, I'm afraid so,' Daniel said emptily. 'I'd better head back to London.'

'On that score, Danny, there's something else. Some not so good noises at Scotland Yard. Nothing immediate because – as my inside information has it – Frank Searle there has resisted putting everything fully into motion without something more concrete from Paris. Apparently that could now be on its way, and – brace yourself, Danny – it sounds like it might involve *you* as well.'

Nabens paused – but at the other end Daniel was too stunned, too winded to comment. With Leorah and Mendel, he thought he had hit bottom, but now the trap-door was opening again. Something slipped, something clinging and dark in his mind.

'. . . If that happens, there's no knowing how the directors will react. Of course, I'll protect you in so far as I can by claiming no knowledge, but, well . . . you know how shaky this one has been with them. From your own end, Danny – if you're heading back to England, it's best you do that fast, because pretty soon you won't be able to. If that Paris confirmation comes through, every dock and airport officer will have your picture and description, plus half the country's police.'

Part Seven

Scotland Yard Press Office: Associated Press

22

It has today been announced from the office of Inspector Frank Searle that a nationwide search has been mounted for Daniel Grade, a Fleet Street journalist, and his student daughter, both residents of Wentworth, Surrey. They are wanted for questioning in connection with the murders of two Swiss residents, Anton Reiner and Kent Ehnbridt. Mr Grade and his daughter were originally sought by French police, but it is now believed they are in England.

Scotland Yard Press Office

The mist had only half cleared from Dover harbour, and a light drizzle was falling when Jaalgen entered England. It was almost midday.

He hired a car in the centre of town, and called in at the first service station outside for a map of southern England. Two miles further on he stopped again and unfolded the map to study it. Although it had been two years since his last trip to England, his memory of the main routes around London was good. He traced an ink line along the A2 into the city, then circled Wentworth.

Daniel Grade had arrived in England at 6 a.m., three hours before Frank Searle's announcement. Fog was heavy at Heathrow airport, and his plane from Beirut had been diverted to Gatwick.

With the scant attention paid to him by passport and customs officers, he assumed that no alert had gone out yet –

but he had to be completely sure. He could set off to see Catherine at home, but it would be the first place they would start looking. He could well find a squad car parked at the end of his road. Before he made a move, he'd better contact Nabens for confirmation.

One thought, among the tangled mess, had begun to preoccupy him more and more – and now he felt he couldn't any longer hold back the urge to know. Seeking out the Swissair desk, he headed over. After a few minutes expressing the urgency of his call to the girl at the desk, he had the telephone in his hand. He dialled Simon Mendel's number in Zürich.

Mendel's secretary answered. 'I'm sorry, he's at a private conference in Paris.'

'When will he be back?'

'Not for about ten days.'

'I see. Thank you. Please tell him I called.'

Ten days? A conference. Daniel called the Swissair girl over and explained that he had a message to pass for a Herr Broeding to a certain Simon Mendel, but because his German was non-existent, he was having trouble with the secretary. Would she be kind enough to do the talking for him? Broeding, Daniel recalled, was a main director of SBECSA, and if anyone's name got him through, it would be his.

'If you get Mr Mendel, hand it back to me. He speaks very good English.' Daniel dialled the number.

Taking the receiver, the girl said in her best Swiss-German. 'Yes. I have a message from Herr Broeding. Could I speak to Mr Mendel please? There was a slight pause and then she held the receiver out.

'He's there now?'

'Yes. Apparently.'

But with the receiver suddenly before him, the confirmation so close at hand, Daniel hesitated. Mendel's avoidance tactic alone had surely told him what he wanted to know. After that, any conversation would be lame, probably full of wounded, incredulous denials . . . Certainly, Mendel wouldn't admit anything under such circumstances. It could be a fiasco.

'Please . . .' the girl was thrusting out the receiver more urgently.

Daniel took it from her and laid it gently back in its cradle. Flustered and slightly embarrassed, he peeled off a ten-pound note, muttered, 'I'm sorry,' and with her puzzled eyes on his back made his way to the car hire desk.

Everything seemed louder than normal, almost as if inside his head: the tannoy's echo, the background whining of a jet, the clatter and bustle of people. His legs felt weak, and he felt sick. *Mendel!* However much he thought he had already partly accepted Mendel's involvement – along with the rest of Leorah's nightmarish claims which he had slowly come to terms with on the long and tedious flight over – he had been fooling himself. He had felt the shock like a hammer-blow! Mendel had been the last grain of sanity in that nightmare.

After hiring a Cortina 2000 saloon, Daniel drove to the nearby Gatwick Inn. There, over a coffee, he waited for Nabens' London desk to open.

His thoughts had gelled as they had on the flight over for a number of reasons, he contemplated: Leorah had gone so far that it appeared pointless for her to hold back on the rest; Al-Hakim being still alive and the unlikelihood of him plotting against his own nation; and, finally, Mendel's close knowledge of his own family – the painful yet indisputable truth that really nobody else had been so well positioned to weave the elaborate plot involving Xavier, Julie and himself. And now the phone-call. The only thing which eluded him now with a Swiss-inspired plot – and which had done so almost from the start – was *why?*

Daniel drained his coffee and ordered another, still waiting. Tiredness from lack of sleep began to catch up with him.

At two minutes past nine he phoned Nabens.

'I'm sorry, he went into a meeting straight away,' he was informed by Nabens' assistant Penny. 'Try again in about half an hour.'

Daniel phoned back after twenty minutes. Nabens was now available.

'Any news?'

'Announcement first thing this morning, I'm afraid. I've just come out of a meeting – Bob's still in there.'

'What's the bottom line?'

'Not good. Nationwide search for both you and Julie, Home Counties concentration mainly. They've added Ehnbridt's name to the list, too. From the mood so far, the directors will speak up for you on past merits – but they won't actually defend you until they know more.'

Daniel had gone beyond the brink. *Ehnbridt?* A day before, the accusation would have seemed madness, but now he felt merely numb; just another detail – along with the confirmation that the *Post* would no longer back him – added to what was previously the impossible, the unthinkable – levering even further open his frightening pit of acceptance.

'What about handing myself in, explaining the whole thing?'

'If you think you can do it successfully, go ahead. But if you're in doubt, forget it. You won't get bail on a double murder charge like this, Danny. And it could be at least three or four months before it comes to trial.'

Daniel was considering this when Nabens added. 'They found your fingerprints all over Ehnbridt's room, apparently.'

Nabens again broke the long silence which followed. 'Are you okay, Danny?'

'Yes.'

'We had something else from Swenkel. Perhaps you can make more of it than I can. '*No* body discovered by the rail parapet you described. However, the people of a nearby village, Ferleiten, have told Austrian police of a man who claimed he had fallen from the train. He was suffering from severe snowburns, bruising and mild hypothermia, and later killed the doctor who treated him. Police descriptions match that of Jaalgen . . .'

*

Daniel drove into London almost blindly.

The countryside, then Croydon, then the urban sprawls of Streatham and Brixton passed just as a vague background. Finally he was heading over Vauxhall bridge, over the Thames and into Victoria, heading for the West End and the City, the heart of it all. *His* London. Or that's how it had felt only days before – and all through the years he had driven those all so familiar roads: Buckingham Gate, The Mall, Trafalgar Square, then up the Strand and into Fleet Street.

But now it all felt strangely alien. Each person looking aimlessly from the roadside, each car driver that might glance over in passing, made him wonder if there was something more meaningful behind their gaze. Half his life spent tracking clues and people for stories, and now he was the one being hunted and tracked! As if he was suddenly in a giant cage – an arena. Everyone a spectator, a potential hunter or hunter's guide. None of the buildings or streets held the magic they had done before. Merging in with the misty sky, they seemed dull, formless and, like the people, silently threatening.

Daniel looked to one side. An old lady was staring at him quizzically as her car rolled forward. He suddenly realized he was gripping the steering-wheel unnecessarily hard. The lights had already changed. Changing gear, he moved off.

He remembered reading somewhere that you were always safer, more anonymous, in a crowd, so he headed for Oxford Street. He parked the car in North Audley Street and walked from there.

Oxford Street was thronged with Christmas shoppers. The growing urgency, almost panic, of there being only seven shopping days left to Christmas was obvious in the crowds. Merchandising was brash, consumption conspicuous and voracious, but overall, with the reindeer lights strung the length of the street, the atmosphere was festive. Daniel felt none of this. Occasionally people brushed and bumped against him, but he hardly noticed. He walked for quite a while, without awareness of time passing, glancing aimlessly into shop windows. From the corner of his eye he noticed a news-stand, and headed across.

A few yards away, he froze, panic rising. Even from there, he could pick out part of the headline: JOURNALIST SOUGHT . . . He walked over anxiously, bought a copy, and opened out the newspaper a few steps away . . . JOURNALIST SOUGHT IN DOUBLE MURDER ENQUIRY. It was the bottom of the front page, continuing onto page two. Daniel read only half of it, his eyes glazing, the chill that had numbed him the past hours turning icy, paralysing. He scanned the top of the page: it was the early evening edition. By later editions they could have a photograph!

The hubbub of people passing broke his concentration. Folding the paper again, he shuffled forward. The activity of the street began to drown his senses. He could imagine them all looking at him intently, recognizing, then converging on him with fingers pointed, accusing. When a couple close by locked eyes with his he suddenly picked up pace. By the time he had gone fifty yards, pushing and weaving his way frantically through the surge of people, he was almost at a run. *Oh God* . . . He had to get out of this street. The people, the traffic, the gaudy colours of the shop windows began to revolve in his mind, turning into a nightmare kaleidoscope. He reached the top of North Audley Street quicker than he expected, and started along to where he'd parked his car.

For a moment his breathing stopped completely. Two policemen were standing beside it, one writing studiously in his note-book. Daniel stood staring only a second longer, then he turned briskly away and headed for Oxford Circus tube station.

Isolation – the feeling was complete.

First the discovery of Leorah's betrayal, then Mendel's, now the *Post*'s desertion. It had never struck him how alone he could be until that moment.

The only time he had ever felt like this before was in the boxing ring. The crowd was there but you were always alone, punching out at your opponent through the glare and sweat. This time he was in there with Jaalgen, striking out desperately but never connecting, with Mendel and Leorah among the crowds, *jeering*.

Julie? He knew that Jaalgen would be going after Julie, to bury the link to Reiner's letter-bomb. He tried to remember if at any time he had mentioned the cottage or its location to Mendel. Nothing came to mind. Was there any other way Mendel could know of it? *No*. She was safe there. The only way Jaalgen could find out was through Catherine. So if he couldn't risk going home, he should at least phone, check that everything was alright.

But if he traced Jaalgen – or if Jaalgen found him – what would he do? What *could* he do? Jaalgen would be armed; so he would need a weapon. And another car. Who could he turn to? Where could he even start?

It felt unreal that Jaalgen was still alive. He looked at his reflection in the darkened window of the tube-train. The intensity of the darkness outside seemed to match this mood. With the clatter and motion of the train, he could imagine Jaalgen falling past the window – as he had done on that night – but Daniel had never looked out to see *where* he had fallen. The parapet appeared so high, it had seemed pointless. He shook the image away.

On the train it was different: it had been a matter of self-defence, spur of the moment. But, now, this was cold planning – weighing the pros and cons of where and how to kill a man. It was still self-defence – with his own life and Julie's at stake – but having the time for thought somehow made it more cold-blooded.

It was odd, but all his life he had felt something separated him from the Tony Dwyers, the Billy Stoners of this world. They had all been brought up in the same neighbourhood, but that gap – through fate or fortune, or just changing influences and ambitions – had seemed to be there from almost his earliest boxing days. Now he'd crossed over again, been thrust back into their world, with a vengeance, and it struck him how narrow that gap had been all along.

What were the words? *There but for the grace of God go I.* Perhaps he felt the alienation, the desperation, all the more because this path had been forced upon him; theirs had been chosen. And he had more to lose!

Julie . . . *Where? How?*

Their worlds . . . *Don't tell 'em the fix, Danny . . . we were mates at one time – remember. Successful wholesale greengrocer goes back to blagging, what for? If at any time . . .* The harsh fluorescent strips of Charing Cross tube station broke his concentration. He stood up as the doors slid open. Suddenly he'd remembered Billy Stoner's favour owed.

Jaalgen parked at the edge of the roadside behind the trees bordering the fourteenth green at Wentworth. It was early evening and the winter light had died early. He killed the headlamps.

From where he was he could see the house on the far side of part of the fairway and green. It was quite a large house in Georgian style; he'd already identified it from its front view. With the dampness of the fairway grass, mist had begun to settle heavily in the cool air, partly obscuring it. He pulled on his ski mask and got out of the car, picking his way through the trees. Getting to the edge of the green, he crouched down, studying the house more attentively.

One light was on, downstairs. Probably the lounge or kitchen; he couldn't make out any of the details inside. He circled around, getting part of a side view of the house. No other lights showing there either. Whoever was inside was probably alone. He checked his gun and started heading across.

Catherine Grade was pensive. She had so many mixed feelings about Daniel's call an hour earlier that she wasn't sure what to make of them.

He'd started by asking about Julie – was she alright? Yes, Catherine had spoken to the Lancings at the nearby farm just the other day, and Julie was fine – *why?* Daniel had changed the subject abruptly. Had she heard the news? No, she hadn't. Had anyone called? Yes, a man, about two hours before. He hadn't given his name and had rung off abruptly. It was only then that she'd asked, 'What is it, Danny?' And he'd blurted it all out: the investigation now including him as well as Julie, Scotland Yard's co-operation with the French police, the fact it was already in the newspapers . . . He was almost screaming with rage and incredulity as he'd talked of Mendel's involvement . . . *Would you have ever believed it?* Catherine had said little, stunned by the total incredibility of it all, and knowing that few words could have been of any consolation at the time. But she hadn't understood it when Daniel said, 'I'll be at Billy Stoner's till tomorrow, and I *don't* want you staying alone in the house tonight.' She'd asked him why not, but he'd just evaded the issue.

It wasn't that she resented the idea – the size and emptiness of the house always affected her more when she was alone there, some nights worse than others. His request just seemed odd; if the police hadn't called already, it was unlikely they'd call now. And even if they did, they were hardly accustomed to harassing suspect's wives.

But she complied with his wishes anyway, phoning Jenny as she'd promised. There was no answer – then she remembered Jenny had mentioned attending a pottery course in Weybridge. It was now 6.20 p.m. Jenny would probably be back in about half an hour. Catherine went upstairs; she might at least get a few things together. While she was packing, going through the routine motions to keep her mind off everything, the terrifying implications of what Daniel had said, finally caught up with her, and she burst into tears.

Of course, she *had* heard the news – on the radio in the mid-afternoon. But she had wanted to hear it from his own mouth; forced explanations were so often defensive, unrevealing. Like all those other secrets she had held back so well through the years, waiting on proper admissions. If she had admitted to hearing the news, Daniel would have expected outrage and a barrage of questions, and she wasn't sure if she was up to that. She'd cried then too. *Christ alive, you've really done it this time, Danny*. Was that why she had developed such a paranoia over this case – Daniel's total, almost frightening absorption? Perhaps that had been the warning signal.

Sometimes it seemed she had always been protecting him from something, cushioning him. After months of deliberation, he had finally left boxing on their sixth wedding anniversary – mainly because of her, she often felt, despite the easily damaged eyes – and there had been a painful period of readjustment, for which she again felt to blame. And then she found herself protecting him again – but this time from the rigours of journalism, with the long haul of his book inbetween. At times this role had seemed hard to break away from: the lonely, bored housewife, always opinionated and all too often over concerned. But now she just felt powerless, frustrated.

Reaching out to place a brush in her vanity case, she stopped her hand halfway.

A noise, only faint, but she knew all the house's familiar noises. She held her breath. There it was again: a light scuffing – coming from the far side of the garage.

She went out of the bedroom onto the landing, trying to judge its source more accurately. She heard nothing for a moment – then more sounds, footsteps – this time from inside the garage. After a second clicking noise – all the lights went out.

Catherine felt as if her stomach was being scooped out. She tried the landing switch. Nothing. She felt her breath coming in tiny gasps, and put one hand to her mouth.

The footsteps were now moving around the side of the house. They were light, barely audible, but long hours in the house alone had tuned her senses fine. *The garage* – whoever it was had turned off the main electricity junction-box.

I don't want you staying alone in the house tonight . . . Oh God, Daniel, what is it you haven't told me?

She looked down the stairs. Darkness obliterated all but the first few steps, and there another small pool of light showed through by the front door from a nearby streetlight. She started making her way down. The telephone stood on a side table in the hallway below.

Another sound now. She halted, listening intently. A latch or handle being tried, somewhere round the side of the house . . . probably the lounge. *The french windows!* Her eyes shifted sharply to the door leading from the hallway into the lounge. It was half open.

She heard a handle being tried again – and then a scratching noise. God in heaven, they would be inside in minutes – and then she would have no protection. She looked desperately towards the lounge door again. The key was on the other side.

The scratching noise was becoming more insistent.

She started down faster, almost skipping, but keeping her progress silent. Only a few yards from the bottom now . . . *please, two more seconds and I'll reach the door* . . . Halfway across the hallway she froze. She recognized the sound immediately: the french window swinging slowly open.

Her skin crawled, and for a moment her body swayed unsteadily. Every nerve was tuned as tight as a cheesewire to the sounds inside the room; her vision was filled with the door handle only a few paces away.

She heard faintly two or three footsteps at the far end of the room, then a drawer being opened . . . then another. Some papers being rustled.

She risked a step closer, and listened. The papers were still rustling; he hadn't heard her. She took another tentative step . . . the door handle was virtually within reach . . . and in that instant she saw him through the half-open door, saw the dark silhouette of his figure crouched over Daniel's desk at the far end of the room. And whether her step alerted him, or a tiny gasp unconsciously emitted, she didn't know – but suddenly he looked up, his eyes locked on hers. And he was moving.

Catherine lunged for the door handle. Jaalgen was

halfway across the room by the time she had wrapped her hand around and onto the key.

Shocked by his sheer speed, size, and the ominous appearance of his black clothes, Catherine's nerves felt stretched beyond endurance. A scream ripped from her insides, but sounded somehow distant – not her own. Her hand trembled, threatening to drop the key. She slammed the door with Jaalgen only two paces away, and turned the key quickly. She heard his weight coming hard against the other side – and she jumped back in fear.

She saw the handle turn once . . . then twice more after a few seconds. Then it stopped.

Biting on the back of her hand, she moved over to the telephone. She had done it. A nervous, barely audible laugh escaped from her lips.

Her first thought was the police, but then she remembered Daniel's and Julie's situation. Running her finger along a number written at the top of the telephone pad, she started dialling.

Art Swenkel had arrived at London's Heathrow airport late that afternoon.

He had intended all along to keep the Mossad out of the picture as much as possible. The fact that an increasing quota of 'dirty tricks' was being tagged to them, more even than to the CIA in recent years, was one of Samuelson's growing concerns. Reiner and the whole affair in Zürich had been skirting close to the edge from the start.

But with the reports suggesting the likelihood of Jaalgen's reappearance, and with the growing international police investigation, he felt he just couldn't stand in the shadows any longer. 'If the police get hold of Grade, he'll tell the whole story on Reiner, anyway,' he'd answered to Samuelson's objections. 'That is, if they believe him.'

From the airport Swenkel had phoned Grade's home. A woman had answered – presumably his wife – and said that he wasn't home, and no, she didn't know where he was.

Swenkel had rung off without announcing himself.

Hastily he drove away from the airport and up the short link to the M4 motorway. Not for the first time, the words turned through his mind: *'Julie's safe. She's at a cottage I used to live in in Berkshire . . .'*

Billy Stoner's house stood in a small, tidy mews between East Sheen and Kew; with the advent of New Covent Garden, he had moved there from the East End. 'Accessibility,' Stoner explained. 'And the punters in the East End aren't what they used to be. The money's all on the west side now, Danny.' After a few strained and curtailed niceties and two cups of extremely strong tea, it took Daniel over forty minutes to finish his account of the seventeen days that had passed since their meeting in Ye Olde Cheshire Cheese.

'You look awful, Danny.'

'Thanks a lot.'

'No offence, though. With all that, you've got a right to.' Stoner stood up, pacing thoughtfully. 'I didn't believe a word of it, when it all came on the radio earlier. Gawd, it made me sit up, though. Seen the photo in the latest *Standard*? Doesn't flatter you much.' Daniel barely managed a smile. 'Sounds like the sort of friends you can do without, especially that Mendel. Right cunt.' Daniel was still expressionless, and Stoner could see that he was deeper gone than he'd first thought. He understood what Daniel must be feeling, but its intensity concerned him. 'Anyway, I'm sure you didn't come here just to hear me prattling on. What can I do to help you, Danny?'

'I'll need another car.'

'Yer, well that's no problem. I can get you that within a couple of hours. Mate of mine's got a clean Granada. I would have lent you my own' – Stoner pointed out the window at the metallic green 4.2 Jaguar in the driveway – 'but it sounds like you could be in a bit of bother, and I've just had a respray. Probably a bit shouty for what you want, anyway. Anything else?'

'Yes. This Jaalgen's probably armed. I'll need a weapon.'

'You mean a shooter?'

'Yes.'

'You're not going to top anyone with it, are you, Danny?'

Daniel didn't answer, and Stoner's face clouded. 'Don't you think this is all getting a bit out of your depth?'

'I *need* it Billy.'

'I mean for me as much as you. I've been out of it for years now, Danny. Now, I've got a shotgun, but it's straight – the licence is in my name. You go topping somebody, it'll come straight back to me.'

'If I had to, it would only be in self-defence. But I can't go up against him without it, you can see that.'

'I don't know . . .' Stoner cradled his head in his hands, looking down. This was a new Danny Grade, one that he wasn't used to. At one time, within the sphere of a few Mile End Streets, he'd thought that Daniel might opt for the villian's life. When he'd turned to boxing, that too had been okay; that was the other main option of those streets. Everyone could imagine himself as another Ronald Biggs or Henry Cooper. Attainable heroes. But when Danny had turned to journalism and written the book on Dwyer, that had gone so far beyond their normal sphere of thinking, it had become difficult to measure. Now, hearing him talk of shotguns and killing a man, it jarred. But a favour – Mile End or East Sheen – was a favour. He hedged awkwardly. 'How can something like this get so out of control?'

'I don't know, Billy. It seems just as mad to me as it does to you.'

Stoner appeared deep in thought for a moment longer. 'Look . . . fuck the self-defence. That's a courtroom job, which I don't trust. If you have to use it, *use it*, but just make sure you get rid of it. There's another reason why I say that . . . I sawed the end off, so it's illegal anyway, even if you don't do anything with it.' Stoner laughed nervously, as if both excusing the action and brushing off the rashness of his decision. 'There aren't too many rabbits in East Sheen.'

'Thanks, Billy.'

Stoner noted a new expression this time; but it wasn't a smile, more rising determination. His faint uneasiness returned, but he covered it hastily.

'If you want some other advice, Danny, I'd do something about that barnet – it stands out like a beacon. Any copper in London could match you just on a description – curly, stone-grey hair. You stay here a minute – I've got just the thing.' Stoner reappeared from the kitchen with a glass containing black liquid.

'What is it?'

'Liquid boot polish and oil. Just the thing. Here, you dab that on your hair while I get the stuff together.'

First Stoner phoned his friend about the car, then he went upstairs. Daniel heard him rummaging about for a while, the sound audible through the floorboards. When he came back down, Daniel had almost finished combing the black liquid through his hair.

Stoner held the shotgun in one hand, a small box in the other. He placed both on the coffee table, then appraised Daniel's hair.

'Just the ticket. Makes you look like John Travolta.'

Again that cold, distant expression. Stoner was frightened. He had only felt this way once before in someone's presence; less than a month later the man had set fire to his own house, with his wife and two children inside. Stoner gripped the shotgun to steady his hand.

'Be careful, Danny – with a sawn-off, the spread's wide. It's not loaded right now. Now, out of the box of twelve shells, I've used . . .'

The phone rang suddenly. Stoner broke off to answer it.

He listened for just a second, then shouted, 'Come here, Danny. Quickly!'

Daniel grabbed the receiver.

'*Danny!* Someone's broken into the house –'

'Who? Where are they now?'

'*Right here* . . . What is it you haven't told me, Danny? What's going on? Try to get back quickly. Or send . . .'

'Who is it? I don't understand . . .'

Daniel stopped; he realized he was talking to a dead line.

Instantly he called his home number back. It gave the engaged signal.

Then he phoned the operator, who reported back quickly. 'It's ringing unobtainable. The line's probably been disconnected.'

23

The cottage was full of memories.

Just how many and how deep they went, Julie had come to realize in the last few days. This place marked so many transitions, so many major events and changes in the family's life.

Her earliest memories of it were when she was four years old, and they'd first moved there from the East End. Her father had fought his last bout, and had turned to boxing journalism four months before. The cottage, he'd felt, better suited his new line of work. The grass was higher and wilder now, and the flowerbeds were partly overgrown with weeds due to the sparse tending the garden received. But the interior had, if anything, expanded subtly in character through the years. Once it had been their home, full of life and activity, though pleasant and quiet due to its remote position – the main road a quarter of a mile down a dirt track and the nearest neighbours a mile away. Now it was used purely as a weekend retreat, and for her father's bouts of concentrated writing. The walls and shelves were filled with boxing memorabilia, newspaper articles and books, and a large desk dominated one side of the lounge, under the main window. It was here that most of her father's more difficult battles had ended.

If he ever managed to sort this one out, he could be sitting there soon, she thought wistfully. The phone had been cut off nine years ago, when they'd moved to the new house, as a necessary deterrent against interruptions. Any messages had to be passed through the Lancings a mile away.

Among the books, *Demise – the rise and fall of a champion* dominated, eleven copies in all: the English and American editions and the various translations. She traced her hand along them. The book had changed their lives in so many ways, it was difficult to measure: the money, the increased prestige to her father's journalistic career, the move to Wentworth, the expiation of his guilt over having exposed Tony Dwyer's corruption in the first place, and that painful yet all so necessary last door closed on his past career. It had been his only book; he had written on a subject so heartfelt, so much what he knew, that it had been difficult to repeat. He had resisted producing 'clone' books, a cycle which he felt trapped so many authors.

Julie laughed. She remembered when they'd heard it was hitting week nine on the *New York Times* bestseller list. Her father had merely brushed off its popularity as a symptom of the nation as a whole; that because the accent on 'making it' was so strong, maximum pathos was gained for those who tried and failed. When she'd questioned his ridiculous modesty, he'd paraphased Marlon Brando's classic lines from *On the Waterfront*. 'That's how I saw Tony Dwyer, I suppose: a wasted contender . . . hopelessly lost and trapped by his old neighbourhood and allegiances. Only he didn't see it until too late.' Her father had cried the night he'd finished the book.

As she walked about the cottage now, with everything signifying some achievement, some progress in time, his presence seemed very close and warming. The radio had been her only companion the last few days. *The radio*. She stared at it accusingly, and felt tears and jumbled emotions welling up again inside. Her father now implicated as well? *'Wanted for questioning . . .'* Surely they were just using his name to get to her.

The news had put her in cold shock for an hour, slowly worming itself around to fear and panic. She'd thought of Xavier again then, the nightmare still with her – Xavier's body falling . . . the chase through the Paris streets . . . the night time flight from Le Touquet. But the foreboding which slowly began to overwhelm her was that, even apart from the police hunt, her father was in danger, that something tragic and terrible was going to happen to him . . . *Christ, stop it . . . stop it!* You're letting the long hours alone get to you, that's all.

At least there was one thing she need no longer worry about. The message received two days ago from her father through the Lancings had been put in a roundabout way, but she understood it clearly: 'The man who chased you in Paris, no need to worry any more; he went the same way as Nobby.' Nobby was a cat they'd owned years ago which had died young.

Lifting her head from her hands and drying her tears, she noticed it had grown dark outside without her realizing. She got up and went to the window. A light mist was beginning to settle heavier on the surrounding fields.

'She's at a cottage I *used* to live in in Berkshire.'

Art Swenkel did what he hoped any Mossad agent would do, from his years of training new recruits. He went first to the post office at Staines, and was directed to a depot in Hammersmith. There, he started looking through old phone directories.

He first picked the year 1973, and then worked backwards. Three D. Grades were listed in Berkshire, but when he reached 1968 four appeared. He wrote down the extra one and tried the number; it rang unobtainable. He tried the other D. Grades. Two were still there, a Doris and a David Grade, and the other was a new occupant who thought the Grades had moved to somewhere around the Canterbury area.

Swenkel made a note of the address listed beside the fourth number.

The car lights flickered rapidly along the trees bordering the golf course. Daniel swung the wheel hard and turned into the maze of lanes that wound through to his home. With the mist, and his beam playing away from it, Daniel didn't notice the police car standing in the shadows at the lane's main junction.

It had taken him less than twelve minutes from East Sheen; because of the urgency, he had borrowed Stoner's 4.2 litre Jaguar. The surge as he opened up the throttle, the sheer power of the car, seemed to match the driving force of terror he felt inside. The tyres screeched as he swung wildly into the driveway, the gravel sluicing from underneath on braking. Reaching for the shotgun on the back seat, he leapt out.

Silence. Darkness and silence, with no lights showing inside the house. Only a dog barking in the distance. The rashness of his action suddenly hit him. If Jaalgen was inside, he would make an easy target standing where he was. He started to run across the gravel, half crouching.

A sound and movement alerted him; as he raised the shotgun, he saw the front door swing open a few yards head of him . . . A panicky split-second of shadows and uncertainty, then Catherine came running out towards him. His first reaction was to look beyond her, but nobody was following.

Catherine fell on him, hugging him tightly; a half-scream turned to sobbing.

'Where is he?' Daniel demanded.

'I think he's gone . . . just a moment ago.' Catherine fought back her tears to make herself more comprehensible. 'I could hear almost every movement. He was right next-door to me in the lounge. I locked the door on him, you see.'

'And he didn't try and break through?'

'For a moment – but when I phoned you he went outside and cut the line. Then he came back, and I could hear him moving about again.' Catherine's gaze became distant. 'I was frightened beyond belief.'

Daniel could feel her shaking in his grasp. If it really had been Jaalgen, he couldn't quite make the sense of it all. He released her gently and moved towards the front door.

'It's the main switch, I think,' Catherine prompted.

Daniel entered the garage, flicked the fuse-box switch, and came past her into the hallway. Warily he studied the lounge door. From where he stood no sound was discernible.

Catherine had partly recovered her composure, but the sight of Daniel holding the shotgun combined with her fear suddenly came home to her.

'What on earth's going on, Daniel? That gun! . . . The man in our house! What is it you've kept back from me?'

Daniel only then became aware of still holding the shotgun – but he wasn't yet sure what lay behind the door. Speaking over his shoulder, he moved towards it.

'It's a long story. I couldn't tell you it all, not with everything else. It would have been too much. Anyway, I wasn't completely sure myself. I thought he'd already been killed.' Delicately he reached out to the door handle, and listened.

'What do you mean – *killed*? You're talking in riddles.' Catherine stood gaping as if she'd been slapped in the face.

'It was Julie,' he muttered. 'The same man that chased her in Paris. I thought I'd killed him on a train – it was self-defence. But apparently I didn't – and now he's after her again.'

Still no sounds from inside. Feeling the sweat on his forehead, Daniel slowly turned the key and opened the door.

Quickly he switched on the light. The room was empty. The far end, by his desk, was in a mess, but the rest looked in order. He went over and started sifting through the disturbed papers.

Catherine broke the silence. 'So now you're going to try again.'

'If I have to.' But Daniel was thinking: why the desk? Everything else had hardly been touched – apart from three drawers in the dining-room dresser.

Catherine could sense the tension he'd endured over the last few days bubbling like a volcano beneath the surface, and at first she put his cold, purposeful attitude down to that. Now the thought of him killing a man was something different, something horrifying if not so incomprehensible – yet now it hit her. Daniel was steeling himself for the act.

'That's what they're calling you on the radio – a murderer! So now you're going to prove them right.'

Daniel gripped her by the shoulders. The unsaid words spun through his mind . . . You don't understand. He's ruthless, a killer. It isn't my decision. I don't *want* to kill him . . . *Or do I?* If Jaalgen came in now, unarmed, with no immediate threat to Julie, would he pull the trigger? Daniel didn't know the answer. In the end, all that came out was, 'It's either his life or Julie's. You make the choice then.'

Catherine stared deeper into his eyes, at the confusion and torment beneath the surface, sensing the terrible intensity of love he felt for Julie – and in that instant's reflection, wondered whether she herself was lacking, in not so readily contemplating murder . . . *She was always your favourite*. As Daniel turned back to sorting frantically through the mess of papers, Catherine collapsed, holding one hand on the corner of the desk for support, her tears brimming uncontrollably again. 'Oh God, *God* . . . how did we ever get into this mess? Is there no way out?'

But Daniel only half heard her introspective question, his eyes falling on something on the desk: the middle pages of an address book thumbed and curled inwards. Flicking through to that point, he turned the pages slowly one by one, then stopped. The entry was at the bottom: 6, Ashacre Lane, Peasemore, Berkshire. Messages to Julie through the Lancings – 0635-5691. Daniel only read the first line before he started for the door.

The two policemen in the squad car at the Wentworth lanes junction had seen the metallic green Jaguar enter, sitting up slightly at its speed – but a brief glimpse of its occupant revealed a dark-haired man, so they'd relaxed again.

Three minutes later when it exited past them at the same speed, their curiosity stirred. One looked at the other.

'What do you think, Len?'

'Golf club dinner, forgot his tie. Lover visiting and the husband was there when he shouldn't be. On the other hand, worth a blow.' He picked up his radio handpiece and pressed the release. 'Tag three to main, anything on a green Jaguar registration number VRN 460M.'

'V-R-N 4-6-0-M. One minute . . . patching through. Hold on.'

The sub-unit at Egham receiving the call radioed it through to Scotland Yard Central in SW1, who, in turn, put it through on a direct VDU link to the main computer at Hendon, the PNC.

The information flashed back on the VDU within thirty seconds: *registered William Ernest Stoner, 14, Beechview, London, SW14.* The PNC only listed offences within the last five years and two parking offences came up, followed by: *14/11/76. Two counts of assault, one a police officer in performance of duty. Driving with undue care and attention. No insurance. No tax. Car tyres defective. Case pending prosecution.*

The operator passed it on to her section head, who reached for the phone with the message still only half in his hand.

Inspector Frank Searle had asked to be contacted at home if anything developed, and he picked up the phone on its third ring.

Stoner, green Jaguar? Assault, undue care and attention . . . SW14? 'No, I don't think it's anything,' he commented ponderously. 'Sounds like just the sort who would be driving like a madman. What was the driver's description?'

'Middle-aged, dark hair.'

'No. Sounds like a no go.' Then, as a faint afterthought. 'South-West 14 – which part of London is that, by the way?'

'Morden, Wandsworth way, I think, sir. I'll just check.' He squinted through his window partition at a large wall map of London split into area codes in the office nextdoor. 'East Sheen . . . part of it looks to run into Mortlake.'

Searle's mind ran through dates, times and messages received since the enquiry started, most of them flooding in since the main articles and photos. *East Sheen?* The total number was over forty, and impossible to categorize except simply as likely hoaxes, crank calls and 'possible leads'. But from the eleven that afternoon, one was from a woman who claimed she'd seen the man in the *Standard* at North Sheen railway station. He remembered it because the sergeant who had taken the call mentioned her being posh, 'not the sort that usually calls in'.

'Wait, I think we have a possible ID in that area,' he said. 'It's only slim, but perhaps worth following up. Get the squad car in question to follow, and radio through to others in the area with the details.'

On Searle's instruction, the squad car crept out of the shadows of the Wentworth lanes three minutes after its first call, and the alert touched another thirty squad cars covering the network of motorways and 'A' roads over a five-mile radius.

'. . . and in parts of southern and south-western England, stretching as far west as Dorset, the mist built up through the day has developed into fog, particularly heavy in north Hampshire, and parts of Surrey, Berkshire and Wiltshire. Some flights have been delayed at Heathrow and a full stoppage and diversion of flights is possible later. Roads out of London affected are . . .'

Daniel switched off the car radio. He'd kept it on since leaving Billy Stoner's house for any information on the progress of the police investigation. Most of it had been repeats of what had appeared in earlier papers: *journalist and daughter sought, believed now to be in England, double murder . . .* He didn't need it on to tell him what the weather was like.

Ahead the fog lay in patches, and Daniel watched the

bonnet cleave its way through. In the denser patches it was almost impossible to see, the fog clinging like layers of fine gauze to the windscreen, then lifting suddenly and miraculously again. But new patches came up just as thick, without warning; and they were becoming more frequent, the intervals shorter.

Each one seemed like a barrier in his mind, something trying to halt his progress towards Julie, a challenge, and he kept his foot down hard, powering his way through. Would Jaalgen be keeping up the same speed through the fog? He doubted it – and so each patch he went relentlessly through brought him that bit closer, gave him a bit more edge. *A chance*.

Some red tail-lights loomed up suddenly, then the hazy maroon form of a car. Daniel flashed his lights. It didn't move. He flashed again, and was almost upon it, clearly seeing its number plate and the shapes of people inside. Then he weaved inside of it quickly and without warning. A truck was a hundred yards ahead in the middle lane, and he swung wildly back in through the fast-closing gap between the two.

Sweat bathed his body, and his nerves were at screaming pitch. He heard a horn blaring – whether from the truck or car he wasn't sure; he could only afford a split-second glance in the mirror, then yanked his eyes back to the road ahead. it was a tense game. Mist and shapes and indistinct lights.

If he slowed up he would be too late, yet if he had an accident he wouldn't get there anyway. He shook his head. Don't think about that factor! Just keep going. Play the odds, hope for luck. Hone the senses, strain the weary eyes, each mist patch, each tail-light an obstacle, an enemy almost as much as Jaalgen.

Past thoughts plagued him, past and present jumbling in the mist, unthinkable options, dilemmas, dangers. *No!* No options . . . *no choice*.

How long a start did Jaalgen have on him? 'A minute or so ago,' Catherine had said. He hadn't noticed any unfamiliar cars near their house, or heading out of their lane, so it was likely Jaalgen had parked in a back lane and cut across the fairway. That would have taken Jaalgen possibly two minutes, and he himself had been only a few minutes inside the house. So, perhaps a minute or two lead. At sixty, seventy miles an hour, one to two miles ahead. *One to two miles?* Peasemore was about twelve miles away, so he'd have to hope he was going at least fifteen miles an hour faster to catch up. But then what if Jaalgen was going faster than seventy?

He looked at his speedo: it flickered just over ninety. At that instant he flashed past a squad car parked on its raised ramp at the side of the motorway – but he didn't notice it because of the fog.

The squad car driver was doing a crossword and his co-officer saw only the rough shape of the Jaguar, looking more like grey than green to him, and a vague *VR*, or was it *VB*, at the beginning of the number.

'Did you see that?'

'Yes,' the driver lied, glancing up. 'Going fast, wasn't he.'

'Not that so much. I think it was the Jaguar on the alert a moment ago.'

'Hard to tell in this pea-souper.' The driver hesitated for a second, then put aside his crossword and started up the Rover 3.5. 'But even if it wasn't, he was going fast enough to warrant us following.' He put the car into gear, and they snaked down the ramp and onto the motorway.

Jaalgen had been contemplating the tail-lights of the juggernaut on the inside lane for almost a minute now. He'd seen the car lights appear at the house as he'd almost reached the far side of the fairway. A Jaguar, or perhaps a Triumph Stag; it had been hard to tell with the heavy mist. At least, something sleek and fast-looking. It had been a fast, breathless scramble then, the rest of the distance to his own car. The thought began to concern him more and more with the passing miles.

If it had been Grade in that car, and Grade had discovered he was on his way down to the cottage, he could be after him within minutes. What sort of chance would he have then? All he had was a Morris, the most convenient to hire in Dover at the time. He was unfamiliar with the car's engine capacity, but all he knew was that however hard he pressed on the accelerator, the needle stayed obstinately between seventy-five and eighty.

Not long after that his eyes had fixed on the juggernaut and an idea began to form. But he had to wait for the right moment.

His speed now was only sixty as he tailed it. It was a delicate balance: the longer he held back his speed, the more chance Grade had of catching him, yet if he didn't implement his plan, Grade would catch up with him anyway! Time could work either way. He glared at the road ahead and cursed inwardly. *Come on!*

In a way it seemed ludicrous that he was worrying about a man like Grade – himself a professional, and Grade nothing more than a tinpot journalist. Yet the incident on the train, the desolation of the mountainside, the wind whistling through the tall pines – the visions he was still fighting so hard against had built up an inexplicable feeling of foreboding connected with Grade, some *borzeichen*, warning him not to take Grade lightly. To be cautious. This time, he wouldn't make the same mistakes.

The girl, too, had foiled him in the chase that night through the streets of Paris. It was uncanny. In some recess of his mind, he realized that the two incidents represented a vulnerability, a flaw in his personality, something that could grow like a cancer, out of control – and so he dared only half plumb his motives – pushing on only to clean the slate, finish what he had started before the feeling claimed him totally. When he caught up with the girl, he . . .

A roadside sign broke into his thoughts: the diagram of a road narrowing over a bridge. It was followed after fifty yards by another sign: NO HARD SHOULDER FOR 300 YDS.

Jaalgen accelerated and started flashing his lights at the juggernaut. The juggernaut driver didn't see him at first, and so Jaalgen started beeping his horn as well as he came up alongside. After a second the driver looked over in puzzlement. Jaalgen drew closer to the cab and mouthed, 'Your back wheel,' and pointed behind.

They came onto the beginning of the parapet. The driver looked straight ahead again, and with no sign of him slowing down, Jaalgen thought: Christ, he's not going to stop in time.

Then suddenly on the last portion of the parapet, the juggernaut braked sharply and pulled in thirty yards beyond the start of the fresh hard shoulder. Jaalgen pulled in just in front of him and got out.

The driver looked a bit bemused that he should actually stop. 'What's up mate?'

'Your back wheel. Looks like a bad wobble.'

'Felt alright from the cab. Let's have a look.'

The driver reached for a canvas bag of tools behind and got out. Jaalgen followed him back.

'It's this right-hand wheel,' Jaalgen prompted. 'But the inside more than the outside.'

The driver nodded, took out a wheelbrace and leant underneath to test the tension of the wheelnuts. Jaalgen started to sneak the gun out from inside his windcheater. The driver was about to look up after testing the second wheelnut when Jaalgen brought the gun butt down on the base of his neck. The driver was only slightly stunned, starting to swing the wheelbrace around, and so Jaalgen hit him again, slumping him to the ground. Two cars had passed, but Jaalgen was sure their own figures and movements had been indistinct in the fog.

Jaalgen quickly searched the driver's body for any spare keys, and finding none, dragged the body to the roadside. Then he ran to the cab and did the same search, looking under the sunvisors, in the glove compartment and spare workbags.

Satisfied, he started up the Juggernaut's massive engine, slammed her into reverse, and – checking that nothing was coming immediately behind – backed her up quickly, swinging her around as he came up to the start of the parapet, broadsiding her so that she was blocking all three lanes. He checked the mirrors, still edging a bit. *Good.* He pulled on the brake. Hardly room each end for a motorbike to pass. Switching off the ignition, he yanked out the electrical wires beneath; then, climbing down, he opened the bonnet and took out the rotor arm.

Images of Mannheim, the accident and *Polizei* sirens came to him, but he pushed them into the background. With the rotor arm and ignition keys in his pocket, he ran to his car – and as he started to head off, heard the first collision on the juggernaut's far side.

The orange warning sign flashed 50 mph as Daniel sped past. Daniel turned on the windscreen wipers for a second to clear the residue of moisture from the mist patch he'd just gone through.

Murderer! Catherine's words still rang in his mind. It was odd, that word and all it signified had never really hit him. He felt as if he was about to fall into a void, yet never did quite fall, just looked down upon it; as if the cold terror of what might happen to Julie was the only cord keeping him suspended, and when it snapped he would fall, and would have to face everything else: the fact that he might by then be a murderer; Leorah's and Mendel's betrayal; the paper's non-backing; the ruining of his career. Or perhaps the whole whirlwind of events had been so numbing that he'd wanted to phase them out of his mind anyway? Self-preservation or just sheer terror? He wasn't sure.

A Volkswagen was going slow in the fast lane and he flashed his lights. It moved hastily and, as he passed, it flashed back at him. He glanced in the mirror, and in that instant caught his own reflection, the intensity of his eyes. He ripped his vision away and back onto the road, afraid of having to admit Catherine was right, afraid of weakening his resolve if he delved too deep – and yet afraid of that inner part he'd glimpsed and didn't recognize, or perhaps didn't want to recognize.

The Volkswagen was flashing again. Why the hell is he still flashing? But as he looked up at the mirror, he realized it wasn't because he'd pushed past, but because of something in front, and he caught a glimpse of it in that instant himself: a small fire in the inside lane and a large shape beyond, parts of it still indistinct in the fog, but, looming larger, then larger still . . . *Oh my Christ!* A red and grey mass of tangled metal spread out across the lanes. Daniel was hammering towards it; there was no way around it . . . and the terrifying reality dawned on him that he wasn't going to stop in time.

Daniel braked hard and swung the wheel. The car spun, and the juggernaut was at his side, its trailer towering high above him as he careened towards it; at the last second, he could see the print on the trailer clearly, and held one arm up in protection. The impact threw his entire body forward. Some glass shattered, and he felt fragments of it cut into his arm and forehead. His vision spun suddenly into darkness.

The squad car following had lost a mile on Daniel in coming down from its ramp, and yet another half a mile in building up to his speed. When they'd radioed in, the report had come back: 'Suspect probably armed. Proceed with caution. Other units in area will assist.'

Daniel looked up. His blackout had lasted only about six seconds, but the nightmare had only just started. The Volkswagen behind him had pulled in on the inside lane, but with no hard shoulder it could move no further, and as Daniel watched with horrifying fascination, a truck appeared behind it, bearing down quickly . . . and he wanted to wave his arms or shout or flash his lights at them, but it was futile, and by then *too late*. The truck driver saw the Volkswagen at the last moment, swerved and clipped its corner, jamming the Volkswagen into the parapet . . . the truck tilting, upended, spinning lazily onto its side as it flew towards Daniel. It came to rest and burst into flames less than fifteen yards away, and he clearly saw the face of its driver lit horribly and ghostly inside as he burned.

Daniel felt sick, terrified. Not just for himself, but for

Julie. If he was now ensnared in an accident, he wouldn't be able to get past and on. There would be nothing to stop Jaalgen. *No!* He squeezed his eyes shut, mumbling to himself, feeling the sweat course down his body. Get past? He almost laughed insanely: what way past was there anyway?

His nerve ends tingled, searching wildly for messages, working their way around and finally prising his eyes open. He had to . . . *had to*. He looked to each side: two cars had already collided with the juggernaut before the truck and Volkswagen arrived. A man was visible in one and clearly dead, but he couldn't make out anyone else. He checked his own damage: the car's rear side was badly dented and the front side window smashed. He felt badly shaken, with a few superficial cuts, but apart from that there was nothing immediately apparent. The Jaguar had stalled in the collision, and he tried to start her up; she coughed and ground down, and he tried again.

The engine sparked to life, roaring as he revved harder. He put her into gear and edged forward, straightening up. Apart from the rending of metal as he disentangled, it felt and sounded fine.

He had to get past, and there was only one way. Some portion of his mind passed it down through his frayed nerve ends – but it was a ridiculous, terrifying, insane answer, hardly better than no answer at all. But it was the *only* way: heading back the wrong way along the motorway. He swallowed and wiped his forehead as he contemplated it. The nearest gap in the central partition was probably half a mile away; if he could make it to there, it would probably be almost a mile down the oncoming traffic lanes before the next gap beyond the juggernaut. The chances would be slim. With the fog, even slimmer.

He closed his eyes for a second more, steeling himself, and opened them wide again to the rolling waves of fog . . . waves of *death* they almost seemed now. Then, with a last prayer of resignation, he let out the clutch and started rolling forward. Within fifty yards, he was doing forty – and realized that unconsciously he had been holding his breath. He kept to the middle lane, so that he could switch to either side more easily.

Some lights, glaring yet distorted, plunged towards him . . . but the car was in the inside lane. It slowed drastically on seeing him, passing slowly, and Daniel looked fleetingly into the mirror and saw that it had stopped far short of the juggernaut. The residual fires from the truck and a car provided a warning to people.

Another set of lights – faster, more startling. Coming in the fast lane. Daniel made out its shape only as it was almost upon him – a police car! He caught the startled expressions of the two officers inside as it flashed past. Its brakes screeched furiously and it slid broadside, part of it colliding with one of the cars by the juggernaut. It appeared to start up again after a second and edge after him for a few yards, then give up the ghost. Then everything behind was lost in the fog.

'The guy's fucking crazy,' the squad car driver screamed. 'I'm not following him in this. Let's radio on.'

'What? That there's someone heading back up the wrong lane towards you. I'll put it out – but he's not going to get far anyway.'

'Where the hell is he going?'

The mist was denser ahead. Daniel peered at it intensely. With the way those lights had loomed so suddenly out of it, his sense of foreboding was overwhelming. His palms were slippery on the steering wheel. So far he'd been lucky, but if anyone came straight for him in the middle lane, he wasn't sure he'd have time to move out of the way.

The mist swirled to one side, and he could see the gap in the central reservation, about a hundred yards ahead. He put his foot down a bit, picking up to fifty. The mist crossed his bonnet in rapid, more closely grouped clouds. He cut his speed at the last instant, braked, swung around – and was through.

And his brain started screaming before the wave of relief even hit him. There were two sets of lights, one further away, bearing down *fast*. He had been so intent on getting through the gap that in that split instant he had taken his eyes from the opposite lanes.

Panic igniting every nerve in his body, he accelerated hard across in front of them. Lights and mist and blaring horns and straining engines became all one horror for a suspended moment. He felt the rush of air from the farther vehicle buffet his car – then something rending behind, twisting him around.

Looking round to get his bearings, he found he was in the inside lane. The car that had hit him was pulling to a halt behind, but the clock in his mind was ticking ever faster . . . *Julie!* Not much time left now! Putting his foot down again, he fishtailed back into the middle lane.

Sweat was streaming into his eyes. His nerves were on a taut thread, ready to snap. The yards rolled by, seeming to take hours, yet only seconds passing. Mist and lights and sounds and briefly-lit frightened faces, a last-second swerving, the bumping and grinding of metal, and distant, muffled screams. Three cars he'd almost hit head-on . . . or was it four? Two cars he'd brushed against, or was it three? Each was an obstacle, an *enemy*. And Jaalgen? Daniel gritted his teeth. How much further now? It was impossible, almost beyond sanity. Part of him yearned to give up, just for the release, to slip peacefully into surrender. Jaalgen would get there before him anyway. No way could he make it in time. It would all be for nothing . . . And then he noticed he was now passing the juggernaut in the lane opposite, and a flicker of hope entered his mind. Six hundred yards more, maybe only four hundred if he was lucky.

He powered the car on, the fog rolling towards him ever menacingly.

A van passed him on the inside lane, flashing furiously – and then in a brief break in the mist, he thought he saw the gap. The fog was a tease, swirling back and forth, uncovering and then obscuring again, offering him sight of his posibble escape, then yanking it away. It was there, then gone. He strained his eyes harder, pacing the car to where he thought he had seen it. Just one more glimpse, if only for a second . . . that would be enough.

The blaze of lights distracted him: two sets close, and one further behind! In that split instant he contemplated swinging around the two, then cutting up before the third . . . but suddenly it occurred to him that the space between them wasn't enough. And even if he did get through, what if he'd then missed the crucial gap? *Where was it?*

If it was where he thought he'd seen it, could he reach it before they reached him? It looked to be about sixty yards ahead.

The lights bore down on him. No time for a decision . . . *no time!*

Daniel put his foot down hard – the bonnet tilting as he surged forward – heading at an angle for the central gap. Still the mist shrouded it. Lift . . . *lift!*

The lights were closer now, dazzling – bathing the mist all around. A horn blared.

If he was wrong, or misjudged its position, he would crash into the barrier, be swept along like a toy with the force of them hammering along. He shook the thought away. Come on . . . *come on!* Forty yards . . . *thirty!*

The mist cleared. Suddenly it was there – *the gap*. But it lay to the right of where he was aiming . . . He didn't think he could make it! The shaking of his body threatened his grip on the wheel.

Searing lights and the cacophony of sounds and the madness of the day, Jaalgen, Julie, memories – all tumbled back upon themselves, and Daniel closed his eyes, praying and screaming to unseen gods, his nervous exhaustion leaping into some new boundary . . . and when the battering and rending of metal registered on his senses, he opened his eyes expecting oblivion. But instead he saw that two of the vehicles which had just swept past had collided with each other. Then fog, thick rolling fog . . . and he realized he was clear and moving away on the far side.

*

At the end of a news bulletin, Swenkel heard the alert on his car radio: 'M4 motorway blockage between Bradfield and Frilsham, nine miles west of Reading . . .' He took the next motorway turn-off, signposted Theale. *Damn!* Having to head through on the A roads would slow him. He glanced at his watch, then at the rifle resting on his passenger seat.

The cottage was quiet. Julie had gone to bed early, deciding to take a good book. It was that year's smash seller, *Shogun*, and at moments she felt totally transported to medieval Japan, thankfully shutting out the surroundings of foggy, rural Berkshire. A small lamp was on at her side.

She was almost halfway through the novel, having started it the night before, and was just reading of Blackthorne's bluff to commit *seppuku*, when the sound of footsteps outside broke her thoughts. That was odd; she hadn't heard a car. She put down the book and moved over to the window. A dark blue Morris Marina stood about twenty yards up the lane. But she couldn't see anybody. The bedrooms were set in the eaves of the cottage, and the slant of the roof blocked her view for about twenty feet. Whoever it was was probably close to the house now, approaching the front door, she thought. She listened intently: nothing for a second, and then a light clicking noise.

She opened the bedroom door and stood listening at the top of the stairs. This time the doorbell rang. She went halfway down and called out.

'Who it it?'

'A friend of the Lancings. I have a message for you.'

Julie made her way briskly down the rest of the stairs. The lounge lay in darkness below, and she started across it – then stopped. A slightly clipped tone to the voice disturbed her. A friend of the Lancings? No, it was probably okay – how would he know of them otherwise? But then what about that small noise she'd heard beforehand: had it just been a tap at the window, or the latch being tried?

'One minute,' she shouted, suddenly conscious that she had paused.

The only light in the lounge was where she stood, a widening bar slanting down from the stairs. Beyond that everything was dimmer. She looked towards the window by the door, but could see only a black blanket of darkness beyond. On moonlit nights, one could pick out the front porch and part of the garden. She moved another few paces, out of the pool of light from the stairs.

Some movement came close by the window, within inches of the pane, something indistinct – but it made her start. The face appeared almost immediately afterwards – and she had already jumped back in horror a split instant before the glass shattered and the bullet embedded itself in the chair only a foot away.

Another bullet followed quickly, ripping into the top of the chair as she lunged to the floor. Then another one, lower, burying itself into the floor inches from her feet as she scampered for cover behind the chair and coffee table.

Then silence.

Julie held her breath. Her mind hammered: it was *him!* It had been only a fleeting glimpse, but she was almost sure. Confusion over her father's message, images of Xavier by the river, the night time chase through the Paris streets, the face in the window superimposing, matching – all jumbled. No, it can't be, he's dead. *You told me! He's dead!*

Shots sounded again, splintering wood. Julie looked up: they were pumping into the door, around the lock.

You're dead . . . Cling to that; refuse to believe what you've seen. Sweating with fear, eyes half closed, she started mumbling, almost chanting . . . Her mind felt frozen. But if it wasn't him, who was it?

The bullets grew ever more alarming, some passing through the door and striking the walls and floor around. The lock was working loose.

Julie's eyes were wide open again. She fought to free herself from her trance. She felt paralyzed with tension and confusion. The sound of one of the rivets coming free finally broke the spell: he would be inside within seconds! And she would still be sitting there, as if waiting for the bullets to pump into her. With raw fear and self-preservation surging up, she looked around for some means of protection – a weapon.

It was the wrong room for weapons: a fireplace, but no tongs or poker. There wasn't even normal dining-room cutlery; it wasn't used as a dining-room anymore – there were only books and papers and pens. Julie became frantic; her eyes darted to each corner of the room, searching. But all she could see were more books, boxing trophies, photographs, gloves, training weights . . .

Another rivet sprang free, the lock hanging by only two now.

Weights. Her eyes went back to them. They were stacked by the wall, just a yard away. They might be too heavy to throw, hard to direct accurately, but the bar lay at their side. Would *that* be too heavy to swing?

Kicking sounded at the door, the last rivets flying free.

Nothing else – no time left for contemplation! Julie leapt over and gripped the base of the bar.

The door swung open and Jaalgen stepped inside. His eyes darted around adjusting to the light, and studying the room. He took a step closer, but she waited: another step and he would see her, but then she wanted to make sure she caught him right. She would probably have only one chance at it. Faint shuffling, his feet turning. Her heart pounded so loud! She was sure he could hear it. A frozen second, his eyes seemed to be on her, then he moved – and she swung.

The bar came up in a blur, striking him full square in the chest, and he flew back, gasping for breath, against the desk below the window. Julie came up to swing again – but saw he was recovering his balance, bringing the gun barrel around towards her.

A trophy and two photographs behind her exploded as she ducked. Then everything fell silent, only the sounds of some distant crows coming to them through the half-open door.

Jaalgen knew that the blow to his chest had cracked some

ribs, knew that he was bleeding somewhere deep inside – a rib jagged and pushing through. He didn't know how long he'd last, perhaps long enough to get to a hospital, but he'd finish the girl first. That he would make sure of. He screwed up his eyes: the shadows were heavy and shapes were unclear at her end of the room. Was that part of her leg? He fired at it and heard a slight scream, sinking to a muted whimper. He fired again, but in that instant the object moved.

His eyes suddenly widened, startled by the speed of the reprisal. The bar was swinging up towards him again – but this time he was sure he had her clear, and fired. He saw a splash of red on her arm, but the momentum of the bar had already started . . . and he only managed to move slightly to one side. He felt it crash into his shoulder, almost knocking him over, the gun flying from his hand and skittering across the floor.

The bar swung at him again, smashing viciously into his thigh.

Jaalgen was suddenly afraid. The arc of the weapon was very long. First the chase in Paris . . . then her father on the train . . . the mountainside . . . It was slipping away from him again. The bitch was *killing* him. But it wasn't just a fear of death, more the fear of dying before he completed his task – of dying pointlessly . . . Like his father going to the gallows before he'd struck a real blow for the Third Reich, for his dream . . . Blind determination pushing him on, he lurched forward, aiming his head at Julie's stomach. The bar swept down on his back, but left only a numbing feeling as he grappled her to the floor.

Jaalgen struck out and hit her in the stomach – then twice rapidly. The bar rose again and he gripped it halfway, yanking it roughly from her grasp and hurling it to one side.

Below him Julie screamed in terror. He lashed out and hit her in the face. Let the bitch suffer like he had. Coiling her long blonde hair round one hand, he yanked her back hard as he reached over for his gun. A faint sound behind, a fleeting look in her eyes – not quite terror anymore – made him look round.

Daniel Grade stood in the doorway, levelling his shotgun. The light flicked on above them.

Jaalgen squinted in the harsh light, his spirits sinking. Daniel looked wild, formidable – and seeing the dark hair, Jaalgen had to puzzle for a second before he was sure. It was a replay of the train. The shotgun would erupt at any second, and the fulfilment so close at hand would be blown away, along with his own broken body. It seemed unfair – yet somehow ludicruous, something to make him laugh insanely if he hadn't felt so suddenly empty inside.

Jaalgen noticed that Daniel was mumbling something under his breath as he surveyed the scene, but he couldn't make out the words. Then the shape of the shotgun dawned on him fully – *a sawn off!* Something heavy lifted from his mind. He started to smile and reached for the gun at his side. The shotgun moved a fraction in the corner of his vision.

'If you know your guns, Mr Grade, you will also know that with that weapon there the spread is wide. To take me, you would take both of us.'

Jaalgen got to his feet, yanking Julie up with him, moving his grip to around her neck, and pointing the gun in front of them. It was perfect. He couldn't have planned it better if he'd tried. Now he had both of them – and the ultimate test for the father.

Jaalgen's smile widened, taunting. 'Why don't you try it? Go on.'

Daniel tightened his grip on the shotgun, fighting to control himself. Julie was bleeding, but alive and conscious. Jaalgen's eyes were fixed on him intently; he could see now where the plastic surgery had been performed; the skin around the eyes was unnaturally taut. He noted the fleck of blood below Jaalgen's lip, his unsteadiness. He didn't look as if he could remain standing much longer. Delay – *play for time.*

'You were the dupe, you know. Right from the start.'

Jaalgen ignored this. 'How does it feel to be on the other side, Mr Grade. Now it's my turn.'

'He could have done it all without you, the way he's

planned this last bit so elaborately. Reiner, the letter-bomb, Ehnbridt, all of it pointing around to me. Oh yes, he's very clever, Mendel.'

Jaalgen glanced fleetingly over Grade's shoulder at the window as a noise was heard. It sounded like one of the crows flying off. *Mendel?* The name meant nothing to him. He felt a flicker of uncertainty, but tried not to let it show. 'I don't have time for your word games. I knew who it was from the start – Emil Schaarer.'

"That's what you were meant to think. That's what Mendel *wanted* you to think.'

The moment hung between them; the only sound was the open door swinging slightly in the wind now trying to pick up and clear the fog. Jaalgen's breath showed in the cold air coming in. He wiped at his forehead with one hand. His expression was momentarily puzzled, then slowly it changed. Blood trickled thicker by his lips. He smiled again.

'You will remember that on the train we didn't talk at all. So you will know that when someone is about to kill, he doesn't have time for words. The many different ways I've visualized this moment – Oh, you *couldn't know.*' Jaalgen shook his head slightly. 'But the reality is something else again.'

Jaalgen raised his gun higher.

Daniel was aware of Julie screaming. 'Go on, do it, dad . . . *do it!* Save yourself! He'll kill me afterwards anyway.' His finger trembled on the trigger; a shudder passed through his entire body . . . he couldn't, just *couldn't.* A faint ringing sounded somewhere inside his head.

At the last moment – as the gun barrel pointed straight at him – he closed his eyes. The cord snapped, and he was finally released, falling into the void . . . Julie was still screaming, but now she seemed further away . . . and the mist was rolling towards him again, the faces rising up out of it: Reiner, Mendel, Leorah, his own picture in the newspaper, the headlines, Catherine, the crowds in Oxford Street pushing, surging, pointing . . . *murderer!* The shot sounded distant in it all – and he was falling away, blood erupting from his neck and mouth. But the face was Jaalgen's . . . The gun was rising again, then suddenly he was lunging on top of Jaalgen, hitting and hitting and hitting, his fists flaying raw, the face dissolving into the same pulp as the neck . . . feeling Jaalgen's blood all around, soaking him, the red merging with the blackness of the void, dragging him back down. Then someone said, 'You'd better get out of here . . .' But still he was hitting – and he didn't look up until he felt a hand grip his shoulder.

Swenkel stood there, a rifle in his hand, and was shouting at him.

'You'd better get out! The police will be here any minute.'

Daniel stared up at him, mesmerized, disbelieving.

'I'll sort out this mess. You'd better take my car as well, the police know yours. It's a Renault, about fifty yards back up the lane.'

Daniel stared at the dangling keys. But it wasn't until he saw Julie, saw the release from terror in her face, that he knew that the dream, the *nightmare* had really ended, the last waves of it spilling away from him, and with a half-scream, half-cry he fell on her and hugged her tight in his arms.

EPILOGUE

It took four days to clear up.

The investigation was held 'pending', on receipt of Swenkel's information. Swenkel had actually been present shortly after Ehnbridt's murder and before Daniel's arrival, and with the depth of his knowledge about Reiner and the movement and activities of Jaalgen, it had been fairly straightforward. The only delay had been Searle holding back while Swenkel travelled to Paris to meet with Inspector Laboille. Then the file was closed. The slate clean.

Both murders were attributed to Jaalgen, although no link was provable to Mendel; the letter sent had been anonymous, impossible to trace. It was the only nagging loose end.

And still he didn't have *motive*.

Daniel looked around the newsroom from his desk. At each stage, he considered, Mendel had covered himself well. Except for one element: the Hilal. From everything – Mendel's report, Jaalgen's actions, Leorah's admissions, all the information pieced together – he was sure Mendel didn't know about the Hilal.

He had called Mendel's office three times in the last two days only to be rebuffed by his secretary. Why did he bother, he'd wondered. Now that the Hilal knew of Mendel, it would only be a matter of time; he would go the same way as Al-Ben Salmad. But the thought of Mendel dying before Daniel knew *why* – why his daughter's life had been threatened, why Xavier, Reiner and Ehnbridt and all the others had been killed – rankled him deeply. The Hilal? It was then that the thought occurred to him of playing one against the other.

He made yet another call to Mendel, informing the secretary that he knew Mendel was there, and that he had vital information which Mendel wasn't aware of: '. . . Tell him that an old friend of Al-Hakim and Khourem is very eager to know his name, and that if he doesn't accept my call this time, I'll be only too glad to pass it on. I'll call back in half an hour.'

Daniel looked at his watch: twenty minutes to go. Outside, some Christmas carollers were singing in the street. Daniel smiled to himself. Two days to Christmas! Julie would be home for Christmas day, out of hospital. The leg injury had been only superficial, a flesh wound, and on her arm the bullet had passed clean through. Thankfully, it hadn't damaged any tendons, only muscle tissue. 'She'll feel a slight loss of power in that arm when it heals,' the doctor had informed them. 'But unless she's planning to contend at Wimbledon, it shouldn't really bother her.' Daniel had heaved a mammoth sigh of relief.

The atmosphere in the newsroom had changed noticeably; not only charged with Christmas merriment, but through the reaction to his own plight. Most people on the paper already knew him, but the few that didn't had been reached by the news story of the police investigation. He'd muttered to Golding, 'If I receive one more slap on the back, condolence or congratulation from someone I don't even know, I think I'll scream!'

Even with Catherine it had been more condolence than reprimand. She'd known about Leorah and him – call it woman's intuition, or whatever, but she'd known. Of course she didn't specifically know it was Leorah, but she'd sensed that he'd had an affair.

He'd tried to talk about it, but she held up her hand to stop him. She didn't want to know the details, or any explanations. It was as if she felt he had been *away* for a while, not just in body but in spirit too, and she was now just glad to have him back; as if he had had some temporary mental aberration, some foolishness, and was now over it. In a way, she was right, he could see in retrospect. He *had* been foolish over

Leorah – yet another of those bitter-tasting lessons in the never-ending maturing process. But the real key to Catherine's reaction, he felt, was that for years she considered he was already having an affair – with his work. And she felt that this time, with the terrible consequences his unreasonable absorption had brought, the point had finally been hammered home to him. Painful to admit, she was right; for probably the first time he saw her view of it.

It hadn't helped his sense of guilt much either when she'd accepted his offer of a New Year's holiday in the Seychelles in the way he'd intended it – not just as a peace offering, but more for the time that they both needed to work it all out, discover things anew. There might be no startling discoveries, but already he was realizing just how much strength he drew from Catherine, how people thought he had it so much together, but really how lost he'd be without her. He'd had that feeling in their earlier days, but with the pace of his work the last few years, he had grown away from it.

Daniel noticed the clock on the far wall. He was five minutes over. When he dialled Mendel's number, the secretary put him through almost straight away.

'So you got through to me at last,' Mendel stated flatly. 'Obviously you *know*.'

'Yes.'

'I thought you might. I knew it would only be a matter of time. This friend of Khourem and Al-Hakim – you intrigue me. Tell me about this.'

'I said that only to get you on the phone. They know already. It's a number of men actually, an organization.'

'I see.' Mendel fell silent for a second. 'So tell me about them.'

'*No*, you first. I want to trade information.'

Mendel laughed briefly. 'What exactly do you want to know, Daniel? You want now to play the outraged journalist, the outraged friend – wondering how I could possibly do such terrible things to you. Is that what you want?'

Mendel's calmness, his cool sarcasm now bit inside

Daniel. 'Save it. The fact you could do it sickened me enough. I didn't call for a replay, to sit through excuses, or listen to you crawl.'

'Crawl? Now that's an interesting expression, Daniel. I would never *crawl.* But I think you should know anyway – you would find it interesting. You see, I didn't betray a friend, because you never were a friend.' Mendel let the emphasis hang. 'Reiner's secretary contacted me halfway through the pharmaceutical investigation – as one might naturally approach the Swiss Institute over such a matter – asking if I knew of any good investigative reporters, ones who've had experience of Swiss affairs. I passed her your name, but by then I knew something of where Reiner's enquiry would be heading. First I tried to mislead you by falsely indicting Schaarer, clumsily I might add . . . to make it *look* like a false indictment. I'd been discreetly hiring a nine-seater Mercedes for a while. I simply had the plates changed to that matching a car registered to Schaarer, then on one occasion I had someone stand in for Reiner. With a brown toupee and steel-rimmed glasses, from a distance the effect was very good. When you discovered Schaarer had been largely responsible for Reiner's non-promotion, Reiner would be discredited. Conveniently, it also misled some others. Of course, it was when Reiner first contacted me that I decided to cement our relationship more solidly. Something which you probably mistook for normal courtesy and helpfulness – I knowing full well that you would have to come back to me when . . .'

'Look, fuck you, Mendel. I told you I don't want to know! All I want from you is motive – *why* all this happened in the first place? Now either you want to know about this organization or you don't.'

'I just explained it so that you could see how ideally placed I was to control everything, to keep an inside track. Anybody with possibly damaging information on the Swiss community would naturally come to me. Of course, you never did find out motive, did you?'

Mendel's patronizing tone turned Daniel's stomach. He

didn't answer. At a desk behind him two phones were ringing almost simultaneously.

There was a long silence at Mendel's end, then a sigh. 'I suppose you'd get to find out in the end anyway. And there's really nothing that can be tied in, absolutely nothing can be proved.' Mendel's tone changed, taking on a new pace. 'Everything was worked out so well, so scrupulously, right down to the last detail. Literally scores of brokerages and exchanges were used, going back now over the last eighteen months and still continuing – and the amounts never large enough to raise eyebrows and still even more difficult to trace. And even if they did, they would find at the end of it only individual men – men who have had reason to consult me through the years – investing normally, doing something perfectly legal, part of *no* consortium or grand plan. Of course, it was easy to control from Switzerland, because there are no restrictions on that type of trading here. What might give you the clue is what the Arabs have been investing in most since the war. My part in it all was to create a certain situation in the Middle East, the correct investment atmosphere, then control and monitor everything – as I was ideally placed for in the Swiss Institute, you'll agree. But no connection, apart from passing consultation, exists between me and these men, some of them the world's richest . . . Certainly nothing that could be proved, at least.'

Mendel's tone needled Daniel even deeper; the way he was so totally caught up in his plan, almost gloating.

Mendel became condescending. 'Let's see, Daniel. Let's see how clever you are now, if you can work it out. What do people put their money into most in times of trouble, of war, monetary devaluation.' Mendel paused for a moment, then continued. 'Commodities of some type, antiques sometimes, precious stones, silver – but most popular of all is gold. Purely and simply gold. Haven't you seen how dramatically the markets have risen with the advent of trouble in the Lebanon? Money, but particularly Arab money, has literally poured into gold.'

Daniel *had* seen it. In the last eighteen months, gold prices had risen from $130 an ounce to nearly $250 an ounce. Wetherall predicted they could almost double again in the next year or so. He felt his mouth go dry. It had been so obvious – so infuriatingly close at hand all along.

'Of course, some of that initial rise was due to our inflow into the market. But everything above $150 an ounce could be virtually considered gain. It was a tailor-made situation. Massive increases in wealth in the Middle East, with greatly expanding banking to absorb it. Hit at Beirut, the centre of Middle Eastern monetary trade and power, and people's faith in banking and money markets in general is shattered. The next time it could be Bahrain . . . Abu Dhabi. Gold becomes a safer bet.'

'And *that* is what it was all for, everything – the war, the assassinations . . . all the deaths since? For gold?'

'Perhaps you don't fully understand. We're talking about a great deal of money. In the final count, probably in excess of forty billion American dollars.'

The pictures were running through Daniel's mind: the bombed-out buildings of Beirut, the slums and refugee camps, the basement of the hospital with Leorah that first day . . . the torn limbs and wrecked bodies and lives, the Israeli children on the bus . . . Julie's frightened face that night in Paris, Reiner, Xavier . . .

'The best part is that nobody will ever know. Now, with Jaalgen finally dead, the last traceable link to me is dead as well. And I'm sure your reputation has been shaken enough recently that you wouldn't be stupid enough to write up a story without background.'

'We'll see. Don't count on it.'

That washed over Mendel. 'In the end, of course, the banks will have to do something to compensate. They'll probably put up their interest rates to attract investors back. But I foresee we will have at least another eighteen months or so, and by then have made handsomely enough to be prepared to pull out.'

The chase down the motorway . . . the people dead by the

juggernaut, Julie fighting for life at the cottage . . . The pictures were burning deeper. Daniel felt physically sick. 'Is that how things measure on your scale – money, manipulation, exactness. People, the strife you've caused . . . *lives* don't count.'

'Don't try and dehumanize me! The war was a symptom that was already there, and would have flared up at some stage or other. That process was merely catalyzed. Al-Hakim and Khourem were necessary, of course, but they would have ruined the country with their policies anyway. As for the other deaths, they were unfortunate, a bit messy, and I would have avoided them if . . .'

Daniel slammed the phone down. He'd had enough of the taunting voice, the calm, rational, almost gloating pride in it. The worst part was that Mendel was probably right – nobody would ever know! He wasn't sure what was more sickening, the sheer size of the scheme or the irony. Traced back to Switzerland, first the Mossad, then Reiner had thought it must be a banking-inspired plot. Gold prices would continue to rise, and people would think it just a symptom of the times! *Forty billion dollars?* What could be proved with a couple of dozen unconnected investors receiving advice through the Swiss Institute, as they might well do in the normal course of events. Invest in gold? Nothing unusual about that advice either, with the market rising. And no link existed between Mendel and Khourem's assassination, the sparking off of the war, except his name muttered by Al-Ben Salmad, now dead.

The Hilal? It suddenly struck Daniel that he'd forgotten to warn Mendel about the Hilal, and he reached out for the telephone again – then stopped. Pulling his hand back, he smiled and got up, lifting his jacket from behind his chair. *Kismet*, Leorah would probably term it. Who was he to interfere with the path of fate?

Daniel walked briskly along Fleet Street. A light snow was falling and he turned up his collar. Thirty yards down, he stopped at a news-stand. Ben, the vendor there for the past fifteen years, greeted him knowingly.

'Glad to hear that that little business of yours is now all cleared up, Mr Grade. Never believed a word of it meself from the start.' He cocked his head mischievously as he handed the paper over. 'It's an exciting life you lead at times, I don't know. P'raps I should swap places with you for a few days.'

Daniel smiled back as he paid. 'Have a good Christmas, Ben.' He tucked a large cigar into Ben's coat pocket and walked on.

Many of the offices had closed early for the holiday, and the street was quieter than normal, with only the light traffic of people heading home. It would have been funny but for the disappointment. The only thing they had gained newswise from the whole affair – apart from a detailed account of the bus hijacking, and a different slant on affairs surrounding the war in the Lebanon, including a strong 'rumour' that Al-Hakim might still be alive and living in exile in Bahrain – were the dramatics of his own dilemma. He glanced at the paper in his hand. The headlines read: CHRISTMAS CEASEFIRE GAINED AT UN. At least a token peace offering – until next year. He heard St Paul's chime six o'clock, and glanced up at its lighted dome a few hundred yards away looking somehow magical on that night with its light covering of snow. Then he turned into Wine Office Court. He'd arranged to meet Billy Stoner in Ye Olde Cheshire Cheese, the pub where they'd met a few weeks before, the day the messenger had walked in on them to say Reiner was sitting at his desk; the day the nightmare started.

Stoner was already there, two drinks on the bar before him: a pint of beer and a Scotch.

'I thought I'd get you a double, what with the snow.' Stoner winked and handed the glass over. 'Two days before Christmas, down it comes – you could almost set your bloody watch by it. Cheers!'

They drank silently for a second. The bar was quite full, and noisy.

'Well, you got out of it clean in the end, Danny. It's all over now. You can give a sigh of relief.'

'Yes, thanks. How about your case – hitting that copper?'

'Still pending. But I'm going to take your advice – eat humble pie.' Stoner sipped his beer, then his expression changed. He squinted at Daniel warily. 'You know, you were a different man last week. I don't mind telling yer now, I was frightened. Really had me going.'

Daniel put one hand firmly on Stoner's shoulder. 'Yes, well, I was going to talk to you about that, Billy, you know, about keeping the shotgun. There's this guy in the office I've never really liked, and . . .' Daniel broke out laughing at Stoner's expression, then leant over and whispered. 'It's safe under the back seat of the Jag. Nobody ever saw it. And I've polished it up a bit – you could almost display it at Sotheby's.'

'Yeah, well, it can go back under the floorboards where it belongs.'

Daniel took a belt of his Scotch. 'Look, I'm sorry about not getting the car back to you earlier. What with the whole mess, everything being so hectic . . .'

'That's alright. I understand.'

'Want to go up and see it now?' Stoner shrugged and held a hand up, but Daniel persisted. 'Come on . . . I'll show you where I've parked. I might not have the time later. We can leave the drinks here for a sec.' Daniel shouted to the barman, 'Set us up a couple of cigars and two refills for when we come back, Harry.' He pointed to the glasses and led the way out.

Stoner followed him up out of the basement and they headed across the cold street, then into a small side street opposite. Daniel stopped after twenty yards and held out one hand.

Stoner stood rigid. He stared first at Daniel's dead-pan face, then back at his car – gradually taking in the mass of dents and scrapes, twisted metal and broken glass. When he finally spoke, it was in little more than a hoarse whisper.

'I thought you said it was *alright*.'

'It is, Billy. It is.' Daniel leant over, pointing. 'Bit of filler here. Bit of filler and padding there. It'll be right as rain.'

Stoner's voice was slowly returning. 'Come on . . . look at it! It's *fucked.* A write-off. Even if it could be knocked back into shape, it'd take months.'

'No, never. A few days in the body shop, it'll be fine.'

Stoner lapsed into nervous laughter. 'This is a joke, isn't it?' But Daniel just stared back at him, almost morosely, and Stoner stopped laughing, the icy uneasiness biting deeper. Then he saw something just past Daniel's shoulder, a shape in the next side street. He took a step to one side, for a better look. A few more paces and it was fully in view: a brand new Jaguar 4.2, metallic green. White ribbons stretched from the front emblem to the boot, and on the side, written in crazy foam, were the words 'MERRY CHRISTMAS, BILLY'. A light layer of snow on the bonnet and roof put the final seasonal touch to it. He stood transfixed for a second.

'You bastard!' Stoner muttered under his breath. 'You absolute fucking bastard.' His face cracking into a widening smile, he turned to Daniel.

Daniel held up his hands defensively, backing away. 'Now wait a minute. Let's not be hasty.' Then he started to run.

'You wait till I catch up with you! Winding me up like that.'

They were both laughing now, breathless, mock abuse flying, when Stoner caught up with him halfway across Fleet Street, slapping one arm across his shoulder. Swaying like two drunks, the sound of their laughter filled the street, disturbing some pigeons alighting for breadcrumbs in front of the Law Courts a hundred yards up, and momentarily drowning out the sounds of a record-player from a nearby office party . . . 'So this is Christmas . . . And what have you done?'